For Orion, my writing buddy

About a Rogue

"My dear Mrs. St. James." She started at the name. "I'll thank you not to tell me what to do. After all, I am not the one who vowed to *obey and serve.*"

The flush ran down her neck. "How dare you— This is not a real marriage!"

He came off the door, closing the gap between them so quickly she gasped. "Not real?" he bit out. "It most certainly is, madam. Solemnized before all of Marslip and bound by Church law. Don't *ever* say it's not real." He paused, his gaze running down her again. "If you're fearful I shall force you to your wifely duties in bed, set your mind at ease."

"Then you accept this will be a chaste marriage?" she said as he went back to the door.

He paused, looking back at her. Some of her hairpins had come out, setting a long tawny curl loose to graze her bare neck. He could see the beauty mark, dark and taunting on the plump swell of flesh.

Well, wasn't he a fool. He wanted the woman, even though she despised him.

"Of course it won't be," he said. "Someday you'll come to me—"

She gasped in fury.

"—and when you do, it will be for pleasures that most women only dream of." Max gave her another sinful smile and opened the door, leaving her staring after him in openmouthed indignation.

Also by Caroline Linden

CAROLINE LINDEN

ABOUT A ROGUE

Desperately Seeking Duke

AVONBOOKS

An Imprint of HarperCollinsPublishers

This is a work of fiction. Names, characters, places, and incidents are products of the author's imagination or are used fictitiously and are not to be construed as real. Any resemblance to actual events, locales, organizations, or persons, living or dead, is entirely coincidental.

ABOUT A ROGUE. Copyright © 2020 by P. F. Belsley. All rights reserved. Printed in the United States of America. No part of this book may be used or reproduced in any manner whatsoever without written permission except in the case of brief quotations embodied in critical articles and reviews. For information, address Harper-Collins Publishers, 195 Broadway, New York, NY 10007.

First Avon Books mass market printing: July 2020

Print Edition ISBN: 978-0-06-291362-3
Digital Edition ISBN: 978-0-06-291363-0

Cover design by Guido Caroti
Cover photograph by Glenn Mackay
Cover illustration by Allan Davey
Additional photographs © Deklofenak/Depositphotos (shelves); © Ravven/Depositphotos (windows); © kodoruk/Depositphotos (flooring); © Reinhold Leitner/Shutterstock (texture)

Avon, Avon & logo, and Avon Books & logo are registered trademarks of HarperCollins Publishers in the United States of America and other countries.

HarperCollins is a registered trademark of HarperCollins Publishers in the United States of America and other countries.

FIRST EDITION

20 21 22 23 24   CWM   10 9 8 7 6 5 4 3 2 1

ABOUT A
ROGUE

Prologue

1787

News of the untimely death of the vicar of St. Mary's parish of Kittleston spread on a tide of dismay, causing sincere mourning among his parishioners. A mere forty-five years old, he had been well-liked, a calm, cheerful presence who always had a kind word, a helping hand, or a sympathetic ear for anyone in need.

The ladies of the parish gathered to console the deceased's fiancée, Miss Calvert, who was just as beloved in the town and whose devastated sobs brought more than one neighbor to tears of their own. Everyone in the parish murmured to themselves how terribly sad it was, for poor Miss Calvert and for the parish, for how could either hope to find another such man?

Twenty miles away, in the sprawling grandeur of Carlyle Castle, the news spurred a very different sort of mourning, as well as a tremor of despair that seemed to unmoor the great house. Stephen St. James was not only the beloved vicar of St. Mary's, he was also the youngest brother of His Grace the Duke of Carlyle.

"It was a wound from an old scythe," said Mr. Edwards, the family solicitor. He had received the news of Lord Stephen's worsening health two days ago and come at once to the castle. "He was using it in his garden on some pernicious vines, and accidentally cut his leg. By the time the doctor was sent for, the wound was deeply inflamed. I am told his suffering was brief," he added quietly.

Her Grace the Duchess of Carlyle stared out the window. Her eyes were dry and her chin resolutely steady, but she gripped a crumpled handkerchief. "Thank heavens for that much. My darling boy," she said softly. "He did so love being in his garden . . ."

"Miss Calvert was with him when it happened. She did urge him to send for the surgeon, but he believed it to be a trifling injury." Mr. Edwards shared this with great reluctance, but he had promised he would. Emily Calvert had been hysterical, pleading with him to beg the duchess's forgiveness and mercy. She thought herself a murderer for not insisting upon the doctor immediately.

"That poor girl," replied the duchess, still staring out the window. "She must not blame herself. No one could persuade Stephen to worry. It was not in his nature." Her voice trembled at the last. She took a deep breath. "Send someone to see if Miss Calvert is in want of anything we can supply."

Mr. Edwards coughed. "She would like to visit his grave."

The duchess was silent. "We must put him in it first." She sighed, her hands moving restlessly for a moment. "Of course she may. I could hardly deny her that."

Mr. Edwards made a note of it as the porcelain clock on the table ticked steadily along. "Have you any wishes for the funeral, Your Grace?"

"Heywood will know what to do," she said, naming the august Carlyle butler. "As it was for—for Lady Jessica."

Lady Jessica had been the duchess's beloved only daughter. They had buried her just seven years ago. Her Grace's voice still broke when she said the name.

"Yes, ma'am." His pen scratched a few more notes. "I suppose His Grace has been told."

The duchess's face spasmed. "No. I will do it later. He was not well this morning."

"Of course," murmured the solicitor. Formidable though she was, the duchess was also a mother who had just lost her youngest son, and now must tell her last surviving child that they would open the family crypt again, to bury his brother. It was doubtful the conversation would be brief or easy. The duke's mind was neither quick nor agile, and his understanding was always uncertain.

But there was nothing he could do about that. Mr. Edwards hesitated, then put the pen back into the stand. "There is one more subject I must broach . . ."

"Yes, yes," she snapped, now glowering at the window. "I know."

He waited, but when she said nothing more, he reluctantly went on. The matter was urgent, as the duchess herself would tell him, were she not so grief-stricken. "I have taken the liberty of examining the records . . . It is always better to be excessively informed, I believe, although I am deeply sorry it has become necessary . . ."

"Are you?" The duchess made a visible effort to gather herself. Mr. Edwards averted his eyes, in case she required a moment of privacy. "Get on with it, then," she said crisply, a moment later. "Who is he?"

Lord Stephen had been not merely the duke's younger brother; he had also been his only heir. A terrible accident years ago had left the duke with the mind of a child. He had never married, never had a son, and never would. Lord Stephen's death meant the dukedom must now pass to a distant cousin.

It had been fiercely hoped by all at Carlyle Castle that Lord Stephen's marriage would yield an heir. Miss Calvert was not a very young woman, but she was by no means past the age of bearing a child, and there had been genuine affection between her and Lord Stephen. Now those hopes were dashed, which meant the heir presumptive was wandering about somewhere, in complete ignorance of the monumental inheritance about to befall him.

Mr. Edwards drew a paper from his case. Thirty years ago, the second Carlyle son, Lord William, had been killed in the American colonies, shortly before the duke's accident. As the years passed and Lord Stephen did not marry, the succession had become precarious. Quietly and discreetly, Mr. Edwards had begun investigating three men, against the grim possibility that this day would arrive.

Even so, despite the urgent necessity, this must be done delicately. Edwards had been the Carlyle solicitor for over twenty-five years, long enough to know the family secrets and stains. He chose to begin with the easiest point. "Captain Andrew St. James, of His Majesty's Scots Guards. His grandfather was the younger brother of His Grace the fourth Duke."

"Yes," she said, her expression unreadable at this mention of her late husband. "I remember. He'll be Adam's grandson. Is this young fellow anything like his grandfather?"

Mr. Edwards cleared his throat. Lord Adam, by all accounts, had been both sensible and charming. That had not saved him from a vicious falling out with his older brother, the fourth duke, and Lord Adam had left the family estates decades ago. "I've no idea, Your Grace. My reports are that Captain St. James is an honorable and respectable man."

She harrumphed. "Of what age? Is he married?"

"About thirty years, ma'am, and he is not married, to the best of my knowledge."

She sighed. "It *would* be a military man."

Her second son had gone into the British army, and never come back from it. Her opinion of the army was not high.

After a moment she roused herself. "I suppose we should be grateful that he's survived this long. That may mean he's very clever—or extremely stupid. I am not sure which I prefer. Who else?"

Edwards withdrew another sheet of paper. "Mr. Maximilian St. James."

"I can tell from your tone of voice this one is not so respectable."

The solicitor gazed at her evenly. "He is a gamester, Your Grace. He has no other income that I can discern, but he is well-known at the gaming hells.

He is descended from the second duke, is about twenty-seven years of age, and also has no wife."

"Such dissolute fools the young men of Britain are these days." She frowned ferociously. "Are there no more?"

"Er—perhaps." He hesitated; this was the most delicate territory of all. "His Grace the fourth Duke had two younger brothers."

"Oh yes," she said after a moment, a lilt of surprise in her voice. "Good heavens. I forgot about him."

Mr. Edwards nodded. Nearly everyone had, because the duke had ordered it so. Lord Adam had been banished, but his name was still spoken at Carlyle Castle. Lord Thomas St. James, on the other hand, had disappeared at the age of five as if he'd never existed. He had been his mother's favorite son—so much so, that she took him with her when she fled her husband, the third duke, and returned to her native France. Rumor held she had gone back to the French vicomte who had been her lover. It was whispered that Lord Thomas might be his child.

It had been an enormous scandal, and the third duke had declared both his wife and son dead to him. On one notorious occasion, half a dozen servants had been whipped for gossiping about her. After that, the names of the runaway duchess and her son were never mentioned by any of the Carlyle servants or staff. The fourth duke had been no more forgiving of his mother's desertion, and in time Anne-Louise and her son Thomas had been all but forgotten.

"I have made a few attempts to trace him and his

mother, without success." Mr. Edwards paused. "It has been several decades. Who knows where Lord Thomas may be?"

The duchess sniffed. "His grandchildren, you mean. He would be a man of eighty or more, if he were still alive—Carlyle men do not live that long." A fresh spasm of grief contorted her face for a moment before she went on. "And those grandchildren, if he had any, would be *French*."

"Likely so," Mr. Edwards murmured. "I would have to launch a determined search to trace Lord Thomas and any of his descendants."

"Must you?" she snapped.

He hesitated. "If a son or grandson of Lord Thomas should survive . . . His claim would be preeminent, Your Grace."

For a moment the duchess sat in grim disapproval. "An army man, a cardsharp, or a Frenchman," she said sourly. Her gaze moved upward, over the exquisitely adorned ceiling of the room, over the tall gleaming windows, over the graceful furnishings and paintings in gilt frames. "And one of them will have Carlyle." She turned back to Edwards. "Send for them. All of them, if you can find any relict of Thomas in France, but I want the other two here, as soon as they might come. I shan't allow any callow fool or heartless scoundrel to take my son's place."

"Yes, ma'am."

"Attend me through next week," she went on. "I will have some instruction regarding this decidedly lackluster lot of heirs, and there are some urgent matters about the estate which must be settled as well."

Mr. Edwards sighed. "Your Grace, I cannot handle all the affairs of the estate, even if I were to take up residence in the castle. You must allow me to engage a new estate steward. Mr. Grimes assures me he is utterly unable to return to his post, and I fear he never will be—"

Irritably she waved one hand. "Very well. But on a trial basis only," she added as the solicitor breathed a sigh of relief. "Grimes suits me very well and I shall hold out hope for his return."

Mr. Grimes was nearly seventy and had developed a lung condition; he would not be returning to his post. Mr. Edwards had already arranged his pension, needing only the duchess's approval—and a replacement. In the meantime, the responsibility had fallen onto Mr. Edwards himself, and these six months had nearly driven him into his own retirement. "I shall make inquiries as soon as I reach London, ma'am."

"Hmph." She gave him a dark glance and shook her finger at him. "A sober, reliable fellow, Mr. Edwards, with a vast experience of managing such an estate. Not one of these hungry young men who wishes to experiment with improvements to things that need no improving!"

"Naturally, ma'am."

"You may go," she announced, and the solicitor got to his feet, gathered his papers, and bowed his way out of the room.

Sophia Constance St. James, once one of the most eligible heiresses in England, sat in her silk-upholstered chair, her bejeweled fingers clutching a handkerchief of finest Irish linen, and gazed vacantly through the tall mullioned window at the rolling sweep of lawn, prosperously dotted with sheep on the distant hills. It was Carlyle, as far as the eye could see and acres beyond.

Almost sixty years ago she had come here as the young bride of George Frederick, the fourth duke, a man twice her age. On her wedding day her mother had whispered in her ear to stand her ground early, or to give way forever. She had chosen to stand her ground; she was the only child and heiress of a wealthy banker who brought immense wealth to her marriage, and she demanded that her husband recognize her worth. And he, tyrannical and arrogant though he was, had done it, because she gave him no choice.

When he died, she'd expected a life of more ease and comfort, only to suffer the devastating loss of one son, a nearly fatal injury to her eldest child, and the death of her only daughter. Still, she had not quailed from her duty. For nearly thirty years she had been guardian of everything she could see, in her son's stead, fiercely determined that Carlyle would be preserved and whole for the next generation.

Now it would go to someone else's son, and she would bury hers—affectionate, charming, beloved Stephen, her heart's darling. Her throat tightened with misery. Three of her children, dead; all of her dreams and loves, gone. Although her eldest child still lived, he was no longer her Johnny, and he hadn't had the sort of life she'd ever dreamt of for him. The vast, verdant vista out her window might have been a mirage.

A rustle at her skirts disturbed her morose thoughts. "Oh, *really*, Percival," she exclaimed as the ginger cat leapt into her lap.

"I am sorry, Your Grace," said Philippa Kirkpatrick, closing the door behind her. "He was lying in wait outside the door."

The duchess smiled, holding up the cat so they were face-to-face. "Never willing to be excluded, are you, my great beast?" She let him down and he curled up in her lap, lashing his tail across his face.

"Shall I put him out?" asked Pippa.

"No, no, let him be," the duchess said, her fingers ruffling then smoothing the cat's fur. "He is a comfort."

Quietly Pippa took a chair beside her. She folded her hands in her lap and waited.

The duchess was grateful for that. Despite her youth, Pippa wasn't one of those flighty modern girls, wild for dancing and flirting over cards with a beauty patch on her cheek. She was kind and sensible, with a tender, loyal heart. She had always been a sweet girl, from the first moment the duchess had seen her, on the day Jessica married Pippa's father, Miles. Snug in his arms, young Pippa had gazed at her with big dark eyes and smiled, and the duchess had been instantly smitten.

"See, Mama," Jessica had said with a luminous smile, smoothing the little girl's hair. "I've got a husband and a daughter at one fell swoop!" Jessica had loved Pippa like her own, and the duchess had followed suit. The girl had grown up to be very like Jessica, and privately the duchess wished Pippa *had* been her granddaughter.

She sighed silently, sorrow flooding her again. She would never have grandchildren now. "Has Mrs. Humphries brought out the crepe?"

"Yes, ma'am. The maids are covering the mirrors."

The duchess glanced at her, noting the color of her dress. "I see you've anticipated her."

Pippa smoothed her hands over her black skirt. "Lord Stephen was always very kind to me, ma'am. It's not right for him to be gone so young."

"No," murmured the duchess. Not right at all. "Edwards wanted to speak about the heir."

The girl's eyes widened. "So soon? Oh, madam, how inconsiderate!"

She flicked one hand, disturbing a meow from Percival. She resumed stroking his fur. "It's not soon. I ought to have done it years ago, if I had not been so confident of Stephen . . ." She closed her eyes at the sudden memory of Stephen's boyish laugh, his voice assuring her he knew his duty to Carlyle. *Never fear, Mama*, he'd promised when he came to tell her about his engagement to Miss Calvert. *I shan't let you down.*

With an effort she wrenched her mind away. She was surrounded by ghosts today. "Now the likely candidates are grown men, most certainly set in their ways, and surely unequal to the responsibility before them." She paused. "I have no intention of letting Carlyle descend to an ignorant fool. I may have no say in which of them inherits, but I can and will exercise all leverage at my command to *make* them worthy of the title. I have sent for them."

"Yes, ma'am," said Pippa after a startled pause.

"I would like your help," continued the duchess. "They will be quick to grasp my role, and, I have no doubt, attempt to flatter and appease me. But you . . . you, they will not be so eager to please. You must be my eyes and ears for their true feelings and intentions."

"Of course, ma'am. If you wish."

The duchess turned to her, smiling ruefully. "I do rely on you so, Pippa."

Pippa smiled back. "I shall do my best, Your Grace."

"I know you will. That is why I depend so heavily upon you, poor girl."

"Not poor at all! I'm pleased to be of some support to you."

The duchess patted her hand. "You always have been, child." She gazed out the window again in silence for several moments. "The most likely heir is a military officer. I have hopes for him," she said at last. "Thin hopes, but there you are. Mr. Edwards reports that he is a respectable man, whatever that means in the army. But the other . . ." She clicked her tongue in displeasure. "A gambler! And only very distantly related. No, I have no good expectations of him."

"They may surprise you, ma'am," ventured Pippa.

"And they may not!" said the duchess tartly. "But either of them is preferable to a Frenchman, of all people. How my husband would turn in his grave, to think of Carlyle going to a Frenchman." She brooded on that for a moment before rousing herself. "The gambler is most likely a hopeless case. Once a gamester, always a gamester. It's like an infection in the blood. As for the Frenchman . . ." She sighed. "I shall hope he does not even exist, or at the very least refuses to be found. No, we must pray for the best, and that means we pin our hopes on Captain St. James."

Chapter One

Maximilian St. James could see that his reputation had preceded him.

It was obvious in the face of the periwigged butler, stiff and disapproving as he ordered Max's baggage conveyed to a guest room upon his arrival. He discerned it in the weary, jaundiced glance the solicitor gave him when they met, reminiscent of the tutors who had sized him up before trying, vainly, to instill in him some scraps of Greek and theology.

And he saw it mostly plainly in the face of the Duchess of Carlyle herself, who sat on her throne-like chair and fixed an unblinking, gimlet-eyed stare on him as if she expected him to slip pieces of the silver into his cuffs and steal them.

Well. Max was used to that. And he did not care.

After all, if the duchess didn't want him here, she ought not to have sent a letter that strongly resembled a royal decree, imperiously demanding that he present himself at Carlyle Castle on this day, as if he were a servant or a dog to be summoned with a snap of her fingers.

It had, alas, pricked his curiosity just enough to make him respond to the duchess's letter instead of tearing it in half in front of the stiff-lipped servant who delivered it. There was just enough suggestion of advantage that he couldn't ignore it.

Max never ignored anything that could be put to his advantage. And this summons, for all its mystery and condescension, was very promising.

Thus far his instincts had seemed on target, both with regard to the mystery and the potential advantage. After a solitary breakfast this morning, he'd gone exploring. The castle was a sprawling pile of stone but pristinely maintained, with ancient tapestries on the walls and priceless antiquities on the mantelpieces. No bankrupt aristocrats here, but wealth and power in abundance.

And while he was here . . . Max took the opportunity to look up someone he'd heard about all his life. Trailed by a stone-faced footman, he strolled through the castle corridors until he found the gallery.

There was his quarry, at the far end of the gallery: the second Duke of Carlyle, his long curled wig cascading over his polished armor, his face narrow and almost delicate, save for the thin mustache along his upper lip. A length of fine linen or lace was carelessly knotted around his neck, and fields and hills—presumably Carlyle—spread behind him into the distance.

Max had always been well aware that a duke figured in his lineage. It had been his father's favorite point of pride, and his mother's main source of hope. He himself had used the fact to his benefit whenever possible, with the occasional fond thought for the ancient Frederick Augustus, whoever he was. Invoking his name, and hinting that Max was still close to the ducal branch of the family, had got him out of more than a few scrapes, even if it had never once led to actual improvement in his circumstances.

He studied the man, his great-great-grandfather. Was there some resemblance? He doubted it. That fellow posed with arrogant command, confident in the wealth and power he held. Max, on the other hand . . . Too many scoundrels and hellhounds, all of them penniless, had come between the two of them for any kinship.

"Cheers," he quietly told the painting, giving his ancestor a brief nod. Then he turned and walked away.

And now he sat in an ornate salon, enduring the suspicious eyes of his hostess with a faint smile, waiting. The duchess sat on an elaborately carved chair that would have made the Queen herself envious. She was a plump old lady, seventy if she were a day, her gray hair frizzed and piled fashionably high. Even though it was morning she wore a black silk gown, and the rings on her fingers could have kept even a very rakish gentleman in style for a year. Max could see the toes of her slippers, propped up as they were on a lavish gilded footstool, and the diamonds on her shoe buckles glittered at him.

The solicitor sat at her elbow, a sober fellow in unrelieved black. The morning sunlight shone on the thinning hair atop his head. He was busily making notes on the papers in front of him, and only when he glanced up appraisingly did Max suspect that the notes were about him.

Another guest had arrived, presumably just this morning. He hadn't been at breakfast two hours ago, and there was still dust in the creases of his trousers, as if he'd hastily brushed them while still wearing them. He was taller than Max and surely outweighed him by a few stone, a rough-looking common sort of fellow. A soldier, was Max's idle guess, even though the man wore regular clothes. He had that way of sitting in his chair that suggested he was accustomed to a sword on his hip. He must also have been summoned, for he took the chair beside Max's and faced the duchess.

No one bothered to introduce them.

"Good morning," said the duchess abruptly, before the two men could do more than exchange polite nods of acknowledgement. "I trust your journeys were without incident."

Max's mouth curled. On the godforsaken mail coach, until he managed to charm a nearby innkeeper's daughter to let him have a horse on credit. The roads were atrocious, it had rained the first day, and if not for the accommodating innkeeper's daughter, he would have arrived bedraggled and on foot, baggage in hand, like a traveling peddler.

"Yes, Your Grace," said the soldier politely.

"It was perfectly delightful," drawled Max. He crossed one leg over the other and draped his wrist over his knee, the picture of rakish insolence.

Her lips pinched at him. "Excellent. No doubt you wonder why I summoned you to Carlyle." She turned to the solicitor. "Mr. Edwards will explain."

The solicitor adjusted his spectacles. "On the fourteenth of April last, Lord Stephen St. James, youngest brother of His Grace the Duke of Carlyle, fell ill and died."

The soldier had penetrating green eyes. He turned

them on the duchess. "I offer my deepest sympathies, madam."

"Thank you, Captain," she replied. "That is very kind of you."

"Unfortunately," continued the solicitor, "Lord Stephen was His Grace's nearest living heir. Carlyle himself has no children or wife."

The soldier jerked in his chair with an audible intake of breath. Max flicked a glance at him, but his face was expressionless.

An odd thought lit up the back of Max's mind. But no; it couldn't be. He and the duke were only very distant cousins, and if anyone at Carlyle gave a damn what happened to him, they had never showed it. Eons ago, in Max's childhood, his mother had appealed to Carlyle for aid, when his father had run off with another of his flirts and left them without money. He still remembered his mother's tragic expression at the curt reply, with but five pounds enclosed. They had nearly starved that winter, being forced to stay with his mother's family. Max's father had returned home in the spring, drunk, penniless, and utterly unapologetic.

He glanced at the soldier again. That one seemed to have a sense of what was up. He sat as alert as a pointer, all but quivering with eagerness to please.

Max shifted in his chair. The captain must be another St. James relation. Nearer, or more distant? he wondered. Because there was only one reason it could possibly matter to either of them that the Duke of Carlyle's heir had just died.

And then the duchess confirmed it. "Lord Stephen has also left no wife or children. In their absence, it appears the dukedom will pass upon my son's death to one of his distant cousins." Her unimpressed gaze moved over each of them. "In short, to one of you."

Blessed Christ and all the angels. Max's heart skidded violently in his chest before he could rein in his reaction. A *dukedom*—and not just any dukedom, but Carlyle, large and prosperous.

But he did rein it in, because the next words out of the soldier's mouth squelched his moment of euphoria. "That is most unexpected news, Your Grace," he said in his deep, gravelly voice. "May I inquire how . . . ?"

"Certainly," she said crisply. "Mr. St. James is the great-great-grandson of the second duke." She raised her brows at him, and Max inclined his head in agreement. "And you, Captain, are the great-grandson of the third duke."

So the soldier outranked him. Max silently let out his breath. It *had* been too incredible to be true.

"This is quite shocking news, ma'am," replied the captain. If the news had shocked him, he had recovered well. "But is there no one—?"

The solicitor cleared his throat and opened his mouth. "No," said the duchess shortly. "There is no one nearer."

A weighty look passed between them, and then the solicitor picked up the thread. "As you may not know, His Grace the Duke suffered a tragic injury many years ago. It has rendered him unable to take a wife and father direct heirs, which means there is no chance either of you will be supplanted by an heir apparent." He drew a wide sheet of paper from under his elbow and spread it on the front of the table, facing them. "I have taken the liberty of documenting the family here."

He paused as Max and the soldier leaned forward in unison, craning their necks to see. "This documentation will be invaluable when the time comes to assert a claim, particularly as neither of you is a direct descendant of the current or previous holder of the title."

For the first time Max's eyes met those of the captain. The other man looked as startled as Max felt. The Duke of Carlyle was incapable of fathering a child. His only heir was dead. And he was . . . Max took a brief glance at the neatly scripted family chart. The duke was nearly sixty years old.

This . . . this was a pressing concern, he realized.

"I see this has been something of a surprise to you," announced the duchess into the silence. "It has been no less alarming to me."

Max's hackles rose. He knew exactly what she meant. It might not have been so horrifying to them if they'd taken any interest in him years ago. "I wouldn't precisely call it alarming," he drawled. "A surprise, I'll grant."

The duchess's expression should have turned him into a pillar of ash. The solicitor sighed in disappointment. Even the captain gave him a disapproving look. Max simply smiled back at all of them.

"The rules of inheritance are firm," said the duchess, still eyeing him with distaste. "The title and entailed lands must descend through the male St. James line, and they will. One of you will be the next duke—Captain St. James, most likely, or Mr. St. James in the event tragedy befalls the captain." From her expression, Max thought she'd consider his inheriting a calamity verging on the apocalypse.

"There is a considerable fortune attached to the

estate, naturally," she went on. "It is an enormous responsibility, and neither of you have the slightest preparation to assume it."

"Naturally," murmured Max.

"I have had both of you investigated," she went on, ignoring him. "The results were hardly reassuring, but we must deal with what we must. Neither of you has taken a wife yet."

"No, ma'am," said the captain.

Max could hardly feed himself some months, let alone a wife and the children who usually followed. The duchess, with her jewels and satincovered footstools, hadn't the slightest idea about him. "Not one of my own," he said languidly.

The silence was like a bubble of surprise. The lawyer took his meaning first, pressing his lips together and looking down. The captain cleared his throat, and the duchess glared daggers at him.

"Nor have you taken any pains toward respectability, sir," she shot back. "That is what troubles me, and that is why I sent for you. The Duke of Carlyle wields great power, and must do so with dignity and decorum."

Max thought of the last duke he'd seen—the young Duke of Umberton, gambling away eleven thousand pounds in one night and taking down his breeches to piss upon the faro table in a fit of pique. Dignity and decorum, indeed.

"It is an awesome responsibility," the captain was saying, as sober as a judge, lapping up her words as if they were scripture. "I hope I may become worthy of it."

His manner, obsequious to Max's disdainful eyes, was nonetheless thawing the duchess's frosty demeanor. She nodded at him. "I expect it of you, Captain." The glance she gave Max was cold again. "And of you, Mr. St. James."

He dipped his head in acknowledgement.

"I understand this may be a difficult request," she went on. "I am prepared to help. Mr. Edwards will disburse to each of you five hundred pounds, immediately. I trust you will use it wisely, and return to Carlyle Castle in six months' time more sober, refined gentlemen. If I am satisfied with your progress, I shall grant a further sum of one thousand five hundred pounds per year, to continue as long as you remain respectable."

Good Lord. Five hundred pounds now, fifteen hundred a year. For a moment he couldn't believe his ears.

But he had also heard the *if* in her statement, and realized this was not as heaven-sent as it appeared. "And if you are not satisfied?" he asked politely.

She sighed at Max's question. "If you do not, you shan't have a farthing more from me. Are you really so stupid to throw away such a chance, Mr. St. James?"

No, he certainly was not. Max tilted his head in deference. "I merely wished to know."

"I shall monitor your progress during the next six months." She shot him a look of warning. "I am not the enemy. This offer is intended to help you. Do not delude yourself that Carlyle runs itself, or that a steward can be hired to do it all. You are both young men, neither raised with this expectation. It will be difficult for you to adjust, but you must rise to the occasion. I urge you to accept this proposal and take it seriously."

The captain cleared his throat. "Yes, of course, Your Grace. It is extremely generous of you."

"It is not generosity," she retorted. "I have no wish to see Carlyle run into the ground. I wish to see it descend to someone who will appreciate its majesty, care for its dependents, and preserve it for future generations. To that purpose, you have six months to establish yourselves as someone capable of becoming that man. And you needn't fear that the funds would cease if I should die," she added, her dark eyes on Max again. "I will leave instructions in my will to continue the annuity so long as my conditions are met."

Max no longer felt like taunting her. By God, he'd never imagined a chance like this. She meant it. When a man's luck turned like this, only a fool would ignore it.

"What shall those conditions be, Your Grace?" he inquired.

"Respectability," she said crisply. "No outrageous behavior. Sobriety. The Dukes of Carlyle have long held positions of power in Westminster, and you would do well to take an interest in politics so that you are prepared to acquit yourselves well when you sit in the House of Lords. If you do not, someone else will be happy to take advantage of you, sooner or later." She paused. "And I have always felt a wife settles a man. The next duke will need a legitimate heir. A suitable bride is necessary, and I advise you to turn your attention to finding one."

"We must marry?" asked the captain, a faint frown touching his face.

"The Duke of Carlyle will need an heir," she repeated. "If you do not provide one, Captain, Mr. St. James would become the heir presumptive."

Max and the soldier exchanged a fleeting glance. *Not bloody likely*, thought Max of his chances of becoming heir to the dukedom under that man. The captain was the sort who did what was expected of him. No doubt he was thinking of a woman right now who would leap at the chance to become his future duchess.

Not that Max could blame him. Everyone in this room knew *he* would be a terrible duke.

"Mr. Edwards will answer any further questions," said the duchess as the clock chimed softly. She got to her feet, and a large ginger cat strolled from beneath her chair with a yawn and a stretch.

"If I may, Your Grace . . ." The soldier leapt forward to help her, bending solicitously near as he offered his arm. Max caught a few quiet words as they walked toward the door, and gathered the captain was concerned particularly about the question of a wife. Max could have sworn the fellow was asking the duchess to choose a woman for him.

Thank God he wouldn't have that problem. He turned to the solicitor, who sat with smooth hands folded neatly on his papers. "An annuity for good behavior."

Edwards's spectacles gleamed. "Her Grace wishes it."

"And are you the man who shall judge that her conditions are met?"

"I am."

"Marriage," said Max thoughtfully. "Sobriety. Those are well-defined; a man is married, or he is not. He drinks, or he does not. Respectability . . ." He made an equivocating motion with one hand. "That is less objective."

"I grasp your concern." Mr. Edwards removed his spectacles. "My advice would be to consider whether or not you would be content to acknowledge your actions in the town square. If you would proclaim them proudly, I believe you'll have little to fear from Her Grace."

Max thought not. He thought that the duchess would be appalled by a solid half of the things he had done in town squares, to say nothing of what he'd done in gaming hells and theater boxes and pleasure gardens. But then, Her Grace had no conception of what his life had been.

"I see," he replied politely to the attorney.

The captain was still speaking with the duchess, his shoulders hunched over as he bent his head down to hers. Max rested one hand on his hip and tapped his fingers. The velvet of his coat was worn there from the nervous habit. What was the captain so eager to know?

He couldn't shake the feeling that the man was trying to steal a march on him somehow. But how? The captain, as the duchess had spelled out earlier, had a nearer claim than Max, and nothing either of them did would change that. The captain had the inside lane already.

But if the duchess approved of the captain's bride, she might settle an additional amount on him. Was that what the man was after? Fifteen hundred pounds per annum was significant—a bloody fortune, in Max's eyes—but it was surely a trifle to the mistress of Carlyle Castle. "Does she expect to choose our brides?" he murmured, only partly to the solicitor.

Mr. Edwards's face grew pained. "Indeed not. Surely—surely you wouldn't think of wedding an actress or a courtesan?"

"No," said Max, smiling faintly at the confirmation that the attorney did, in fact, expect him to do precisely that. "Nothing like it." His gaze lingered on the captain. That fellow wanted the duchess's approval desperately, and he wasn't hiding it.

Max instinctively recoiled from doing the same. The duchess thought he was a thoroughgoing rogue already, incapable of making a correct decision. If the captain—who obviously stood far higher in her favor—allowed her to ride roughshod over him, she would think Max deserved it, too, if not worse.

Max wasn't about to let the duchess, or anyone, pull his strings.

But perhaps . . . perhaps she had handed him the chance to cut those strings once and for all.

Chapter Two

For almost sixty years, a pottery works at the bottom of Marslip Hill had produced earthenware by the Tate family. It was in all respects a family business; each new generation of children was exposed to all aspects of the industry, to see where they might fit in best. Brides were wed from neighboring families, knowing what to expect and proud to ally themselves with the Tates.

Like many family businesses, it had been the desire of each generation of Tates to see his sons join him and take over the works eventually. For three generations it had happened just that way. But the current owner, Samuel Tate, had no sons, only two daughters. And although he loved them both dearly, never had he wished for sons more than on this day, in the middle of this blistering argument with not just one but both daughters at once.

"Papa!" Bianca was in a full-fledged fury. "You've gone mad!"

"Not a bit," he returned. "It's a brilliant idea and will be the making of us."

"The making of *you*," she flung back. "Not Cathy! You're trying to ruin her life!"

They both turned toward the elder sister, who

had sat mute and morose through the entire argument. At their regard, tears obligingly welled up in her big blue eyes. One streaked down her pink cheek as if trailed by the brush of an artist. "No, Bee," she protested, her voice raspy from tears. "That's too far . . ."

Bianca was having none of it. "*Ruin*," she repeated forcefully. "Break her heart and overrule her will!"

Their father made a face and waved one hand. "Spare me the dramatics. It's an excellent match! She said herself it wouldn't be anything like ruin."

Bianca's fingers itched to throw something at him, and a compotier stood obligingly nearby, waiting on the corner of the table for approval. Unfortunately it was one of the new ones, shaped like a hollowed-out strawberry leaf with curling vines forming the handles and charming little clusters of berries nestled around the base. It had been made by their best modeler, a truly beautiful piece—so she reluctantly refrained. "Cathy should not have to say anything. *She* should have been the one who came to *you* about her marriage, not the other way around."

"Now, Bee," Samuel said, putting his hands out diplomatically. "Would you have me throw aside a great opportunity for either one of you? St. James is a gentleman—what's more, he's a gentleman who's heir to a duke." He shook an admonishing finger. "Your sister, a duchess! And you want me to sit quietly by and tell him no, without even considering it?"

Bianca folded her arms. "So you're only considering it? And Cathy shall decide, freely and absolutely?"

His gaze veered away. "I shall counsel her, of course . . ."

"You've already made up your mind!" She paced the room, her skirts swinging and threatening the safety of a row of egg cups on the lower shelf, before abruptly stopping in front of her sister. "Cathy, do you want to marry Mr. St. James?" she asked, as evenly and calmly as she could manage.

The tears pooled again. "It—it is a very eligible match," said Cathy hesitantly. "And a great honor to be asked . . ."

"And do you wish to be his wife, to live at his side and bear his children, to subjugate your desires to his own, to suffer his temper and indulge his vanities, from now until the day you die?" prompted Bianca.

"And you accuse me of influencing her!" exclaimed their father, erupting from his seat.

Another tear rolled down Cathy's face. "Bianca . . ."

"Do you?" Bianca repeated.

Her sister's eyes darted to their father, now glowering from his side of the room. "I—I don't wish to disappoint Papa . . ."

"See?" Samuel stalked over and took Cathy's hand. "Catherine, my dear, I want your happiness—as well as your security and comfort, and a man like St. James can amply provide both."

"Not with any money of his own," put in Bianca.

"He's a cousin of the Duke of Carlyle," continued Samuel, his attention fixed on his elder daughter. "Imagine that! You would move in the finest circles, with duchesses and countesses—perhaps even princesses. Why, one outbreak of smallpox and you might become a duchess yourself."

"Perhaps you can ask the vicar to add that to the marriage service," Bianca added snidely. "Blessed Lord, may it please you to smite the following persons with smallpox . . ."

Samuel's ears were red. He resolutely kept his back to her. "And he's a handsome fellow, isn't he? All the girls could hardly stop speaking of him when he came to dinner last month."

"Perhaps he'll have one of them," muttered Bianca. "Or more likely, all of them. He has a dissolute air about him . . ."

"Young and clever, handsome and eligible," finished Samuel in a growl, shooting a furious glance at his younger daughter, who only shrugged. "If you'd brought him to me, I would have given my blessing at once. Does it really matter who introduced him to you?"

"Does it really matter who shares his bed and belongs to him?" Bianca tapped her chin as if in thought.

"Enough!" roared Samuel, his patience gone at last. "That's enough from you!"

"And from you!" she blazed back. "Mama would be appalled!"

That charge vibrated in the air. Cathy sucked in a frightened gasp. Samuel snatched off his wig and threw it on his desk, looking as though he were choking on a curse. "Enough," he snarled. "Enough!" He stalked around the desk and put his hands on his hips, the sign he was done speaking to them, and they were expected to go.

Still sniffling, Cathy rushed to the door. There she paused, clutching her apron, her flawless cheeks mottled red and her eyes waterlogged. "Bianca," she said softly. "Come, Bee."

Bianca struggled, but there was no choice. Something must get through to her father about the barbarity of his actions. No—there was nothing else—it must be done. The compotier struck the wall with a satisfying, expensive crash. Ignoring both her pang of regret at destroying the piece and her father's bellow of outrage, she stormed from the room, catching her sister's hand and pulling her along, down the stairs out of the shop, and up the hill to their home.

"How dare he!" she seethed, slamming her way into the sitting room and sending Jane, the young maid, scuttling out with a yelp of panic. "He must have been struck by some horrible malady—perhaps stood too near the kilns and melted his brain—"

"You know he didn't." Cathy, still gasping for breath after the furious charge up the hill, staggered to the settee and sank down. "An advantageous marriage is not an unreasonable thing for a father to suggest . . ."

"Don't ever say that!" Hands jammed on her hips, Bianca leaned over her wilting sister. "He proposed to sell you like a suckling pig in the market, without so much as asking your opinion!"

"Now, Bianca." Cathy shook her head in reproach. "That's not the way it was."

"Why are you defending this?" Bianca was honestly amazed. "I thought you didn't care for Mr. St. James at all."

The man who had lobbed his grapeshot shell of a marriage proposal into their happy family was not entirely a stranger to them. Maximilian St. James had met their father in London at a philosophical meeting, during a dinner at the home of one of

Papa's business associates. Samuel had come home impressed with the fellow, praising his intelligence and manners.

Bianca, thinking him nothing more than another idle gentleman taking advantage of Lord Sherwood's famed hospitality, had paid little attention. There was far too much for her to tend to at home to expend much care on any idle gentleman—for St. James was clearly a gentleman, not a working man. Despite Samuel's obvious infatuation, he made no mention of anything useful that the man did, unlike Lord Sherwood, who had founded a practical school for artisans, or Mr. Hopkins, who crafted the most beautiful clocks when he wasn't reading Diderot's *Encyclopédie*.

Then Samuel invited the man to Staffordshire, to their home. Dinner parties fell under Cathy's purview: which tablecloths to use, how to arrange the silver to best reflect the flowers and candles, whether the goose should be dressed with watercress or stuffed with sage and bread. She had their mother's flair for style and entertaining.

That time Bianca did take note of Mr. St. James. It was hard not to, as he arrived like a peacock strutting into the midst of a bevy of plain, sober grouse. Tall and lean, he wore his dark hair unpowdered and long, not caring that it curled around his shoulders like a Boucher Madonna's. The embroidery on his burgundy velvet coat sparkled in the candlelight, and his sharp London wit set him aside from the earnest scientists and philosophers who filled the table.

Still, her feeling then had not been negative. Despite being so attractive, he was obviously well-read and, as Papa had said, intelligent. If he were pottery, though, he would have been a tureen: handsome and expensively made, drawing every eye around the table, but hollow, and good for nothing more than holding the humble soup. Bianca expected he'd got his fill of philosophy and commoners, and wouldn't be back.

Instead he reared his head mere months later— just yesterday in fact, proposing to marry Cathy, with whom he'd barely exchanged an hour's conversation.

"He's a very eligible gentleman," Cathy replied to her demand. "He is cousin to a duke, you know."

"Which makes *him* nothing," Bianca retorted. "It has given him pretensions, though . . ."

Cathy flushed. "But he's not from Marslip, he's from London. To be singled out by a gentleman is an honor, and you know that a connection to the Duke of Carlyle would mean so much to Papa."

"I don't know what great benefit Papa hopes to reap from being able to say he dines with the distant cousin of a duke. There must be a thousand such people in Britain."

For the first time her sister frowned at her, returning somewhat to her usual poise. "You're being deliberately obstinate."

Bianca's lips parted. She sank down to the floor and grasped her sister's hand. "Oh Cathy—you're considering this mad proposal, aren't you? Why? Was I wrong about Mr. Mayne?"

A minute shudder rippled through her sister at that name. "I find—" Cathy stopped and cleared her throat. "I find that if I don't think of him, Papa's plan is very . . . sensible."

Sensible. Not exciting, or thrilling, or even desirable. It would please Papa, and Cathy, ever anxious to do that, would throw aside the man she did love for one she did not. Bianca's temper began to smolder anew.

"All right. Perhaps it is," she said quietly, watching her sister's face. "I suppose you'd be married here, in the church at Marslip. Shall you have Mr. Mayne read the banns, do you think, or will Papa insist on a license?" Cathy said nothing but her chin trembled. "In that case we could have the wedding here, in this room. I'm sure Mr. Mayne won't mind, and it would be more convenient for Aunt Frances. After that, I suppose Mr. St. James will prefer to live in London."

The color drained from Cathy's cheeks.

Bianca went on. "It's such a long way away. I do hope you'll come visit at times—it won't be the same without you. How shall I know which tablecloths to use, or whether Mr. Mayne should sit beside Mrs. Arlington or Mr. Soames, when you're not here to—"

"Stop!" Cathy shot off the settee and flung herself against the wall in the corner. Her shoulders shook. "Stop, Bee!"

"I'm not doing anything," she pointed out. And then she waited.

Unlike Bianca, Cathy hadn't inherited their father's iron will; she had more of their mother's desire to please, especially to please Samuel. Papa had overwhelmed her this time, like a sudden hurricane blowing in and flattening her to the ground before she knew what was happening.

But Cathy was Samuel's daughter, too, and once she recovered from the shock of her father's suggestion and realized what it would mean, she would pick herself up and discover her spine.

And she did. After a few minutes of silent sobbing against the wall, Cathy straightened, dabbed her eyes dry, and hesitantly turned back to face Bianca. "You think I'm a terrible coward, don't you?"

She shook her head.

Cathy went to the window and drew aside the curtain. The pottery works lay down the hill, smoke puffing industriously from the kiln chimneys. "Papa thinks it's a good match," she murmured, almost to herself. "But he can't want me to move so far from Marslip . . ."

Bianca said nothing.

"London is a massive city," Cathy went on, her voice growing stronger and more despairing at the same time. "And so far! I might not see you or Papa again for years!"

Bianca pinched a loose thread from the hem of her apron and bided her time.

"And Mr. Mayne—" Cathy stopped. Her knuckles were white where she gripped the curtain.

After a fraught minute of silence, Bianca stirred. "I suppose it would be a great surprise to him."

Her sister made a noise like a sob. "It would."

"I always thought he was so fond of you," Bianca went on carefully. "And you of him."

Silence.

Bianca climbed to her feet. "Only you know what you want, Cathy. You're right—Mr. St. James is very eligible, and perhaps he will inveigle Carlyle to buy a large and expensive dinner service from Papa. He might exhibit it, like Mr. Wedgwood did—the Duke's Service! Papa would like that very much, I grant you, and it wouldn't be bad for our factory, either, for the world to see our work on a noble table. So Papa would be pleased as anything, and you would have a charming, intelligent gentleman for your husband." Cathy seemed turned to marble, she was so still. The devil inside Bianca prodded her to add, "And he *is* devilishly handsome. Rather puts the Marslip lads to shame, in fact, even Mr. Mayne—"

Cathy turned on her in a swirl of skirts. "Don't," she growled. "Don't say it!"

Bianca relented. She could tell her arrow had hit its mark; it wanted only time to do its work. "I won't," she promised, squeezing her sister's hands. "It is your decision, after all—your life, your marriage, and your heart. I will support you and help you, no matter what you decide, so long as it is what you want."

Pale and somber, Cathy nodded. "Thank you, Bianca."

She kissed her sister's cheek. "Of course! Now I should get back to work. That red glaze isn't quite as bright as I would like it to be, and it has an appalling tendency to blister if it's not applied just perfectly." She made a face. "Since no handsome strangers have seen fit to ride up and offer to marry *me* and sweep me away from glazes and pots and Marslip!"

Cathy laughed. Bianca smiled. They both knew she would never leave her workbench, where she experimented with glazes and minerals to improve Tate pottery, and Bianca's setdowns of any local young men who sidled too close to her were legendary.

And they also both knew Cathy was desperately in love with Mr. Mayne the curate. Mayne hadn't asked for her hand yet only because he was waiting for his waspish elderly grandmother to die and leave him her modest fortune.

Time, Bianca thought to herself. That was all they needed. She only had to stall Papa long enough for Cathy to realize what he was asking of her.

Chapter Three

This time Max rode to Marslip on a horse of his own, which allowed him to study the property at some leisure.

Samuel Tate came from a long line of potters, though none of them had had his business acumen. Under his hand the pottery factory had grown and prospered, and he'd built a small empire at the foot of Marslip Hill, rather grandly named Perusia. Tate produced very handsome dinnerware, with brilliant glazes and beautifully done etchings and ornamentation. Numerous wealthy and aristocratic families in Britain dined off Tate platters and plates. By a stroke of good fortune, Tate's brother-in-law had been one of the engineers when the mania for canals swept the country, and so a branch canal ran near enough for Perusia wares to be shipped to Liverpool and London quickly and efficiently.

With quality wares and a reliable shipping method, Tate should have been the richest potter in the country. He was a clever man, and ambitious. Max had been impressed when they met at the home of a mutual acquaintance, Lord Sherwood.

But Tate had curious blind spots as well. Sherwood confided that the man had had difficulties collecting payment from some of those aristocratic patrons, even as the patrons exhibited their custom dinnerware with pride.

Max wasn't surprised by that. He *was* surprised that Tate seemed to accept it, even as it cost him dearly. Max could see a dozen ways to improve the profitability of the business, and when he'd mentioned this—idly, almost absently—to Tate, the man seemed struck by the thought. It had led to an invitation to Perusia itself, which Max had accepted even though it lay in the wilds of Staffordshire.

He could see exactly how large and prosperous Perusia was. The factory occupied four long brick buildings, arranged in the shape of an *E* a short distance from the canal. The tall bottle-shaped kilns stood in a cluster at one end, smoke welling industriously from the chimneys. The workmen were neat and purposeful, and always hurrying about their business. A steady stream of barges came and went at the factory landing.

It was an opportunity, and Max was ever ready to seize an opportunity. He saw brilliant possibilities in a partnership: Tate managing the factory as he'd been doing, while Max assumed the chore of marketing and selling the wares, not just in London and Liverpool but across Europe and even into America.

Alas, at that dinner Max had sensed that Tate was less enamored of a partnership than he was. Everyone in the Perusia business appeared to be family—a cousin traveling to the warehouse in Liverpool, a nephew managing the books, the engineering brother-in-law. It had seemed yet another opportunity just out of his reach, another chance he would helplessly watch slip away, until the Duchess of Carlyle dropped the key into Max's hand. She may not have intended for him to use it this way, but Max was quietly sure of two things.

First, that he would never be the Duke of Carlyle. Captain St. James had spent the entirety of their visit to Carlyle Castle ingratiating himself with the duchess. Over dinner he'd talked of taking a house near the castle, to better study the workings of the estate from Mr. Edwards, and of his hope to meet a respectable woman and settle down as soon as possible. The soldier virtually oozed earnest sincerity and dogged determination. It was almost amusing, really, how transparent his solicitude was. He all but kissed the duchess's shoe, and practically begged her to choose a wife for him, all the better to please her.

But it worked; the duchess seemed more satisfied than amused at his fawning, and promised to introduce the captain to women she deemed eligible and appropriate. Max thought the duchess would have him married before the harvest was in, and securely under her thumb as well.

So the captain would be the next duke, but Max was still promised an income. He didn't like the prospect of having to prove himself every year to get it, though, and he wanted no part of giving the duchess any sort of control over his behavior, even if he wasn't quite the wastrel she clearly believed him to be.

That had been the germ of his plan. Tate required a keener, more ruthless eye; Max possessed that, but required an opportunity to put it to use. And by a most fortunate coincidence, Tate also had a beautiful unmarried daughter, who'd kept an excellent table and blushed very prettily at Max's compliments during his visit to Perusia.

So secondly, Max meant to seize this chance to make his own marriage and secure his own fortune. With five hundred pounds—less the two hundred required to settle a few pressing debts and other expenses, get a horse, and refurbish his wardrobe a bit—and the promise of an income of fifteen hundred, plus a close kinship with the Carlyles, he was perfectly poised to sweep a lovely, sheltered country girl off her feet.

Particularly if that country girl had no brothers and a prosperous father who was already disposed to like him.

Max sensed this proposal would appeal to Tate. Not just a business partner but a son-in-law, who could care for the man's family after he was gone. Not a fortune hunter, but a gentleman with an independent income, even if one dependent on a duchess's whim. Not just a London gentleman but one with connections to a duke, elevating the man's status now and his descendants later.

And Miss Tate was a beauty, petite and delicate. She came to his shoulder, with inky dark curls and wide blue eyes. Her voice was soft and musical, and she had presided over dinner with grace and a sweet, innocent charm.

Max couldn't help smiling in anticipation as he dismounted in front of the handsome brick house. It was new, built less than a decade ago when Tate's fortunes began to rise. Max had lived in too many old houses, with smoky chimneys and crumbling plaster and leaking roofs, to have any affection for them. He heartily approved of this snug new house, as well as the lovely, wealthy bride who would come with it.

Samuel Tate came out to meet him, a broad smile on his square face. "St. James! Welcome to Perusia."

"It is my very great pleasure to be invited again." He handed off the reins to the lad who came for his horse and swept off his tricorn hat as he bowed.

"Come in, come in! I'd begun to fear the rains would wash out the road and delay you."

Max smiled. "Yes, the road was in bad shape. Perhaps I shall propose to Carlyle that he put up a bill to extend the turnpike to Marslip."

Tate's eyes brightened. "An excellent idea, sir! The other potters and I have asked for such a thing before, but I'm sure His Grace's approval would be an immense aid."

"No doubt," agreed Max, still smiling. The current duke would probably ignore his request, but the soldier seemed a practical fellow, and Max suspected he was the sort to feel responsible for family. A skillful presentation and a little emotional pressure might bring him around.

He didn't mean to be a parasite on Tate. Quite the opposite; Max intended to make Perusia the most successful pottery works in all of England—perhaps Europe.

Together they walked down the hill to the factory, talking of London. Tate was intrigued by all the news from town, particularly of the enduring passion for antiquities from Rome and Athens. Max answered equably, deducing that the man was thinking of new items for his factories. And this was, after all, his expertise. Max spent his life among the most fashionable set, even if he couldn't afford that life himself.

"Now, then," said Tate, clasping his hands when they had reached his private office, overlooking the humming workshops below. "I suppose you're anxious to hear my reply on the matter you wrote about to me."

Max inclined his head. "I am."

Samuel shifted in his seat. "You have the devil's own timing, sir. That question had been on my mind lately." He paused, his gaze assessing. "You're not from Marslip, but you've got a clever head on your shoulders, and I admit I was struck by our conversations earlier about improving and spreading the reputation of our wares. But one thing concerns me greatly, and that is the depth of your interest."

"In the business," asked Max, "or in your daughter?"

"Both," replied Samuel bluntly.

"Of course." Max crossed one leg over the other. "I would call it sincere and fathoms deep, on both counts. I am deeply impressed by what you've built, sir. After our conversation at Lord Sherwood's, I considered proposing a mere business arrangement, whereby I would manage showrooms in London and other cities, and split the profits from it. A fair and equitable partnership.

"But then I was invited to Perusia and met Miss Tate." He leaned forward and rested one elbow on the table. "I sense that you are a man devoted to two things in life: this pottery works, and your family. It only made my admiration for you grow. We may not have been raised in similar circumstances, but I envy you both of those dear concerns."

Tate harrumphed. "You're cousin to a duke."

Max opened his hands almost penitently. "We did not presume upon the St. Jameses of Carlyle Castle. My mother preferred I grow up not thinking too highly of myself, but to have humility and a sense of self-reliance. And it's served me well," he added in the same humble tone.

It was not a lie. He merely omitted that there had been no alternative, nor any desire to debase himself by begging them after that callously sent five pounds.

"But recently those relations have become more cordial," he went on. "I spent several days at Carlyle Castle becoming acquainted with Her Grace the Duchess as well as my other St. James cousin. It may not be known widely, but His Grace's brother recently fell ill and died, leaving the dukedom without a direct heir. My cousin is the heir presumptive, but until he marries and has a child of his own, I am *his* heir. It renewed my own sense of family, and made me appreciate your devotion all the more."

"Admirable," said Tate in approval.

"A man like you will want to see not just his fortune preserved, but also—and more importantly—his children cared for, with the fruits of that fortune." He smiled a little. "I also confess Miss Tate's beauty and gentle nature made a very striking impression upon me."

Tate's head was bobbing faintly in agreement. "'Tis a great honor you do her, sir."

"The honor," said Max gravely, "would be all mine, if you were to bless my suit."

"Well." Looking quite pleased, Tate smacked his

hands down on his knees. "I must say you've persuaded me. Your ideas about a showroom are rather grand, but with a gentleman such as yourself in charge of it, I think we might pull it off and really make something of ourselves." He paused, something flickering over his face. "Of course, you'll have to win my daughter's approval as well."

Max smiled. "I wouldn't wish it otherwise."

Tate laughed. "You'll have plenty of chance tonight at dinner! She presides over my household in her late mother's place, you know. Every arrangement is done at her command, from the flowers to the table setting. I can't think you'll find anything lacking, sir, in her skills or in her person."

"I have no doubt of it," replied Max, who had already made his decision weeks ago.

BIANCA DRESSED FOR dinner that night as she might for battle.

Papa had invited That Man to visit. He had arrived earlier and been installed in the front bedchamber before vanishing to the offices with Papa. She'd heard Jane marveling to Cook about how elegantly he dressed, how charming his manners were, and how incredibly handsome he was. They had already guessed downstairs that he was courting Miss Cathy—not merely because every unmarried man who came to the house wanted to court Miss Cathy, but also because Samuel was treating the fellow as if he were already one of the family.

And in that case, thought Bianca grimly as she clasped on Mama's necklace of pearls, he would be treated as one . . . for better and for worse.

She went downstairs to the parlor. Aunt Frances

was already there, looking just as irate as Bianca felt. To be fair, Aunt Frances always looked irate, but tonight Bianca was pleased to see it.

"The chimney in my sitting room is blocked," was her greeting. "Tell Samuel to send a man over to clear it." Papa had built Frances a home of her own when he built Perusia, declaring that he couldn't throw her out but neither could he share a roof with her. Her Ivy Cottage was down the hill, away from the factory.

"Of course." Bianca stooped to pet Trevor, the fat white bulldog who went everywhere with Frances. As usual, the animal growled low in his throat even as he submitted to her attention. Trevor acted very fierce but was virtually a lapdog, if treated the right way. Bianca scratched between his ears until his bandy little legs quivered and gave way, and Trevor collapsed onto his back and presented his belly for more scratching.

"Trevor," said Frances sternly. "Get up! No cheese for you."

Bianca quietly slipped the dog the small piece of cheese she'd concealed in her handkerchief for him. Trevor lapped it silently from her fingers as if in conspiracy to evade Frances's temper. Having got what he wanted, the dog flipped over onto his feet and waddled off to examine the corner of the settee.

"Has Papa told you about our guest?" Bianca rose to her feet and fluffed her skirts. Papa had decreed they must look their best tonight and she had obeyed. She wore her newest gown, deep burgundy with lace flounces and velvet trim on the stomacher, and had even let her maid tame her hair into smooth curls.

Frances sniffed. "A gentleman, he says! Bosh. A good-for-nothing ne'er-do-well, with his eye on Samuel's fortune."

"Oh no, Aunt," said Bianca somberly, even though she agreed with every word. "Papa likes him very much."

Frances clucked. "More fool him."

Cathy came in then. She looked glorious, radiant in a rose-pink brocade gown with silk ribbons, silver combs glinting in her dark hair. But her eyes were red and her mouth was a sad droop. "Good evening, Aunt," she murmured.

Frances was not really their aunt; she was Samuel's, the younger sister of his father. In her youth Frances had been considered a handsome girl, but her father's ambition prevented her from marrying the prosperous farmer she'd fallen in love with. He insisted she wed the man who kept their business accounts, to shore up the fellow's loyalty to the business. Frances dutifully married the bookkeeper and retaliated by making everyone around her miserable for the next forty years.

Now she looked Cathy up and down. "Are we attending a dinner party or a funeral?"

Cathy gave her a look of reproach. "A dinner party for Papa's guest. You helped me choose the menu."

Frances glared and took a sip of her port. She always drank port before dinner, claiming it settled her stomach. Bianca thought it did more to loosen her tongue. "The London rogue."

A strangled squeak escaped Cathy. She bent her head and fussed with one of the bows on her gown.

"Why do you say so, Aunt?" Bianca was deliberately prodding a hungry bear. Frances hadn't had anyone to exercise her temper on in weeks. Samuel had been in Liverpool for almost a month and only returned recently, and Cousin Ned, the factory office manager, had learned to avoid her. In Samuel's absence there had been no guests. Frances considered it beneath her to browbeat servants, and despite her crotchety manner, she cared for both Bianca and Cathy. Mr. St. James was fresh meat, as it were; prime prey.

Now their great-aunt raised her brows. "What other sort is there? London is the font of all vice, my father used to say." She sipped her port. "I recognized his sort when he was here last. Very sure of himself. Not as clever as he thinks he is. Too handsome by half. I wonder he left London at all, to consort with the ordinary people of Staffordshire."

"Not ordinary at all," said a voice from the doorway. They all three turned to see Mr. St. James, blinding in green satin with glittering gold embroidering. He wore his hair neatly queued tonight, and made a very elegant bow. "There are quite extraordinary people here in Staffordshire, judging by the inhabitants of this room alone," he added gallantly.

Aunt Frances's shoulders went back and her chin came up—all the better to peer down her nose at him. "What effrontery to say such a thing. We're hardly acquainted well enough for you to know."

He smiled. "I could honestly say it based solely on appearances. Mr. Tate did not warn me there would be three lovely ladies at dinner tonight."

Frances stared at him a moment, gave another sniff for good measure, and turned her back on him. "Have us a touch more, dear." She held out her glass, and Bianca obediently poured more port.

"So why have you come all this way, if you were not eagerly anticipating our company?"

Mr. St. James smiled. He had a deep dimple in one cheek, a very masculine slash that hardly deserved the delicate term *dimple*. "A man always hopes, madam."

"More fool you," muttered Frances. Bianca smiled happily.

"Welcome to Perusia, Mr. St. James." Pale but poised, Cathy went to greet him. "Won't you come in? I hope you remember my father's aunt, Mrs. Bentley, and my sister, Miss Bianca Tate. We are very informal here, with only family tonight."

"Thank you, Miss Tate." He bowed beautifully over Cathy's hand. Bianca grudgingly admitted his manners were perfect. "If you are informal tonight, I vow I would swoon away at the mere sight of your formality. You would outshine any lady in London or Paris."

"Trevor darling, don't piddle on our guest's shoe," drawled Frances, turning Bianca's private disgust into glee once more. Mr. St. James looked down with a startled expression at the grumpy bulldog inspecting his shoe, and sidled a step away.

But then he went down on one knee and let Trevor sniff his hand, and—to the astonishment of everyone else in the room—the bulldog sank down and pushed his head up into Mr. St. James's hand.

"That's a good boy," said the man in a deep, rough voice, stroking hard down the dog's head and back. Trevor's tongue lolled out of his mouth until he lay down flat and gave a guttural moan of happiness.

Turncoat, thought Bianca in pique. After she'd smuggled him cheese, no less.

Papa came in then, looking quite pleased with himself. "My apologies, St. James. Cathy my dear, have you welcomed our guest?"

"Yes, Papa."

"That's my girl," he said in approval, before complimenting her dress and hair. Cathy blushed scarlet at this unexpected flattery, Cathy who was so beautiful she looked lovely in a coarse linen smock and who never expected to be told so.

Bianca rolled her eyes at this blatant fawning. Her father loved them both, but he wasn't the type to lavish praise on anyone—least of all on his daughters. In the workshop, she and her father were notorious for arguing furiously over new designs and technique, and Papa treated Cathy's attentions as he'd treated Mama's: his due, and nothing out of the ordinary.

To her chagrin, she happened to glance Mr. St. James's way. Papa was exclaiming over Cathy's hair combs, which had been their mother's, and the cursed man who wanted to marry her was watching Bianca instead.

For a brief moment their eyes met—his dark and assessing, hers probably shocked and hostile. That was how she felt, at any rate, and Bianca made a point of tearing her gaze off him and pretending great interest in the clasp of her bracelet. Such an *impertinent* rogue.

They went in to dinner, Aunt Frances on Papa's arm, Cathy with Mr. St. James. Bianca trailed silently behind, plotting how best to achieve her ends.

She had schemed to invite a large party of people, including Mr. Mayne the curate, all the better to contrast him with Mr. St. James, but Papa had put his foot down. "Family," he'd barked at her, "and no one else."

That meant it was up to Aunt Frances. And fortunately, the older woman seemed spoiling for the chance.

"Who, pray, are your people, sir?" she asked him over the fish course. "I have forgotten."

He smiled. "Have you? I'm sure I never mentioned them at all."

Frances bared her teeth at him. "That explains it! My memory is usually faultless. Do tell us, that we may all know."

"My father," he said easily, "was, as you know, a St. James, a relation of the Duke of Carlyle."

"How distant?" asked Bianca innocently. "My goodness, sir, were you raised amidst the splendor of Carlyle Castle?"

Cathy gave her a reproachful look and Papa growled under his breath. Bianca only batted her eyes at their guest, who sat smiling back with the self-possession of a panther, biding his time.

"No, Miss Tate," he replied. "I am only a distant cousin, and had not the privilege of visiting the castle often."

"Oh," she said. "Only on visiting days, I suppose?" Visiting days, when any strangers passing by would be permitted to stroll the castle grounds and see the house.

He continued smiling at her as if he knew exactly what she was up to. "Not even then, I'm afraid. I have resided in London for some time. Much too far away to drop in for a cup of tea, or even a visiting day."

Bianca's mouth flattened. Thankfully Frances rushed into the breach.

"Yes, yes, Carlyle." She dropped a bite of turbot on the carpet, and Trevor noisily slurped it up. "Who are your mother's people?"

"I doubt you will know them, ma'am. My grandparents came from Hanover."

"German," said Frances with a whiff of disdain.

Mr. St. James only bowed his head in acknowledgement. "Their parents were retainers of His Majesty George the First, when he came from Hanover."

Frances directed a frigid look at him, for mentioning that the recent kings had been more German than English. "Retainers! Who were they? A Groom of the Stool, perhaps?"

Bianca almost spat out her wine. She cast an admiring glance at her great-aunt for suggesting St. James's ancestor had been in charge of the royal chamber pot.

"Not at all," he said easily. "I believe my great-grandfather was a falconer."

"Falconry!" Papa seized the point. "Very noble sport, what? Fit for a king!"

"I daresay it is considerably less noble when one must clean the mews," said Frances tartly.

St. James laughed. "Perhaps that is why they gave it up for farming, ma'am."

Frances's mouth pinched. She regarded farming as a proper and hearty occupation.

"Enough of grandparents and farmers," declared Papa. "St. James, you've been in London. Tell us all the entertainments to be found there. Cathy was just reading to us from *The Lady's Magazine* about a fencing match at Carlton House, between a Frenchman and a lady, of all people! Are such things common there?"

"Would that they were," murmured Bianca, imagining running an épée through the rogue who sat across from her.

He, rudely, heard her. "I would not call it common, Miss Tate, but enthralling nonetheless."

"At Carlton House, I'm sure all was as proper as it should be," said Cathy, giving Bianca a look of warning. "It is the home of the Prince of Wales."

"And yet we have seen how even the noblest of gentlemen, like His Highness, may harbor a wild and scandalous nature," replied Bianca with a simpering smile. "Wouldn't you agree, Mr. St. James?"

He sent her a searing glance across the table. "I would, Miss Tate," he said with a faint smile. "In the case of the prince."

"We'll not be gossiping about His Highness," warned Papa, before forcing the conversation toward inane topics like the weather and the state of the roads near Marslip. Bianca ate in silence and hoped Mr. St. James was as bored by this excessively polite conversation as she was.

By the time Aunt Frances led the way to the drawing room after dinner, she was seething. Thanks to Papa's dry conversation, St. James had come across as faultlessly polite and capable of discussing roads and turnpikes until everyone in hearing fell asleep. It was one of Papa's favorite subjects, though, and even Aunt Frances had recognized how unlikely she was to deter him from it. The ladies had retreated from the dining room to avoid falling face first into the pudding.

"He's very much a London gentleman." Bianca returned to her first plan, persuading Cathy that St. James was too snobbish and too elegant to make a good husband. "No wonder he agreed so enthusiastically with Papa's raving about the roads. It must have been a vicious shock to his person to make the journey north."

Cathy looked at her sadly and said nothing.

"He seems hearty enough." Frances was having more port. "Solid farm stock."

"Yes, how astonishing! I never would have guessed, from the amount of lace on his coat."

"Don't you disdain a farming man," said Frances sternly. "It makes a man ever so strong and firm-minded, well grounded in his passions and purposes."

"I shudder to imagine Mr. St. James's passions," said Bianca before she could stop herself.

With a faint noise of distress, Cathy jumped up and fled the room.

Frances raised her brows, mellowing with her second taste of port. "What's got into her? I declare, that girl needs a husband. She's been very emotional lately. One dinner with a man and she's in tears!"

Bianca scowled. Contrary to all previous indications, Aunt Frances sounded almost like Papa. "You do know St. James wants to marry Cathy?" she said.

Frances's brows snapped upward. "What, what? Cathy?"

"He's already made Papa an offer for her," she replied. "That's why he's come to Marslip—to win a bride and secure a handsome income from Perusia, no doubt. And Papa approves." She gave a tiny shrug. "Only I don't believe Cathy is coming around to the idea."

"Fool girl," said Frances stoutly. "She could certainly do worse."

"Yes, of course," said Bianca innocently, "the great-grandson of a Groom of the Stool! Or no—forgive me—a *falconer*. The honor! The prestige! We shall be elevated above everyone in Staffordshire."

The older woman shot her a dark glance. "I see what you're up to. You disapprove, and you want me to blow it all up. Well, I won't! Making foolish marriages is a Tate family tradition."

Bianca flushed at being caught out. "But Cathy and Mr. Mayne," she began hotly.

"Pshh!" Frances rose and aimed a stern finger at her. "If *that* were meant to be, Mayne would have been here on his knee, begging Samuel for her hand. Has he even made her a proposal?"

Bianca scowled in furious acknowledgement that no, the gentlemanly curate had not.

"Nor will he," finished Frances with savage coolness. "Between the two of them, nothing would ever get decided, let alone accomplished. I never met two more docile, agreeable people in my life! They both require someone with more backbone. At least this St. James fellow has that. He didn't let *you* rumble over him, did he?"

Bianca shot to her feet. "Why can't two people who are matched in disposition make a happy marriage? Why must there be one with backbone and one who gives way? I daresay two gentle, accommodating people would sort things out quite well, if left to their own devices."

"No?" Frances leaned closer, her sharp blue eyes pitying. "Then why hasn't Mayne gone to your father, even in the face of a determined rival? Why is your sister sitting by accepting St. James's compliments and flattery? You always think you know best, miss, but this isn't your problem to solve." She threw up one hand. "You can't save people from getting what they deserve!"

She swept out of the room, Trevor waddling after her with a startled yip.

Bianca seethed. Did no one see that Papa had been dazzled to the point of imbecility by the Londoner's manners and elegance? Did no one realize Cathy had been cowed into silence, not charmed into agreement? She reserved judgment about Mr. Mayne, who certainly *could* use more backbone, but he ought to have a chance to prove himself, and this hurried rush to get Cathy to the altar seemed specifically designed to prevent him having one.

She stormed up the stairs and banged on her sister's door before flinging it open. "Cathy, I—"

She stopped cold. Her sister jerked upright from the open bureau drawer, red-eyed and with a petticoat in her hands. An open valise sat on the floor at her feet. "Don't try to stop me, Bee," she said, her voice trembling. "Don't you dare!"

Bianca closed the door. "From doing what?"

Her sister's wild eyes darted to the door, then to the window. "I'm eloping with Richard." She took a crumpled paper from her skirt pocket and thrust it out, almost defiantly. "I'm going."

Bianca read the first sentence of Mr. Mayne's scrawl—*My darling, I am in agony; if you love me half as much as I love you, let us fly to Manchester this very night before we are divided from each other forever*— and smiled.

"Of course I won't stop you," she said quietly. "I've come to help you."

Chapter Four

Max's plan was proceeding brilliantly, by any objective measure.

The business was as solid as he'd thought, with far more potential to grow. Tate had shown him some spectacular samples of a brilliant cerulean glaze, unlike anything he'd ever seen. Max pictured services painted not with bucolic country scenes but with replicas of the great works of art— not merely Fragonard and Rubens but Michelangelo's Sistine ceiling. He was sure the painters Tate employed had the talent to do it, given what he'd seen so far. It would cause a sensation in London.

His marriage proposal had been accepted. Samuel Tate had given his blessing, and Miss Tate had blushed and stammered in gratitude when he spoke to her about it. Max stayed only one night in Marslip before dashing back to London to wind up his affairs there, keen to see the thing through.

Within a fortnight it was all but done. Tate had eagerly received the marriage contract. It was more fashionable to marry by license, so Max went to the effort of visiting Doctors' Commons to secure one. He gave notice on his rooms, packed his things, and hired a manservant away from a friend who had recently suffered a disastrous loss at the gaming tables.

This time the journey to Staffordshire seemed easy and familiar, as if he were going home. In fact, Max reflected with satisfaction, he was—not only a new home and a new bride, but the first settled, fixed home and family he'd known in many years. Tate had offered him the former family house on the far side of the hill from the potteries. It wasn't as fine as the house atop the hill, but it was solid and comfortable, and would allow Miss Tate easy access to her family while Max was traveling, spreading Tate wares around the country.

Max spent considerable time contemplating how best to make Perusia the preeminent source of fine pottery wares. He must establish contacts in Edinburgh, Antwerp, Calais, eventually Paris . . . Now that the war in America was over, trading was resuming with Boston and Charleston as well. The colonials must be starved for anything elegant after so many years of blockade. Yes, the Americans had enormous potential, particularly if Max made an early, bold strike to seize the market.

He said as much to Tate that night as they shared a cold supper in Max's new home. Tate had met him at the door to hand over possession. His daughters, Tate explained, had begged off, to prepare. In the morning Max would marry Catherine, and she'd seen the house comfortably furnished and supplied. Just stepping over the threshold filled him with such a feeling of contentment that he knew, deep in his bones, this was his destiny.

"I thank God we crossed paths," said Tate at the end of the evening. "You're a rare one, St. James."

Max could not agree more. "Mr. Tate," he replied, "I might say the very same to you."

At that moment, it seemed as though everything he had ever wanted was in the palm of his hand. And it was.

Until the next morning, in the church.

BIANCA'S PLAN WENT off almost perfectly, if she did say so herself.

Cathy never had been one for scheming. The night she tearfully declared she was running off with Mr. Mayne had proved that. Her plan—if it could be called such—had been to pack her valise, lug it down the hill to the church after everyone had gone to bed, and tell Mr. Mayne that she was ready to elope. In the middle of the night. With no preparation whatsoever.

"Don't be a goose," had been Bianca's reply to that. There was no need to flee in the dead of night; St. James was returning to London in the morning. They had days, even weeks to prepare, and the better they prepared, the better off Cathy would be with her curate.

First, they'd gone to the vicarage together. Any doubts Bianca had about Mayne's stoutheartedness were swept aside by the way he seized Cathy and bent her backward in a passionate kiss. It went on so long, in fact, she had to turn her head and clear her throat twice to regain her sister's attention.

This time Mayne rose to the occasion. Far from the dithering fool Aunt Frances called him, he arranged for a travel chaise. He plotted their journey to his elder sister's home, where they could be married in peace and propriety. He took the money Bianca offered him without blinking an eye or saying a word of protest. He gazed at Cathy with rapt devotion, and swore to protect her with his life. Cathy twirled home with stars in her eyes and roses in her cheeks.

A week later Papa announced he had received the marriage contract from Mr. St. James. Cathy grew quiet and nervous, but bravely ventured a protest that it was perhaps too soon to wed someone she'd barely met. She spoke fondly of Mr. Mayne, and how much more at ease she felt around him. Deceiving Papa had not sat well with Cathy, and she seized that last chance to change his mind.

Up until then both sisters had hoped he would yet see reason. Papa was bewitched by St. James, but he could still come to his senses and recognize Cathy's unhappiness and Mayne's worth. Cathy especially hoped he would reconsider, no matter what it cost his business. By nature she was kind and caring, and she hated to hurt anyone's feelings, let alone her beloved father's.

Papa overrode her, saying firmly that Mayne was nothing but a country curate while St. James was a gentleman—and cousin to a duke, if she hadn't forgotten—and that she would have years to become acquainted with him. It was a very advantageous marriage, and he was certain she would thank him someday.

After that Cathy stopped fretting about how upset Papa would be when she was gone.

As for Bianca, she had such an argument with her father over his callous dictating of Cathy's marriage that he hadn't spoken to her for a week. This time it suited her perfectly. It gave her freedom to help Cathy smuggle her trunk to the vicarage and plan how to slip out of the house the night before the wedding. It gave Cathy leisure to write a long letter to her father explaining everything—Cathy refused to leave without doing it, but Bianca was relieved to see that her sister's eyes were dry at the end. There was a certain poetic justice in the thought of Papa dining with the interloper St. James on one side of the hill while Cathy sneaked down the far side of that same hill to meet her true love.

And now it was the morning of the wedding. Papa had invited half the town to celebrate his daughter's marriage to a gentleman. Bianca had argued against that, too, but been overruled again. Mayne, of course, was nowhere to be seen, although Papa hadn't been coldhearted enough to ask him to perform the ceremony. Mr. Filpot from St. Anne's in Waddleston Grange had come, and was cooling his heels in the morning room, trimming his fingernails with a penknife.

Aunt Frances, as if scenting something on the wind, had walked over that morning and was installed in the breakfast room with Trevor, calling for a rasher of bacon and more preserves for her bread.

Maximilian St. James, Bianca presumed, was somewhere gazing fondly at himself in the mirror, preening at how he'd gulled an ambitious country potter and his simple daughters, and tallying up the many ways he could spend Cathy's inheritance.

Bianca had also risen early, to monitor the maids and keep them from telling Papa about Cathy's absence for as long as possible. She sent Jennie and Ellen running for water, the iron, the curling tongs, more water, then a cup of chocolate, until both maids eyed her resentfully and Ellen finally declared she must go to Miss Cathy, who was the bride after all—condemning Bianca's unusually demanding behavior with a severe look.

And thus it was Ellen's scream that announced to all of Perusia that Cathy was not in her room dressing for her wedding. Papa came thundering up the stairs in alarm, until Bianca calmly handed him the letter her sister had written. The concern on her father's face, however, did not last long.

"Eloped!" Papa thrust the page to arm's length, then held it up to his face as if the words might change shape up close. "With Mayne!" He turned on her even before reading the second paragraph, let alone the next two pages. "You knew about this?"

"Yes."

For a moment his face went so red, she feared it would give him an apoplexy. Her grandfather had died of one, after all, and Papa had such a temper—

"Bianca," he said in a savage whisper, "come with me." He took her arm roughly and marched her into Cathy's room and slammed the door behind them. "What have you done?"

"*I* didn't do anything."

He gripped his wig with both hands, but didn't tear it off. "I know you," he growled. "And I know Cathy. She would never do something like this on her own."

"There's where you're wrong, Papa," she replied. "It was entirely Cathy's idea to elope with Mr. Mayne, because she loves him and he proposed to her. She tried to tell you! When you said you'd got the marriage contract from St. James, she *told* you she cared for Mr. Mayne. You didn't listen!"

"A country curate!" He stared incredulously. "She can't want a country curate when she could have a gentleman from London, an eligible, elegant gentleman with connections to a—"

"A duke, yes," Bianca finished scornfully. "I know. She knows. *Everyone* knows, Papa. But there is far more to a husband than connections, and Cathy didn't want St. James."

"And you encouraged her to thwart me!"

"I supported her in following her own heart!"

"Keep your voice down!" he whispered harshly, even though his voice had grown as loud as hers. "Someone might hear you!"

Bianca's brows went up. "Someone who didn't hear Ellen shrieking?"

He cursed, which took her aback. She'd heard him bellow the same language at other people, workmen who broke a whole crate of dishes or a potter who showed up to the factory drunk, but never at her or Cathy.

For the first time it crossed her mind that Papa was not merely upset but truly angry. He stood with his hands on his hips, staring at the floor, one toe tapping angrily. Instead of his usual gray wool, today he wore his best suit of dark blue satin, with the silver buckles on his shoes. He had gone to great lengths to bring about this wedding, and now he would be humiliated when he had to tell St. James that the bride had fled rather than marry him . . .

And yet it was his own fault. He ought to have listened to Cathy.

"This is not some girlish prank, is it?" he asked after a moment, his voice more controlled. "Cathy's not hiding somewhere—perhaps at Frances's home—waiting to emerge when I promise her a new wardrobe or a carriage if she goes to the church?"

Bianca was shocked. "No! Cathy's never done anything like that."

"But you have." He looked up, a glint in his eye. "You ran off and spent the night in the woods when I wouldn't let you become an apprentice potter."

"And see how wrong you were," she returned, flushing angrily that he would bring that up again almost fifteen years after she'd done it. "I'm a good thrower and a better glazer."

He conceded with a nod. "Aye. And you got your way. Just as you did when I refused to let you accompany me to Liverpool."

She quailed inside, just a little, at that. It was true. Papa had been going to see a man about printing designs on his pottery. She had been eighteen and had questions about the process. It wasn't a new technique, but a refined version that promised more flexibility and colors, subject only to the engraver's talent. Bianca wanted to see it in person, and she'd waged a fierce campaign to persuade her father until he finally threw up his hands and took her.

"That was different," she said, before pivoting back to, "even though it was very fortunate I went."

She'd struck up a friendship with the printer's wife, and because of it they had secured the printer's exclusive services for two years. Even Papa had admitted it was better than he could have done.

Her father put his hands on his hips. "Was it?

And how shall you turn this circumstance around to the better?" He swept out one arm. "I've agreed to a marriage contract. St. James can sue me for breach, because you helped your sister run off with the penniless, soft-mouthed curate."

"I warned you not to do it."

"But I did." He leaned closer. "What's more, I'd do it again. He's got an eye for the business, Bianca. He's also got connections among the highest society in London and knows how they think. He's a clever gent, no matter what you think, and I gave him a share of Perusia."

She reeled at this shocking news. "What? Why?"

"Because he was to be my son-in-law!" her father replied. Too late she realized his temper had not died down, it had only burned low, into a white-hot fury all the more dangerous for being smothered and contained.

"How much?" she demanded.

"A one-quarter interest," was his horrifying reply.

Bianca felt incandescent with rage. She had expected to inherit half, with Cathy getting the other half. It was true she had envisioned Cathy wed to an amiable, pliant husband like Mayne, leaving her effectively in charge of Perusia, but now Papa had given one quarter to this *invader*, this usurping, grasping, fortune hunter—

"And if you want any hope of saving Perusia and placating St. James so he doesn't drag us into court and end up owning *half* of Perusia," her father added in the same ominous tone, "perhaps you ought to put on your sister's bridal dress and fulfill the contract."

For a moment she thought *she* would have an

apoplexy; she could barely breathe, she was so angry. Cathy's dainty chip hat decorated with pink cabbage roses lay on the bureau, next to the lace fichu that had been their mother's. Knowing she would be eloping with her love, Cathy had happily gone through all the motions of preparing for the wedding. With shaking hands Bianca jammed the hat onto her head and tossed the fichu around her shoulders.

"Very well," she said coldly. "If that's all you care about, and what I have to do to preserve Perusia, I will."

She threw open the door and went out of the room, knocking over Ellen, who was crouched down at the keyhole listening. "Get up, Ellen, we'll be late for the wedding."

Down the stairs she marched, hands in fists and head high. Aunt Frances emerged from the dining room, nose twitching in expectation and Trevor yapping at her skirts, and Bianca pushed right by her and out the front door. Her father was roaring at the servants upstairs, but stormed after her in time to catch up as she reached the gate, hauling the flustered Mr. Filpot behind him.

For a moment they both paused. This was the moment, Bianca would acknowledge later, that she ought to have said something. Not necessarily an apology—she would never be sorry for helping Cathy marry a man she loved instead of a man she didn't know—but some word of understanding, to let her father know that she did regret some consequences of her actions.

She *was* sorry that Cathy's elopement, on the eve of a much-trumpeted marriage, would be humiliating to Papa, particularly given that all of Marslip as well as the jilted bridegroom would witness it. She did *not* want to let her temper get the better of her again and lead her into making a massive mistake that all of them would rue for the rest of their days. She *didn't* like quarreling with her only remaining parent, who was so like her in temperament and humor, making them the closest of fathers and daughters—when they weren't quarreling like mortal enemies.

But before she could bring herself to say any of that, Papa opened the gate for her, and Bianca stalked through, carried along by fury and outrage.

Ironically, it was a glorious day. The sky was a peerless blue, dolloped with billowing clouds of pure white. The honeysuckle was in bloom, its sweet scent rising to meet her as she strode down the path toward the small stone church. Peevishly Bianca hoped the roads to Wolverhampton were dry, so that her sister at least would remember this day happily.

Guests were loitering outside the church—no doubt waiting for the bride to arrive. Bianca cut through them like a scythe, ignoring their scandalized and fascinated stares, until someone touched her arm.

"Good morning, Bianca," said her friend Amelia impishly. "That hasty to see your sister wed, are you?"

She opened her mouth, then paused.

"Such a lovely thing for your papa to invite us to the wedding celebration. Mum's beside herself; unpicked her best gown and turned and pressed it." She wrinkled her nose at this waste of energy.

"Where is Cathy?" Amelia craned her neck. "Is she already a fashionable London lady, late to everything?"

Bianca seized her hand. "Amelia, go home," she whispered. "Tell everyone—take them all away—"

"Bianca!"

She looked over her shoulder. Papa had come back for her. He barely managed a nod at the astonished Amelia before taking Bianca's arm and leading her, firmly, into the sacristy. "A moment," he barked at Mr. Filpot, who was trying to don his vestments. The startled fellow fled, collar in hand, and Papa closed the door behind him.

Too late Bianca realized Mr. St. James was also in the room. Today he was magnificent in an ivory coat over emerald green breeches, his coal-dark hair as sleek as a seal's fur. At their entrance, he looked up from the book in his hands, his brows raised in idle inquiry.

"St. James," said Papa with determined cheer. "Good morning, sir."

"Sir. Miss Tate." The man made a languid bow. He was so elegant, so handsome, Bianca glared at him in fulminating disgust. In return he gave her a sinfully intimate smile. Not at all the sort of smile a decent man would give any woman except his bride, on his wedding day.

Then she remembered that *she* might now be that bride. Not that St. James knew it, which left him firmly in the category of rogue.

"I have some unfortunate news," went on Papa. "It appears my daughter Catherine has . . . left."

St. James's brows snapped together. "Left?"

"She's eloped with someone else," said Bianca

before her father could reply. "A man she is desperately in love with. No doubt they are exchanging their vows at this very moment."

St. James didn't move a muscle but the room seemed to grow at once smaller and hotter.

"I cannot vouch for that," said Papa, holding his palm out toward Bianca as if to push her physically from the conversation. "But it's true she's run off with the fellow."

"Our agreement, sir," began St. James.

"I have another daughter," said Papa, almost defiantly. "If you'll have her."

The man blinked. He turned to Bianca as if just realizing, very belatedly, that she was there.

"Bianca's agreed already," said her father. He turned toward her, that bullheaded glint bright in his eye. "Haven't you?"

Angrily she shrugged.

If asked, at that moment, she would have said that she fully expected St. James to cry off. There would be some shouting, perhaps; at the very least a blazing argument. Not because he cared for Cathy, whom he'd only met twice, but because Cathy was beautiful and gentle and eager to please, and only a madman would take Bianca in trade for that. She would have wagered everything she had that by now, St. James had taken her measure, enough to be well aware that she despised him and saw right through the fraud he was trying to perpetrate on her father.

Slowly his gaze, now as bitter cold as ice, ran down her figure, then back up to her face. Bianca's temper began to boil.

"Very well," said St. James, as coolly as if he and

Papa had just agreed to the sale price of a different horse.

Papa nodded once. "Excellent. Bianca, come with me." And he pulled her from the room before she could say anything.

Cathy would have been in tears by now, incoherent with despair. Bianca felt only righteous fury as she stomped down the path with her father. All he cared was that *someone* marry St. James. He cared that much for St. James's connections and business proposal, that he would marry any daughter of his to the man, one way or another.

Fine, then. Papa would have his distant-cousin-of-a-duke son-in-law. He would have his elegant new London manager, flattering lascivious countesses into buying some dinnerware so that Papa could boast of the aristocratic tables his soup tureens sat upon. He would be rid of both spinster daughters, and she hoped he reveled in having that big, empty house to himself.

As for St. James, he would have his share of Perusia and a wealthy bride. Bianca meant to make certain he bled for every farthing, though. If he could consider marriage purely a business arrangement, so could she.

The only thought that consoled her was that Cathy would be blissfully happy as Mrs. Mayne.

Papa opened the church door. Amelia was standing there, holding the posy of flowers she had offered to provide, craning her neck looking for Cathy.

Bianca snatched the flowers from her and started down the aisle. A confused murmur arose from the guests awaiting them outside as Cathy failed to materialize. Inside, Aunt Frances was all but falling from her pew, her face flushed with interest. Bianca ignored them all and fixed her eyes on the mercenary rogue at the altar.

And he, of all people, wasn't even looking her way.

Chapter Five

There was a genuine possibility, growing stronger by the moment, that Max had lost his mind.

No more than ten minutes had elapsed since he had agreed to switch brides, and wed not the lovely, gentle Catherine Tate, but her fiery sister, Bianca.

You remember her, Max savaged himself mentally. *The one who hates you.*

He wondered if this had been Tate's plan all along. Perhaps Max had been just as much the prey as the pursuer. Perhaps he'd been tricked, coerced into marrying the shrewish sister so Tate could win a better suitor for his more appealing daughter, and be rid of both in one neat trick. Max vaguely thought there was a similar case in the Bible itself. Tate could have got the idea right here in church.

Not, Max admitted, that Bianca wasn't a beauty as well, in her own way. Her hair was somewhere between blond and brown, her eyes shifting from gray to blue. She was taller than her sister, and curvier, too. He had not missed the fact that she possessed a spectacular bosom. She moved with purpose and energy, not gentle grace, and her wit was as sharp and keen as a rapier.

She wielded it much the same way a swordsman might a rapier, too.

If he'd had more time to consider, would he have agreed to the switch? Max pondered the question in some remote, analytical portion of his brain as he took his place in the church, before the handful of whispering guests and the minister, who was still fumbling through his book of Common Prayer for the marriage service.

He would like to know if either, or both, ladies had been in on the scheme all along. Miss Tate had never refused his attentions; she'd appeared flattered by them, with her shy blushes and murmured thanks. He didn't imagine that it meant her feelings were engaged, and frankly he had not hoped they were.

Now, of course, it was clear her feelings *had* been engaged . . . just not by him.

As for Bianca, her feelings toward him had always been crystal clear: disdain, disgust, and dislike being chief among them. At the time he'd been amused. He'd thought she might be jealous of her older sister, betrothed at last while she remained a spinster.

More fool you, he told himself. Perhaps he should have recognized the chance offered in the sacristy to reject this mad plan, and cut his losses.

But Max had learned to seize opportunity when it crossed his path. Dame Fortune hadn't smiled upon him often in life, and she rarely allowed him the luxury of pondering and debating her offerings. He still half expected the Duchess of Carlyle to withdraw her support and cut him off without warning, which was why he had moved so swiftly to propose this arrangement to Tate.

No, he reflected, he didn't think more time would have changed his answer. He was used to making the best of things, and this last-minute adjustment did nothing, really, to change his plans.

A murmur of amazement signaled the appearance of the bride. Max kept his gaze on the cross standing on the altar behind the minister as she strode up beside him. He didn't need to see her face to sense her fury; it fairly streamed off her, like heat from a fire. With whom? he wondered idly. With her father? With herself? She could have denied agreeing to it, but she hadn't.

Still, when the minister reached the admonishment to anyone who wished to protest the marriage, Max tensed. All she had to say was one word and everything would be ruined.

Nothing. The silence in the church was absolute.

The minister, Filpot, cleared his throat and turned to Max. "Wilt thou have this woman to thy wedded wife?"

Max barely heard the rest of the charge as Filpot droned on. He would. He would have her, and keep her, and be just as good a husband to her as he'd meant to be to her sister—which was to say, probably not a very good one, though he intended to atone for that by being away as much as possible. The best marriages, after all, were ones conducted at some distance. The only times his parents had seemed at all fond of each other was when they were apart—far, far apart. As Max planned to spend most of his time away from Marslip, it didn't much matter which wife he left behind.

"I will," he answered with calm certitude.

Filpot nodded once, darted a nervous glance at Mr. Tate, and turned to the bride. "Wilt thou take this man to thy wedded husband?"

Aside from a faint noise of derision as Filpot read, "Wilt thou obey him and serve him?" she made no protest. When Filpot raised his eyes warily at the end, Bianca said, quietly but clearly, "I will."

It sounded to Max's ears like a threat.

He was smiling in mild amusement when he took her hand from Tate's. She still hadn't looked at him, but kept her fierce gaze fastened on the minister. "I, Augustus Crispin Maximilian, take thee, Bianca Charlotte, to my wedded wife," he recited. At his name, she finally glanced at him, horror stamped on her face at the terrible moniker. Max's smile widened as he gripped her hand tighter. "According to God's holy ordinance, and thereto I plight thee my troth."

She pulled loose at the last word, only to take his hand again when prompted. In a flat voice she repeated her own vow. Max laid the ring on the minister's book and listened with the same detached amusement as Filpot blessed it.

At the last moment he worried it would not fit. It had been chosen for her sister, after all, and Max had spent some time deliberating over it; women liked jewels, and Max liked to make a good impression. But when he took Bianca's hand and tried it, the ring slid smoothly onto her finger. She made a fist, causing the gold to sparkle in the sunlight, and he couldn't resist another smile.

"Those whom God hath joined together, let no man put asunder," Filpot pronounced.

Bianca raised her eyes to his. *No man, and no woman*, Max silently promised her. He was under no illusions that Bianca came to this happily, but she'd done so willingly, and that was all that mattered. They were married, and she could not undo it now.

When the service was concluded, the minister led them to the chapel. Tate followed closely at their heels, jovial once more, shaking Mr. Filpot's hand and slapping Max on the shoulder as if this outcome had been the dearest wish of everyone involved. It only deepened his cynical wondering if Tate had planned to foist Bianca onto him from the beginning, but he obligingly accepted the congratulations with a smile. What was done, was done, and if he'd been deceived into doing it, there would be time for redress later.

After the marriage was properly recorded, a legally binding record in the parish register, Filpot and Tate walked out. The minister seemed vastly relieved everything had gone off smoothly, chattering rapidly though quietly to Tate, and Max saw the coins Tate dropped into the man's palm. Almost like a bribe not to raise any complaint.

But for the first time, he was alone with his lawfully wedded wife. Max folded his arms and leaned back to look at her.

Now that he really paid attention, she was rather lovely. Not in the way of her sister, who was like a delicately crafted porcelain doll with every hair in place . . . and yet. There was a fine pink flush in her cheeks, and that splendid bosom rose and fell appealingly. She wasn't the wife he'd expected, but Max found that hadn't decreased his desire for the marriage.

There was a real chance it had done the opposite.

She noticed his scrutiny. Her eyes were as turbulent as a summer storm as she advanced on him. "What a horrible name you've got."

He smiled. "The bane of my existence since birth."

"No wonder you use Maximilian," she went on. "Augustus Crispin!"

His mother had named him after his father's father and grandfather, hoping that would spur the family to look after him. It hadn't worked, and Max only acknowledged those names when forced to do so. "Maximilian was my mother's father's name," he said instead. Old Maxim had been a silent, stern type, refusing to speak anything but German despite living twenty years in Britain. Max had infinitely preferred him to anyone from his father's family.

She sniffed. "How did you know my name?"

Max raised a brow. "We've been introduced more than once, my dear."

"My full name," she said acidly.

"Your father showed me the family Bible," he replied after a moment's pause. Tate had shown him the lines, including the spaces left for his daughters' husbands. Again Max wondered if Tate had expected, even then, to write *Maximilian* next to *Bianca Charlotte* instead of *Catherine Louisa*.

His wife's eyes flashed. Odd, how he already remembered to think of her as his. "Did he?" She paced away, her yellow skirts swinging in agitation. "You need to be disabused of some of the notions my father gave you. Firstly—"

"Firstly," he interrupted, "we shall go to the wedding breakfast. Everyone will be waiting for us."

The color rose in her cheeks again. "A pox on all of them."

"As you wish." He tugged his cuffs into place and headed for the door.

"Don't you dare walk out on me!"

Hand on the latch, he turned and raised a brow. "My dear, we have the rest of our lives to disabuse each other of faulty notions. Today, at this hour, our neighbors and family are waiting to celebrate our union in holy wedlock. They will wonder if we spend the next hour shut up in the chapel shouting at each other."

"Oh?" She widened her eyes. "Did you mean to shout?"

Max had not bumbled ignorantly along the path toward this marriage. He'd spent considerable time sorting out how Tate's factory worked, which employees were clever and hardworking, what skills were vital. Buying a few rounds of ale at the local tavern had taught him a great deal.

Some of the more interesting tales had been about Bianca. At the time Max had listened in detached interest, not expecting to see much of her. Now, though, he found it much more valuable intelligence. Bianca didn't spend her time in the house, arranging flowers and being domestic, as her sister did. She had a workroom in the factory and was nearly as demanding as Tate himself in pursuit of quality. Many of the men didn't like a woman working in the pottery, but they tolerated it—though they took unwonted pleasure in the times Bianca and her father got into loud arguments, which all the factory could hear. Max had no doubt that she *would* begin shouting at him, if given the chance.

He laughed. "No. I rarely shout. A great waste of breath, generally."

At his riposte, she put up her chin. "Neither do I," she said in a frosty but not shouting voice, "at reasonable people. If you can be reasonable, we shall have no quarrel."

And Max smiled again. "I am always entirely reasonable, madam."

He meant it: reasonable, rational, cold-bloodedly logical. He'd learned the hard way not to trust anything else. Bianca, he sensed, was led more by her feelings, instinct, and passion. It would be an oil and water marriage, but Max meant to make it succeed, one way or another.

At least, as *he* defined success.

She came right up to him, raising her face. Up close her eyes were more gray than blue, and there were faint freckles across her nose. There was also a small beauty mark on her breast, barely visible under the lace fichu across her shoulders. Max had to fight back the urge to stare at it, and tried not to think of peeling away her yellow silk gown to explore the rest of her skin.

"I hope that is true," she said, "for both our sakes. Since neither of us wanted to be married to the other, we're going to have to be very reasonable indeed, or there *will* be a great deal of shouting. The first thing you should bear in mind is that these pottery works are *mine*. My father may have given you a share, but I've twenty years of experience and knowledge on you. Besides, we both know that what you want isn't the manufactory. It's the money." Her lips curled in a condescending little smile. "That's perfectly fine. You shall have it—a reasonable allowance, provided you stay out of my way."

"Hmm," he said, torn between laughing incredulously and being deeply offended. "An allowance."

"You don't know anything about pottery," she said in the same belittling tone. She turned and walked back to the desk, where she'd left her frivolous straw hat when signing the register. "You would only be in the way! Take the money and amuse yourself, I don't care how, and we'll get along famously."

He sighed. "My dear Mrs. St. James." She started at the name. "This is not a strong beginning. Firstly, I own one quarter of Perusia, and I intend to participate in the business. Not throwing pots or stoking the kiln—all things you no doubt excel at," he added, just to see that furious color in her face again. "But in my own inestimable way. And I'll thank you not to tell me what to do. After all, I am not the one who vowed to *obey and serve*."

The flush ran down her neck, toward that intriguing beauty mark. "You— How dare you— This is not a real marriage!"

He came off the door, closing the gap between them so quickly she gasped. "Not real?" he bit out. "It most certainly is, madam. Solemnized before all of Marslip, sealed in God's eyes and bound by Church law. Don't *ever* say it's not real." He paused, his gaze running down her again. Damn that beauty mark. "If you're fearful I shall force you to your wifely duties in bed, set your mind at ease. I would never force a woman."

"Then you accept this will be a chaste marriage?" she said as he went back to the door.

He paused, looking back at her. Some of her hairpins had come out, setting a long tawny curl loose to graze her bare neck. Despite the fichu he could see the beauty mark, dark and taunting on the plump swell of flesh.

Well, wasn't he a fool. He wanted the woman, even though she despised him.

"Of course it won't be," he said. "Someday you'll come to me—"

She gasped in fury.

"—and when you do, it will be for pleasures that most women only dream of." Max gave her another sinful smile and opened the door, leaving her staring after him in openmouthed indignation.

Chapter Six

Bianca resolved before noon on her wedding day that she would hate and despise her husband for the rest of her life.

She saw now why Frances had devoted her life to spiting the people responsible for her miserable marriage. St. James, she seethed, deserved to be broken on a rack. Papa deserved to be shunned by both his daughters for all eternity. Bianca deserved a sharp smack in the face, for letting her temper get the better of her, and Cathy—

Her anger lessened. Cathy deserved to be happy. She pictured her sister, wrapped in Mr. Mayne's arms, her face glowing with joy, and told herself it was all worth it. Cathy had practically raised her since their mother's death some thirteen years ago. If Bianca had any grace or manners, it was due to Cathy, who somehow absorbed everything feminine without effort. When she was eighteen, Papa had offered to take Cathy to London to search for a husband, and her sister had refused. "Not without Bianca, too," she'd said, even though Bianca was only fourteen at the time and would have been, at any age, an unqualified disaster in London.

In the years since, Cathy had loyally supported

Bianca in all her quirks and oddities, helping persuade Papa that she ought to be allowed to pursue her interest in making pottery, then in formulating new glazes. Cathy had even supported her when she refused those other marriage offers, when Papa had torn out his hair and raged at her for being stubborn.

Not that Bianca couldn't have stood up for herself, but Cathy had smoothed things over and warded off the violent arguments that would have ensued—that always *did* ensue—without her, keeping peace between Bianca and their father. If this was the way Bianca had to repay her sister, she was only glad that she could do it.

That didn't make the wedding breakfast less of a nightmare, though. St. James greeted all the guests cordially, already acting like a gentleman of the manor. To look at him, no one would ever guess that he hadn't married the woman of his heart's desire that morning. *Lying rogue*, she thought in disgust.

Papa had also regained his bonhomie, thanking everyone for coming and accepting congratulations with a smile. Bianca decided to ignore him, as she was no longer speaking to him.

For herself, she could only act as normally as possible, reminding herself that she was neither ashamed nor sorry, that this marriage would have very little impact on her life, and that it was all to the greater good anyway, enabling Cathy to be with her love and allowing Bianca to continue her work unimpeded. After all, if St. James wished to keep drawing his allowance from the business, he couldn't very well oust her from it, since her work helped make Perusia pottery uniquely attractive. And now that she'd given in to Papa's mad proposal, not only was she a married lady, no longer under his hand, but Papa owed her a monstrous debt.

Aunt Frances, of course, had to put in her word, as pointed as a needle. "Now I see why you were so keen on matchmaking between Cathy and the curate," she murmured, her gaze raking over St. James. He stood across the room from them, smiling faintly at something Mr. Murdoch, Papa's head modeler, was saying. "You sly minx," added the older woman in a soft, almost spitefully delighted tone. "What fine prey you've bagged."

"You think I wanted him for myself?" Bianca cast a scathing gaze toward the man. What a peacock he was, in his emerald satin breeches and ivory velvet coat. His lace alone was finer than anything any woman in the room wore. It made her own beautiful silk gown, a bright cheery primrose, look plain and simple in contrast.

"I assure you not. It's strictly a marriage of convenience," she told her aunt. "I see little difference between him and Mr. Murdoch."

Frances raised her brow. "None at all?"

Mr. Murdoch was fifty, his fair hair faded to white and his hands callused to leather from handling the clay. He was a talented modeler, invaluable to the business. No one would ever confuse him with Maximilian St. James, who was far more attractive and far less useful.

"None," lied Bianca. "If you'll pardon me, Aunt, I see Amelia awaiting me."

Amelia was agog, and Bianca was forced to employ some license in her retelling of the story. Cathy's love affair became a bit more passionate, St. James's courtship much more mercenary, and Papa's motives a vast deal more paternal instead of mercantile. As for Bianca's actions . . .

"You really had to marry him to save the pottery works?" whispered Amelia in scandalized shock.

"It was the only choice." Bianca nibbled her slice of cake. Cathy had ordered it made, and Bianca loved cake. It would be silly to let it go to waste.

"But Cathy—!" Amelia clapped one hand to her mouth. "Does Cathy know?"

Bianca paused. "No," she said carefully. "I had no time to ponder it, or write to her about it, but had to decide in the moment."

That was not strictly true. She'd had well over half an hour from the time Papa snarled at her that perhaps she ought to step into her sister's shoes and marry St. James, and the moment Mr. Filpot had cleared his throat and recited the charge to her. Not nearly enough time to consult her sister, who must have been halfway to Wolverhampton by then, but enough time to have put a stop to it.

"Bianca, she'll be overset! Surely she never dreamed you would have to go to such lengths for her!"

"She will understand," said Bianca firmly. "And she'll be happy. It's all I want her to be. I shall make the best of things for myself. Besides . . ." She lowered her voice. "It's not as if St. James wants a real marriage, you know."

Amelia goggled at her. "No! A man like that?"

Bianca looked at That Man, her husband, the scheming rogue. He looked perfectly at ease, chatting to her neighbors and friends as if he'd known them forever.

He also looked far too attractive for words—and for her. Bianca had not spent much time thinking about marriage, which didn't look very appealing to her. But when pressed, she'd always pictured herself, if she married at all, wed to someone comfortable, a little older, much more amiable. In her mind he was neither handsome nor ugly, easy in manner and kind in spirit.

Instead she found herself yoked to this spectacularly handsome but soulless snake, who glided into Marslip intent on gaining her father's company and stealing her inheritance.

"Look at him," she said quietly to her friend, without looking away from him. "A London dandy, handsome and sophisticated and as slippery as oiled glass. What can he want, all the way out here in Staffordshire? Is he a potter? Is he a modeler? Does he know anything at all about pottery? No. He saw an opportunity, and he seized it, didn't he? It was all the same to him whether he married Cathy or me."

As she spoke, he glanced her way, his dark eyes gleaming. When he saw her watching him, he smiled—that wicked, knowing smile—and made her a very handsome bow.

"Are you certain?" Amelia bobbed a hasty curtsy and leaned closer to whisper in Bianca's ear. "That one doesn't look like he holds what is his lightly."

Bianca stiffened. "I am not *his*," she hissed.

"You are." Amelia nodded sympathetically. "His wife, his property by law. Even if you think he doesn't care for *you*, that doesn't mean he isn't possessive of what's his."

That would clearly be the first notion she disabused

him of. Bianca gazed back at him, expressionless, her resolve hardening. She and Mr. St. James were going to have a very blunt conversation.

She managed to avoid him the rest of the day. After the guests left, he disappeared, a circumstance that pleased her greatly until she overheard Ellen tell Cook that Mr. Tate wanted a hamper for him and Mr. St. James at the offices. Bianca scowled at the thought of That Man invading her workshop, but she could not slip away. In Cathy's absence she had to oversee the tidying up after the guests, the distribution of the remaining food to the workers' families, and the transfer of her own possessions to Poplar House.

That last drove home to her what she'd done. Poplar House had been their house before Papa built the large new Perusia Hall. It was at Poplar House that Bianca had been born and spent her childhood. When Mama died, just weeks before Perusia Hall was to be ready for them, Papa had moved them all up the hill to the Hall, disregarding its unfinished state, and promptly let Poplar House to his cousin.

None of them had been back to the quaint little house since. Papa had preferred the grander Perusia Hall, and the cousin's wife had been a sickly woman who didn't entertain guests.

Today Bianca walked down the hill to Poplar House as mistress of it, not a child but a married lady. With a sense of detached amazement she approached the familiar blue door under the freshly thatched roof. The cousin had moved out six months ago, having saved enough money to take his wife to Bath in a bid to improve her health. Upon St. James's proposal, Papa had given orders for the house to be cleaned and repaired, making it ready for his daughter and new son-in-law.

No one had expected it would be Bianca stepping over the threshold, keys at her waist, to explore her new . . . old . . . home.

Cathy had furnished it very comfortably. It was a good thing she had, thought Bianca, wandering silently through the rooms, so familiar and yet so strange. Not only did Cathy have an eye for pleasing design and arrangement, Bianca would have been tempted to paint the master's bedchamber black, including each pane of the casement windows.

Instead it was a welcoming shade of sage, complementing the new linen bed hangings of dark blue. The furniture had been polished to a warm glow, and the grate in the hearth was freshly blacked. A clutch of fresh daisies stood in a double-handled vase on the windowsill.

Bianca stood in the doorway for a moment. Her gaze lingered on the large bed. *Pleasures that most women only dream of,* echoed his arrogant voice in her mind.

"Ha," she said to the empty room, and closed the door.

Her bedroom was far more to her taste, even if it did adjoin his. It had once been her mother's, and just setting foot in it made her step lighter. So many happy memories here, of listening to stories at her mother's feet . . . practicing her lessons while her mother sewed . . . showing Mama her own embroidery here, as proud as anything of her work even though she despised embroidery.

The sadder memories Bianca had always tried to ignore. That she'd spent so much time in here with Mama because her mother's health was never robust. The numerous vases of flowers, because Mama could not go outside anymore. How many handkerchiefs had been scattered around the room, ensuring there was always one at hand when a coughing fit seized her mother.

Cathy had obviously wanted to banish those memories as well. She'd chosen a buttery yellow for the walls, with pale green bedcovers and brocaded upholstery. The windows faced west, and the afternoon sunlight made the room glow like a spring day after the rain.

Jennie had already unpacked her things. Bianca had changed earlier out of her morning finery into one of her everyday linen dresses, lacing up herself and tying on a much-mended apron. Now she brushed out the curls and pinned her hair into its usual twisted knot, peering into the small beveled glass to secure it.

There. She smiled at her reflection. That was better.

A stream of servants brought more things from Perusia. She supervised and organized and set up the rest of the house. It was hard not to think of her mother here, as she directed them to push the settee next to the front windows, where Mama had used to sit in the summer with her sewing.

This was *her* house, she decided then. It had been her home as a child and held her memories. She might have to share it with St. James, but it would never be his.

Chapter Seven

Max made his way home in the dark, lantern in hand. A neatly graveled path led down the gentle hill, just far enough away from Perusia, to the half-timbered farmhouse. Poplar House wasn't as grand as Perusia Hall but it was the finest house he'd ever been able to call his own—the finest, and the first. Tate had presented him with the deed this afternoon as a wedding gift.

He wasn't fond of old houses as a rule, but in this instance, he was prepared to make an exception.

The stout door was a cheery blue, a surprising note of color against the dark timbers and white plastered walls. A long wooden bench sat beside that door, its swaybacked seat hinting at generations who had sat there before, smoking a pipe and watching children chase a hoop across the grass. Max let himself in, savoring the prospect.

The door opened into a central hall, long and narrow. To his right was a wall of stone, with a fireplace set in the middle. A banked fire smoldered there, chasing away the late spring chill in the night air. Through a partly open door at the far end of the room, he could hear muted laughter and voices over the splashing sounds of dishes being scrubbed. The scent of freshly baked bread lingered on the air. It was all so . . . homelike.

Slowly Max set the lantern on the mantel.

He pushed open the door to his left and found the parlor—it was too comfortable and lived-in to be called a drawing room. A bank of windows set high in the wall looked out toward the hill he'd just descended. The candles in the wall sconces were out, but the linen draperies were open, letting in enough moonlight to see. A pair of wingback chairs stood drawn up before the hearth, and a long settee was beneath the windows, heaped with plump cushions. A round table was off to one side, holding a vase spilling over with flowers.

Max regarded it in silence. How easy it was to picture himself reading in front of that fireplace, his foot on the fender and a glass of claret on the table beside him. He had no idea if the wind whistled through those windows or if that chimney smoked—for all he knew, this room was beastly hot in summer and an ice house in winter—but it was *his*. Reverently, he closed the door.

He didn't go to the back of the hall, where the servants were still moving about in the dining room and the kitchen beyond, but up the doglegged stairs behind the main door. Tate had warned him the house was old; Max narrowly avoided banging his head on the low ceiling as he climbed the stairs.

A broad corridor stretched in front of him, two doors to the left and two to the right. A massive chest sat between the doors on his left, beneath a large portrait of a family from some decades ago. As he took it in, a maid popped out of a disguised door at the far end, an ewer in her hands. She gave a startled gasp and bobbed a quick curtsy at the sight of him. Max nodded once, and she hurried through the door at the near right.

Candlelight shone across the dark planks of the floor in the corridor, glinting off the sconces on the wall. Female voices spilled out, including one Max identified immediately as Bianca's.

How he knew this with such certainty, he couldn't say. He'd never heard the maid speak. But somehow he knew it was she, in her bedroom, preparing for bed, and his feet led him there without any decision by his brain to go.

She sat at a dressing table, her back to him as she ran a brush through her hair. The maid was emptying the ewer into the basin in the corner, relating something about a pig in an animated voice.

Max folded his arms and rested his shoulder against the doorjamb. Bianca was smiling as she brushed and plaited her hair, listening to the maid's silly story. He could see it in the small mirror in front of her. In the light of the lamp on her dressing table, her hair glowed with amber glints. Each stroke of the brush made the long, loose curls bounce.

Another homelike moment. His house. His wife.

She turned toward the maid then, caught sight of him, and promptly burst that thought like an errant bubble of soap. Stiffening in her seat, she gave him a frigid glare. "Did you want something, Mr. St. James?"

"To wish you a good evening, dear wife," he returned. The maid whirled to stare at him, clutching the ewer in both hands, her mouth hanging open. "You may go," he told her, stepping aside as she scurried out of the room. He closed the door behind her and faced his bride.

He'd spent the day with Tate in the pottery offices, reviewing the marriage contract and concluding all the business related to it. A piece of his brain, though, had been working away all day at the question of Bianca. Things had not begun well between them, and Max was quite sure he would have to make the first effort if he wanted their relationship to improve. But he also sensed that any appearance of craving her good opinion would only inspire contempt, not the amiable regard he wanted.

Nor, it must be admitted, the physical desire he craved. He wanted her, and he wanted her to want him.

Bianca wound a strip of linen around the end of her braid and tied it. "There was no need to frighten off Jennie."

"Did I frighten her?" He affected surprise. "If I did, she takes fright very easily. Might as well get it over and done with, I suppose."

"None of us here know you," she replied. She rose from her seat and tugged the ties of her dressing gown tighter. "Nor you, us."

"Ah. Yes. That will change." He clasped his hands behind his back and strolled toward her. She watched him, her expression calm if a shade condescending. "We are married, after all, until death shall us part."

"Well." She smiled sweetly, looking coy and mischievous for a moment. Max's sangfroid faltered. She was rather . . . bewitching like that. "At least there is an end in sight."

He laughed. "No, really? I was counting on another forty years or more."

"And I've already begun counting them down," she replied as if struck by delight at the coincidence. "What do you want?"

He lowered his gaze at that question. "What any husband might want, with his new wife." Idly he picked up one of the delicate little pots from her dressing table and opened it. "To become closer acquainted."

She made a sound like a faint snort. "It will take very little effort for that, since we aren't acquainted at all."

"And yet, we aren't entirely strangers, either." The pot was crafted to look like a ripe plum, deep pinkish-purple with a pert pair of leaves on a stem forming the handle on the lid. It was very finely made, and Max removed the lid. It glowed translucent green when held in front of the candle. The pot itself was delicate porcelain, and held a fragrant salve of some kind. He inhaled the scent of sweet almonds, honey, perhaps lavender. "What is this?"

"A remedy for pernicious itching in sensitive places," she said evenly. "Do you need some?"

Max's gaze jerked up, startled.

"A balm for my hands," she said, an impish smile tugging at her lips. She was pleased to have wrong-footed him, the minx. "The clay can be quite abrasive."

"Right." He studied the little pot. It was as dainty and lightweight as an eggshell. It bore the Tate mark on the underside—or rather, a variant on it. Not the usual, stately Roman TATE encircled by a laurel wreath, but the name, scripted, enclosed in a rosette. If he had to guess, it was Bianca's personal mark. He put down the jar of balm. "You work in your father's office."

Her lips flattened. "I work in my own workshop. I am a Tate, too, you know."

Max cocked his head. "Not any longer."

At that, temper flashed in her eyes and she brushed past him. "Don't be so certain of that."

He only smiled.

"Since you're here, you might as well sit down." She took a seat in the wingback chair by the window and nodded at the opposite chair. "There's a great deal you need to learn."

I might say the same, he thought as he accepted her invitation to sit. "Should I fetch a quill and paper, to make notes?"

"Only if you're too simple to remember." She eyed him dubiously. "On second thought, perhaps you should."

"Why do you think I'm simple?" He leaned back in his chair and crossed his legs. Max was frivolously vain of his legs, and he smiled as her gaze flickered to his calves in their silk stockings for a moment.

"Let's see." She put her head to one side and ticked off her fingers. "You coldly proposed marriage to a woman you didn't know. You married a woman you knew even less, after pondering the question for a matter of minutes. You—"

"And how long, pray, did you ponder that same question?" he drawled.

She took his meaning at once. Her slate eyes turned flinty. "Are you suggesting I *planned* to marry you?"

Max lifted one shoulder. "It must be considered,

you know. Perhaps that bit about your sister running off with another fellow was a convenient story. Perhaps you envied her. Perhaps you schemed to bring this about."

"Good God, why would I?" she exclaimed in horror.

Max spread his arms wide, as if to display his person, and smiled engagingly.

He did not think Bianca had engineered their marriage. He did not really think Tate had done so, either, not after the way the man blustered about it all afternoon. But the switch of brides had been done with breathtaking speed, requiring a healthy bribe to encourage the curate to read the proper lady's name and amend the license. It was all very suspicious, and while Max didn't regret his own actions—he rarely wasted time on regret—he was curious about hers.

Her mouth fell open and her brow creased indignantly. "You!" she cried. "You? You think I wanted *you*?"

"It must be remarked," he said in a low, silky tone, "that you got me, while so many other women have failed."

A bright flush rolled up her neck. "Would that any of them had succeeded!"

Max shrugged. "To your great benefit, they did not."

He wasn't sure why he felt compelled to needle her. It might be a dreadful mistake. Sometimes it was better to let someone vent their spleen, get their shouting done, and then stealthily work his way into their good graces.

But he just couldn't, not this time, not with her.

Regardless of how and why, she was his wife, the supposed helpmeet of his life. He found her intriguing, if challenging, and there was that bloody inconvenient charge of attraction that went through him every time he saw her.

And most importantly, he sensed that if he ever let Bianca trample over him, he would never, ever win her respect. That would be the single greatest mistake he could make, and Max wasn't about to make it.

"My benefit!" She stared at him as if he'd gone mad. "Of all the—"

"You know, I took care to discover what sort of wife your sister would be," he said idly. "No one said aught of you. Perhaps you wish to tell me yourself?"

"It doesn't matter," she replied in the same careless tone after a moment's pause. "We aren't much of a husband and wife, are we?"

"Now that is where you're wrong." He clasped his hands over his stomach and let his gaze drift toward her bed for a moment. "We are most certainly husband and wife."

A fine flush of pink colored her face again. "Bollocks."

His brows shot up, half-surprised, half-amused. "I say, madam!"

"You say." She shot to her feet, her dressing gown swirling around her legs. "*You* say! All this time, it's been what you say, and what you want. I must tell you, sir, that shan't continue." Pacing a path in front of the fireplace, she eyed him narrowly. "You might as well acclimate yourself to a few truths, Mr. St. James. I may be your wife before the law, but I do not belong to you. This marriage was, and is, merely a business arrangement. My father, fool that he is, made you a partner in the pottery works, but I daresay he didn't tell you how much of its success is due to my efforts—efforts which I intend to continue. And if you have half a brain in your head, you'll not argue."

"I see," he murmured.

"In addition, this is my bedchamber, and I'll thank you not to walk in and out as if you own it."

He did own it. Max said nothing, entertained beyond measure.

"And lastly . . ." She sat in the chair again, this time leaning forward, her gaze intent on him. "When my sister returns to Marslip, you'll not say one word to her about our discussion in the church."

"Our discussion in the church . . ." He pretended to think. "I don't really recall much of one. Your father said she was gone, you declared she had run off on some great love affair, and that was it."

"There was your coldhearted willingness to marry a perfect stranger on the spot," she said, two spots of pink burning brightly in her cheeks.

Slowly Max leaned forward until their faces were barely a foot apart. He could see the flecks of blue in her eyes, and the damned beauty mark on her breast. Her pacing had dislodged the sash of her dressing gown, and it gaped open just enough for him to see that tempting spot.

"Was it?" he asked softly.

A line of bemusement appeared between her brows. "Was it—was it what?"

This time he openly surveyed her, not hiding his brazen appreciation of her flushed skin, full bosom, long legs, and dishabille. God help him, why did he find temper and passion in a woman so mesmerizing? He'd tried to choose a demure, quiet wife who wouldn't provoke him, who would make it easy for him to leave her be.

Instead . . .

"Was it coldhearted?" he whispered. "Are you certain, Mrs. St. James?"

She blinked. "Obviously—"

Max clicked his tongue. "Don't be so sure. I'm not as simple as you want me to be." As she stared in amazement, he got to his feet, bowing low in the same motion to keep his face near hers. "Until tomorrow."

Unhurriedly he rose. There was a door beside her bed, which could not lead to the corridor or to the back stairs to the nursery. Tate had showed him the house, and Max vaguely remembered this door led to the master's bedchamber. He hadn't taken much notice of it at the time, not thinking he would use it often. "This connects us, I take it?" He opened the door and gave her one last lazy smile. "How convenient."

"Go!" She snatched a cushion from her chair and hurled it at him. Max caught it and flipped it onto her bed, then let himself out. He paused, waiting, and heard her exclamation of disgust when she realized the door had no lock.

"Good night, my dear," he called.

His only reply was silence. But Max still thought things were already improving between them, all things considered.

Chapter Eight

Bianca went to bed in a rage but woke the next morning restored to her calm, practical self.

So Mr. St. James would not back down quietly; she was silly to have thought he might. That man was trouble, and even worse, he was clever and canny. From what he said last night, he was pursuing a long game.

"Forty more years, indeed," she muttered as she tied on her petticoat. With his sly smiles and blatant suggestion that she must want him because he was so incredibly attractive, he'd be lucky if she didn't poison him within forty days.

It was tempting, once she'd put on her shoes, to stomp about loudly and disturb his rest. The other room was still silent, and she pictured him holding a pillow over his head to drown out the sounds of her own toilette. In the end she decided against it, on the idea that it was better not to let him believe she thought about him at all. She cast one last baleful glance at the door to his bedroom as she left. Perhaps one of the men from the workshop could come over the hill and nail it closed.

She went downstairs, absently reaching up to tap her knuckles on the low ceiling where the stairs turned. When she and Cathy were small, she used to jump off the top step and try to touch that bit of ceiling. Once she jumped too hard and fell head over heels down the stairs to the hall, sending Cathy running, screaming for their mother. Mama had held her and kissed her and made her stay in bed for three days to settle her brain and let her bruises fade—but she'd sat by Bianca's bedside for those three days, telling her stories and singing songs.

This had been such a happy house then.

She went into the dining parlor. It adjoined the kitchen and as such was much too informal to be called a dining room. Unlike the dining room in Papa's house, with its tall windows and silver chandelier, this room was just as worn and cozy as the rest of the house, with floors that sloped and uneven whitewashed walls and a fireplace permanently blackened by the many years of fires. It was still furnished much as it had been in Bianca's youth. None of the furnishings had been fine enough for Papa's grand new Perusia Hall, not the walnut dresser and plate rack, nor the ordinary oval table and spindle chairs, and especially not the tall-backed settle by the fire. It had all been as Bianca remembered it, when she explored the house yesterday.

Today, though, she threw open the door to the familiar room and stopped short. That Man sat at the table, and from the looks of things he'd been there awhile.

At her appearance, he looked up from the papers in his hand, over the round spectacles perched on his nose. "Good morning, my dear," he said with a faint smile. "Mary, bring Mrs. St. James's chocolate."

The maid cast a nervous glance at Bianca, but nodded and whisked out of the room.

Bianca reminded herself to breathe deeply, because it did not matter to her what he did or said. She seated herself as far from him as possible. The table was sadly too small—far smaller than she remembered it.

"You rise early," she remarked coolly when he continued to watch her with that small, knowing smile.

"Always have done." He sipped his coffee. From the dishes in front of him, he'd already been served, and eaten, a healthy breakfast. She hadn't heard a whisper of noise from his room, making her wonder with an unpleasant start if he'd been downstairs before she even woke. "How delightful that we have it in common."

"Not so delightful," she returned. "Papa blows the horn for the workers to begin at seven. Everyone in Marslip rises early."

"Ah. Then I shall blend in seamlessly."

"Like a polecat among the lambs." She smiled at the irritated twitch of his brows, and spread fresh butter on a soft, plump roll. Mary brought in the small pot of chocolate, steaming gently, and set it before her. Bianca inhaled greedily. She lived for her morning chocolate.

Particularly today.

St. James had gone back to his reading. Bianca ate in silence, trying to savor her chocolate without looking at him. Instead of his usual finery, today he wore ordinary clothes: a dark blue coat over a gray waistcoat, dark brown breeches. It was ordinary cloth, too, linen and wool instead of satin and velvet. It ought to have made *him* more ordinary, and to her intense disgust, it did not.

His dark hair was neatly queued, though not as sleekly as yesterday; slightly tousled, as if he'd gathered his hair with one hand and tied it in a hurry. One loose strand curled just behind his ear. Bianca glared at it, both for being out of order and for being so mesmerizing.

As she poured out the last of her chocolate, he flipped a page of his document, and she caught sight of the writing on it. She set down the chocolate pot with a clink. "What are you reading?"

"The contract with Albert Brimley."

Her mouth set. Mr. Brimley owned the warehouse in London where Papa shipped some of his finest wares. "Why?"

St. James glanced at her over his spectacles. "Someone ought to. Is it standard, this quota on breakage?"

"Some breakage is unavoidable, with the roads as they are, so yes, I presume it is the usual."

"Presume," he echoed under his breath. "The roads are terrible, but this contract allows Brimley to claim up to one fifth of every shipment arrives broken."

A fifth? That sounded excessive. But Bianca was forced to admit, to herself if not to him, that she didn't know if it were reasonable or not. She had never taken a great deal of interest in the particulars of any contract, only the choosing of the merchant they wished to deal with. Mr. Brimley, she felt, was an honorable man.

"Whatever made you read a contract?" she asked

instead. Surely Maximilian St. James, London dandy, couldn't possibly know more about shipping pottery and chinaware than she did.

"I've been reading them all," he said, dropping the papers and removing his spectacles. "Are there any you wish me to read with particular attention?"

"No." She gave a huff of astonished laughter. "Why would I?"

He smiled, his dark eyes fixed on her. "Why would you not?" Her smile faded at his pointed tone. "Perusia potteries are important to you, are they not?"

"Of course!"

"Then you ought to know what your contracts say."

"I do, mostly—"

He cocked one brow. "And do you *mostly* make your wares high quality?"

She flushed. "Read them all, if you please. They're already signed, though, and Papa won't break his word. Those men are his friends as well as his partners."

He smiled again. Damn the dimple, carving his cheek. "I never said he should break his word. Nothing I've seen is too dreadful."

"Then why bother?" Bianca drank the last of her chocolate. "Are you well-versed in shipping contracts? I can't imagine so."

"I read law for a year," he answered, to her immense surprise. "Not well-versed, but not ignorant."

"Then you're a solicitor?"

Finally his eyes dropped. He folded the spectacles into his waistcoat pocket. "No."

Bianca wondered, but he said no more and she refused to show any interest in anything about him.

The horn blew in the distance, and she plucked a roll from the basket on the table. "I wish you a pleasant day reading contracts," she said, rising from the table and heading for the door. She said it to twit him; he would sit up here in the house reading while she did something actually important to the factory.

To her astonishment he also rose, gathering his papers with one hand as he drained his coffee cup with a flick of his wrist. "Shall we walk together?" He gave her another of his wicked smiles.

"There's no need for you to go to the factory," she said, but he was at the door, waiting for her with his arm offered.

She did not take it. Out the door she went, tucking the roll into her pocket for later. St. James followed without a word.

Chapter Nine

Around the hill and down the slope they went, in perfect silence. The sun was in the trees now, just barely, and the morning dew wet her skirts and petticoat as she walked. Bianca made a mental promise to ask Papa to widen this path, to spare her arriving damp to her knees.

As always, when Bianca came over the crest of the ridge and saw Perusia laid out before her, pride and happiness swelled in her chest. It was no palace or ducal manor, and wouldn't impress anyone expecting such grandeur. Instead it was an industrious little village, with the factory buildings bustling with workmen, the canal sparkling in the rising sun just beyond, dotted with bargemen delivering coal and readying other barges to receive crates of Perusia wares.

The courtyards of the factory were alive with activity as well, workers driving wheelbarrows of unfired pieces to the kilns, to the glazing and paint workshops, to the drying room. A thin trickle of people still hurried through the spinney of birch trees from the workers' cottages and boarding rooms. Everything was neat, well kept, and prosperous, overseen from the top of the hill by Perusia Hall.

She must have made some sigh of contentment, for St. James stepped up beside her. "Are you tired from the walk?"

Bianca scoffed. "That little stroll! Of course not. If *you* are," she hastened to add, "pray stop in at Perusia Hall for a while. Mrs. Hickson, the housekeeper, will see to your comfort."

His mouth curved. "I shall bear it in mind." And he stayed at her side as she strode down the hill.

At the gate to the factory, Bianca turned right, toward her workshop. It was in the southern arm, where the light was best, near the glazers and painters. To her surprise, St. James came with her.

"Papa's office is that way," she said, indicating the entrance to the central block. Papa liked to be in the middle of everything, and from there he could look down into the main workshop, where the pieces were made.

"I know," was his calm reply.

Bianca stopped. "That is where you should go, sir. To the office, to read your contracts and discuss business with my father."

"We did that yesterday," he said. "I would like to see the rest of the factory. Would you guide me on a tour?"

Her eyes narrowed. "I haven't time for that. If you enter there, you'll find Ned's office. Ned oversees the factory and will gladly show you around." Her cousin would roll his eyes at being sent on such a tedious chore when he had other, more important things to do, but Bianca sacrificed him without hesitation.

"Yes, he's a capital fellow, but I would hate to tear him away from his duties first thing in the morning." Squinting up at the offices, St. James suddenly smiled and made a small bow. Bianca looked up to see her father looking down at them. Papa lifted one hand, and she turned her back. She had not yet forgiven him for the scene in the sacristy.

Without another word she stalked to her workshop; she had work to do. She unlocked the door with the key she wore on a thin chain around her neck and let herself in.

Here she took a deep breath, feeling at home for the first time in a week. It smelled of wood spirits and enamel, with a faint whiff of turpentine, but it was her own space, just as she'd left it before she'd had to throw herself into the wedding diversions.

Then That Man stepped into the room behind her, and her moment of peace was extinguished like a snuffed candle. "Your workshop, I presume?"

"Obviously." She took her thick work apron from the peg behind the door and tied it on. "I prefer to work in quiet."

He smiled. "Of course. I shan't disturb you."

He was determined to cling to her. Very well; let him. He could watch her ignore him all day. With any luck at all he would expire of boredom within an hour and go away.

Instead he sat down in the chair next to her workbench and returned to his contracts. Bianca drew breath to protest, then silently let it out. She didn't care. She would ignore him no matter where he sat.

And she tried. She truly, truly tried. She sat on her stool and spread open her notebooks, skimming her notes to remind herself what progress she'd made a few days ago. The ruby glaze was intractable, coming out too dark for her taste. She wanted it to be the color of ripe strawberries, not burgundy wine.

St. James turned a page. In the frosty silence it sounded loud. Bianca made an impatient noise low in her throat.

"Your pardon, my dear," he murmured.

She tried to fix her attention on her formula. It was so close. Perhaps a little more potash? A bit less alum? She took down her mortar and pestle to grind another batch from the jars of minerals on the shelf above her head.

A tap at the door sounded, and Billy stuck his head inside. He was twelve, an apprentice in the firing workshop. "More samples for you, ma'am."

Bianca abandoned the mortar. "Bring them right in! Has the red mellowed?"

Billy shrugged as he carried in the tray of tiles. "A bit." They'd been fired three days ago and were only now cool enough to examine.

Bianca bent over the tray, scrutinizing each one. "This one looks good . . . This one is nearly orange, though. What happened? These all had the same sample applied."

"Edge of the kiln, perhaps, ma'am." Billy cleared his throat. "Good morning, sir."

"Good morning," said St. James pleasantly. "Billy, was it?"

"Yes, sir." Billy looked at Bianca nervously. "Billy Tucker, sir. My da works in the throwing house."

"I believe I made his acquaintance yesterday. Tall fellow with sandy hair?" asked That Man, as if he'd already met and memorized every person at Perusia.

Billy perked up. "Aye, sir! Quite tall. Mum says

I'll be tall like 'im . . ." His voice petered out as Bianca looked up from her samples. "Are these not right, then?"

"They're very close," she replied. "How is your da, Billy? Hands still sore?"

"No, ma'am, that salve you sent over helped that."

She beamed, pleased. "Lovely! I hope that makes it a bit easier on your mother." Mrs. Tucker had had a baby only a few months ago. If her husband's hands had stiffened too much for him to work, they would have been without income.

Billy nodded. "Aye, ma'am."

"These ones are good. The rest are rubbish." Bianca picked up the chosen tiles and flipped them to see what she'd marked on the reverse, to be sure she used the right formula. Billy took the tray and left, closing the door behind him.

She made notes in silence for a few moments, until her neck prickled. That Man was watching her. "What?" she snapped.

"How do you formulate the glazes?"

"With a close study of mineral properties, some chemistry intuition, and extensive trials," she replied without looking up.

"Very impressive," was all he said in reply. She stole a peek from the corner of one eye to see him holding one of her tiles. He caught her watching and laid it down. "Brilliantly impressive."

Bianca went back to her work, reminding herself to hate him. He hadn't the first idea what she did. Calling it impressive was empty flattery from him.

When she glanced at him again, he was once more absorbed in the contracts, turning the pages silently.

"It would surely be more comfortable to read in my father's office," she couldn't stop herself from murmuring.

"Not so," he replied. "The din from the workshops is disturbing."

"You might ask him to close the casements." Papa liked to be able to survey the entire workshop from his office, but even he acknowledged it could be loud, with the lathes and potters' wheels. There were casement windows to dim the noise.

"I am quite comfortable here," said St. James. "Though I do treasure your tender concern for my comfort."

"Should I not?" She consulted her notes and added a gram of soda to her mixture. "As your wife, I insist you retire to a more refined space, befitting a gentleman who once read law." She bit off the word *wife* with emphasis.

"My dear, I would not be parted from you, not even by a regiment of workmen hammering away," was his silky reply.

She imagined chasing him from the room with a pair of fire tongs, the sturdy tool that lifted items from the kiln. It cheered her enough to carry on, but not enough to allow her to forget he was there.

And that was what Bianca really craved. This man had already taken up too much of her attention, and now he was spoiling her concentration simply by sitting there, his legs elegantly crossed and those spectacles on his nose again. How did a man look more appealing with eyeglasses, instead of like a nearsighted quiz?

Even worse, she could see his leg from the corner of her eye. He had very shapely calves. Bianca wasn't above noticing a finely muscled leg on a man, but before it had always been passing curiosity and nothing more. There had never been the remotest chance she would do more than look.

But this man . . . The world expected her to go to bed with *this* man.

She had tried not to look at his legs the night before—nor at any part of him—but he seemed determined to draw her eye. Even in his plain, sober clothing, wearing spectacles and reading a dust-dry contract. Obviously he knew he was a handsome man. Bianca was wildly annoyed that she had to know it, too.

She made a valiant effort, but it was too much. Within the hour she gave it up, threw down her pestle, and jumped off her stool. "Very well, I shall lead you on a tour. After that I expect to have this workshop to myself."

He removed his spectacles and studied her. "Do I unsettle you?"

"I prefer to work in privacy." She stressed the last word. "You unsettle me as much as anyone being in the room would. There is a reason my workshop is in this wing, quiet and removed. Shall we?"

"Of course." He stowed his eyeglasses and tucked the contracts under his arm, then followed her out the door. "A strong lock," he observed as she put in the key.

"Very strong. What I work on would be quite valuable to a rival." She tucked the key back into her bodice, flushing as his gaze followed, and lingered on her bosom. "This way," she said brusquely, tugging up her fichu as soon as she'd turned her back to him.

Outside in the southern courtyard, she turned to him. "Do you know how pottery wares are produced?"

He smiled at the blunt question. "In broad strokes."

Bianca shook her head in disgust. "The way I know how to play the harp! In other words, not at all. This way."

She led him first to the clay house, with its sloping ramps to the canal and the road, to allow barrows and wagons to be drawn up to the door. "Here is the first step," she said, striding through and pointing as she went. "The clay is brought in to be inspected and weighed. It must be clean and pure or the wares produced from it will be rubbish. Charles there is responsible for making sure it is so." She nodded to her distant cousin, who was watching her and St. James with undisguised interest.

Bianca's face heated. Today she deeply regretted how enmeshed her family was in the pottery works. They had all been invited to the wedding festivities the day before, and all had seen her, instead of Cathy, emerge from the church on St. James's arm. She knew what they must all be thinking: Bianca the outspoken spinster had somehow ended up with her sister's intended husband! *Poor fool*, she supposed they were thinking when they looked at St. James himself, the man who'd almost won the sweet, lovely Cathy and instead had got her.

She hoped Amelia was busily spreading word that Cathy had run off with her true love, and that Bianca had acted only out of concern for the future of the pottery works, making a marriage for purely business reasons. If there was one thing Bianca couldn't bear, it was people staring at her. And while her marriage might be a scandal, there was nothing interesting about it.

"From here the clay is brought to be mixed." She led the way through a doorway and down a wide ramp. "Different pottery requires different mixtures of clays, precisely measured."

St. James stepped up and peered into one bin. "Which is used in making your plum pot?"

She flushed at the memory of him in her bedroom, inspecting her private things. "That is something else—porcelain, not pottery. There is a different workshop for it."

"Oh? How is it different?"

"Entirely," she said brusquely, and no more. The porcelain workshop was a tender subject, and not one she wanted to discuss with him.

From the clay rooms they went into the production hall, which was a collection of workshops divided by shoulder-height walls. A walkway ran the length of the hall, with periodic staircases descending to the floor, and it was not unusual to see Papa storming down one of them in a temper, having spied a workman neglecting his work or engaging in unsafe or illicit behavior.

She led her husband through the hall, pointing out and explaining the throwers and turners, making items on the pottery wheels; the modelers, carving out of clay; the grinders and polishers, smoothing the surfaces of the unfinished pieces; the slip-makers and mold-makers, making delicate ornaments from the water-thinned clay called slip.

"This entire workshop is for teapot spouts," she said in one doorway. Trays of neatly made spouts lined the shelves by the door, like the fat little tails of upside-down piglets.

"Odd-looking little things, aren't they?" St. James studied them with a faint smile. "I never thought of the spouts being made separately."

"As are the handles," she replied. "And the lids."

He slanted her an amused look. "Are they? Who might have guessed?" Bianca rolled her eyes. "Where, pray, are the lids created and when are they attached?"

"They aren't—" she began, before catching herself. He was laughing at her. "The body of a teapot would be made in the previous rooms, while the spouts and handles are made here, then sent along to be attached before firing. You confessed you knew nothing about the pottery works. I was trying to be helpful and explain them."

"Ah." His dark eyes glinted at her. "And now I know that lids are not attached to the pots. A mystery I have pondered all my life, solved."

She smiled sweetly back. "I'm sure there are innumerable others to perplex you."

He gave her a sizzling, knowing look, up and down. "Perhaps there are, but I intend to solve them all."

Meaning her. Her pulse roared in her ears, and she had to grip a handful of apron to keep her temper in check. "That should keep you occupied for an eternity."

That Man leaned closer. His hands were clasped behind his back, and he didn't touch her, but Bianca tensed all the same. "If that's what it takes," he said quietly. "I don't quit, my dear."

She inhaled raggedly. If he were anyone else, or

if they were anywhere else in the world, she would ring a peal over him. But the very last thing she needed—even less than she needed St. James's company, let alone his smoldering looks—was to spark rumors that the two of them were already quarreling on the workshop floor.

"Spoken with the sheer idiocy of Pyrrhus himself," she returned, and marched away.

Chapter Ten

Max understood exactly what Bianca was up to, and it amused him to no end.

She was going to keep him at arm's length; she was going to lose no opportunity to put him in his place and let him know she thought very little of his intelligence and ability.

Max was accustomed to being underestimated: by landlords and merchants, by the Duchess of Carlyle and her solicitor, by his own father. None of them had thought he had any brains in his head, nor any ambition beyond running up debts and being as languidly elegant as possible. So he was neither surprised, nor even upset, that Bianca felt the same. Like the rest of them, she saw what she wanted to see, and like the rest of them, she would be astonished when she eventually realized the truth. He looked forward to that day.

Also, he had seen the covert way she looked at him, and especially at his legs. Max wasn't above displaying himself to best advantage in the hopes of piquing her interest, and unless he'd completely lost his touch, he sensed she was more interested, and attracted, than she would admit.

He followed her through the factory, docile as a

lamb. Samuel Tate had showed him all this before, and Max had read a number of tracts on the subject of manufacturing and pottery production. He let slide her needling about him being perplexed until the end of time by her, as well as her smart retort about Pyrrhus. Nothing he'd seen so far made him think the costs would outweigh the benefits of victory. To the contrary—everything he saw and learned about Bianca made him think they would be an incomparable team . . . once he persuaded her they ought to *be* one.

In the packing house he couldn't stop himself from asking questions. The issue of breakage in the contracts lingered in his mind. If Brimley and other merchants insisted on being able to write off a fifth of all wares sent to them as broken on arrival, there was a significant opportunity for improvement. Max expected there would be many such opportunities, but this one seemed an obvious choice to attack first.

So he watched workers nestling cups and plates into straw-filled crates, and he questioned every step. "What sort of straw?"

"The dry sort," Bianca answered shortly. "It's straw."

Max scooped up a handful and crushed it in his palm. "Not so. Some straw is little more than dried grass. Some is as stiff as a willow. After the considerable effort it takes to produce these fine wares"—he lifted a finely wrought pot, awaiting packing, from the shelf nearby—"you would toss it into a crate filled with anything?" He shook his head and replaced the teapot. "But perhaps this is not an area of the business which concerns you."

Her mouth was hanging open. "How— What—
Of course I care!" she said furiously. "How do you
know so much about straw?"

*From the many nights I've spent scrounging for a spot
to sleep, and never turned up my nose at any safe, warm,
straw-filled stable,* he thought. "I know many things
that might surprise you," was all he told her.

Incensed now, Bianca hailed a workman passing
by. "William, what sort of straw is used for packing
the wares?"

"Wheat, mostly, and barley," answered the man,
barely breaking stride.

"Wheat and barley straw," she snapped at him
and strode off.

Max contemplated the straw in his hand and let
it fall back into the crate. "Use more straw when
packing anything going by road," he told the worker
lingering curiously nearby. "One quarter more, on
Mr. St. James's orders." The fellow nodded and scurried away, and Max went after his wife.

She led him back to the main offices and up the
stairs to throw open the door and march in. Max
followed, unhurried.

"And here is a place you must remember well,"
said Bianca as he entered. "I believe you had some
questions about contracts for my father?"

Samuel Tate came around his desk, his eyes sharp
and interested. "Well now, I didn't think to see either of you at the factory today. It was your wedding
yesterday! Take a day free, man, to recover your
strength."

"Yes," said Bianca warmly. She gave Max a smile
he'd never seen before, one which made his heart
stutter in surprise. Her eyes sparkled and her lips

curved in true pleasure. "Do, Mr. St. James. This is all so very new and taxing to you! You must want a week's respite at the very least."

Max smiled back at her, letting the full force of his appreciation show. "New and fascinating, my dear. I find myself entranced, and utterly lost in my study."

Tate laughed. "I knew it! I told you," he said triumphantly to his daughter, whose face had turned pink. "I knew it would work out for the best. Wasn't I right?"

She ignored him. Max could only guess what was in her mind as she made a graceful little curtsy. "If you are so happily occupied, sir, I shall leave you here and return to my work."

"Of course." He bowed, catching her hand when she tried to brush past him, and raising it to his lips. "I would never dream of interrupting your work, knowing how important it is to you and to Perusia." Her mouth flattened. Max released her hand. "Until later, my dear."

With a twitch of her skirts and a glare of pure aggravation, she swept out of the room.

Grinning broadly, Tate closed the door behind her. "Well! Seems a promising beginning, aye?"

All yesterday the man had alternated between fretting, apologizing, and fulminating about his daughter's temper and obstinate will. Max wasn't sure if Tate regretted his actions at the church, or merely wanted Max's assurance that all was well. It had not escaped him that his wife had not spoken one word to her father either yesterday, at the wedding breakfast, or just now, when she'd kept her back to him the entire time she was in his office.

But she'd come into the office, and apparently that was enough reconciliation for Tate. Today the storm had passed, in his mind, and he was ready to resume course.

Max had a feeling Bianca took after her father in that. The first time he'd been invited to Perusia, for that dinner a few months ago, he'd noticed that Catherine Tate would listen politely to anyone prattle on for as long as they could talk. Not Bianca; she'd whittled a long-winded philosophical argument down to its essence, and left the two philosophers blinking at her in bewilderment. She had a sharp, quick wit, with no patience for idle chatter. She walked briskly, spoke boldly, and was delightfully easy to rouse to a passion.

Max admired her confidence—and envied it. He, however, had learned that there was a time for that boldness, and a time to hold his tongue and listen. Time to erupt in fury and time to swallow his pride, even to grovel. Time to act, and time to watch, and wait, and learn, until precisely the right moment arrived to seize what he wanted.

So he smiled at Tate's hopeful query. "It was all very sudden for both of us. Of course it will take time to become acquainted, as husband and wife." He paused. "But I do believe it is a most auspicious beginning."

WHEN THE BELL rang at six o'clock that evening, Max was waiting at the main gate. He had spent the day in the offices, as Bianca had told him to do, but now was time to devote some attention to his wife.

After several minutes she emerged from the far

workshop. Her head was bent, the flat straw hat hiding her face as she tugged on her gloves. Her head came up. He saw the flash of her wide smile as she lifted one hand in greeting to the woman who had called to her.

Max's gaze lingered on that smile. He'd only seen it a few times, true and carefree instead of tight and grim. But it transformed Bianca's face, brightening her eyes to blue and accentuating her lush mouth.

All day long he had kept his ears open, keen for any new glimmers of insight into this intriguing, infuriating woman who was his wife. Max thought they were more alike than not; she'd taunted him about how quickly he agreed to the bride switch, but had no reply when he turned the query back on her. He suspected they had both acted on impulse, even if her impulse sprang from passion and fury while his came from an iron-willed determination not to let this opportunity slide through his grasp.

Perhaps, he thought idly, watching the sway of her skirt as she crossed the courtyard toward him, she had felt the same. *These pottery works are mine*, she'd said in the church. Tate had assigned him a quarter share of the business upon his marriage— the business being of course Tate's and not his daughter's, not yet. Max had probed a little, and Tate admitted he had always hoped to leave Perusia to his children.

Tate had hastened to add that he'd been reserving ultimate judgment on that score until his daughters were married, for he did not intend to leave his life's work to be frittered away by an indolent son-in-law. That last had come with an appraising look, to which Max somberly agreed that it was a wise precaution to take. It seemed to have satisfied Tate, who had quickly moved on to doubting the sensibility of the erstwhile curate, who was presumably his other son-in-law by now.

Bianca looked up and caught sight of him, watching her, thinking about her, and her smile dropped away. She walked right by him, but Max fell in beside her without missing a step. "Good evening," he said.

"Good evening, sir," she replied coolly.

"It is now," he said with a smile.

"Is it?" She widened her eyes innocently. "I felt a sudden chill."

"Allow me to lend you my coat."

Her lips parted and she stared at him in astonishment, until Max began removing his coat. "Please, no," she said hastily. "Don't do that!"

Max paused mid-shrug. "I don't mind," he said in a low voice, gazing at her. "I grew rather warm and flustered as you approached."

Her color deepened. She snatched back the hand she'd put out to stop him. "It must be a fever. Pray, keep your coat on so you don't develop an ague."

"I've never felt fitter," he assured her, tugging his coat back into place. With a huff, she strode off, the ribbons on her hat fluttering.

"Did you make good progress on the scarlet glaze?"

She gave him a sideways glance. "Some."

Max nodded once. "I am delighted to hear it."

If Bianca was so dedicated to her work, he would encourage her to pursue it. It did not escape Max's mind that here was an easy way to please them both: she could continue in her glazing experiments unchecked, while he was free to improve the rest of the business.

After several silent paces, she said, with the air of one forcing herself to make conversation, "I trust you spent a pleasant day reading contracts."

"Oh yes," he agreed.

She eyed him warily, but he said nothing else. Let her wonder. Let her come to him, wanting more.

"You needn't come to the factory again," she said, facing forward.

"Why are you so keen to keep me from the factory?" he asked. "A factory which is one-quarter mine."

"I believe Papa meant for you to be a silent partner."

"That's not what he told me."

"I said," she replied sweetly, "that's what he *meant*."

Max smiled grimly. He knew she was wrong—he knew it was what *she* preferred, and nothing to do with her father's wishes—but her insistence on it did drive the knife deep into his pride. "Did he? Sadly, it's not what *I* meant when I accepted it."

"No doubt you'll learn how to interpret his words," she said with mock sincerity, "in time."

"Do his remarks require a great deal of interpretation?" Max pretended to think. "Odd. It didn't strike me as though they did. An honest, open fellow, I thought him."

"Of course *Papa* is honest," she said, casting aspersions without hesitation. "I suppose that is unusual in your world."

Max laughed. "My world is Perusia." And because he couldn't resist the devil inside him, he added in a quieter tone, "And you, my dearest wife."

Bianca gave him a jaundiced look. "Does that

sort of folderol seduce ladies in London? Because I think it makes you sound an idiot."

He grinned to hide his flash of pique. "I've never tried to seduce a London lady by marrying her! Who knew that's what it took? Too late now, I suppose."

"Yes, much too late." Her smile was dangerous. "And it didn't work anyway. You ought to have thought of that before wasting your chance, making a chaste marriage of business."

"You keep saying that word, *chaste*," he remarked. "I'm not entirely sure what you mean."

She opened her mouth, blushed, and closed her mouth. "It's when a husband and wife live separate lives. Very separate. Very *widely* separated, in fact." She raised her hands and held them out, two feet apart. She eyed the span, and increased it to a generous three feet. "Preferably by a league or more."

"Well, that's not what we've got," said Max smoothly. "Barely two hundred yards apart all day!"

"Yes, barely," she muttered. "Tomorrow we must strive to do better."

They had been following the path back to Poplar House, skirting the hill of Perusia Hall and winding through the trees. By now they were out of sight of the factory and all the workers leaving it, as well as hidden from view of Perusia Hall—and Poplar House. Max slowed his pace.

"You spend a great deal of time thinking about the state of our marriage," he said.

His wife rolled her eyes, but he noted that her steps also slowed. "Far too much. Would that I could stop thinking of it entirely, or better yet, forget it ever happened."

He laughed. "Perhaps you ought not to stop thinking about it, but change *how* you think about it."

She raised her brows. "And become a simpering, silly bride who never puts up a word of protest to anything you say? *Tsk*, Mr. St. James." She shook her head. "Wouldn't you find that perishingly dull?"

"I would," he agreed. "I like a woman of passion and spirit."

"But not to marry, obviously," she said, with a sly glance at him.

"Perhaps not originally, but Fate seems to have guided me in that direction." He gave her another smile. "Just as it did to you."

He'd wondered if she had another suitor, or someone she fancied for a suitor. It had been one of the questions in the back of his mind as he kept his ear open for any intelligence about his new wife. If she harbored feelings for someone else, it would wipe away any suspicion that she'd schemed to cause their marriage.

Of course, it would also affect his strategy. He didn't like to think of his wife pining for another man.

"I never thought to marry at all," she said.

"Never?" Max had not expected that answer, and wasn't sure she meant it.

"Of course not," she said firmly, her lips turning up. "Certainly not to anyone like you."

"I understand," he said with mock gravity. "Most women never dare even dream of *that*."

She stopped. "You—you conceited rake!"

"I'm not a rake at all," he countered. "I'm a happily married man. Why didn't you want to marry?"

She rolled her eyes. "A married woman has no right to anything, even that which was hers before her marriage. Her money, her lands, her business, even the clothes she wears are his. If she bears a child, risking her health and person, it's his child, and he can take the child from her at his whim." She looked at him levelly. "Would you surrender all that in any bargain, sir, for yourself?"

"Hmm," said Max thoughtfully. "When a man marries, he becomes the legal guardian of his wife, responsible for her room and board, liable for her debts. Men have gone to prison for their wives' debts. If she bears a child, any child, while married to him, he is obliged to support that child as his own, even if half the town knows his wife was unfaithful to him and the child is another man's."

"Good heavens," she said, laughing a little. "It sounds a miserable business for both people. I can't imagine why anyone would desire it."

Max grinned. "There are . . . certain pleasures that compensate for all that." Their walk had brought a very fetching flush to her cheeks and her fichu had slipped; her breasts plumped up above her bodice, ravishingly tempting.

Still amused, she waved one hand. "Not for us. I told you this is a chaste marriage."

"And it's beginning to hurt my tender male feelings," he told her.

Bianca laughed—a full, throaty laugh he'd never heard before. Max's smiling éclat faltered; she was bewitching. No porcelain doll but an earthly goddess, the sort of woman who would keep a man on his toes but be a worthy partner, at dinner, at a ball . . . and in bed.

He hadn't expected much in that regard from his marriage. Catherine had given little sign of attraction to him, even for a reserved lady, and Max had presumed they would find their own bedmates.

But Bianca . . . Lord above, the sparks of attraction were scorching him on all sides.

"Do you know," she said, reluctantly amused, as Max tried to absorb this new realization about his bride, "I think I might have liked you, if we weren't married."

"Oh, you mustn't hold that against me."

"But it is by far your greatest fault, and one I cannot overlook." She heaved a sigh of regret. "We must resign ourselves to being adversaries, or at best indifferent housemates."

Max shifted his weight toward her. "Surely not. I can think of things far, far better than . . ." His gaze dipped once more, almost against his will, to her décolletage. "Indifferent chastity."

Her eyelashes fluttered, and her throat worked. "What a tragic waste of imagination."

He grinned at her. Oh God yes, he did like this woman. For the first time he was completely glad his intended bride had eloped with another man. "Imagination is never wasted." His voice dropped to a murmur. "Fortunately, I know how to bide my time . . . and my imagination will keep me very warm while I do."

She smiled widely. "For your sake, I hope so," she said. "For *I* certainly shan't."

She marched off, leaving him to follow in her wake, his blood running hot and his thoughts very happily occupied imagining how it would be when he finally won her over.

Chapter Eleven

For the next fortnight and more, things went as they had done that first day.

No matter how early Bianca rose, That Man was always at the table before her. In aggravation she told Jennie to wake her earlier, and earlier, and even when she staggered downstairs, yawning in the pre-dawn darkness, he would be waiting and rise, fully dressed and not looking tired at all, from his seat at the breakfast table to wish her a good morning.

In disgust Bianca gave it up. He could win this battle; she was going to sleep.

There were plenty of other battles to fight, of course. During those breakfasts, he always had a book or a pamphlet or a contract in his hand. Once she spied schematic drawings of a kiln and some device she didn't recognize, annotated in writing she didn't recognize. Bianca knew her father's hand-writing, as well as Mick's and George's, who were the heads of the firing house crew. Since she would have chewed off her hand before asking That Man to explain, she was reduced to asking Billy what was being built by the kilns. Twelve-year-old boys, alas, were not reliable spies; he did not know, and she was forced to swallow her curiosity.

And her husband persisted in walking to and from the factory with her. Some days they walked in silence, unless Bianca was forced to offer her thanks for some gallantry of his, like pitching a fallen branch from the path. Other days they sniped and sparred the whole way to Perusia's gate. One day Amelia, meeting her in the courtyard after That Man had left her, commented that she looked unusually well that morning. "You have the look of victory about you," teased her friend. "Flushed and bright-eyed. What problem have you solved?"

Bianca forced a smile and made up something innocuous, but seethed inside to think that there was no true reason other than her conversation with Max. He'd provoked her into speaking to him and then almost made her laugh. She would have to be more on guard with him.

And, perhaps, with herself. Holding her grudges was beginning to wear on her.

She still was not speaking to her father. A few times she had caught him watching her at the factory, when she came down to inspect some newly fired wares glazed in her now-perfected scarlet. To her joy, they glowed like June strawberries, bright glossy ruby-red without any purple or orange undertone. It was exactly as she'd wanted it.

Normally she would have borne the scarlet-glazed dishes off to her father's office, to share her triumph with him. He'd raved when she showed him the delicate green glaze that had occupied her for several months, and which now graced many a tea set in the very fashionable Chinese style. He'd declared she was cleverer than half the factory put together, and more determined than all of them. Bianca had basked in his enthusiastic approval.

This time she was reduced to hearing from other people that Papa was pleased with the scarlet glaze. It took the shine off her triumph, particularly when That Man was one of the people telling her how splendid it was.

"It's unmatched," he said as they walked home one evening. "As red as the blood of the martyrs."

She couldn't stop a small smile. "Thank you." And then, because of the rage she'd felt at his earlier slighting of her work, "Now perhaps you understand why I go to the workshop every day."

"I certainly see the benefit to Perusia," he said, smiling in that way he had that made Bianca—very much against her wishes—want to smile back. "It was a surprise to me that you would be so driven in pursuit of glazing formulae."

She stopped. "Why was it such a surprise to you?"

He also stopped, and faced her. Bianca had to give him that—when she spoke to him, he turned his full attention on her. Many men did not. "Most ladies of my acquaintance are not given to such serious occupations."

London ladies, she thought with an edge of irritation. Women who did not need to work or do anything practical. "Here, they are," she replied. "Over one quarter of the workers at Perusia are women."

"Yes," he acknowledged, "and some of them are highly skilled artisans. But they work for the income, which you do not need."

Bianca put her hands on her hips. "No? That suggests my work has no impact on Perusia, that the orders would be streaming in even if we couldn't produce teacups that look like they're carved from jade." She shook her head. "Any potter can produce a double-handled vase or a competent teapot. There are dozens of factories producing wares virtually identical to ours. It's a cutthroat business, you know—"

"I do," he murmured.

"—where everyone copies any competitor's popular designs, and Perusia must stand apart. We do that with the delicacy of our decoration, from uniquely colorful glazes to the detailed paintings to the whimsical little touches other manufacturers don't spend the time to create. Papa has always taken great pains to hire the best artists and to train our workers to his exacting standards, and that is why we succeed. The glazing is only a part, but an important one, as it is often the first aspect of a piece to catch someone's eye. My glazes, sir, are unique to Perusia. So if I went home and sat in the parlor all day," she finished with a pointed finger for emphasis, "it might well decrease our income. Which we do need, to support not just our workers but our family." She arched one brow at him. "Even you."

Throughout her speech his demeanor had gone from sober seriousness to open appreciation. Now he laughed, and swept a deep bow. "Pax, madam! I intended no offense. Only . . ." He tilted his head, his face still relaxed in amusement. "You have been a great surprise to me. Daily I am astonished anew."

"That is no surprise to *me*," she told him. "I suspected all along you had no acquaintance of clever, ambitious women."

"Ah, now, that's where you're wrong." He kept pace with her as she started walking again. "London women have their own ambitions, and there's no shortage of cleverness and cunning among them."

"Oh? Then what do they pursue?" Bianca had seen fashionable magazines from London. She'd read their descriptions of needlework and playing the harpsichord and dancing. It all sounded rather useless to her.

"Influence," he said after a moment. "Whether it be in leading the fashions or influencing the government."

"Women must find power where we can, I suppose."

He gazed at her for a moment. "You have far more within your reach than you think."

Bianca scoffed. "You mean as a wife, or as a daughter. Thank you, no. I prefer to make my own mark."

His forehead wrinkled ruefully. "I had no doubt of that."

"I admire you for acknowledging it." Although she tried to conceal it from him, Bianca was somewhat amazed. Even her father, who did value her contributions to Perusia and gave her credit for them, confidently expected that she would give it all up to be a wife and mother.

At this, her husband smiled his slow, simmering rake's smile. "Perhaps I'm not what you thought I was."

The smart retort stuck to her tongue. What he said was true, and she didn't know what to make of it. She settled for ducking her head in a nod, and walking faster. And St. James, maddeningly, didn't irk her by belaboring the point.

When they reached Poplar House, Mary was waiting with a letter. "From Miss Cathy," she said—unnecessarily, for Bianca had gasped in joy at the sight of her sister's handwriting.

"Thank you, Mary!" She seized the letter and tore off her hat and shawl, unloading them into the maid's hands before carrying her prize into the parlor.

Bianca did not regret helping her sister elope, but now she realized how anxiously she'd been waiting for some word from Cathy that all had gone off well, that she was married to Mr. Mayne, that she was happy. Just the sight of this letter, free of tear stains—she looked closely for them, as she unfolded it—caused the pressure inside her chest to ease.

She sat on the settee by the window and broke the seal.

Dearest B—

I am married! And more happily than I can express in ink and paper.

We made the journey to Wolverhampton in good time, due primarily to your great assistance in helping us get away from Marslip unseen. The journey was not easy but Richard was so tender and caring of my comfort, I hardly felt a moment's trouble. Richard's sister, Mrs. Taylor, was astonished to see us, but she listened to our story and instantly agreed to help us. Where would we be, I asked Richard, without our sisters? He agreed we have both been singularly blessed in you and Maria.

There was some trouble about the license, which took several days to remedy. Richard had to ride to Lichfield, which caused a delay, but all is right now. I have been Mrs. Mayne for an entire day and have never been happier and know that I owe it all to you, dear Bianca.

I am sorry not to have written to you sooner but I felt it better not to stir up any trouble that may have erupted between you and Papa. I hope he was not too terribly angry with you for helping us. Do write as soon as you may and tell me if he has been horrible to you, or if Mr. St. James kicked up a terrible fuss about it.

Bianca stirred uncomfortably. She still had no idea how to tell her sister what had happened with Mr. St. James, let alone why she had gone along with Papa's mad, angry suggestion. Papa would no doubt argue that he had been caught off guard, while Bianca had known for days and days that her sister would not be standing up beside St. James in the church. She ought to have been more prepared for his burst of fury, and not let herself get caught up in it.

What would Cathy say about this?

"I trust she is well." St. James's voice made her start. He had followed her as far as the parlor doorway, where he stood with his arms folded and his shoulder against the jamb.

Bianca cleared her throat and angled the letter away from his view. "She is."

"Happily married?"

"Yes—very." He continued to gaze at her until, uneasily aware that she had schemed to deny him the bride he'd wanted, she muttered, "Did you want something?"

"You look unsettled. Not as one might expect upon receiving a joyful letter from a beloved sister."

"Are you an expert on sisters?" she parried.

"Not at all," he said, a faint smile appearing. "I've never had one. But I am well-versed in disappointment and dismay, and you have the air of it about you."

She wondered at that, but feared asking how he was such an authority would only invite more questions about her own behavior. "She asks how our father has taken her elopement." She chewed on her lower lip, then added quietly, "And if you made a fuss."

He strolled into the room and took a chair by the table. "Will you put her mind at ease?"

"Will I assure her all is well, or will I be honest?" She fiddled with the letter. "I don't know."

"In this instance, I recommend honesty." Bianca glared at him, and he lifted one shoulder. "It can hardly be concealed forever. Might as well break the news and be done with it."

"I suppose." He was right, though she hated to admit it. "She is more concerned with how our father reacted to her disappearance."

"Will he forgive her quickly?"

Bianca stared at the floor. Papa had always adored Cathy, who reminded him of their mother. One plea from Cathy, with tears brimming in her big blue eyes, and Papa would relent and fold her into his arms. Bianca, on the other hand . . . *She* was the bullheaded daughter, the one who got into arguments with their father, the one who stood up to him. *She* was the one he hadn't spoken to in three weeks despite seeing her almost every day. "Perhaps not immediately, but he will."

"He's fond of her, then."

"Very." Bianca folded the letter. Cathy had written more, but she would read it later. The prospect of telling her sister what had happened, in all its incredible, furious detail, had dimmed her delight at receiving it.

She did not relish telling her sister that she, Bianca, was now married to the man who had courted Cathy. Even without sparing Papa and St. James generous shares of blame, even explaining how angry she'd been and how Papa threatened the loss of Perusia, it would shock her sister. Cathy would be stunned and horrified that Bianca had agreed to it.

"A forgiving father is a blessing," her husband remarked.

Bianca blinked out of her thoughts. "Yes."

St. James shifted in his chair, leaning a bit toward her. "He misses you, you know. He had no one else to regale with your triumph at the scarlet glaze, so I have heard it all twice."

She blushed. She'd known all along her father would be enormously pleased with the scarlet. "Is your father kind?" she asked on impulse.

There was a second of hesitation. "He's long in his grave," said St. James easily.

"Oh." She had suspected as much, but felt, for the first time, a flicker of curiosity about his family— and a twinge of shame that she'd never spared them a thought until now, when it felt too awkward to ask. "I'm sorry to hear it."

"Thank you." It was politely said, but invited no

further questions. St. James rose. "Convey my felicitations to your sister on her marriage."

Bianca's mouth fell open. "Your . . . felicitations?"

"Of course. She is my sister-in-law. I am delighted to hear she is happily wed." His eyes gleaming, he gave a brief bow and walked out, his shoes ringing on the worn wooden floor. Despite his newly sober clothing, he still wore the raised heels of a London gentleman.

Bianca realized her fingers had clenched around Cathy's letter. She exhaled and smoothed it on her skirt. St. James obviously was suffering no regrets about their marriage—or at least not great ones.

She tried to tell herself everything was still as she'd thought before, that he cared only for his share of Perusia and it was all the same to him no matter which Tate sister he had to marry to get it. It was no trouble for him to be pleased for Cathy, because he'd got the other daughter and ended up as he wanted to be anyway.

But deep inside, she was beginning to suspect there was much, much more to him than that.

MAX'S STRIDE REMAINED unhurried and calm all the way up the stairs and into his bedroom. He even managed to close the door normally instead of flinging it shut behind him.

But he couldn't hold back the curses, and his hands trembled as he ground his palms against his temples. "God damn it," he whispered in the still room.

A noise outside the door made him tense, until the sound of a maid's footsteps pattered past, accompanied by some off-key humming.

Max exhaled. His head bowed heavily. Eyes closed, he slid one hand into the pocket in his coattail and retrieved the letter. Mary had handed it to him after Bianca had carried off her sister's letter to the parlor. Max had smiled and thanked Mary and swiftly hidden it in his pocket. Not quickly enough to avoid seeing the direction on the front, in the spidery familiar handwriting that always gave him nightmares, but he hoped he'd done it smoothly enough that the maid wouldn't pay the letter any mind.

For a moment he debated burning it without reading. Never had one of these letters brought good news; at best they taunted and mocked him, at worst they made him contemplate murder. The world would certainly be better without the man who sent them, and Max had entertained many a fantasy about showing him out of it.

Still, after a moment, hating himself, Max broke the seal. There was always a slim chance . . .

But no.

Money, he thought grimly as he read the short message. It always came down to money. For the last year penury had been Max's shield, but now it seemed news of his marriage had found its way into the ear of this poisonous viper, who never missed a chance to feed off anyone who came near him. Max had hoped Staffordshire would be far enough away to avoid notice, but the viper had found him, and decided he was ripe enough to attack again.

Another noise made Max start. The muffled sound of Bianca's voice drifted through the door. She would be changing for dinner.

He stared at that door for a long while. By now

he could tell her mood from the timbre of her voice, and tonight she was happy. The letter from her sister must have contained very comforting news. Jennie's voice answered, and then the two of them laughed. Bianca had such a warm, vibrant laugh.

Max inhaled. He'd forgotten to breathe, listening to her voice, light and lilting with carefree delight. She still held him at arm's length, but her manner was thawing, slowly but steadily. He had encouraged that warmth at every turn, keeping his calm even when she provoked him and making good-humored replies to any smart comments from her. Today, just minutes ago in the parlor, she had looked at him with wondering, almost dazed eyes, her mouth gone soft, and he'd felt a surge of elation. Things were turning his way.

And he wasn't about to let anything interfere.

His gaze dropped to the letter. The viper preferred to bleed his victims from afar; not once had he approached Max directly. Perhaps he sensed it was better for his health that way. Max had promised to kill him the next time they met, after all.

With steady hands he struck the flint and lit the lamp, then touched the corner of the paper to the flame, and watched it burn until the heat singed his hands and he let it crumble into ash in the grate.

Chapter Twelve

Max was learning far more about pottery and ceramics than he had ever expected to know. Even though he had vowed to apply himself and learn it all, it interested him more than he had anticipated.

Tate had created an impressive system in his factories, where he trained workmen in a limited number of skills until they excelled at them. Not only did it speed production, it led to a uniformity in the quality of the wares they produced.

Tate was inordinately proud of this. "Each one as fine as the last!" he told Max, gesturing to long shelves filled with vases on one visit to the workshop. "A man does better when he's allowed to develop one skill to the best of his ability, rather than having to learn the entire process."

Max surveyed the line of double-handled vases. It was indeed remarkable that each one had been crafted individually. He couldn't have told any one of them from the other. "That must have required an immense amount of training."

Tate waved one hand. "Some didn't take to it in the beginning, but I can pay higher wages to a man with more skill, can't I? Everyone likes to be paid more." His mouth twitched in irritation. "And I've got to, or bloody Mannox across the river will poach them from me. Ten men last year alone, Mr. St. James, he stole from under my nose! Well, I won back eight of them, and that will teach Henry Mannox to think he can hire my men away and pick their brains for my designs and formulae. His wares are inferior quality in every aspect, and everyone knows it."

Max raised his brows. "How did you win the workmen back?" If the answer was higher wages again, he foresaw a problem; every workman in here would go work for Mannox for a few months, then allow himself to be "won" back by Tate, for an increase in his wages. A man might change factories twice a year, playing the owners against each other.

His father-in-law harrumphed. "Mannox treats his men like dogs. Most of them recognized it and came back. And . . ." He hesitated. "Six of them wanted the school."

"What school?"

"For the children." He paused, his mouth puckered up. "Bianca set it up in the old workshop after we built these new premises." With that, Tate stalked out of the room, arms folded. Max had divined by now that indicated some displeasure or reluctance on Tate's part—most likely due to the mention of Bianca. He followed his father-in-law.

"I take it Mannox has no schools."

Tate snorted. "Mannox has filthy factories and poor methods. Ah well—everyone learns that once they've worked for him for a few months."

"Yes," said Max smoothly, "but those months of their labor are then lost to Perusia. I wonder how we might persuade workers to want to stay."

"That would be ideal," acknowledged Tate. "I've

done my best, sir. When I built Perusia, we had to relocate a good way away from the old works, and there weren't enough rooms available. A man won't work for me if he can't house his family, so we built the village." He waved one hand at the neat rows of cottages and houses visible beyond the copse. "Mannox ain't got that," he added with a smug air.

"Bianca, though, insisted it wasn't enough and she made a school for the little ones." Tate shrugged. "I suppose it helps."

"Aren't the workers' children set to become apprentices?" Max was surprised. Not only would it ensure the child a good job when he was older, it was good for the pottery works to have a new generation of workmen being trained at all times.

"Aye, many of them do." Tate beamed again. "Men are proud to work for Perusia, sir—proud! I pay good wages, have a doctor in once a month, and charge only a pittance rate for the cottages. But Bianca—" He stopped and looked away. "She's got rarefied ideas," was all he said, a moment later.

"I see," murmured Max, wondering what they were. He already knew his wife had a romantic streak, from the way she had conspired to help her sister elope. Did she have an egalitarian one as well?

Tate waved it aside. "It's her project, none of mine. And if it persuades a few fellows to come back, all the better! What's the harm in letting her have her little passions, eh?" He winked at Max. "Good advice for any husband, if you ask me! Keeps a wife happy, and out of your way to boot."

It was so at odds with Bianca, this vision of her as an idle woman needing something harmless and feminine to keep her occupied, that Max couldn't repress an amazed glance at his companion. Tate nodded, eyebrows raised encouragingly as he waited for Max to agree with him.

Ah. Tate *wanted* his daughter to be more idle and more feminine, caring for the children even if she took too enlightened a view of that endeavor. Bianca, however, wanted to be useful. How had she described her work? *A close study of mineral properties, some chemistry intuition, and extensive trials*, she'd said. She cared about her glazes, and that made him think she also cared about this school.

So in reply to Tate's comment, he merely smiled and dipped his head, neither agreeing nor disagreeing. "One thing I've not seen. Where are the smaller items produced?" he asked instead, remembering Bianca's little plum pot. "My wife has some charming pieces on her dressing table."

Tate flicked one hand. "Those bits of paste," he scoffed. "Frippery."

"Oh?" Max had seen many an elegant lady's dressing table, with little silver pots full of pomade and powders. Fripperies they might be, but they were in demand. "More than that, I think."

Tate rolled his eyes. "Bianca wanted to experiment with the porcelain. There's no harm in it, but earthenware is more lasting. Stronger, too." He strode back into the workshop, pausing now and then to examine a piece. At one bench he paused, taking down a vase and turning it from side to side. Having kept pace, Max scrutinized the piece, too, searching for the flaw that had put a frown on Tate's face. He couldn't find it, but expected it would be pointed out soon.

Then, to his astonishment, the older man flung down the vase with a violent crash. "Who made that?" he roared. "Craddock!" A stout fellow with ginger hair rushed over. "Who is responsible for this?" Tate demanded, waving one hand at the remnants of the vase, lying in shards on the floor.

"Martin, Mr. Tate," said Craddock uneasily.

Tate threw up his hands. "It's not good enough for Perusia! Does he need to be sent back to making plates? Don't let that happen again."

"Right, sir. Never." Craddock ducked his head and gestured for a boy with a broom to come sweep up the mess.

Tate stepped over the broken vase and strode onward.

Max regarded the shattered vase. Its faults had been small, imperceptible to any casual observer, but Tate had spotted them, and destroyed the vase in consequence.

It seemed a waste of clay, of labor, of potential income. The smooth handle of the jug was intact, a sinuous curve of biscuit. It had been fired once, but was still devoid of Bianca's glossy glazes. It looked as perfect as the rest of them to him. Tate had higher standards, and that was entirely admirable. But smashing a vase that looked perfectly fine to the unskilled eye—that is, to the vast majority of the population—rankled. Max, who had long had too little of everything, despised waste.

With a lingering glance at the boy crouching over his broom, the rows of bowed heads in the silent workshop, and the shelves of otherwise indistinguishable vases, Max went after Tate.

Chapter Thirteen

Bianca would never have admitted it to herself, let alone to anyone else, but she was coming to like her husband.

She didn't understand him, and she still thought there must be more to his decision to marry her than she knew. But every day that went by seemed to bring evidence of some endearing thing about him, and it was becoming harder and harder to keep him at a distance.

His response to Cathy's letter was the most surprising, but far from the only sign that she might have been slightly wrong about him. There was the way he waited for her at the factory gate every day, and seemed to sense from her mood whether he should speak to her or be silent. The faultless manners he always displayed, to everyone from Bianca herself down to the lowest scullery maid. That he never lost his temper with her, not once, since that stern warning in the sacristy. Since Bianca had been guilty, at times, of trying to provoke him into an argument, this last impressed her immensely.

It was obvious that Max was not merely the shallow, fortune-seeking rogue she had labeled him, and trying to divine his true intentions was driving her mad.

In an effort to relieve some of the strain, she reconciled with her father. She marched into his office, held up Cathy's letter, and announced, "My sister wishes you to know that she is well, and very happily married to Mr. Mayne." She curtsied to her parent, and almost walked back out the door before he recovered from his astonishment.

"Bianca, wait!" Papa caught her arm. "You have heard from her?"

Her jaw worked. "Surely you already knew?" She meant St. James, who spent a portion of every day in the offices with Papa. He must have told her father that she'd heard from Cathy. Even if he hadn't, there was a very large chance Mary or another servant had told someone at Perusia Hall that a letter had arrived. The housekeeper there, Mrs. Hickson, was mother to her maid Jennie, and there wasn't much news that didn't eventually travel from house to house.

"By my soul, I did not!" Her father couldn't keep the yearning from his voice. "Tell me how she is."

Bianca turned toward him. Papa released her, giving her arm a small pat. He cleared his throat and nodded at the letter in her hand. "She's happy, then?"

Bianca nodded. "Very happy."

Papa's lips pressed together. "I suppose I should be relieved that curate did the proper thing."

"He always meant to," she said in withering tones. "It was obvious to everyone in Marslip that he wanted to marry Cathy."

"And it would have cost him nothing to ask my permission and my blessing," her father fired back. He threw up his hands as she drew an irate breath. "Never mind! 'Tis done, and there's nothing to gain by quarreling over it now."

"No," said Bianca stiffly.

"And you?" he asked cautiously. "Are you . . . happy?"

Bianca drew a controlled breath. "I am content with the choices I made."

He didn't look pleased. "Content."

"Well, what else can you expect me to be?" She raised her brows. "Condemned for helping my sister pursue her true happiness—"

"Condemned!" he growled indignantly.

"—told that my birthright was to be given to a stranger, and then told I could reclaim it only by marrying the stranger." Bianca lifted one shoulder. "I did what I must."

Her father's face worked. She braced herself for a fiery row; this was the first time she'd spoken to him since the disastrous wedding day, and Papa rarely missed a chance to put in his word.

But instead, with almost visible effort, he swallowed whatever it was, and gruffly said, "I hope you warm to the fellow. He's a good man."

The fact that Bianca was coming to agree, however reluctantly, did not make her admit it now. "I have little choice now but to make the best of things," she said. "And I will."

"That's a start," Papa replied, his face brightening. "Your mother and I did the same."

Bianca blinked. "What?" She'd always thought her parents had cared deeply for each other.

But before he could respond, Ned tapped on the door. "Beg pardon, Uncle Tate, but Mr. St. James requests you to join him in the drying room."

"Aye, of course," said Papa. Ned nodded and left. Bianca looked at him inquiringly, but Papa shrugged. "I've no idea what he's about. You're . . . welcome to come along and see."

She gave a stiff nod. It was a truce, and possibly the first time they had reached one without any shouting at all.

And what could Max want? Bianca had slowly got used to seeing him in every corner of the factory. He'd spent time with every single group of workmen, learning something of their trade. Not only was he there every day, in one office or workshop, he'd taken to speaking to all the workers, from the women painting scenes on custom platters to the gilders applying delicate gold leaf to teacup rims to the men hauling up clay from the barges. Not everyone welcomed his attention, but everyone admitted he was polite and displayed deep interest in each and every skill.

She knew he'd helped unload clay and inspect it. He'd even gone to the firing house, the blistering hot warren of rooms where the kilns were, and tried his hand at unloading the kiln.

Bianca knew all this because Amelia's brother worked in the firing house and told her Max had dropped a piece. It was only a fruit bowl, but it shattered, and Max had amazed all the workmen by apologizing. Papa would never have done that.

That was all startling enough. But every day when she came down to dinner, he was waiting, no longer humble and ordinary in wool and linen but the elegant, sophisticated rogue again in velvet and lace, smiling at her with unwavering attention and interest.

He was provoking her curiosity to no end.

With her father at her heels, she went down the stairs and through the factory to the drying room. Here were endless shelves of newly sculpted wares, carefully set apart from each other so the clay could dry throughout. After this some pieces would be fired, then glazed and painted and fired again, while others would be fired and left as biscuit ware. The colored clays made very striking pieces unglazed.

Max stood at the far end of the room, examining a teapot. He looked up as they came in, and set it down. A warm smile crossed his face as his gaze flickered between them. "How good of you to come."

"Well, well, such a mysterious invitation! Who could resist? What are you about, St. James?" Papa folded his arms and waited expectantly.

Max nodded. "As you know, I've applied myself to learning how Perusia operates, from the clay pits to the sales warehouses. A few points of interest have struck me. First, Perusia has conceded that a large percentage of all wares may be broken upon arrival at the warehouses. That is lost income."

"The roads are to blame," said Tate. "Bloody awful."

"Yes," Max replied, "but the canal is not. More wares are going via canal, yet the contract still allows Brimley to declare one fifth breakage. And he does, very nearly."

"What!" Papa looked thunderstruck.

Max put up his hands. "I would like to see it for myself. I intend to pay a call in Mr. Brimley's offices and inspect Perusia crates as they arrive."

Papa frowned. "Brimley's run our warehouse for years."

"I only want to see if it's true that twenty percent of wares arrive damaged. If they do, we must improve our packing, to reduce that much lost dinnerware. Don't you agree?"

Still scowling, Papa nodded once.

"But if they don't . . ." said Bianca, letting her voice trail off.

Her husband didn't smile, but she sensed he was pleased she asked. "Then we should review our contract."

"Brimley wouldn't lie," said Papa, recovering. "By all means inspect the deliveries."

Max bowed in acknowledgement. Bianca turned away to study one of the vases on the shelf beside her, to conceal her astonishment. He'd been serious when he asked about straw and packing and that contract allowance. She'd thought he was trying to annoy her—and because she'd already *been* annoyed, she hadn't paid proper attention to what he actually meant.

"Secondly," Max went on, "I have a proposal." He held out the teapot he'd been studying earlier, and Bianca took it. Now that it was in her hands, she noticed the spout was slightly off-kilter, and there was a nick in the handle. "This is from a young potter who's still learning to attach handles and spouts. Normally it would be cast aside."

"As it should be!" exclaimed Papa. "It's not good enough for Perusia!"

"We can't sell wares of such low quality," added Bianca, horrified that he would suggest such a thing. "Are you mad? Perusia wares are the best, bar none! I wouldn't put our mark on that piece for anything!"

"Of course not," said Max easily. To her further astonishment, he took the teapot from her, raised it up, and hurled it onto the flagstone floor. Both Bianca and her father jumped at the crash.

"It's not good enough to be sold as Perusia ware, but producing it costs Perusia the clay, the potter's work hours, and now we've nothing to show for the expense. In fact, it will even cost us someone's labor to sweep it up and take it out back to the rubbish pile. And tomorrow, that potter will come in and use more clay, and produce another teapot that's still just shy of perfect, because he's barely more than an apprentice, and we'll incur more wasted clay, time, and money."

"Apprentices must learn," objected Bianca. "The only way to learn is to do it. Have you some idea of how to train them without letting them touch clay until they are master artisans?"

He grinned. "Not as of yet. I do have an idea, however, that may reduce the costs of their training."

Bianca glanced at her father, who still wore a scowl. Part of her wanted to remind Papa that she'd warned him Max knew nothing about their business, but—mindful of his valid points about breakage and straw—she asked, "Well, what is it?"

"Instead of putting them to work on Perusia ware, we give them simpler tasks." Max took a plain cylindrical teapot from the shelf. Its spout was straight, not curved, and its handle had no flourish. It was a simple piece, but Bianca knew it would be glazed and painted. The flat surface would better display the landscape scene it was destined to bear.

"A teapot such as this, or even simpler, would be an ideal item for a novice potter."

Papa snorted. "We do that already, St. James! You didn't think we gave them the difficult work straight off?"

"I did not, but I'm thinking of a new level of simplicity. Perusia wares stand out by the beauty of their design and the brilliance of their glazes," Max said, his gaze meeting Bianca's for a heartbeat. "Delicate, exquisite design is the hallmark of Perusia. I want to create a new standard, still quality, but simpler in design, less expensive to produce, and sold for less."

"Cheap goods!" Papa's face grew stormy. "Never, Mr. St. James. You'll not put a Perusia mark on anything less than the finest—"

"A new mark," said Max quickly. "Not Perusia. That must remain the premier standard. But this mark will be one that ordinary attorneys and bank clerks and military officers can afford to buy for their tables."

"You mean to put the less experienced workers onto it," said Bianca slowly. "To train until they are accomplished enough to make Perusia wares properly, but in the meantime producing items we can still sell."

Max turned the full brilliance of his smile on her. "Precisely."

"Ridiculous," declared Papa. "Have you any idea how long it takes to train a good potter?"

"Years," acknowledged Max. "And most of what

they make in the first year is smashed. Imagine if they spent that year instead making simple, ordinary items, turning plain bowls and teapots until they can do it to perfection. Then they will be ready to move on to curving spouts and frilled rims and pressed ware, and eventually to the Perusia workshops."

Papa folded his arms and said nothing. Bianca wet her lips. "It's a good idea." Her father glanced at her in amazement. "Worth trying, at least," she added. "Don't you think, Papa?"

"I won't sell low-quality ware," he repeated. "I won't damage the reputation of Perusia."

"Nothing shall interfere with sales of Perusia ware," Max repeated. "I mean to create an entirely new line of dinnerware." He glanced at Bianca. "And other items for customers of some means, who aspire to some level of taste and style, but cannot afford anything with the Perusia mark."

Papa was still scowling. "We're already short of workers. If I knock men down a rank to make this new dinnerware, they'll all leave for Mannox."

"No one would be knocked down or take a reduction in wages. It would be a proving ground, of sorts, after finishing an apprenticeship. The income from the new line will be a gain, even without considering the losses it will avoid." He paused expectantly. "Will you consider it?"

"Yes," said Bianca before her father could refuse. "Perhaps you could prepare a description of this new line, where you plan to sell it, as well as a list of the workers you would divert. There's no harm at all in looking at that, is there, Papa?"

Papa harrumphed. "I suppose I could read a plan.

Nothing is settled," he warned her, shaking his finger at her.

"Of course not," she retorted. "But only a fool wouldn't consider a potential plan to create a new line with minimal disruption to the factory. You know how long it takes to train men on designs."

Papa grunted. "Only a fool, eh?" He shook his head and turned to go. "Write your plan, St. James," he said over his shoulder. "And give it to Bianca. She'll let me know if she approves." He strode down the row, pausing now and then to scrutinize a piece on the shelves.

That left Bianca alone with her husband.

"Thank you," he said, a smile playing about his mouth.

"For listening to an idea to improve our business? I will always do that," she said pertly. Then, somewhat reluctantly, she added, "It sounds very promising."

She had not expected that from him. He had only been in Marslip a month; how could he think of something she never had? With some chagrin, she told herself *that* was her answer. She had lived here her entire life, steeped in Papa's philosophy and way of doing things. Perusia had prospered under it, so she had never spent much time considering doing something radically different.

But Max had lived elsewhere and seen more of the world than she had; he had told her he wasn't as simple as she thought he was. She supposed it had only been a matter of time before he surprised her like this. It was a just comeuppance, she told herself.

At her compliment, he gave a brief bow. "I am delighted you agree."

"What made you think of it?" she asked.

His gaze dropped to the shards of the teapot he'd smashed. "I despise waste."

"Yes," she agreed, "but some is inevitable—"

"Do you know how many items are unfit for sale as Perusia work?" he interrupted. "It approaches one in ten some months. I commend your father's devotion to quality, but the workshops are producing too much that is inferior."

"So you wish to create an extended apprenticeship."

"Something like it." He was watching her closely. "Did you support the plan just to oppose your father?"

Finally Bianca smiled, a bit ruefully. "Am I that contrary? No, I assure you, I would never support a bad idea. This one may not prove worthwhile, but it has enough to recommend it that I think Papa should consider it." Her smile turned impish. "You must write a persuasive proposal if you want it to go further than this conversation, though."

He grinned. "I mean to, complete with a list of the shops in London that might sell such a line of dinnerware." He paused. "Come with me."

Bianca blinked. "What? To—to London?"

"Yes." He appeared serious, to her amazement.

"But I have work to do here," she protested.

"You've just perfected the scarlet glaze," he pointed out. "The work of months, completed and found true in repeated trials. The glazers have got it down and can reliably reproduce it. Now we must display it to patrons so they can begin yearning for it on their own tables. Come with me to London to show it off."

Bianca bit her lip. What he said was true, and she had been spending less time in her workshop after the long hours tinkering with the red glaze. And she'd never been to London.

But it would mean going with him, her husband, who was still a stranger to her despite the gradual weakening of her antipathy. Here she had Amelia and Papa and Aunt Frances to distract her; here she was at home and he was the outsider, while in London it would be the opposite. He would be back among his elegant, arrogant friends, and she would be the common country wife he'd wed for her money.

"I also hope to view several locations suitable for a Perusia showroom, and would very much like your opinion of the choices," he added as she said nothing. "A setting to display Perusia wares to their very best, and an agent to collect orders. Bring the finest scarlet pieces and we can show them in private previews of our coming work."

"You want my opinion?" She shouldn't let this tempt her, she shouldn't, and yet . . .

"I would hesitate to take any premises without the advice of someone who knew Perusia intimately," he said, a faint smile spreading over his face. "And I would far prefer your company to your father's."

He was a cunning devil. Even so, Bianca couldn't stop the flush of pleasure at his words, that her opinion was equated with that of her father's. And she *would* like to see London. "Very well," she said, smoothing her hands down her apron to ease their sudden dampness. "I'll go."

His face lit up. "Brilliant!" His attention never wavered from her face. "Thank you."

And that *thank you*, more than anything else, made Bianca think she might end up liking her husband after all.

Chapter Fourteen

Max had invited Bianca to accompany him to London on impulse, but the moment he said it, he found himself tensing up in anticipation of her reply.

It shouldn't matter to him if she came with him or stayed in Marslip. He had a long list of things to do in town, after all, plenty to occupy his time. In fact, logically it would be easier if he went alone, and could take plain quarters and be out until all hours without any guilt that he was neglecting her.

And yet, as she looked at him, her clear eyes bright with surprise, he all but held his breath hoping she would say yes.

He hadn't thought he would spend much time with his bride. He hadn't thought he would mind finding other lovers. If he'd married Catherine, he never would have invited her to come to London, where he would almost surely cross paths with a former lover or flirt, and a wife would have been grossly inconvenient. But looking at Bianca, Max couldn't quite recall what he'd found so thrilling about any other woman.

He admired her intelligence; he'd known many intelligent women, though. He marveled at her boldness; he'd met bolder, brasher women, but none quite like her. He knew her resistance to him was a challenge, and he thrived on challenge, but this was the first time he felt the hovering weight of failure. Failing with her wouldn't be something he could walk away from and begin anew elsewhere; she was his wife, 'til death divided them. And he wanted . . .

Oh God how he wanted her. He wanted her to smile at him, laugh with him, curl up under his arm, run her hands through his hair and pull him to her, push him onto his back and straddle him. He wanted her mouth on him, soft and teasing, hungry and rough. He wanted her under him and twined around him and sleeping peacefully at his side, her head on his shoulder.

Max had never expected that from any lover. It shook him how desperately he wanted this unexpected wife of his. Wanting anything that much was only a portent of how badly it would hurt when he didn't get it. If he had any sense at all, he would hold back, never let her see how he felt, wait for her to come to him . . .

Instead he watched every minute flicker of her eyelashes, the slightly deeper breath she took, the way she unclenched her hands and pressed them flat to her skirt. "Very well," she said, her voice a shade throatier than usual, and he couldn't hide his elation.

Because he'd been planning this trip to London for a month, most of the arrangements had been made. Now that he would have his wife with him, though, he sent a flurry of new instructions ahead to his man in town. They needed better accommodations, a hired carriage, and a larger staff, particularly a cook. New possibilities opened before him as well; they might entertain, socialize, attend the theater. He was almost like a boy, eager to show off and please her, Max thought, shaking his head at his own behavior.

The days until they left were filled with packing and planning. "What should I take?" Bianca asked him directly, throwing open the door between their rooms and facing him with her hands on her hips. "What will we do in London?"

Max leaned against a bedpost. "What would you like to do?"

"I've never been," she exclaimed. "I've heard it's beautifully elegant, and disgustingly filthy. You've lived there. What should I prepare for?"

He smiled. "A bit of everything, I suppose."

Her mouth flattened in frustration. "You're not very helpful." She turned back into her room.

"Right. Wait." He crossed the room in three steps, putting his hand on the door before she could close it. "I've been preoccupied. I'm sorry."

"If we're only to view shops and warehouses, I needn't take any but ordinary clothes. But if we mean to go elsewhere, or to entertain, I ought to take some gowns. But which ones?" She frowned at the array of clothing spread out over every surface in the room. Jennie the maid stood sheepishly in the corner next to an empty waiting trunk.

Max glanced at Bianca from the corner of his eye. Her lower lip was between her teeth and there was a thin line between her brows. So accustomed to seeing her bold and confident, he realized with some surprise that she was completely thrown by this.

He drew breath to offer encouragement and platitudes, and then changed his mind. "Those dresses." He pointed. "And these. A good cloak and your favorite bonnets. Sturdy shoes and dancing slippers. We'll buy the rest in town."

Her patent relief dissolved into surprise at the last. "The rest? I have plenty of clothes. Why would we—?"

"As you said, I have experience of London." He winked. "You'll want more."

"I won't need more," she muttered as he went back to his own packing.

Max paused in the doorway and looked back at her. "Let it be my wedding present to you, my dear. You shall choose everything, of course, but I would like to indulge you this once."

And he had the pleasure of seeing her eyes grow wide and her mouth fall open before he bowed and closed the door.

BIANCA RECOVERED FROM the indecision of packing for London. After what Max said, she reasoned, it didn't make much difference what she took, so she told Jennie to pack her usual garments, including her burgundy gown and the gown she'd worn to her wedding. Two gowns ought to be enough, no matter what Max thought.

Matthew was to drive them the five miles into Stoke on Trent, where they would hire a carriage to London. Bianca wondered at this extravagance, but Max said it would be economical, since they were three, with Jennie, and all the baggage. Max had sent his manservant, a fellow named Lawrence, ahead several days ago to await them in town.

Papa came to wish them well. He and Max had been closeted for days, discussing Important Matters, as Bianca referred to them in her mind—much too important to mention in front of her. She and her father had made peace, but they still had not reached the equable give-and-take they had had before . . .

Before Max.

Bianca watched from her window as Max directed Matthew how to tie the trunks onto the cart. Jennie was milling around uselessly, excited beyond measure at getting to see London. Ellen from Perusia Hall had gone into a sulk when she learned Jennie, five years younger than she, would accompany Bianca, even though she had never been Bianca's maid. Ellen had been Cathy's maid, and since Cathy's departure she'd become prickly about her position.

Max said something to Jennie, who nodded and spun around toward the house, almost treading on a passing goose as she did. The goose flew up with a great honking, Jennie cowered and shrieked, and Max laughed.

Bianca leaned nearer her window, staring. It was rare she had the chance of seeing him without him knowing she watched. He was still a puzzle to her, this man who did menial tasks himself but who dressed in satins and lace for dinner. He read contracts and quizzed the workmen, but reminded her that he owned a quarter of the factory.

And he looked at her with such a range of expressions she couldn't begin to sort out what he thought.

As if feeling her scrutiny, his head tilted back

and he looked directly at her window. Could he see her? Bianca tensed, but didn't move.

He swept off his tricorn hat and made an elaborate bow. When he stood upright, he was grinning broadly at her. Awkwardly Bianca raised her hand, finding to her surprise she was smiling in spite of herself.

Blushing, she let the curtain fall and took a large step backward. Good heavens. What had got into her?

Out of breath and flustered, Jennie burst into the room. "Oh, ma'am, are you ready? Mr. St. James says all is prepared and they only wait for you."

"Yes." She busied herself pulling on her gloves and fussing with the cuffs. "Have you taken down everything?"

"Yes, ma'am!" Jennie was almost dancing.

"Then let's go." Bianca closed the window and secured the latch.

She came out into the courtyard, where the wagon was waiting with the baggage. Jennie scrambled up onto the seat beside Matthew, waving at the servants who were not going. Ellen lifted a hand morosely, but Mary swung her arm, and Timmy from the stables waved his hat at her. With a jolt Matthew started the horses, lurching down the rutted lane.

Bianca turned to her husband, brow furrowed. "I thought we were to ride with Matthew as well."

"Did you?" He made a face. "I'd rather not ride a wagon from here to Marslip Green, let alone to Stoke on Trent."

"I'm sure it can't be that bad," she began, but something flickered over his face.

"It's worse," he said in a low voice, then immediately cocked his head and smiled. "No fit way for a lady to travel. I made other arrangements." As he spoke, the stable boy pulled up in the gig.

Bianca drew a tense breath. The gig was what they used for short trips into Marslip, or the slightly larger, somewhat more distant town of Burslem. The seat was well padded but small; she and Cathy fit comfortably, but Max was larger than either of them, and she was wearing her thick wool traveling skirt today. They would be pressed up against each other the entire way to Stoke on Trent.

"The gig's not meant for such a distance," she tried to argue.

"But it will serve." The stable boy jumped down and Max walked over to check the harness.

Bianca chewed the inside of her lip and thought hard. The gig would be more comfortable than the wagon. Even if they'd ridden in the wagon, she and Max would likely have been squashed together amidst the trunks. She was probably being silly, just because she didn't want to touch him.

Touch was the line she had promised herself she would not cross. It was ridiculous to pretend she could survive this marriage without speaking to the man, and once they were speaking, it might as well be cordial. She could admit he was intelligent and could have some good ideas about Perusia. It was even acceptable to find him amusing from time to time.

But his smoldering good looks hadn't diminished, not even when he wore his little wire-rimmed spectacles and let his hair curl around his temples. Bianca was keenly aware that he was the beauty in their marriage. Whenever he smiled at her in that slow, seductive way he had, every time she caught his dark eyes lingering on her, she reminded herself that if she gave way and let him seduce her, he would have won everything: her father's approval, a share of her business, her very person. A chaste, cordial marriage was the best she could hope for, and where she must hold her line.

He turned to her expectantly. The wagon was out of sight down the lane. If she wanted to go to London—and Bianca could admit that the idea had grown on her, quite a bit—she had to ride with him in the gig.

"It's an extravagance," she told him, coming forward. "Now Matthew will have to bring home the gig and the wagon, not to mention the inconvenience Aunt Frances will be put to if she requires a carriage, but since you've already done it, I suppose there's no choice."

"How kind of you to say so," he said with amusement, holding out one hand.

Bianca let him help her up. She fussed with her skirts, discreetly pushing the bulk of the fabric to the side just as her husband settled into the seat beside her.

"Ready to be off?" he asked, holding the restive horse in check with one hand.

Bianca glanced at him, unsettled by how near he was. She could see the faint laugh lines around his eyes, and how smoothly shaven his cheek was. "Yes," she said, curling her hand around the outer corner of the seat. Ready, and fully conscious that she would have to be on guard at all times.

And not just for the ride into Stoke on Trent.

Chapter Fifteen

It was by far the easiest journey Max had ever taken. What a difference money made.

He suspected Bianca thought he'd driven the gig to Stoke on Trent to be alone with her. That had been a happy consequence, he acknowledged, but the truth was he had ridden in too many filthy, jolting wagons to want to do it ever again. Bianca obviously hadn't traveled rough, as he had done most of his life, if she thought it an extravagance to choose a gig. To Max it was deeply significant.

Lawrence, his manservant, had done his job well, and there were comfortable rooms waiting for them at each inn. The first night Max noted Bianca's tight-lipped expression before he made an offhand mention of her room being across the hall from his, and offering his assistance if she required anything. He had the pleasure of seeing her thank him while trying to hide how very relieved she was.

It had been tempting to request only one room. Max wasn't having any better luck fighting his attraction to her than she was having at repressing hers to him. Of course, he wasn't trying to fight his, but he did mean to play a long game, and that meant waiting until she couldn't resist him any longer. He wanted his wife—rather painfully at times—but he also wanted her to come to him, not just amenable, not just willing, but fevered with desire. As he'd said on their wedding day.

Max was accustomed to being denied his desires, but this one was the greatest trial yet.

From Stoke on Trent they traveled in a comfortably sprung chaise. The farther they got from Marslip, the more interested Bianca grew in the passing scenery. She leaned out the window when their chaise had to pull over to allow the mail coach to barrel past, horn blowing. She gasped in awe at the grand house Max pointed out to her on a distant hill. When they crossed a canal, she wanted to stop and see if there were any shipments from Marslip, but Max persuaded her there were not.

"How can you be sure?" she asked, still watching the bargemen as they rolled across the aqueduct.

"I know the route of every shipment from Perusia."

She whipped around, eyes wide. "You do not!"

"Try me," he answered equably. Years spent tuning his mind to count cards and figure odds had left him with a prodigious memory, at least in the short run. He was able to answer every question she asked, until she finally pursed her lips and looked back out the window.

"Is it possible?" he couldn't resist teasing. "Have I possibly learned more about one small aspect of Perusia than a Tate?"

"I'm sure Papa knows all the routes as well," she retorted without looking at him.

Max laughed, allowing her that. It was enough that they both knew he'd proved his point, however minor it might be. "I'm sure he does."

"Did you memorize them just to show me up?"

"Of course not."

She waited, then burst out, "Then why would you? Not the destinations, nor how the wares will be conveyed, but the precise routes? Why would you commit that to memory?"

"When I first approached your father," he said, "he questioned me closely as to my interest in Perusia. I assured him my interest was deep and abiding. I did not lie to him, and learning the shipping routes is simply useful information I was keen to have."

She pursed her lips. "That is a deep interest. What has it gained you?"

I surprised you, he thought. "Nothing but the satisfaction of knowing it," he said lightly. "Who knows when it may come to my aid?"

"You're a strange fellow," she said, turning back to the window—to hide how impressed she was, he thought with amusement.

"My dear," he told her, "that's only the beginning."

If anyone had told Bianca that a long journey, trapped in a chaise with her husband, would be pleasant, she would have called them a bald-faced liar.

And yet, it wasn't dreadful. His good humor never faltered. He never missed a chance to say something mildly flirtatious, but didn't even propose sharing a room at the inn. They talked of business, or London, or the sights they were passing. It was . . . pleasant.

They reached London late in the day. The dusty roads of the turnpike changed to the rattling cobblestones of town, and Bianca pressed her face to the carriage window again, undeniably curious. Her mouth fell open in wonder.

She'd seen engravings of London, with buildings so tall and densely packed the sun didn't reach the pavements, of streets lined with shops and filled with carriages. Nothing compared to being in the midst of it herself. Engravings gave no sense of the bustling activity, even this late in the day. Everywhere she looked there were people: peddlers crying their wares, boys with brooms rushing out to sweep the streets for those on foot, sedan chairs carrying well-dressed people, ladies walking the pavements with small Black servant boys trailing behind, liveried servants rushing on errands, young men throwing dice on a barrel outside a pub. And to the east, above it all, she could see a golden dome that Max said was St. Paul's Cathedral. It was a spectacle she'd never imagined.

The carriage rolled onward before turning into a quieter street. Tall lamps stood in front of every third house, and there were iron railings lining the pavement. They stopped in the middle, before a narrow but gracious house of pale brick. The door was a welcoming blue, just like Poplar House, with a glazed light above.

"This—this is ours?" Bianca looked at him to be sure.

Max nodded as he threw open the carriage door. "For the next month."

She barely felt his hand as he helped her down. Four stories rose above her, a dizzying height to her eyes. Even Perusia Hall, which was grand indeed, had only three floors.

As they reached the step, the door opened. "Welcome to town, sir," said Lawrence, Max's man. Bianca supposed she ought to call him a valet, but Lawrence seemed to do far more than a valet. More than most servants did, to be honest.

As Max spoke to the man, Bianca walked through the hall to look into the front room. It was handsome, though furnished rather sparsely. With Jennie at her heels, she climbed the stairs and found the dining room, with an elegant parlor behind it. Up again she went, finally stepping into a large bedroom, dominated by a massive bed in rich damask hangings. Jennie, her excitement revived after so many days of travel, went to the connecting door and disappeared. Bianca followed and discovered a small closet, furnished with a writing desk and bookshelves, beyond which lay another bedroom, smaller and cozier than the first.

She stared at that bed. Bianca had pictured a few rooms, not an entire house, let alone one so elegantly appointed. She had braced herself to argue against sharing a bedroom, and a bed, and now found that she had perhaps been anticipating Max's attempts to persuade her.

Not that she meant to give in. But somewhere between Stoke on Trent and London, his flirting had grown flattering. She still didn't quite believe he meant every word of it, but like a steady flow of water over stone, his attention and suggestive words were wearing away her resistance.

A footstep behind her made her start. "What do you think?" asked her husband, leaning his shoulder against the doorjamb.

"It's so large," she said.

He smiled. "Comfortable, I say." He came into the room and moved around the bed to peer out the window. "Do you like this room, or would you prefer the other?"

Bianca blinked.

"It's got a view of the garden," he said, still looking out the window, "but the other bed is larger."

Large enough for two people. Bianca flushed from head to toe, and said the first thing that came into her head. "This one will do, thank you."

He glanced at her, as if he knew what she meant, but only nodded. "I'll tell Lawrence to send your trunks."

"How did you find such a place on short notice?" she asked.

"The previous tenant wished to remove from town sooner than his lease required," said Max. "It was quite reasonable."

"How much?" she asked without thinking.

Max raised a brow, and she blushed. "Reasonable," he repeated. "You must trust me in this. Any London rent would sound appallingly high to you, but to one well acquainted with the rents in town, it was economical." He nodded at the windows facing the garden. "I wouldn't bring my wife to a shabby set of rented rooms."

She flushed deeper. Her face would be burned as scarlet as her glaze, after a month in such proximity to him. "I'm sure I didn't ask for such indulgence . . ."

He smiled, that lazy rogue's smile that both put her on guard and made something inside her soften treacherously. "But I wanted to give it, my dear." He turned and walked out of the room, calling for Lawrence.

Simultaneously irked and touched, Bianca pulled loose the ribbons of her hat and handed it to Jennie, who had just come in, out of breath from exploring the rest of the house.

"'Tis beautiful, ain't it, ma'am?" asked the girl rapturously.

"Yes."

"And so near the shops! I confess I do hope you'll be wanting to visit them, as I've longed to see Bond Street all my life." Jennie put away the hat and tugged the drapes fully open. "Look, miss—I mean, madam, such a neat garden!"

Bianca smiled reluctantly at the girl's enthusiasm. Perhaps Jennie had the right of it. "I suppose we shall visit a great many things."

Their London adventure was off to a strangely exciting beginning.

MAX CLOSED BOTH doors between his chamber and Bianca's. "Well done," he told Lawrence. "It cleaned up well."

The valet grinned. "Aye, after four days of frantic scrubbing. Had to pay the charwomen extra. I trust that's acceptable."

Max waved it away. "How is he?"

"In good health."

"So she didn't kill him, then," said Max, and the man raised one finger in salute.

The house was let to Lord Cathcart, who had been, at times, one of Max's best mates. They'd also fallen out and not spoken to each other for months at other times, but this spring, when Max learned of his stroke of immense good fortune, Cathcart had been the first friend he told. The viscount thought it terribly amusing.

The previous resident of the house had been Cathcart's mistress, a plump, doe-eyed creature whose porcelain cheeks and dimpled smile had concealed the heart and soul of a vicious harpy. Max, along with most of Cathcart's other friends, had wagered on how long it would be until Mrs. Robbins fell out with him. It was a habit of theirs, as Cathcart ran through mistresses as though they were coats that must be changed with the season. Max had won the pot, with his wager of seven months and one week coming within days of the final rupture.

And now he'd won even more, by remembering that Cathcart would still have almost two months owing on the lease. His friend had been only too happy to unload the house for a pittance. *Be certain to check the cupboards for any dead animals skewered to the boards*, Cathcart had written in a postscript.

But the house itself was a find, particularly this late in the Season. The fact that it was virtually free made it all the better.

"It still needs a bit of work," Lawrence went on. "I wouldn't advise letting Mrs. St. James take up the carpets."

Max had been to a few parties here. He knew what Lawrence meant. "We're only here a month, perhaps a fortnight longer."

"As you wish, sir." The valet paused. "Shall I send Mrs. St. James's things to the back bedroom?"

Right. Max nodded even as his gaze lingered on

the wide bed. It was big enough for two—or three or four, as Cathcart had once boasted.

Max had never let himself get drawn into that. He too rarely had the funds to support a mistress, and he preferred to keep his lovers to himself, unlike Cathcart, who couldn't resist any woman with large dark eyes and an evil temperament. The more misery she promised to inflict upon him, the more desperate Cathcart was to have her.

It had been easy to mock and tease his friend about that. Cathcart had shrugged it all off with a smirk, saying he had his cravings and they had theirs. Max had always told him he was as deranged as the she-demons he took to bed.

Bianca was nothing like those women. But Max was realizing that Cathcart had been right about one thing: every man had his own tastes. And his were running very strongly in favor of confident, intelligent women who took no nonsense from anyone and spoke their own minds. Women who had a purpose beyond acquiring as many new gowns and jewels as their protector would buy. Women who took a practical, clear-eyed approach to the world at large. Women who didn't seem to realize how unconsciously seductive they could be just by blushing.

It was only a bed; Lawrence had replaced all the linens and mattresses, on his orders. But Max eyed that large, elegant bed and silently promised himself that he would woo and win his wife here, in London, before he went mad from wanting her.

Chapter Sixteen

Life in London moved at a faster pace than in Marslip.

As Jennie had hoped, they went shopping—more shopping than Bianca had patience for. The house was rather simply furnished, but they were only going to be in it for a few weeks. She had brought enough clothing for that time. There was no need to buy much of anything.

But Max insisted. He took her to a dressmaker, and told the woman they wanted three gowns for evening, several day dresses, and all the hats, gloves, and undergarments necessary. Bianca protested until the dressmaker held up the first gown against her, a glowing ivory robe à l'anglaise embroidered with gold thread and seed pearls.

"It suits you very well, madam," said the dressmaker.

"I— It's lovely," she managed to say. It was beyond lovely, and unlike anything she had ever owned before.

Eyes gleaming, the dressmaker swept it away and motioned for the assistant to bring the next gown. This one was gleaming steel blue, with gold spangles for trim and wide flounces of lace at the sleeves and neckline.

"Yes," said Max behind her, and Bianca jumped.

"What are you doing in here?" She grabbed at the dress, holding it in front of her.

"The color suits you, my dear," he said, before obediently strolling away.

"It does," said the dressmaker warmly, as the assistant helped Bianca into the dress, tugging the tight-fitting sleeves up her arms and pinning it in place. "With a petticoat to match it will be superb."

"Well," said Bianca, flustered. "I suppose . . ."

"Monsieur insisted," replied the woman pertly. "Marie will fit it and you shall have it tomorrow." She tripped out of the room, calling for another assistant.

Even though those beautiful dresses were more tempting and alluring than she wanted to admit, the best part of the visit to London was the search for a Perusia showroom. Max, it turned out, had grander ideas than Bianca.

She pictured a cozy shop lined with rows of shelves displaying their gleaming teapots and tureens, larger than what one found in Marslip but similarly quaint. Max took her to a yawning emporium and walked about, sketching with his hands the displays they could create.

"Displays?" Bianca envisioned her neat shelves of fruit bowls. "What do you mean, displays? We'll set out the wares for people to examine, of course . . ."

He shook his head, catching her arm and leading her to the tall windows that overlooked the street. "Imagine a breakfast table here, set for a family.

The egg cups glowing in the light, the chocolate pot at hand—full of chocolate, to perfume the air—a bowl of fresh fruit tempting customers to sit down and enjoy the meal." He pulled her to the windows on the other side of the door. "And over here a dining table, with the most elegant wares Perusia can offer, fully arranged. Anyone can stack plates on a shelf. I want to show people how stunning their tables will look with a complete service."

She looked around. A space such as this would command a high rent. "It's very ambitious. If we were to start with a smaller shop—"

He slashed one hand impatiently. "Smaller shop, smaller orders. I know society. How do things become the fashion? One person demonstrates how smart it looks, whether it be jeweled buttons or a high-sprung carriage or the angle of a hat, and society follows in a rush. We will be creative—innovative—and people will flock to see the styles we set."

Bianca looked at him doubtfully. "It's an expensive chance to take."

"All chance has a cost," he said. "I never take one I don't expect to pay off handsomely."

For no good reason, she thought of their marriage, and how he had looked her up and down in the sacristy before saying, "Very well." Agreeing to change brides virtually at the altar was certainly a chance . . .

But that was different. She gave her head a tiny shake. He meant business, in pounds and shillings—and if it applied to their marriage at all, it was only because wedding her brought him the same income and share in Perusia that wedding Cathy would have.

"Organizing the shop that way will require far more work," she said, returning to the important point. "We'll have to hire a shop assistant simply to maintain the displays. And how many do you plan to have? This space is enormous."

"Not so. We'll wall it off here, and display the larger pieces on the wall." He paced it off as he spoke. "Behind will be a storeroom and offices, where orders can be stored. If we deliver the pieces here, they can be checked and repackaged, delivered in velvet-lined boxes and unveiled like the works of art they are."

"Velvet boxes!" She threw up her hands. "The expense—!"

"The expense will be worth it," he cut in. "Why does a jeweler display his wares on a cloth of black silk? It sets off the diamonds to their best advantage and suggests they are worth being stored in luxury. The same for our wares. They are priceless, they are valuable, they are a statement of wealth and dignity, they are worth a large sum because the owner's children and grandchildren will savor and marvel at them."

"It would be much better if the children and grandchildren decided to buy their own new dishes," she retorted.

"When they do, they'll remember how finely crafted Perusia wares are," he countered.

She exhaled loudly. "This is not how these things are done," she said, trying to stay calm and reasonable. "Papa has a man in London who takes orders and sees they are delivered. There's no need to take this enormous space—"

"Not so enormous," he murmured.

"—and spend madly on displays with real pots of chocolate and velvet boxes," she went on, raising her voice over his. "If this doesn't work, we'll be out a great deal of money!"

"Your father agrees with me."

"Well, Papa's been spectacularly wrong before!" she blazed back.

For a moment his face went utterly still and blank. Too late she realized what he must have been thinking, about his marriage proposal and Papa's gift of Perusia shares.

And in that moment Bianca felt a prickle of horror. She hadn't meant that, even though a few weeks ago she bloody well would have. Awkwardly she cleared her throat. "Papa is drawn to grand ideas," she tried to explain. "The bigger and more dazzling, the better. He would be inclined to approve anything that suggested advancement, even if it were based on nothing . . ."

Oh heaven help her, she was making it worse.

"I am not persuaded," she blurted out in helpless frustration. "I think it's too great a risk."

Her husband had been watching her, arms folded, expression increasingly stony. At this, though, his mouth eased. He crossed the room, his steps loud and deliberate in the empty shop. He stopped right in front of her, which did nothing for Bianca's inner turmoil.

"Will you give me a chance?" he asked softly. Lazily he reached out and straightened the brooch holding her fichu in place. The brooch was pinned right over the valley between her breasts. "To persuade you that it might actually be a brilliant idea?"

She couldn't stop thinking that this conversation

was more about their marriage than the showroom. Had he been trying to persuade her for all these weeks? At the time she'd thought he was trying to provoke her by being so calm, or to enrage her by being so solicitous. But perhaps . . .

"Allow me three months," he said, his voice growing softer and more seductive. The brooch slipped free of her dress; he'd undone the catch. "Three months to show you how beautiful it can be . . ." His fingers smoothed the fine lawn of her fichu, stroking it into place. "How elegant. How it will make people yearn for what they see here."

His dark eyes never wavered from hers. Bianca felt hooked, pinned in place by that gaze. A tremor went through her as he slid one fingertip inside the front of her bodice and secured the brooch back in place.

"Will you?" he whispered. "Will you allow me to try? If you are still . . . unsatisfied, I will heed your every suggestion."

He didn't mean the showroom, and Bianca wasn't thinking about it, either. Her skin felt alive where he had touched her, ever so briefly, and her nipples had grown taut inside her bodice. She couldn't stop thinking about his hands on her, and what he might do. *Pleasures that most women only dream of,* echoed his potent promise in her memory. What did that mean? What did other women dream of? It was bad enough contemplating doing the things her own imagination conjured up.

With her body in active revolt against her sense and logic, Bianca grasped for any escape. She tore her gaze from his, staring at the much safer folds of his neckcloth. "Perhaps." The word came out husky and tentative. She cleared her throat. "I suppose a quarter is a fair trial. For the showroom. If you can secure a reasonable rent."

Slowly he smiled. "Thank you, my dear. I promise to make the most of it." He took her hand, so lightly she barely felt his fingertips, and raised it to his lips.

She did feel that. His breath was warm on her skin, and even though his mouth only brushed her knuckles, it reverberated through her like a blow.

She made the mistake of glancing up at him again. His eyes smoldered and a little curl of hair had fallen free at his temple. He was magnificent, and overwhelming, and utterly focused on her.

This time there was no question: he meant her. He meant to persuade *her* that he could show her unparalleled pleasures.

And she feared he just might succeed.

IT TOOK FOUR days for her to understand exactly why Max had wanted her to buy so many new gowns. A number of crates arrived at the house as she was writing a letter to her father on their search for a showroom.

The letter was taking longer than usual because she wanted to be diplomatic. She had agreed to let Max go forward with his grand ideas, but she still feared it was *too* grand, and she didn't want to give her father an overly rosy view of it.

The delivery, though, caused a commotion, and she abandoned her letter to go see.

"What is this?" Men were carrying in crates, some so large they barely fit through the door.

"Mr. St. James directed us to bring them, ma'am," said one fellow, swiping off his cap and bowing.

Max appeared as the men were trooping out the door, and Bianca turned on him. "What did you buy?"

For answer he pried off the lid of the top crate and lifted out a plate. It was familiar to her, as it was some of Papa's best creamware, the rim royal blue with a gilded edge and a bucolic scene etched in the center. It was a custom order that had been delayed due to troubles with the gilding, and sent to London only days before they left.

"That's Sir Bartholomew Markham's order—"

"Markham has not paid for it. We're having guests for dinner tomorrow night."

She gasped. "What? Why?"

He replaced the plate, his gaze on her. "To make London swoon over Perusia's finest work. To hint there is even finer work coming soon." Finally a smile curved his mouth. "And for entertainment. I cannot ask my wife to sit idly at home every night."

"Whom have you invited?" Real alarm clutched at Bianca's heart. She had no talent for entertaining. That was Cathy's province.

"Friends. Acquaintances. People who can afford Perusia on their dining table."

"No . . . Wait, I—" She stormed after him as he started up the stairs. "You ought to give me more warning!"

He paused, looking down at her with his brows raised. "I beg your pardon for that, but we're only here a month. I arranged it a fortnight ago."

"Oh." As much as she worried about arranging such a dinner, it was a bit disconcerting that he'd already done it. Still, Bianca rallied, following him to the top of the stairs. He wanted a dinner party, and so he had arranged one. "You ought to have told me sooner."

"Ah." He smiled ruefully. "I should have. I apologize, my dear."

"We can't use Sir Bartholomew's service," she went on forcefully.

Max shrugged. "Until he pays the bill, it's ours."

Bianca bit her lip. Sometimes customers never paid and Papa would despair over the bill and the wasted work. "Has he been asked?"

"Twice," said Max. "Both times he urged that we deliver it and said he would send payment by the start of next quarter."

"How much is the bill?"

"Nine hundred pounds," he replied, "and if a fellow needs to wait for his quarterly income to pay it, chances are he'll ask for more time after that, and never pay in full. I'll grant him the time, but until then, he shall not have the dinnerware."

"All right," said Bianca after a moment. She had a passing familiarity with the accounts, but her cousin Ned handled most of it, under Papa's direction. She knew about unpaid bills primarily when Papa went into a rage over a particularly galling one. "That is sensible."

"I told you I could be," he replied, smiling. "As to the dinner party, trust me. I've chosen the guests carefully, for greatest impact and ability to spread the word."

Slowly she nodded. This was his world, after all, and the reason Papa had wanted him in the business at all. Papa had traded his daughter's hand in marriage for the man's connections to elegant society. She ought to be pleased that he was earning his keep.

"Thank you, my dear." He gave her another gleaming look as he bowed. "I hope to lay all your doubts and fears to rest, and assure you of my complete devotion."

And as he continued up the stairs, his heels ringing on the treads, Bianca thought to herself, *That's what I'm afraid of.*

Chapter Seventeen

Everything hung upon this dinner party, and Max wasn't leaving a single thing to chance.

The guest list had been chosen with great deliberation. He had put Lawrence to the task of sniffing out the latest rumors and whispers, and had carefully molded his ideal party. No one in dun territory; no one in the midst of scandal. No one who had fallen from favor in society, or retired from it.

Fortunately for Max, he knew someone who fit each and every criterion. He also knew a great many more who violated some—or all—of them as well, but those people he shut out of his mind. He had won Samuel Tate over with the promise of his connections. No matter what he had learned, no matter how many contractual improvements he suggested, no matter how splendidly the showroom might work out, Max knew that *this* was his opportunity to win his father-in-law's esteem.

His wife's, he was not as sure of. She didn't argue about the party, and in fact made several suggestions about the menu, to best display the greatest range of Sir Bartholomew's dinner service. She raised her brows when the crates of crystal and silver were delivered, but Max assured her they were borrowed only, and she made no protest.

It gave him some private bemusement, that the daughter of a man as rich as Tate cared about whether they bought silver or not. They could have purchased a complete set of each to take back to Marslip and not dented the family coffers.

He dressed with care that evening, knowing it would send the first and most vital message to his guests about his change of fortune. A dark blue coat of velvet, lined with ivory silk and glittering with golden buttons. Dark charcoal breeches, cut close. A waistcoat of pale blue stripes, embroidered with black thread. Elegant, the pinnacle of fashion, unquestionable quality. He smoothed his hands down his chest, scrutinizing his reflection.

How different from a few months ago, when last he'd dined with Dalway and Carswell. When his linen had been worn to threads and his waistcoat had been a castoff. When he'd had but one pair of shoes, and those scuffed and splitting. He'd won three hundred pounds off Carswell that night, and Harry had loudly proclaimed that he'd lost on purpose, to help Max avoid the Fleet.

He didn't want anyone's pity tonight.

Lawrence dressed his hair, but Max refused to powder it. It was still fashionable for court, but not as much elsewhere; he'd never been able to afford a wig and now preferred his own hair. Likewise he waved off the valet's offer of cosmetics. The last thing he wanted to look like was a macaroni, with rouged cheeks and painted mouth.

He went down to await the guests and survey the

dining room. Everything was in order. The plate sparkled and shone. He had arranged for several pieces in the new scarlet glaze to be sent to London, and they glowed as if they were made of rubies in the candlelight.

"Oh my," said a voice behind him.

Max turned. Bianca stood in the doorway, one hand on her bosom, her lips parted in amazement. She wore the gown of cream silk, with a deep peach petticoat beneath it. Her hair was swept up into a pile of curls, not frizzled in the most modern way, but with a very attractive spill of one long lock over her shoulder, and powdered to a pale pink tinge.

The floor seemed to heave beneath him. "By the heavens," he managed to say, "you are a vision, Mrs. St. James."

She flushed. "Jennie was so eager to do it." She plucked at the curl lying across her shoulder. "It feels so odd. Not at all like Marslip."

"No," he said, mesmerized by her. "We are not in Marslip."

And he'd never been gladder of it.

BIANCA WAS MORE than a trifle curious to meet their guests.

Whom had Max invited? She had put him down as a rake, a rogue, a scoundrel who probably associated with other rakes, rogues, and scoundrels. She had never expected to meet any of them, of course, let alone as part of a plot to spread Perusia's reputation.

But the people who arrived did not strike her as dissolute or depraved. They bowed over her hand, congratulated both her and Max on their marriage, and struck up conversation on a wide variety of topics. Bianca had expected gossip about the king's health or the recently published memoirs of Mrs. Baddeley, the notorious courtesan. She was mildly surprised to hear instead about the excursion to Australia, the new abolition society begun by Mr. Clarkson and Mr. Sharp, and the struggles of the Americans in the wake of the war.

"Taxes," drawled one man, Lord Dalway, in delight. "They're squabbling with each other about taxes!"

"Again?" asked Mr. Farquhar.

"Forever," rejoined Dalway.

"I find it much more amusing now," put in Lady Dalway.

"I only wonder how long until they select a king," said Sir Henry Carswell. "Or better yet, ask for *our* king back, and admit they were wrong on every score!"

Everyone laughed. "I doubt very much they will," said Bianca. The guests turned her way.

"What do you mean, ma'am?" asked Farquhar politely.

"They will never retreat now," she said. "After reaching such a momentous decision, and committing themselves to it in blood, they'll never come back. Indeed not. They may make a mull of it, but it is their chosen course, and they will stay to it and thrash their way through as best they can." As she finished, she caught Max's gaze from the far end of the table, thoughtful and attentive. Bianca flushed but gazed boldly back. *Yes*, she silently told him. *I am that way, too.*

Dalway's brows went up. "I do believe you're right,

Mrs. St. James. They certainly are a stubborn lot!"
He raised his glass to her.

Everyone else joined in, but Bianca still caught
Lady Dalway's murmur to Max: "Oh Maxim, I do
like her!"

When dinner ended, Bianca led Lady Dalway,
Mrs. Farquhar, and Lady Carswell to the drawing
room. The rumble of the gentlemen's voices quieted as the door closed, and Bianca rang for Martha, the maid.

"Well!" Lady Dalway threw herself on the sofa,
managing to end up draped elegantly across the
cushions. "What a treasure you are, Mrs. St. James!"

Bianca smiled politely. "I'm sure I don't know
what you mean."

"You do," said Mrs. Farquhar with a knowing
smile. "I've never seen Maxim so content!"

"Or so civilized," added Lady Carswell—archly,
to Bianca's ears.

Lady Dalway let out a peal of laughter. Like
everything else about her, her laugh was light and
beautiful. She sat up and put out one hand. "Oh
heavens, I must thank you for that! Such a rogue
he always was, but now he's been polished and
brushed to a shine! I've never seen him look better."

"Never?" Mrs. Farquhar murmured, but Lady
Dalway ignored her.

"And so focused! I vow, I didn't think he meant
it when he wrote about the dinnerware but I must
confess I was very struck by it. Weren't you, Louisa?"

"I was," agreed Lady Carswell.

"Thank you," said Bianca. "I'm delighted you admire it."

"Oh yes, indeed. Do you know," said Lady Dalway

dreamily, staring off above Mrs. Farquhar's head, "I always thought Maxim would do well to marry."

Bianca blinked. "Why?"

"Serafina is a romantic," said Mrs. Farquhar with a laugh.

Lady Dalway made a face at her. "Nothing of the sort, Clara! Some men do better to marry and some do much worse—and one does sympathize with *their* brides—but Maxim is entirely the former." She turned a melting, artless smile on Bianca. "I do so applaud you, my dear, for bringing him to the altar. He's quite settled, I can see."

Bianca smiled stiffly and murmured something polite. She suspected she knew what Lady Dalway was saying. "I must ask," she said, before she could stop herself, "why you call him Maxim."

Lady Dalway blinked her large blue eyes. Mrs. Farquhar clucked her tongue. "You don't know?"

Bianca shook her head. "He's not told me much about his life in London."

Nor had she asked.

"Well," began Mrs. Farquhar, but Lady Dalway cleared her throat. With a quirk of her lips, Mrs. Farquhar fell silent.

"His grandfather was called Maxim," said Lady Dalway. "I understand he and Max"—Bianca noted the change—"were quite close."

"Oh." A flash of memory, what he'd told her on their wedding day. "His mother's father."

"The very one," said Mrs. Farquhar. "When his mother—"

Again Lady Dalway made a small sound, and again Mrs. Farquhar went quiet.

"If I had been burdened with his Christian names,

I would much prefer Maxim myself," put in Lady Carswell, causing an outpouring of agreement from the other ladies.

It was very strange, Bianca thought as they chatted of more idle topics, to feel a stranger in her own supposed home. She had been here long enough that this house was starting to feel familiar, and she supposed the same was true of Max. Her husband. He was starting to feel like *hers*, and the fact that these other women knew him better than she did, knew things about him that she did not, was strangely distressing.

It was a relief when the gentlemen came in and the card tables were set up. Lady Carswell asked to partner her, and Bianca agreed before noticing her husband heading her way. He had been in deep conversation with Lord Dalway, and now joined her.

"Have you had a pleasant evening, my dear?"

Bianca realized it was relief flowing through her. She was glad he was beside her, conferring with her. He was still hers.

She shook off that thought. "Yes. Lady Dalway admired the dishes greatly, as did Lady Carswell."

"I knew they would. Dalway plans to put in a large order on the morrow. Carswell may do the same." Max gave her a conspiratorial glance, his dark eyes dancing. "Carswell follows Dalway's lead, although at enough of a distance that he can protest he was *not* following at all, but simply reached the same destination of his own choosing."

Bianca smiled. "Would that they all follow Lord Dalway's lead and order complete services."

He winked at her. "There's still time. Will you partner me at the tables?"

"Oh—that is—" She tried not to gnash her teeth. "Lady Carswell has already asked me."

"Quite right," he said easily, after only the briefest pause. "A husband and wife should never partner at whist in company. Good luck." He took a step away, then paused. "Lady Carswell can never remember the trump. Do your best to remind her if you want to win."

She could only watch in chagrin as he strolled away, speaking to the guests with ease. She felt inexplicably annoyed at Lady Carswell for asking her before Max could. It was irrational, and left her feeling out of sorts, even though she enjoyed cards and always liked to win. Instead she had to watch Lady Dalway link her arm in Max's, and trade cards with him, and clap her hands in glee as the pair of them won hand after hand. Even the pleasure of hearing the exclamations of delight over the coffee service, done in her new scarlet glaze and brought out as the candles grew short, was small consolation.

When the door finally closed behind the guests, she returned restlessly to the drawing room, pinching out the candles. The evening had been a success, and yet she felt out of sorts.

She did not want to admit the reason: jealousy. Not so much that Max was clearly at ease among these elegant people, these women adorned in diamonds and lace, these titled gentlemen of wealth and power. She had expected that.

No, it was something worse. It was that those people—those women—knew him. Her husband was a stranger to her, but not to them. And even if she tried to persuade herself that she didn't want to know all his debauched secrets, she did not want to feel like an outsider in her own marriage.

"I would call that a rousing success," said her husband behind her.

Bianca bit down on her lower lip and nodded. It was. She knew it. But she couldn't stop thinking of those sparkling little glances between the ladies, about him, and the way she'd felt at seeing Lady Dalway take his arm.

"What is wrong?" he asked.

She turned to face him. He stood in the doorway, arms folded and one shoulder against the jamb. He was almost unbearably attractive, broad-shouldered—unlike the whippet-thin Lord Dalway—and lean-hipped—unlike the portly Nigel Farquhar. His unpowdered hair gave him the look of a panther, sleek and wild. And his dark eyes were fixed on her.

Bianca fiddled with a porcelain figurine—average craftsmanship, poorly painted, but still a charming depiction of a girl drawing a bucket up from a well—and set it down. She faced her husband, put up her chin, and said, "They all know you."

"Yes."

"Even the women," she went on. "Rather well." She paused. "Much better than I know you."

He drew a deep breath, then pushed away from the door and started toward her. "I've been friends with Carswell since we were lads. Dalway, since university. Farquhar, nigh on six years."

"They call you Maxim," she retorted. "Lady Dalway and Lady Carswell."

His mouth quirked. "They're teasing when they do."

"They know you well enough to tease." She lifted one shoulder, angry at herself for being upset about this. "I felt ignorant."

He stopped in front of her, hands behind him. Bianca closed her eyes and turned her head away, struggling for poise. "What do you want to know?" he murmured.

She looked at him. His entire attention was fixed on her; his eyes seemed to be peering into her soul. What did she want to know?

I want to know who you really are, she answered in her mind. *And why I can't get you out of my mind.* He was a puzzle to her, and no matter how resolutely she told herself that she didn't care to solve him, the mystery kept pricking at her brain.

Bianca thought of herself as practical and intrepid. In her workshop she never considered stopping until she had solved the problem at hand. Now she wished she could stop thinking of her husband as a riddle even more vexing than that scarlet glaze had been. It was all but guaranteed that there was no simple answer, no precise adjustment of ingredients that would unlock him and lay him bare for her to read.

And she was definitely *not* trying to lay him bare in any other way.

But she was human enough, and woman enough, to bristle at the thought of other women knowing her husband better than she did. There was nothing she could do about his past, of course, but it was awkward and embarrassing to think of these elegant ladies watching her and whispering how gauche and naive she was, and what must Max have been thinking to marry her?

"What is the amusing story behind your name?" she asked instead.

"Crispin was my grandfather, and Augustus his father," he answered readily. "Maximilian—Maxim—was my mother's father."

She had to wet her lips to go on. "Why do you go by Max?"

His mouth curved. "Did you not hear the other options? I liked that grandfather better than the others." He paused, then added, almost reluctantly, "I never met the others, though. I understand they were proper tartars, and there was little to be gained by knowing them."

"Were you close to Grandfather Maxim?"

"As close as anyone could be, I suppose. He was a gruff old man."

Bianca nodded. "What happened to your mother?"

He was silent for so long she thought he wouldn't say. "She died when I was young. My aunt took me in, and sometimes I stayed with my grandfather."

She knew he'd not been wealthy, despite his connections to the Duke of Carlyle. It was the darkest charge she had laid against him when he proposed to marry Cathy, that he was a penniless rogue after her fortune. "Are they in London?"

"No. My grandfather died years ago. What did Lady Dalway say that unsettled you?"

"She— Nothing," protested Bianca. "It was clear she knew you very well—they all did—and I felt a fool, not knowing anything about you!"

"Go on," he said. "Ask it." She looked at him warily. "Ask the question that's been festering in your breast all evening."

She took a deep breath. Might as well do it and be done with it. "Is Lady Dalway your lover?"

"No," he said. "Nor was she ever. Neither were Lady Carswell or Mrs. Farquhar," he added as Bianca slowly exhaled. "Never any wife of a friend."

"But you've *had* lovers," she charged.

"I did," he agreed after a slight hesitation. "Before I decided to marry."

It felt like she could breathe again. Bianca tried to hide it. "That doesn't surprise me," she said, striving for brisk practicality. "Marslip is so small, any indiscretion would be obvious—"

"Because now I want you, and no one else," he said in a low, rough voice.

And like that her thread of composure snapped. She didn't understand it, and she didn't like it, but she was horribly attracted to this man. It was too much to expect of anyone, rejecting him when he declared that he wanted her, and wanted her more than any of the elegant, beautiful society women who had just sat in their drawing room. "Blast it," she said under her breath before stepping forward and pulling his face down to hers.

He let her do it, bending to her will without resistance. But his mouth was not passive. He kissed her softly, almost tenderly. She had envisioned something far more debauched and indecent, but this . . . this was mesmerizingly lovely. She felt worshipped. Treasured.

His hands came to cup her face, so lightly she barely realized it. "Bianca," he breathed, his lips brushing hers.

"What?" she whispered, just as his mouth claimed

hers again. This time he tasted her, his tongue sliding into her mouth. Bianca moaned, her grip on him slackening. Deliberate, unhurried, flavored of brandy and coffee, he kissed her. His thumbs traced whorls on her jaw, his fingertips subtly tilting her head to the best vantage for his ravishment.

Because it was. He kissed her deeply, one hand cupping her head now. Bianca thought she was falling, but it was him, bearing her backward. When she hit the wall, she instinctively arched her back, and his arm was there, drawing her tightly against him.

And instead of feeling restricted, the pressure of his body on hers only sent her pulse spiraling faster. She went up on her toes, kissing him back, shivering as her tongue slid roughly over his.

When he whispered her name again, Bianca's sense flickered back to life. What was she doing? His hands were in her hair. Her hands were behind his neck, pulling him closer. His mouth was on her throat, her skin was glowing like live coals, and her blood was racing. Her good sense was nowhere in evidence.

She twisted loose, and he made no effort to restrain her. "Oh," she said stupidly, putting one hand to her mouth. Her lips were soft and tender, and the touch of her own fingers sent an echoing shock of sensation through her.

Max said nothing. He didn't have to. Hunger streamed off him, evident in every taut line of his body, the rapid rise and fall of his chest, the color in his face. Bianca sensed that at one word, even just a nod, from her, he would carry her off to his large, inviting bed and show her all those pleasures he'd teased her about on their wedding day.

The room seemed to spin and wobble. She wanted to know what those pleasures were—desperately. Her body was throbbing in anticipation. Her thoughts raced in dizzying circles, wondering what he would do and how pleasurable it could be and why was she this indecisive when she had promised herself she wouldn't let him seduce her because she *didn't* want to go to bed with him and yet she couldn't stop thinking about his hands on her, his mouth on hers, how good he tasted, how heart-stoppingly gorgeous he was when he looked at her that way—

"Good night," she said thinly, because it was all she could manage to get out, and then she turned and hurried up the stairs, her heart hammering so hard she was sure she would never make it to the safety of her room.

Chapter Eighteen

London had never been so good to Max.

Dalway ordered a complete service the very next day and admitted he'd been wrong to call Max an idiot for pursuing the Perusia connection. "I thought you were mad," he told Max, "but I see now you spotted a diamond in the rough."

"Not rough at all," replied Max easily. "Obscured."

Dalway laughed. "Is that what you call her?"

"What I call my wife is not for your ears," returned Max with a look. "Will you have a coffee service as well?"

"Aye, aye, in that bloodred glaze. Never seen anything like it! Serafina begged for it all the way home." He eyed Max. "She's pleased for you."

Max inclined his head as he made a note of the order. "I'm delighted to have her blessing."

Dalway snorted. "She wants to befriend your wife! Better watch yourself, she's eager to tell all your secrets . . ."

"She doesn't know anything I wouldn't tell Mrs. St. James myself."

"Wouldn't." Dalway caught his mistake. "Ought to hurry home and tell her yourself, if you don't

want Serafina and Louisa Carswell whispering it into her ears."

Max kept his smile, not betraying the curses streaming through his mind. Between the two of them, those ladies could tell Bianca just enough to make him look like a monster. He didn't think they would do so maliciously—no, even worse, they would do it while thinking they were helping him. Bianca, though, was too intelligent by half to miss anything. "I will. And inform Lady Dalway, with all civility, that I can conduct my own amours, without any help from her."

Dalway snickered. He'd always loved a bit of scandal and intrigue, and had since they were young bucks at Oxford, evading the proctors sent to roust them from the local taverns. Max had only been at university for a year, but Dalway had been infamous even before he got there. "I'll tell her. Don't expect a great lot of good from it, though. You know how she is when she gets something in her mind." He shook his head. "Better you the target of her interest than I."

"One hopes the new dinner service will distract her from your many failings," replied Max.

"For a fortnight at least." Dalway grinned. "If you can divert her for a month, I'll pay double."

"On your own, mate," retorted Max, making Dalway laugh again and flash him a rude gesture.

But after the earl had left, Max let out his breath and pressed his hands to his temples. Serafina Dalway, with her outsized and misplaced sisterly concern, would be the death of him. But she, at least, would listen to reason, if he begged. He was not so sure of Louisa Carswell, to say nothing of Clara Farquhar. Gossip was like air to those two, and even if they promised not to say anything, he didn't trust either to remember it in the throes of sharing some delicious on-dit.

Gingerly he considered what Dalway had urged: telling Bianca himself.

It was the safest choice, in the long run. Unfortunately it was the short term Max was thinking of now, with the taste of her mouth still fresh in his mind. And *she* had kissed *him*. Not only was she coming to look at him with new respect regarding his plans for Perusia, she was beginning to look at him with desire as well. He didn't want to do anything to disturb the very pleasing direction things were going with his wife.

Besides, he reasoned to himself, they would only be in London another fortnight. Back in Marslip, there would be nothing to worry about. He would have plenty of time to tell her everything, at his own leisure, once he'd won her over in other ways.

No, if he told her now it would only spoil things. He wanted more of a hold on her heart and mind before he risked both.

BIANCA WAS SURPRISED—PLEASANTLY—THAT coming to London had been far more productive than she had expected.

After Max was proven right about Lord Dalway ordering a service, Sir Henry Carswell did place an order as well. At that news, Bianca had to admit that Max knew far more than she about Londoners. When a request for a viewing arrived from the Countess of Dowling, and an order from Viscount

Harley, she even congratulated him one morning at breakfast.

He took it graciously, raising his coffee cup in salute. "I knew it was only a matter of making the right impression, and your scarlet glaze did that."

"No," she replied. "The scarlet glaze alone would have done nothing. You knew how best to display it and tempt people like Lady Dalway."

He laughed. "And Lady Dalway is likely to spread the word better than we ever could."

They were cordial now. That was reasonable, she told herself. There had been no mention of the kiss, let alone any suggestion of more. In fact, she told herself this might be the happy balance she had wished for. They were both dedicated to advancing the interests of Perusia. It would please her father—whose twice-weekly letters asked repeatedly how she was getting on with her husband in London—and perhaps it was better to kiss him and be done with it. The only way to rid oneself of an itch sometimes was to scratch it.

It didn't matter that she'd felt that kiss on her mouth the rest of the night, nor that she'd lain awake for a long time, wondering what had possessed her and if he thought it meant he'd won. If there had been the slightest trace of triumph in his attitude the next morning, she vowed, she would tell him it had been a dreadful mistake on her part, never to be repeated . . .

But he hadn't. He had greeted her the next morning in the same way he had always done. Not so much as a lingering glance betrayed any smugness. And somehow Bianca never got around to saying it was a mistake, or that she wished it had never happened, or that it must never happen again.

Even though it never *would* happen again, obviously.

He pushed back his chair. "Shall you come with me today? I intend to view another shop."

"Oh?" She gulped too large a sip of chocolate at his voice and winced as it burned her throat. She'd got distracted watching him talk, thinking about how she was never going to kiss his mouth again, and she'd not been attending to what he said. "Er—where?"

"Cheapside," he said. "'Tis for the proposal your father agreed to read."

Ah. About the new line of dinnerware. One of them had been able to keep their mind on business. Flustered, she also rose. "Of course."

"Are you warming to the idea?" he asked, his eyes dancing and a smile lurking about his mouth. There was a drop of coffee on his lower lip, and Bianca couldn't tear her eyes from it.

"I— Well— Perhaps—" Compulsively she reached out and smoothed away the coffee with her thumb.

Max went still. Bianca flushed. "There was some coffee," she muttered, waving one hand toward his face.

"Thank you," he murmured. And to her shock he took her hand. Her clenched fingers unfolded in his, and then he put her thumb to his lips, sucking lightly. She felt the touch of his tongue and her knees almost gave way. His eyes flashed and he released her. "I'll send for the carriage."

He walked out, leaving her gripping the back of a chair for support. Her heart threatened to crack her ribs. What was she thinking, touching him like that?

She closed her eyes and shook her head. "Don't be foolish, Bianca," she whispered to herself.

"Ma'am?"

The voice of Martha, the hired maid, made her jump. "Yes, yes, quite well," she exclaimed, then bolted from the room when the girl looked at her oddly. Hearing Max's voice at the bottom of the stairs, she turned and rushed up. Her head seemed totally disconnected from her mouth—to say nothing of her hands.

A quarter hour later, she felt in command of herself once more. Max handed her into the carriage and she didn't say or do anything lunatic, but thanked him very civilly. The ride itself passed without trouble as well, and then he helped her down in a busy thoroughfare.

Bianca looked around with interest. This was a very different sort of street compared to the one with the large showroom where Max envisioned well-laid dining tables. Here were ordinary women, bustling servants, working men delivering goods and manning the carts, and merchants welcoming customers into their shops. She felt instantly more at home here than in York Street.

The agent let them in, and a bell tinkled at their entrance. Bianca inhaled happily, despite the dusty air. Here was the quaint little shop she had pictured, with shelves along the walls and a large round table in the middle. There was a wide counter at one side, with wider, deeper shelves behind it, and there was a place in front of the window to display wares to passersby. It was perfect.

"I can see by your face this pleases you," said Max with a smile.

She couldn't help a small laugh. "It does. This is what I pictured when you began talking of show-rooms and shop premises."

"And it's a very good idea," he said, "for Fortuna wares."

"What is Fortuna ware?"

"What I propose to call the new, simpler wares." He drew her forward and turned her to face the windows, stepping behind her to leave the view unimpeded. "Look at the people passing by. People who could never hope to afford the coffee service Lord Dalway ordered, but who would like something quality, something lovely, something above ordinary Delftware and plain pottery. Imagine them eyeing the candleholders and little plum pots of rouge—"

Bianca turned her head. He was right behind her, his outstretched arm brushing hers as he sketched his vision in the air in front of her. "Perusia doesn't make candleholders."

He tipped his head, meeting her eyes. "Fortuna ware will include candleholders, and chamber pots and butter crocks and ink pots. Any item that could be made of earthenware or porcelain."

Bianca wasn't so sure her father would agree to that. "That plum pot was a lark, nothing more than some experiments I tried with soft paste porcelain for my glazes—"

"It was not a lark, it was a brilliant idea," he replied. "Fine ladies have little pots of silver and blown glass. Imagine how pleased a shopkeeper's wife would be to have something just as beautiful, but costing a fraction of the silver, on her dressing table. I picture items made at a cost such that even your own artisans could afford some."

Well . . . when he put it that way . . . "How much do you propose to produce?"

He must have sensed that she was coming around to his point of view. He grinned, looking rather like a pirate who'd just unlocked the chest of treasure. "A modest run to start, but if it does well, I would produce as much as we can sell."

"Perusia is where Papa's heart lies," she told him. "He will always care more about it than anything else."

"So he should." Almost idly he touched the loose curl lying on her shoulder. Bianca had liked the stylish arrangement, so she told Jennie to fix her hair that way again, leaving off the powder and sticky pomatum.

"After all," said Max, his voice deepening, "when you find yourself holding something beautiful and unique, you want to treasure it, and safeguard it. Only a fool would let it slip through his fingers." He twisted the curl around his finger as he spoke.

Bianca inhaled roughly. The letting agent had discreetly vanished, leaving them alone in the shop. She was practically in Max's arms. He wasn't talking about Papa, or about pottery, and she knew it. "When I kissed you the other night—"

"Yes," he whispered.

"It was a mistake," she said, striving for firm confidence and only achieving breathless pleading.

He touched her chin, tipping up her face toward him. "No, it wasn't." And he kissed her.

She could have protested, or stepped away; he

only held her chin, and that but lightly. Instead she stood and let him make love to her mouth, not so hungrily as before but with a leisurely thoroughness that sent tremors through her.

When he lifted his head, she swayed. His arm went around her waist in an instant, and his hand, cupped around her jaw, held her cheek to his chest. For a moment she rested against him. He was the perfect height to lean against, remarkably solid and strong. His broadcloth waistcoat was warm and smelled faintly of sandalwood—like him. And she could hear his heart pounding away, almost as fast as her own.

I want you, and no one else. She wasn't sure she believed the latter part of that, but she was convinced of the first part.

A door opening behind them sent her lurching away from him. As before, Max let her go. It was unnerving. She had thought a rogue would seize every opportunity to seduce her, that he would constantly be on watch for any sign of weakness in her refusal, ready to coerce and flatter and wheedle his way into her affections—before crushing them.

This, though. This was far more insidious. She was beginning to fear that he'd been right on their wedding day. The thought of asking him to show her all those pleasures he'd hinted at—the pleasures she was sure he'd had with his other lovers— was hovering at the edges of her mind until she thought it would drive her mad.

"Have you any questions, Mr. St. James?" It was Mr. Cooke, the letting agent, out of discretion or patience. He stood watching them with a faintly knowing smile. Bianca glared at him, wondering how much he'd seen.

"A few," said Max. Unlike Bianca, he seemed to have shaken off any lingering effects of that devastating kiss and returned to his businesslike self.

So she thought, until she saw the flush on the back of his neck, where his hair was pulled back into a neat queue. Until she caught the swift but scorching glance he sent her way when Mr. Cooke wasn't looking. Until she saw the tremor in his hand as he reached for the door as they left.

And as they rode home in the carriage, once more polite and dignified, all she could wonder was how long she could withstand him like this.

Chapter Nineteen

Despite not being in London long, even Bianca knew about Vauxhall Gardens. They weren't new or novel, but they had outstripped Ranelagh in popularity and fame, and when an invitation arrived from Lady Dalway, inviting her and Max to join a party there in a few nights, she was undeniably intrigued.

To her astonishment, Max was not.

He read the card and put it aside without a word before heading up the stairs. Bianca, having been waiting for him to come home and fully expecting to be told it was all the rage among society and of course they would go, scrambled after him. "Do you not wish to accept?"

He said nothing until they reached the drawing room, and he had closed the doors behind them. "Do you?"

"Oh—well—I presumed *you* would want to."

"Do you want to go?" he repeated.

Warily she looked at him. "Should I not?"

"So you do." His brow quirked wryly.

Bianca flushed. "A little. Vauxhall is famous, even in Marslip." She hesitated, but when he said nothing more, only picked up a discarded newspaper and read the page, she couldn't resist asking, "Why do you not want to go?"

"If you wish to go, we shall," he said instead, still reading.

Bianca pursed her lips in frustration. "Max."

His head came up. He looked at her in surprised awareness. Bianca realized with a small cringe that it was the first time she had called him by his Christian name. Undaunted she forged ahead. "What are you not telling me? If there is a reason to decline, then of course—"

"There's no reason." He let the paper fall and came toward her. "You called me Max."

She jerked her head without meeting his gaze. "It is your preferred name."

His mouth curved. "It is, but I've never heard you say it."

"Of course I have!"

"But I never *heard* it." He paused. "I like it."

That admission, uttered in his low, rough growl that did terrible things to her self-possession, was almost too much for her. Bianca kept her poise by the thinnest of margins. "Why don't you want to go to Vauxhall?"

His chest rose and fell in a silent sigh. "It's nothing. Lady Dalway is very fond of the place, but I'm not."

"Why? What is it like?" She lost all pretense of reserve in the face of his clear reluctance. Somehow sensing that he did not want to go, for reasons she didn't know but was suddenly wildly curious to discover, had made her want to go more than ever. "I read there is an orchestra, and singers, and tree-lined paths in a grove, and even fireworks."

"All true," he said with a smile. He was still very close to her.

"What else is there?" she pressed.

"People who drink too much," he replied. "All manner of scoundrels. There is a spirit of . . . permissiveness that you might find shocking."

"I expected all of London to be filled with scoundrels," she said frankly. "It's not been nearly as bad as I thought."

He laughed. "Then we shall go, my dear." He paused, as if waiting, then prompted, "Are you pleased?"

"Yes."

"Say it," he whispered.

Heat rolled through her. "Yes, Max."

He looked at her with a heavy-lidded gaze that made her feel like she might burst into flame. "I like to hear it. Say it again."

"It's just a name," she tried to say.

"Bianca."

The way he said her name caused a physical twinge of response in her belly. She wet her lips, and noticed how avidly he watched. "Max," she breathed.

"Yes," he said as his mouth touched hers.

Bianca wasn't sure who had moved toward whom this time. She was fully aware that her hands had come up onto his chest, and that she was leaning into him. His hand settled lightly on her waist, and she felt it in her toes.

"This is not what I expected," she whispered, her whole body throbbing as his lips skimmed over her jaw to her ear.

"Why not?" he rasped. His teeth nipped lightly at her earlobe, making her quiver.

"Because I don't like you." She was barely aware of what she said.

"Not even a little bit?" His hand was on her back, easing her closer to him—not that she needed much encouragement. His other hand threaded into her hair.

Bianca couldn't stop a little sigh of contentment. He was kissing her neck and it might be making her melt. "You know I don't want to . . ."

He hummed in disappointment. "I wish you did." He brushed a soft kiss on the corner of her mouth. "At *least* a little bit."

She dragged her eyes open. He was so close, so dark, so wretchedly beautiful. Some of her sense resurfaced. "You didn't want to marry me. You proposed to marry Cathy. It's not me you wanted at all."

His dark eyes glittered. "You think I don't want you?" With a sudden tug he pulled her against him. "If I hadn't wanted you, I would have said no in the sacristy."

She laid her fingers on his lips, forestalling any more kisses for the moment. "Do you mean that?"

A frown creased his brow. "Yes."

"Why did you want to marry Cathy?"

His grip on her loosened. Bianca waited. "I thought . . . it was to be a marriage of business convenience. Your father has no son to inherit the business—"

"He has two daughters," she began hotly, but he put up one hand.

"Two daughters who might eventually marry, putting the business into the hands of someone other than a Tate. In my visit to Perusia I sensed that Miss Tate, your sister, has no desire to direct and lead Perusia." His gaze was serious and steady, as if urging her to believe him. "I *do*. I can help Perusia succeed and prosper for years to come. I hope you agree with that, after our time in London. So I offered marriage to your sister, proposing not just a business partnership but a promise of protection and care for your father's daughters."

Well . . . perhaps that wasn't so coldhearted and mercenary as she'd thought. And Bianca could not deny that he'd demonstrated value and commitment to Perusia in everything he'd done in London. "That doesn't mean you wanted to marry *me*."

"I am fiercely pleased to be married to you," he said in a low voice.

Bianca's mouth was dry. "Because you want me. You want to take me to bed."

His gaze dropped to her mouth, and he didn't bother to deny it. "I want you to want it, too."

Bianca was afraid to admit that she did. She had already been weak and allowed her alleged boundary to flex and shift until here she was, pressed up against him with his arms around her. And just weeks ago she had sworn to hate and despise him forever.

Of course, she was also coming to realize that he wasn't much like the person she had imagined him to be then.

MAX'S ALREADY-LOW DESIRE to go to Vauxhall fell even further upon a closer reading of Serafina's card.

"A bloody masquerade," he said in despair. "She's trying to ruin me."

Lawrence looked on with sympathy. He had formerly been valet to Percy Willoughby, who'd been forced to slink back to his father's estate in disgrace after a disastrous night at Vauxhall's gaming tables. He was well aware of how badly things could go in Vauxhall. "May I recommend a domino, sir?"

Max thought of the outfits he'd worn to previous masquerades, including the white sheet and ivy wreath—and nothing more—he'd worn once to win two hundred pounds from his mate Henry Campbell. He'd proclaimed himself Dionysus and had an extremely debauched evening in the woodland. "Perhaps that would be best."

"Shall I advise Jennie on Mrs. St. James's costume as well?"

Dear God. What would Bianca want to be? "Most likely a domino as well," he said, hoping it was so. She was from Marslip, where women didn't dress as Turkish concubines or Egyptian goddesses for an evening of wicked fun. Surely she'd be more comfortable in a simple black cloak and mask.

Lawrence's gaze cut away. "As you say, sir."

Something about it pricked Max's attention. "What?" he asked.

The valet studied his hands. "I suspect madam will like something more intriguing, sir."

Max went still. "What do you mean by that?"

"Begging your pardon, sir, but Lady Dalway and Mrs. Farquhar have been to visit her, and I have no doubt they've told her all about it. Before the week is out, they'll have her agreeing to dress as an Arcadian shepherdess or a nun."

He let out his breath slowly. "Right." He was being ridiculous. Bianca was too sensible to dress as anything dreadful.

"I shall endeavor to guide Jennie toward the most dignified and proper costume," Lawrence assured him.

Max nodded and waved him away. For a long moment he stood, tapping his fingers on his hip as he stared out the window.

It was one night in Vauxhall. One night with his friends. Bianca wanted to go, and he wanted to please her. He would stay close by her side, attentive and protective, and ignore—as if they were cold in their graves—any former acquaintances who might dare speak to him. It was one night.

Surely everything would be fine.

Chapter Twenty

If asked, Bianca would have said that of course she had friends in Marslip. Amelia, for one, had been her compatriot in all manner of childhood pranks. Cathy, her pillar of family, was the one person she told all her secrets to. Then there were her cousins, who came to dine and would commiserate when her father was in a temper, and even some of the working women, with whom she had set up the Perusia school for employees' children.

Nothing and no one, though, were anything like Lady Dalway and Mrs. Farquhar.

They called upon her almost every day after the dinner party, sweeping in like a perfumed hurricane of feathers, silks, and gossip. Sometimes Lady Carswell came, sometimes they brought someone else. They laughed and talked so gaily, Bianca found herself being drawn into their enthusiasms.

It had been Mrs. Farquhar—who had begged Bianca to call her Clara—who suggested the masquerade. "Don't you remember how amusing it was last year?" she said to Lady Dalway.

Lady Dalway—Serafina—gave one of her perfect, dimpled smiles. "I do! But Clara, we mustn't overwhelm dear Bianca. She's never been to Vauxhall, you know."

Bianca's ears pricked up at the mention of the famous pleasure gardens. "Is a masquerade terribly scandalous?"

"Of course not," cried Serafina, at the same time Clara gave a tiny nod, her eyes gleaming with glee. "Well, perhaps they can be," the countess amended, having seen Clara's gesture. "There are places where one mustn't go, at least not alone. But I daresay Max wouldn't stray from your side all evening, so that is of no consequence."

"Royal princes and ladies of the realm attend Vauxhall," Clara assured her. "Would they do that if it were appalling?"

Bianca had already deduced that Clara had a slightly naughty, fun-loving nature. In fairness, Bianca herself had been the same when she was younger. The fact that Clara didn't seem to have outgrown it, as Bianca had done, she put down to the effects of London society. Bianca had become more sensible because she wanted to work in the Perusia workshops, and being a madcap girl hadn't helped.

Still, part of her was fascinated by this talk of masquerade. "What is different in a masquerade?" she asked.

"It's ever so exciting." Clara leaned forward eagerly. "You may dress as anything, or anyone, you like! And all with a mask, so no one will know your name."

"What did you dress as last year?" Bianca was intrigued and could not deny it.

Serafina laughed. "She dressed as a nun! Can you

imagine? It gave Farquhar the start of his life, I don't wonder!"

Clara only smiled, a touch smugly. "I thought I made a splendid Reverend Mother."

Bianca wasn't sure about that; religious figures were not to be mocked, in her upbringing. She turned to Serafina. "And you?"

Her dimples flashed again. "A queen! I looked very striking."

Serafina *would* be a queen; she had a way of commanding attention without any effort Bianca could discern. "I haven't got anything half that elegant," Bianca said. "I don't want people to think I've gone as a simple country girl, when I've only worn my best gown."

"Oh no!" Both ladies sat up in protest. "We'll see you properly turned out," vowed Clara. "Serafina and I should have something that would suit you."

Bianca doubted that very much. Lady Dalway was petite and slender, and Mrs. Farquhar was as pale and plump as a meringue.

Serafina looked at Bianca with a more critical eye. "We must raid Louisa's wardrobe," she announced, referring to Lady Carswell. "She is more of a height with dear Bianca."

"Oh yes!" Clara clapped her hands. "And I shall send my own Thérèse to arrange your hair. She would be happy to train your maid while she is here," she added as Bianca's brows went up.

Bianca wasn't entirely sure about putting herself into Clara's maid's hands—Clara wore rather more powder and rouge than Bianca liked, although she was very fashionable—but it did sound irresistibly intriguing and amusing, and she found that agreeing to consider the masquerade was enough to set Serafina and Clara on the path to full-scale preparations for it.

Max's initial reluctance took her off guard, but then he kissed her and said they would go. It seemed all was settled, and she began looking forward to the event more than she would have ever admitted aloud.

Until Clara and her French maid, Thérèse, arrived on the day of the masquerade, with a shrouded bundle that produced a breathtaking gown.

"Oh no, I couldn't possibly wear this." Bianca was aghast.

Clara waved it aside. "You can! You must! Louisa will be so downcast if you do not—she said she cannot wait to see you in it."

Bianca touched the heavy brocade skirt. It was surely even more expensive than the gowns Max had bought her here in London. It was also startlingly black, relieved only by gold lace around the neckline—the very *low* neckline. "It's so dark."

Clara blinked. "Oh! Well, that is no matter—bring a petticoat," she said to Jennie, who was watching, agog with interest. "A bright one, red or yellow." She opened a pouch and poured out a mountain of jewels. "These will brighten it as well. All paste," she said airily, as Bianca gaped. "It's for a night of fun!"

So she allowed herself to be laced into the dress, draped in the paste jewels, and her hair pinned up in a thoroughly unfamiliar way. She barely recognized herself in the looking glass as Thérèse fixed the headdress in place.

"My, my," murmured Clara in the silence. "I cannot wait for Maxim's reaction to this."

"What do you mean?" Bianca asked, still marveling at herself.

Clara's laugh was warm and low as she came up behind Bianca, and rested her hands on Bianca's elbows. "He'll trip over his own tongue," she whispered. She handed Bianca a white mask, adorned with red spots on the cheeks, a rosy painted pout on the lips, and a tiny heart-shaped beauty mark beside one eye hole. "Do be kind to the poor man tonight!"

That thought made her mouth go dry. She knew she looked . . . well, striking, even in her own private opinion. Marvelous and mysterious, more elegant than she'd ever thought possible—perhaps even beautiful.

But that didn't mean Max would notice. He'd been surrounded by beautiful women for years, and even in this magnificent gown, made up like a princess, she was still the same Bianca she'd been yesterday.

Clara departed in a flurry of pink skirts—she had come already attired in a whimsical shepherdess costume—calling that she would see them at the gardens. Thérèse was packing up her things, and giving the fascinated Jennie instructions in a quiet voice.

Touching the headdress once more to settle it in place, Bianca slowly went down the stairs. She wondered if Clara would be right—if Max would be pleased and even impressed by her appearance. He'd looked at her so . . . so *hungrily* the night of the dinner party, when she'd had her hair up and powdered and wore one of her new gowns. And she'd ended up kissing him then.

There was no avoiding the truth, that she liked

her husband to look at her with desire. It sent thrills through her when he cupped his hand around her nape. And when he kissed her, she forgot why she should keep him at arm's length.

Perhaps tonight would tip the precarious balance, one way or the other.

Max DRESSED SIMPLY for the masquerade, wanting to send every possible sign that he was a different man now. A black suit, unrelieved by anything but white lace at the throat. Lawrence had located a simple black cloak and white mask to wear. With any luck, none of his former comrades would even recognize him tonight.

He heard Clara Farquhar leave. He thought he also heard her laugh as she passed the drawing room door, too, but he didn't call out and stop her. Nigel Farquhar had warned him she was in high spirits over dressing his wife, and Max knew enough about Clara's high spirits to be wary.

In the distance, the bell tolled seven. They were to meet the rest of the party in the supper box Dalway had reserved. It was most fashionable to go by yacht, but given the nature of the evening, Max had chosen to take the carriage most of the way. They would take a launch from Westminster to cross the river.

"I'm ready to go," said Bianca behind him. "What do you think?"

Max looked up—and almost pitched forward onto his face in amazement.

She wore a dress from the time of the Tudors, hanging in heavy folds of gleaming black brocade over a brilliant scarlet petticoat, visible in front. Her waist was impossibly narrow, girdled by a golden chain, and her breasts were barely contained by the rigid bodice. Ropes of pearls hung in crescents down her front, glowing amidst the gold lace that framed her bosom and face.

Dimly he remembered seeing Louisa Carswell in that dress a few years ago. She'd worn a wide red ribbon around her neck and told everyone she was Anne Boleyn, with her head restored for one night. He suspected she'd been just as faithful that night as the ill-fated queen, but Harry Carswell hardly cared. Max had seen him disappearing into the gardens beyond the grove with two young women clad in very little. Prostitutes, he suspected. The Carswells had always been like that.

But Bianca didn't look like a licentious queen; she looked like a goddess of the night, come to torment him to madness.

At his silence she came a step closer, and took a deep breath. Max's gaze veered involuntarily to the plump swells of her breasts above the black satin. "Clara said it would be very striking, but I was astonished by how much so," she said with an awkward little laugh.

His brain was fixated on her breasts. He was sure if she inhaled like that again, her rosy nipples would pop out of the tight bodice. Louisa was slimmer than she, and it showed in the dress. He could barely breathe, watching, waiting, hoping . . .

Max wrenched his gaze away from her bosom, back to her face. There was the sensible Bianca he knew, his wife, and she was looking at him expectantly—and warily. "I've been struck dumb by how beautiful you look," he said truthfully.

"Truly?" Her eyes lit up. She placed her palms on her stomach, unconsciously displaying her compressed figure. "I had doubts . . ."

Max's doubts centered on whether he would survive this evening. "Are you not comfortable?"

"Well," she confided, "it is laced rather tightly."

And like that he pictured undoing those laces, hearing her sigh in his arms, feeling her smooth, warm skin under his hands. He mustered a smile, hoping it didn't look as strained as it felt on his face. "I shall carry a knife," he said, "in case you need to be freed."

Idiot. Now he'd think about shredding that dress off her all night long.

He cleared his throat. "Shall we go?"

A smile, uncertain but growing stronger, bloomed on her lips. "Yes."

They took the carriage across town to Westminster stairs. Bianca kept peering out the window, remarking on various landmarks they passed. Max had to smile. At the landing, he handed her down and made arrangements with the coachman for the return.

"Why did we not go with Serafina and the others by boat?" she asked as Max helped her down to the wherry.

To avoid being marooned at Vauxhall until the early hours of the morning. "I shall have to spend the entire evening in Dalway's company, and you want to subject me to a boat ride with him as well?" He shook his head with a soft *tsk* and settled onto the seat beside her. The boatman pushed away from the dock, setting the lantern on the hook above his head swaying. "Unkind, Your Highness."

Bianca started. "Highness?"

Curse it. Of course Clara and Serafina wouldn't have told her she was Anne Boleyn, scheming wife of a faithless husband and dispatched to the block for treason and infidelity. "Are you not a young Queen Elizabeth?" Max asked lightly, thinking quickly.

"Oh." She seemed pleased by the thought. "And what are you?"

Max raised her hand to his lips for a kiss. "A lowly courtier, Highness."

She laughed. "Truly? Why did you not dress as something adventurous?"

"Lack of imagination, I suppose," lied Max. "No one shall notice me in any event, once they set eyes upon you."

"Don't be ridiculous." She gave him one of her frank, appraising looks. It was not the first time; Max had always met her gaze boldly, quietly, unflinchingly, letting her look her fill. He thought she liked what she saw, even if she never betrayed it by even a flicker of her lashes. Let her stare at his legs or wipe a drop of coffee from his chin. Every fraction of an inch was that much closer to his goal of winning her over.

Tonight, though . . . he could feel the flames of desire licking at him as her gray eyes moved over him. Tonight he didn't feel like the relentlessly focused, patient man he'd become, but more like the reckless, scandalous rake he'd been . . .

"You don't look like a lowly person of any kind," she said in a low voice. "You look dangerous and wicked—and not easily denied."

She saw him too well, apparently. "Nothing of the sort," Max tried to say, when he could speak. They had reached the Vauxhall stairs, and the boatman's efforts tying up the craft bought him a moment to recover from the thunderbolt of shock her words had caused.

"Oh, precisely that sort." She let him hand her up the stairs, then glanced back with a coy little smile. "Tonight, though . . . I think I like it." With a swish of her ebony skirts, she turned and headed toward the carriages waiting to ferry passengers the short distance to the pleasure gardens.

If Max had been a religious man, he would have prayed for restraint and patience. He should have done so anyway, mindful of what was at stake.

Instead, he felt the old rogue within him, dormant and docile these last few months, awaken with a growl. And he followed his wife toward the familiar grounds of his former haunt, where he had been the most wicked version of himself, feeling more like the old Max than he should have.

Chapter Twenty-One

Vauxhall was a marvel.

Bianca barely remembered to put on her mask as they strolled through the tall colonnade. A wide avenue lay directly ahead of them, disappearing into the darkening evening. Glass lamps on posts and trees glowed in a variety of colors. To one side was a neatly manicured square with a pavilion at the center and a rotunda at the end, outlined with trees, and to the other a line of dinner boxes tucked under the colonnade, enclosed on three sides but open at the front to the curiosity of passersby.

Max led her down the avenue, pointing out details helpfully, because Bianca couldn't turn her head fast enough or far enough to take it all in. It was a fairyland, filled with people in all manner of dress, from a tall, portly friar to a figure wearing a wolf's head and furred cloak, so lean and short Bianca wondered if it were a woman or even a child.

At one of the last supper boxes, right before the avenue grew more rustic and darker, they found the Dalway party. Clara Farquhar was there in her shepherdess costume, while her husband wore the long wig and plumed hat of a cavalier. Lady Dalway was petite and beautiful in an all-white draped gown, saying she was Virtue, and her husband wore a black Spanish suit and pretended to strum a guitar as he sang, very poorly, and said he was Scaramouche.

"Carswell and his wife will be along later," said Lord Dalway, eyeing Max with barely concealed amusement. "I see we have royalty among us tonight, but who, pray, are you, St. James?"

"Nobody," said Max with a smile as they took their seats on the bench. "Nobody at all."

"Oh!" cried Lady Dalway in pique. "How unlike you to spoil our fun!"

"I assure you, if your fun depended upon me, it was utterly doomed to be spoiled," he replied.

She made a face at him and turned to Bianca. "My dear, you look simply splendid! I knew Louisa would have something to suit you in her wardrobe."

"It's magnificent," agreed Bianca, stroking the damask. It was also quite warm, but she didn't mention that. Tonight was not a night for practical concerns.

"There's to be a wonderful singer tonight," Lady Dalway went on, consulting the musical program. "Such a pity! I daresay no one much will listen to her during a masquerade. I do adore Miss Leary, though. I wonder if she will sing some of Mr. Carter's songs."

"Is it to include dancing?" Bianca asked. Clara Farquhar had given her instructions on how to dance in the dress, and she'd paid close attention, not wanting to embarrass herself or damage the gown.

"Not always," Max told her. He lowered his voice and tipped his head toward her. "But if you wish to dance, I would gladly partner you."

She flushed. "We cannot dance if no one else is . . ."

His dark eyes glittered in the candlelight as he looked at her. "In the wilderness we can do as we please."

Her mouth went dry. Before she could muster a reply, a whistle sounded, and a servant dashed by, stationing himself at one end of the box. At a second whistle, the man touched a taper to the lamp, igniting the lamp there. But then—as if by magic—the illumination spread, lamp to lamp, until the whole of the garden was nearly as bright as day. Lady Dalway laughed and clapped, like many other people around them, and Bianca joined in.

"How did they do that?" she whispered to Max. It was as if someone had flung aside a heavy curtain, turning night into day in an instant.

"It's a mystery of Vauxhall," he replied, and she could only shake her head and marvel.

The Carswells joined them after the dinner had come. Louisa was dressed as a Persian princess, with diaphanous veils draped about her, and Sir Henry wore the outfit of a naval admiral. The evening passed in a blur for Bianca, with shockingly small portions of food—"If they could slice the meat any thinner, it would waft away on the breeze," commented Mr. Farquhar forlornly—but large quantities of drink, including something called arrack punch, which Louisa Carswell drank with abandon.

In the grove opposite them, the orchestra played. At some point Lady Dalway thought she heard the singer she liked announced, so she got up and made Dalway go with her to hear better. The earl rolled his eyes and mimed being pulled by a halter, causing Sir Henry almost to fall off his bench in a fit of laughter. The Carswells were both greeted warmly by a passing couple, and invited to take a turn about the gardens with them.

A large number of people tried to hail Max as they passed. Several times someone would stop and exclaim. Most were men, but a few were women. They all seemed extraordinarily pleased to find him there, although one fellow shouted that he barely recognized him. To all, Max raised a hand, almost dismissively, and pointedly turned away. The men laughed, the ladies pouted, and one woman who did not look worthy of the name *lady* strolled off with a small smile on her face. Bianca glanced at her husband as it happened again and again, but he appeared to find it annoying, if anything.

As the night deepened, Max touched her hand. "Do you fancy a walk?" he murmured.

Bianca caught Clara's eye, watching them contemplatively. The conversation had grown a trifle rambling and uninhibited as the wine flowed. Besides, she wanted to see more of the gardens. "Yes."

She took his offered arm without thinking, and they crossed the avenue to the lawn in the grove. Up in the orchestra, the musicians were playing, though without a singer. Max nodded politely but never stopped whenever someone called out to him, keeping up a steady pace.

Finally Bianca, tightly laced and already warm in the heavy gown, stopped walking. Max looked at her in concern. "Can we sit down?" she asked breathlessly.

"Of course." He flagged down a waiter running past and ordered two glasses of champagne.

"I don't think I could drink another," she protested, but he shook his head.

"It's burnt," he said. "So it's not as potent. Try it."

The servant came darting back with the glasses, and Max tossed him two shillings, which the man snatched out of the air without breaking stride. Bianca took a sip and realized it was crisp, cool, and decidedly less potent than the champagne she had already had two glasses of.

"Where shall we go?"

It was crowded in the grove, to say nothing of warm and cloying, under the profusion of oil lamps burning in the trees. "Somewhere it's quiet and cooler," Bianca suggested, plucking again at her tight bodice. Now she saw the benefit of the tiny food portions.

Max's gaze dropped for a heartbeat to her fingers. "Right. This way." He steered her away from the orchestra, past the rotunda, toward the darker paths beyond the winding colonnade and supper boxes. Away from the crowd, Bianca removed her mask again, sighing in pleasure as the cool air hit her face. Max had taken off his mask when the champagne arrived, and not bothered to replace it.

"Welcome to Vauxhall, my lady," said a leering harlequin sauntering by.

Bianca looked at him, startled, but Max put his arm possessively around her. The other man made a moue of regret and hurried off. "Did you know that man?" she whispered as they walked.

"No," he said in amusement. "Did you?"

"Of course not!"

"In Vauxhall, it matters little. He admired you."

Bianca flushed. "I shall never be used to that sort of admiration."

Max laughed softly. His arm lingered at her waist,

and she found it rather comforting. "You should try. I admire you a great deal."

She opened her mouth, then closed it. She had nearly said that he was different, that his admiration didn't make her feel the same way. His admiration made her feel . . . beautiful.

They turned a corner, where a pair of ladies dressed as Grecian goddesses were strolling arm in arm. "Maxim! Oh, Maxim, *darling,*" cried one, catching sight of them. She tore free of her companion and flung herself on him. "You're back!"

Astonished, dislodged by the woman's attack, Bianca retreated a step, too surprised to speak.

Max was trying to untangle her arms from around his neck. "I am not," he said coolly. "Not really."

The other woman had hurried up, and now she pouted under her half mask, sidling close enough to walk her fingers up his arm. "But you are! When shall you come to see us again?"

His jaw set, Max put the first woman away from him, holding her a moment to quell her attempts to throw herself on him again.

"Maxim," she mewed in disappointment. "After all the fun we've had together . . ."

The second girl glanced at Bianca. "I suppose you're his new girl. Lucky little pigeon, ain't you?"

"I am not," said Bianca indignantly. "I'm—"

"Good evening," said Max with swift finality. He seized Bianca's hand. "We're done, Harriette, and you know it."

"Don't have to be," she said coyly, but Max was already striding away, pulling Bianca with him. She stumbled, almost dropping her champagne, as he charged down a path, turning corners until finding a secluded bench.

Bianca dropped onto it with a thump. Max put his hand on his hip and stared at the ground, his fingers drumming on his hip. She had learned his nervous habits by now, so Bianca just addressed the matter directly. "They, I take it, *were* lovers of yours."

He cursed, violently, under his breath.

"I knew you had some," she went on. "I'm only surprised it took this long to cross paths with one. Or two."

He plowed his hands into his hair and sank onto the bench. "I never wanted you to meet *any*."

"Well." It was much darker out here, and blessedly cooler. Bianca finished her champagne, looking into the distance at the blue-black velvet of the sky above to give him a moment to compose himself. "It wasn't a terrible shock."

It was obvious to anyone that he was mortified and furious. She wasn't going to pretend it hadn't happened. That was how Cathy had almost ended up married to him instead of to Mr. Mayne; Cathy had never been able to stand up to her father, to say aloud what really bothered her. Bianca, on the other hand, had never been shy about speaking her mind.

But her husband was silent for a long time, and finally she looked at him. He sat with his hands on his knees, elbows splayed out. She could just make out his profile, his jaw hard as he faced grimly ahead.

"Dalway said I should tell you all," he said at last,

his voice low. "I thought him mad, but perhaps he was right."

Despite her bravado earlier, Bianca felt a strange twinge at the thought of him telling her about all his previous lovers. Women who knew things about him, who knew *him* in ways she did not, even though she was his wife.

"Do you want to hear?" he continued. "Or would you prefer to consider it a closed chapter of the past? I will tell you as much as you want to know."

She thought about it. The idea of listening as he listed all the women he'd taken to bed was viscerally revolting. But he, who had been so close-mouthed about everything, was offering to tell her anything . . .

"I would prefer to know about you, not about them," she said softly. "About your parents, your youth . . . your grandfather."

After a long pause, he let out his breath. "My mother was beautiful." His voice was quiet and wistful. "Dark hair, gentle blue eyes . . . She never deserved what my father did to her. He was a thorough scoundrel. I think he married her only because she held him at arm's length. My father wasn't accustomed to being refused. But she did, and old Maxim refused to give up her funds, modest though they were, until they went to church. So he married her, poor creature."

"What was he like?" she couldn't resist asking.

Max growled in disgust. "The most selfish man I've ever known. Nothing mattered except his own desires and wishes. He would scold her and abuse her, then disappear for a month with no word—and leaving no money. One winter we had to go back to my grandfather's farm in Lincolnshire to avoid starving to death."

"But your father—!"

"He didn't care if we starved," said Max with scathing malice. "He preferred the finer life, and he was determined to have it, even if that meant leaving us behind. That year he'd found a wealthy widow—I don't know if she knew he was married, or if she didn't care—and they went off to France or the Low Countries. He always came back when they tired of him, but never for long. He was never pleased in one place for more than a few months together, never satisfied with his wife and son, although I suppose he might have also wanted to stay ahead of his debts."

Oh goodness. Bianca had never suspected that. Her father would never have left any of their family to starve—indeed, Samuel routinely took on distant cousins or their widows, wives of drunkard nephews and children of feckless neighbors. He gave them employment, annuities, hampers of food . . . And all that in addition to what he gave his workers, above and beyond what other employers did. Perusia supported far more than their own little household in Marslip. Her chest filled with a burst of love for her father, irascible and stubborn though he could be.

But she sensed Max didn't want to talk about his father. "Were you happy at your grandfather's?"

"In Lincolnshire?" His shoulders rose and fell on a sigh. "I suppose. He had a good property and I was a boy, left at liberty to explore. Freedom suited me."

"And your mother?"

"She died when I was a child," he said after a

moment. "In the spring. Too much worry and not enough money."

Bianca bit down on her lip, picturing a broken-hearted young boy, abandoned by his father and left to fend for himself. "What was her name?"

"Adelaide," he said softly. "Adela, her family called her. My father came back long enough to collect anything valuable. He went to France, as far as I know. If there's any grace in the world, he fell into a privy ditch in Paris and rots there still."

She was frozen by the calmness of his voice. "But—but you're cousin to a duke," she faltered.

"*Distant* cousin, and not one worthy of His Grace's kindness. My mother tried to interest them in our plight," he went on, as calmly as if they'd been discussing the weather. "Desperately. My father had been quite boastful of his connections, you see, and she'd thought that meant something. She never knew until later that his father and grandfather considered my father the worst sort of reprobate—not that they were any pillars of propriety themselves, mind. She named me after them, hoping one of them would grant me a living or at least favor me with a position. She thought I might make a fine secretary." He tilted his head, and incredibly, Bianca thought he was smiling. "Imagine that, someone trusting me with their business affairs and correspondence."

That stung, even if he hadn't meant it to. She had met his arrival in Marslip with open suspicion, considered him a shallow fortune hunter and called him simple to his face. She wet her lips. "You did read law for a year . . ."

"Ah. You remember that?" He nodded. "After my

mother died, her younger sister, Greta, took me in. Her husband at the time was a solicitor. She sent me off to Oxford for a year, and then I read law under her husband before he died."

"But then you left," she said slowly, trying to put together these disparate pieces of him into a coherent whole. A useless father, but a loving mother and family. University and a solicitor's office, but no profession. Nearly starving one year, but possessed of the manners and airs of a gentleman. Even the first time he came to dinner at Perusia his reputation had preceded him: a rakish sort of fellow, a gambler, a dangerous scoundrel.

"Yes, I left," said Max, with a dry emphasis on the last word. "It happened that my uncle's partner thought I was bent on seducing his wife. If I hadn't left, he would have thrown me out." He paused. "He told all his fellow solicitors I'd done it, and none of them would take me on. That was the end of my career in law."

Outrage filled her chest. Without thinking she put her hand on his. "What vicious slander!"

He was as still as stone. "Don't you think I *did* seduce her?"

Bianca flushed. No, she did not. "Did you?"

"No," he said softly. "But I am grateful you didn't presume I had."

She didn't know what to say to that. And when she tried to slip her hand from his, she realized his fingers had closed around hers, so lightly she'd barely felt it. "You must have been a very young man," she said unsteadily. It felt shockingly right to sit here, letting him hold her hand.

"Eighteen," he agreed. "Old Tibbets knew his

wife favored young men, and so he only employed older clerks. My uncle persuaded him to allow me, but I expect he set his heart against me from the start, certain I would betray him." His voice turned mildly contemptuous. "She did invite me into her bed, but—not only was she my employer's wife— she already had a young lover. Tibbets never suspected the tailor's apprentice was warming her bedlinen every time he delivered a new coat or trousers. And he was a vain man, who ordered a new coat every month."

Bianca couldn't help it; she gave a little snort of laughter.

"I agree," said her husband in amusement. "Old fool."

"What did you do then?" she asked.

"A single gentleman of no fortune and no profession? The gaming tables, my dear."

"Were you good?"

"Brilliant," he said with a wink. She laughed, and he grinned. At some point during their conversation she had slid down the bench until she was right beside him, and could make out his expressions.

"So you weren't an indolent scoundrel when you came to Perusia," Bianca said, feeling as if the veil had dropped from her eyes. "I believed you were the most unprincipled fortune hunter, wanting Cathy's dowry and my father's factory because you had nothing of your own. I thought you had dazzled Papa with empty talk of your connection to the Duke of Carlyle, and wanted nothing more than money."

His hand twitched in hers.

"I'm sorry for believing the worst of you," she added in real remorse. She had been wrong, and owed him an honest apology. "I hope you can forgive me."

He turned, taking both her hands. "Bianca . . ."

"Yes?"

His face was silvery pale in the dark gardens. The moonlight made him look haunted and drawn, his eyes dark and shadowed. Instead of replying, he kissed her.

This time she was ready for it. She didn't know if she had walked into the woodland in order for him to kiss her, but she had walked out here knowing it was a possibility. She had not missed one iota of the searing hunger in his gaze when he first saw her in this gown, nor the fascinated way his eyes dropped to her bosom every time she took a deep breath. The dress was very snug, but she might, just might, have exaggerated her posture at times to see what he would do.

Now he was kissing her, his mouth moving over hers, his free hand wrapping around the nape of her neck. And she was kissing him back, because he was not the rogue she'd thought he was and she could no longer fight her attraction to him.

"God above, how I want you," he whispered, brushing kisses over her brow.

"We're in a public garden." Bianca thought that if that weren't so, they would indeed consummate their marriage tonight.

"I know." He rested his forehead against hers, his fingers playing with the long strands of pearls lying across her bosom. "But with the right discretion . . ."

She tensed. "What? You would do that in a *garden*?"

He laughed quietly. "Not this time. But there are still . . . pleasures . . . one can find . . ."

Her heart was thumping and her skin was tingling. "What pleasures?" she whispered.

"Will you trust me?" He slid off the bench, onto his knees in front of her. His black cloak pooled around him. He traced one finger over the inside of her ankle.

Bianca glanced nervously from side to side, but they were alone. It was full dark out, and the nearest lantern was barely visible at the end of the path. And his words were so tantalizing: *trust me . . .*

She swallowed hard, and nodded.

Chapter Twenty-Two

I won't hurt you. Never, my love." His voice was a thread of sound as his hand skimmed up her leg. At her knee he paused and slowly moved first one leg, then the other, to the side, spreading her knees apart. She almost choked. Another feverish glance around showed no one.

Max raised her skirts, draping the hem across her knees. His gaze never strayed from her face. Her pulse leapt—with excitement.

"I want to please you," he breathed. His hands were on her thighs, smoothing over her bare skin and sending shivers through her.

"I've never—" she began, not knowing how to say that she—unlike he—had no idea what to do.

"I know," he murmured. "Say one word and I'll stop." His thumbs brushed the curls between her legs, and she stiffened, her breath catching in nervous anticipation.

This was so unlike her. Bianca felt as if she were in a dream, or watching it all from a distance. But when he stroked her *there*, her back arched and she flung her hands behind her to grip the bench at the sensation reverberating through her.

"Max," she gasped.

He paused. Bianca gulped for air and nodded weakly. That wild rakish smile slowly grew on his face, and when he put his hands around her hips, to pull her closer, moving between her knees, she only moaned in encouragement.

Pleasures most women only dream of.

Her every breath was like a spasm as he touched her. His fingers petted and stroked those curls, as leisurely as if he meant to spend all night doing only that. Bianca bit down on her lower lip to keep from urging him on. She was tense and on edge, her toes digging into the ground.

"So soft," he whispered. "So wet." His thumb dipped deeper, sliding easily. She *was* wet, and her skin prickled all over as he stroked her, lightly, slowly, barely enough to keep her from bursting out in frustration.

"You look like a goddess tonight." His voice was a drug, more potent than wine. His words made her muscles tighten and a pulse of desire almost made her fall over. "Dark and beautiful . . . bold and wanting . . . mistress of the night in black satin and pearls."

"So—so you aren't as struck by me every other day?" she managed to gasp.

He laughed, deep and knowing. "I want you when you wear that old blue dress with scorch marks on the skirt, with alum on your sleeve and ink on your fingers. When you've got that little crease between your brows that you get when you're working on a troublesome glaze. I would want you in a nun's habit or a milkmaid's apron. It's you, not the dress."

"Good." Her voice had gone raspy. "It's Lady Carswell's dress, I have to give it back . . ."

"Then I should make the most of this chance." He rose up on his knees, his hand still moving beneath her skirts, tormenting her, and touched his lips to the swell of her breast. Bianca let her head fall back, unabashedly letting him kiss her there. The bench was a low one, and his mouth was right at the level of her breasts, and his kiss was so enthrallingly soft . . .

"Breathe," he whispered, and she realized she'd stopped. With a gasp she filled her lungs, and he hooked one finger inside the bodice and tugged, exposing her nipple. He made a low, primal noise of pleasure in his throat, and sucked it between his teeth, his palm spread on her back to hold her in place.

She whimpered. He pushed a long finger inside her. Her whole body clenched around it, and this time he was the one who moaned. He withdrew it, then pushed back inside, sliding his thumb back into position and stroking harder.

The sudden sounds of laughter almost made her faint in fright. "Max," she wheezed, groping for his arm. "Stop!"

His dark eyes gleamed at her. With his free hand he pulled the hood of his domino over his head and ducked down, his face in her lap. Bianca's panicked gaze jumped over his figure, and she realized his cloak blended into the black of her gown to render him invisible, at least in the weak moonlight.

But he didn't withdraw his hand. On the contrary, she felt his lips on her inner thigh.

Bianca sat bolt upright, holding the edge of the bench in a death grip.

A couple came down the walk, arm in arm and

laughing. From their staggering steps, Bianca guessed they were quite drunk. The man saw her, muttered a good-natured curse, and raised one hand. The woman ducked her head into his shoulder, giggling, and they stumbled away, veering into the trees.

Max's mouth was at the crease at the top of her thigh. His tongue swirled over her skin.

"They've gone," she panted even as her knees closed around him.

He pulled her closer, until she was almost falling off the bench, and she felt the heat of his breath on her throbbing center. And then it was his mouth, his tongue, flicking hard and wet over her.

All thought of being silent and discreet fled her mind. She raised her hips, astonished at herself, at Max, at the brazen, reckless way they were both behaving. He might be used to it, but she was not, and yet it was her own voice, whispering frantic encouragement as he drove his fingers inside her and his mouth suckled, deep and hard pulls that made her shake.

He flung back his cloak and raised his head. His mouth gleamed in the moonlight. "Come for me," he said gutturally, gripping the small of her back while his fingers thrust deep inside her and his thumb teased her beyond all bearing.

She bit her lips to keep from screaming. Tears sprang into her eyes. With both hands she squeezed his wrist until her fingers went numb, and then she came.

She knew what it was; Marslip wasn't devoid of naughty books, and she had plenty of married cousins. In smug whispers and blushing detail, they had told her and Cathy what to expect in the marriage bed. None of them had adequately described this ecstasy, though, this otherworldly lightness and moment of joy so sharp and wild, she thought she might cry or burst into hysterical laughter.

When her shudders subsided, she sagged against him, trying to catch her breath. Max pressed his lips to her forehead, smoothing down her petticoats and skirt. He held her easily, until she had recovered enough to sit upright again.

"That was the most glorious sight I have ever seen in Vauxhall, or anywhere else," he said in that low, intimate growl that always sent shivers through her.

Bianca blushed. She might be blushing all over, given that she felt like she was glowing. "Thank you," she said shyly.

In reply he drew her close, his arms around her. She snuggled against him for a moment, until she realized he was trembling. "Max," she whispered.

"Yes, darling?"

"You didn't . . ." She blushed harder. "You didn't come, did you?"

His laugh was wheezy. "You can tell, can you?"

She sat up, nervous but determined. "Is it as wonderful for a man?"

He just smiled, tight and fierce. Of course it was.

"I want to please you," she said. "It's only fair."

He jerked backward, almost falling over. "*No*. Not here. I'll make love to you in a bed, properly, not up against a tree—" He stopped, his face frozen.

So he'd done it up against a tree, probably here in Vauxhall, perhaps with one of those women they'd met earlier. Bianca pushed aside the spike of jealousy; that was all in the past. She focused on the pertinent issue, namely that he had pleasured her and she wanted to do the same for him. Fair was fair, of course, but she also felt a driving desire to see how he felt under her hands. She *wanted* to touch him. "There must be some way . . ."

He swallowed. His eyes closed. "Well—yes . . . there is . . ." Slowly he unbuttoned his waistcoat and pulled it apart. He opened his eyes and looked right at her as he sat back on his heels and reached for the fall of his breeches.

She moved to the edge of the bench. "Should I—?"

"No," he growled. "You . . . watch. If you touch me, I'll perish on the spot." He peeled aside the front of his breeches, staring at her as if in a trance, and untied his drawers.

Bianca leaned forward to see better as he took himself in hand. Lady Dalway had taken her to an art gallery, where she and Lady Carswell had openly admired the naked figures in the paintings and sculpture. Bianca had studied them more analytically, having never seen a man completely unclothed before. And Max . . .

. . . was not what she had seen in the gallery. His erection was longer, broader, rising rigidly from his groin. He sank back, knees spread wide, and wrapped his fist around himself, boldly displaying himself to her. Slowly he slid his fist down, then released and pushed into his hand from the top.

"My fingers are still wet from you," he said in a low voice. "From your pleasure." Another stroke of his fist.

"Is that why . . . I was wet?" She ought to be fainting of embarrassment to be discussing this, but she couldn't take her eyes off his hand as he raised it for another stroke.

"Yes." His voice broke, and his knuckles whitened. "To make it easier when our bodies become one. To make it exquisitely satisfying for both of us."

She imagined his straining erection sliding into her instead of between his fingers. She felt hot and flustered all over again. "It's much larger than your fingers . . ."

"And how much pleasure did they bring you?" He let out his breath in a hiss at the end of the next stroke.

More than she'd imagined. She watched his strokes grow rough, his grip tighter. "Max," she whispered urgently, "I want to touch you. Please."

He inhaled sharply, and bowed his head. His fingers went still, squeezing his shaft, and liquid spurted over his hand. He threw back his head, his face taut, and let out his breath in another long shuddering sigh.

"Next time," he said in a ragged voice, to the sky. "Next time you shall touch me as much as you desire."

Next time. Of course there would be a next time. And it wouldn't be on a bench in the public garden, no matter how alone they were or how dark it was. Bianca was done fighting. She only nodded in agreement, and offered him her handkerchief.

He buttoned himself back up and helped her straighten her skirts. With touching devotion, he smoothed down her hair where she couldn't see it, and assured her the headdress was on properly. Then he offered her his arm and escorted her back to the illuminated grove, as courtly and proper as ever, as if nothing exceptional had happened.

But it had. It had shaken her world.

Tonight she had seen him, heard him, felt him. In London they had both come out from behind their fortifications—dropped their masks, quite literally—and it gave her a great burst of hope for the future. They could have a good marriage, cordial, cooperative . . . pleasurable. *Deeply* pleasurable. It wasn't love, but it was far better than the cool standoff they'd had to date.

And for the first time, the thought sent a rush of happiness through her.

Chapter Twenty-Three

The night at Vauxhall, unfortunately, turned out to be the pinnacle of their London visit.

Max had lain awake the rest of the night, letting each exquisite moment play again and again in his mind. He'd known that day in the sacristy that Bianca, unlike her sister, had the potential to bewitch and enthrall him, and now she'd done it. If God had seen fit to smite him in his sleep that night, Max thought he would have died a happy man, with his last vision that of Bianca on the bench, her head thrown back in abandon, her skirts around her waist, her pale shapely legs spread wide for him.

That, he thought, was enough for one night. Gambling had taught him never to stretch his run of luck to the breaking point. Better to retire early and secure his winnings than to keep playing, become reckless and risk what he'd won. So he took his wife home, kissed her tenderly, and bade her good night. The lingering, curious look she gave him tempted him to finish what they'd started, and take her to his bed, but he reined it in. He was going to do this the right way, so that when she finally came to him, she would be utterly, completely his.

If he'd known what was to happen in the next

few days, he might not have been so sanguine about that delay.

A letter was waiting for him when he returned home two days later. Lawrence pursued him up the stairs and closed the bedchamber door before handing it over.

Until that moment, Max had been in uncommonly good spirits. He had several more potential orders, thanks in part to Serafina's raving praise of the scarlet dishes, and thanks in part to his diligent schedule of calls. He'd visited every last friend and acquaintance he had in London—everyone who could afford a service from Perusia, anyway. On each call he brought a velvet-lined box with a select few pieces, and left a printed, hand-colored trade card in his wake. An old mate of his was a struggling artist and had been happy to take on the lowly commission, which resulted in Max possessing trade cards far above the usual in artistic quality.

If there was one thing Max had learned in his lean and impoverished years, it was that people with money wanted everyone to know they had money. Rare was the miser who squirreled away his wealth and lived modestly; far more likely were people who lived a life they thought reflected their status.

As he had expected, people wanted Perusia scarlet dinnerware.

So he arrived home freshly buoyed by a request from the Duke of Wimbourne to wait upon him with samples the following day, eager to tell Bianca about it at dinner. They were returning to Marslip soon, and an order from Wimbourne would be the crowning achievement.

And then Lawrence ruined it all. "Here, sir," said the man, holding out the thin letter.

In the blink of an eye, Max's mood plummeted. He stared at it for a long moment. "When did it arrive?"

"This morning, not long after you left."

Max nodded. He'd put Lawrence on guard for this very reason, but he had hoped against all hope that it wouldn't be necessary. "Did Mrs. St. James see it?"

"No, sir. I intercepted it while she was still in her closet, writing letters."

He inhaled and exhaled slowly, grateful for that much. Finally he took the letter. "Who delivered it?"

Lawrence shook his head. "Didn't see. Martha might know, but I didn't know if you wanted me to question her, draw any attention to it."

Damn it. He didn't know, either. "Quite right," he told the valet. "Thank you."

Lawrence grinned in surprise. "Welcome you are, sir. Lord Percival never said thank you to me."

Max managed a half-hearted smile. "I hope to inveigle you into staying with me, even when he recovers from his disgrace."

The man winked, and then bowed. "Doing well so far, Mr. St. James." He left, closing the door behind him.

Max's smile faded before the latch had caught. The letter in his hand almost seemed to buzz with ominous intent, as if it might be written in poisonous ink that would infect him just by touching it.

There was no other possibility, not coming this close on the heels of the previous letter, not while he was in London, uncomfortably close to the viper's nest.

Gingerly he broke the seal and unfolded it.

It was as usual. The viper wanted money, and he tried to extract it with stinging lashes of guilt, shame, and fear. There was no implicit threat, but it was there all the same. Max would have simply burned it, as he'd done the last, but for the last paragraph.

> *Best regards to your bride. Such a lovely lady, in her royal garb at Vauxhall. Does she know you, Maxim? You look enamored of her, my boy. No doubt she would be very astonished to hear your secrets . . . I know you haven't told her all about yourself . . .*

Curse you, Max thought in violent fury. His fingers gripped the page so hard they cramped. He longed to tear the letter into shreds, to soak them in oil and set them on fire, and hope that the blaze consumed the soul of the man who wrote it.

He breathed deeply, forcing his mind to cool. It bore no postmark; the letter had been hand delivered, which meant it had come from London. Did that mean the author had returned to town, or had he sent it to one of his spies in London? He had always had a coven of shady characters willing to abet him.

And one of them had seen Bianca with him in Vauxhall.

With a sudden oath he strode across the room

and flung open the door. He called for Lawrence as he rushed down the stairs, taking his hat and cloak at the door from Martha, who came running at his shout.

Lawrence all but fell down the stairs in his haste. "Yes, sir?"

"I must go out," said Max, mindful of Martha at the rear of the hall. "Urgently." He jerked his head as he flung his cloak around his shoulders.

Obediently Lawrence followed. This time, as he stepped outside, Max scanned the street swiftly. Everything looked as it should be, but it had been a long time since he'd laid eyes on his nemesis.

"When is Mrs. St. James expected home?" he asked the valet.

"I'm not sure, sir. Well before dinner."

Max looked at him.

"Around four o'clock, I would suppose," said the servant hastily. "That's when she usually returns."

Max nodded once. "She's gone to the shop in Cheapside? Or did she have plans with Lady Dalway?"

"The shop, sir."

Damn. He wouldn't have worried as much if she were sitting in some elegant drawing room or millinery shop with Serafina and other ladies. Max nodded again. "I want you to go there and escort her home. Not until she's ready, but make certain she arrives home safely."

"Won't Mr. Cooke be there, sir?"

Max didn't trust his wife's safety to any letting agent. Cooke wanted to lease her a shop, nothing more. "I don't give a bloody damn if Cooke is there. Go, and see that she returns home without trouble."

He had hired Lawrence because the man was available, let go by Percy Willoughby without much warning. The man had a sharp eye for fashion, didn't shirk his duties, and knew when to keep his mouth closed, all of which were essential in a manservant. But Lawrence had three other attributes Max prized: he was intelligent, he was observant, and he had a fondness for boxing. Max had seen him lay out men bigger and broader than himself with one punch.

Max had learned the hard way how beneficial it could be to have a strong, loyal fellow at his back.

"I have some urgent business to attend to," he went on. "If I can, I'll go to Cheapside myself and bring madam home. But if not, I want you there."

Lawrence nodded. "Yes, sir. I'll go now."

Max dug a few shillings out of his purse. "Find a hackney."

"Sir . . . What shall I tell her? She'll be astonished to see me."

Max hesitated. He didn't want to alarm Bianca, not until he could explain things to her himself. "Blame it on my eagerness to see her," he said reluctantly. He didn't like to lie to his wife. "Explain that she may finish her business there, but I desire her to come home as soon as she may."

Lawrence nodded and darted back into the house for his cap and coat. Max strode off, south, toward the river, too tightly wound to ride or take a carriage.

He found his man in Whitehall, near the Privy Gardens. William Leake was lounging against a lamppost, looking dissolute and drunk. At the sight of Max, he unfolded himself from his slump and ambled off toward the nearest tavern, where they met at a back table.

"Any word?" asked Max without preamble.

Leake shook his head. "Not yet. 'Tis a sensitive question, you understand."

Max sighed. He knew that, all too well. "I want you to find someone else now."

"All right," said Leake without hesitation. "Another lady? Or are we done looking for her?"

Max hated to take Leake off that task. The man had made little progress, even though it had been a few months. Max had engaged him with the windfall from the Duchess of Carlyle, and had hoped Leake would succeed by now. "No, not done. I'm never done until I find her. But now I need to know the whereabouts of a man."

"Gentleman?" Leake rested his elbows on the table, his gaze moving restlessly about the tavern.

"Not in any true sense of the word," muttered Max. "But I suppose he thinks of himself as such. He certainly prefers to live like one."

"Don't we all, mate." Leake grinned. "What's he done?" Max glared and Leake shrugged. "Just curious. What's his name?"

"I have reason to believe he might be in London," said Max, ignoring the question. "He is originally from Bristol, and recently resided in Reading."

"What makes you think he's in London?"

"I received a letter from him today, delivered by messenger. He spoke of things only someone in London could have witnessed. It might have been someone else who reported back to him, but the timing makes it unlikely. If he's not in London, he's near."

"What's his name?" asked Leake again.

The very taste of it was foul in his mouth. "Silas Croach."

Leake paused, his roving gaze arrested.

Grimly Max nodded. "It's her husband."

BIANCA WASN'T SURE when it happened, but she had grown rather enamored of Max's idea to create a new brand of dinnerware.

"What do you think of the name Fortuna ware?" she asked Jennie. They had gone back to view the shop in Cheapside. It gave Bianca a happy feeling just to walk inside it. She admitted Max was probably right about the showroom, now that she'd met several London ladies and seen their homes. But this quaint shop appealed to her a great deal, too, and she found herself wanting to agree to the lease and rush back to Marslip to begin designing the new, simpler wares.

And perhaps some porcelain as well, despite how her father scoffed at it. Max's boundless confidence was a heady thing.

"Fortuna ware? What's that?" Jennie was opening cupboard doors and inspecting the drawers. Bianca had asked her to look over the shop with a critical working woman's eye. "It sounds lovely."

"Yes, doesn't it?" Bianca stretched her arms in the cozy window embrasure, mentally arranging pieces on a table in her mind. She thought they ought to start with a simple green glaze, since everyone at Perusia was accustomed to that. She imagined a clean white tablecloth with the pale green dishes and candlesticks, painted yellow. A soup tureen was always impressive; yellow as well, she thought, to match the candlesticks. "It might be the name of this shop. Fortuna by Tate and Sons."

"Selling what?" Jennie came to join her.

"Any kind of household pottery. Dinnerware, butter crocks, rouge pots. Not as fine as Perusia, though still quality."

The maid's eyes rounded. "New pottery! At the factory?"

Bianca didn't actually know where Max intended to produce his new wares. He wanted to employ some of their current potters, though, and presumably glazers and painters as well. It would have to be near Marslip if he wanted to use them. "Somewhere," she said vaguely. "We're still refining the plan."

"Oh. Well, I'm sure it'll come out well, if you and Mr. St. James are in command." The girl nodded confidently at Bianca's startled look. "Aye, between the two of you, not even Mr. Tate would be able to oppose it!"

"Between the two of us," echoed Bianca slowly. "What do you mean by that?"

Jennie blinked. "O-only that Mr. St. James is a clever one, ma'am, and a right smooth talker. Thérèse, Mrs. Farquhar's maid, said he could lead an army if he put his mind to it. She used to know him before, I reckon."

Bianca's lips parted in astonishment. "What did she say about him?"

"All admiring!" cried Jennie hastily, sensing she'd spoken too freely. "She said Mrs. Farquhar thought him the most charming and daring fellow she knew, and spoke often of him."

Bianca's mouth flattened. That sounded innocent

enough, but she'd sensed Clara admired Max a little too much at times. "What else?"

"That Mrs. Farquhar thinks you're a very fortunate woman, to have him for your husband." Jennie blushed bright pink. "Even Thérèse thinks he's extremely handsome."

"Well." Bianca cleared her throat. Her maid ought not to have gossiped so much, but she was at fault, too, for asking. "He is, obviously. Neither Thérèse nor Mrs. Farquhar is blind."

Jennie gave a wide grin of relief. "No, ma'am!"

During this conversation Bianca had been staring out the window. Jennie's revelations had distracted her, but now she realized she'd been looking at a man standing opposite the shop. And—she gave a start—he was looking back at her.

He was tall and lean, his shoulders a bit hunched, making her think he was an older man. His clothes were ordinary, sober colors with no lace, and his hat was tipped very rakishly, shadowing his face. But he was just standing there, leaning on a silver-topped walking stick, looking right at her.

"Jennie," said Bianca, "do you recognize that man across the street?"

Jennie glanced up. "No, ma'am. Who is he?"

"I don't know," she said thoughtfully. The fellow hadn't moved.

The bell over the door jangled, and Bianca stepped back from the window to see who it was.

Lawrence, Max's valet, stood there, hat in his hands. He bowed. "Ma'am."

"Is aught wrong at home?" she asked in surprise. He shook his head, although with a trace of a shamefaced grin. "Not at all, ma'am. Mr. St. James sent me to make sure all was well with you, and to bid you come straight home when you are done here. I—er—believe he's eager to share some news with you."

"Oh?" She couldn't stop the instinctive smile. "What sort of news?"

"I don't know, ma'am," said the valet, "but he was smiling when he sent me."

Jennie giggled quietly, and Bianca's smile widened. She knew Max had called at the Duke of Wimbourne's house that morning, in hopes of seeing Perusia wares grace a ducal table. It would delight Papa to no end, and be a crowning glory to their London visit.

"Very well," she said. "I'm almost done here." She turned around to resume measuring the shelves, and caught sight of the man across the street again. And this time she would swear he tipped his hat at her, before turning and strolling off into the crowd.

"Lawrence," she said on impulse, "do you know that man? In the brown coat."

With a sudden movement the valet darted to the window, pressing his hands against the panes. He peered out intently. "No, ma'am," he said, almost disappointed.

"Ah. He seemed interested in this shop."

Lawrence's hands fell to his sides. "Perhaps he also considered a lease on it, madam."

She laughed in surprise. She ought to have thought of that. "Of course! No doubt. I fear he's to be disappointed. Now, let me finish these measurements and we can go—Jennie, where did you put my measuring tape and notebook?"

But when she glanced at the window again, Lawrence was still staring intently into the street, his arms folded and legs apart. He looked unexpectedly imposing.

How curious.

Chapter Twenty-Four

The next day Max persuaded Bianca to come with him to meet the Duke of Wimbourne. "So you can assure your father I've not been wasting our time in London," he told her.

She wrinkled her nose at him and laughed. "Lord Dalway's order alone would persuade him of that, and you've got several more in hand!"

"Yes," he replied, "but he will want your report as well, that I managed to conduct business without bringing shame upon Perusia."

She gave him an arch look. "You must know my opinion of your efforts."

"Why, I've never heard you express anything at all on that matter." He leaned closer, resting his elbow on the breakfast table and smiling wickedly at her. "What *is* your opinion of me?"

She continued buttering her toast, but her lips curved teasingly. "Cleverer than I first thought, but perhaps not as clever as you think yourself." She slanted a sparkling look at him as she took a tiny bite.

Max laughed. "No man is as clever as he thinks himself. Go on."

"More sensible and pragmatic than I expected,"

she allowed, "particularly given how you dressed when we met."

He bowed his head in acknowledgement. "Thank you."

Her cheeks turned pink. "Too handsome by half."

He leaned even more forward. That beauty mark on her breast was just visible if he tilted his head to the right, and he did so. "How so, madam? Pray tell me more."

"I will not. Saying that much has probably inflated your vanity to monstrous proportions."

He smiled again. "Hearing such praise has indeed swelled my . . . vanity. I cannot swear to 'monstrous proportions,' of course, but it is quite large enough . . ." *God*. Bantering with her like this, hearing her call him handsome and clever and even sensible—possibly the highest praise she could give—had made him hard, just sitting at the breakfast table.

Peering at that beauty mark may have also played a part. He dreamed of kissing that mark again, as he'd done in Vauxhall.

Her lips parted as she took his meaning, and her blush became scarlet. "And you're much too wicked," she replied, but her voice had gone husky, the way it did every time he kissed her and touched her.

"My darling," whispered Max with a meaningful look, "you have no idea how wicked I can be." He gave her a slow smile as her bosom heaved. "I look forward to showing you, though."

The door opened and Martha came in with the ironed newspapers. Bianca's knife clattered on her plate and she jerked backward in her chair as Max resumed his normal posture. "Here they are, sir," said the maid, laying the pages on the table. Martha was a fine London maid, never letting on that she saw anything.

"Come with me to Wimbourne House," said Max, while Bianca was still flustered. He did want her to accompany him for all the reasons he'd listed, but also to keep her close. There had been no word from Leake, and Max had told him to send it immediately, no matter the time of day or night, if he discovered Croach. As long as that viper was out there, Max felt tense and edgy, though he was determined to hide it from his wife.

Lawrence had reported that a man had been staring at the shop in Cheapside yesterday while Bianca was there; she had seen him, but Lawrence had not got a good look at him. It only fueled Max's suspicions that Croach himself was in London.

To what end, he did not know. And that made him all the more anxious to leave.

"Well . . ." Bianca cleared her throat as Martha refilled her chocolate cup and withdrew with the empty silver pot. "All right. If you wish."

He caught her hand and kissed it. "I do wish. Most passionately."

She blushed again, but he breathed easier. Whatever malignant intentions Croach had, he wouldn't touch Bianca.

BIANCA EXPECTED A duke's home to dazzle and amaze her, and Wimbourne House did not disappoint.

It was by far the largest home she had ever seen, set close to the river. Max told her it had a large garden in the rear, with its own stairs to a landing on the Thames. She tried hard not to marvel as they were admitted and shown into a small parlor of such beauty, she could hardly believe it, and she whispered as much to Max.

"Wait until you see the rest of the house," was his reply.

And he was right. She could barely keep from gaping in awe at the artwork, the graceful furnishings upholstered in silk, the plush carpets. The floors were marble, and the chimneypiece was the most ornate sculpture she had ever seen. Only when she caught sight of herself in a tall, golden-framed mirror did she realize how wide her eyes were.

The duke himself came in, rubbing his hands together. "St. James! Of all the people."

"My Lord Duke." Max bowed reverently low. Bianca followed, dipping into a curtsy until her knee almost touched the floor.

The duke laughed and cuffed Max in the shoulder, grinning. He was about Max's age, to Bianca's surprise, and had a mischievous air. He was tall and lanky, with a face that was amiable rather than handsome. His clothes, though incomparable in quality, flapped around him as though they'd been made for someone else. "Present your lady to me."

Max drew her forward. "My wife, Mrs. St. James, Your Grace."

"Indeed." Wimbourne eyed her warmly. "Pleased to make your acquaintance, madam."

"Thank you, sir," she replied. "It is my great delight to make yours."

Wimbourne raised his brows at Max. "Well!" He paced to the sofa and flung himself on it. "Let's see this chinaware that nearly made Lady Dalway weep." And Max had Lawrence bring forward the velvet-lined chest he had built to carry around his sample of Perusia wares.

Now Bianca understood his desire for velvet boxes. In this room beautiful enough for angels to occupy, Papa's finest wares emerged from the ivory velvet trays like rare jewels being unveiled for the first time—like something an angel might dine from. The scarlet glaze on the egg cups blazed like liquid rubies against the pale fabric. Max lifted out the gravy boat as if he were presenting a holy relic, its gilded rim glowing in the sunlight. Plate after plate, bowl after bowl, Max laid down a full setting for two on the polished table nearby, complete with teapot and cups on saucers with fluted rims, finishing it off with a delicate compotier, shaped like a bell flower and supported by three nymphs, garlanded with flowers and ivy.

It was the replacement for the one Bianca had thrown at her father, all those weeks ago when he'd been arguing that Cathy ought to marry Max. Bianca said a silent apology to that destroyed compotier, and to Mr. Murdoch, the modeler who had made it, but she also thought this new one surpassed the previous in every way. If she hadn't smashed his first try, he might not have been pushed to create this one.

The duke was struck by it, too. He picked it up and examined it from all sides. "Marvelous," he murmured.

Max smiled faintly. "I thought you might like it."

"You would," said the duke with a twitch of his mouth. "Well! Of course I'll have some. Can't have

Dalway's table finer than mine. Why was he given precedence, I'd like to know?"

"You were away from town," said Max. "I left my card, and called as soon as you sent for me."

Holding one of the egg cups up to the light, the duke scoffed. "Next time, I want to know first. God above! This glaze has a shine like nothing I've ever seen!"

"It *is* like nothing you've ever seen," Max told him. "Mrs. St. James only completed her formulation of that scarlet glaze a few weeks ago. You're holding one of the first examples of it, and if you were to order a set of it, you would be the first to lay your table with it."

Wimbourne lowered the cup and looked at Bianca. Her heart lodged in her throat at his astonished regard. "You created this, madam? *You?*"

"Yes, Your Grace," she said.

Wimbourne looked at the cup again, then at Max, who still wore a vaguely self-satisfied smile. "You clever scoundrel," he muttered. "I'll be damned! Simply incredible."

"How many settings, Your Grace?" asked Max smoothly. "If I might say so, the larger orders will be given precedence in the factory."

Wimbourne snorted. "Trying to extort me to order more, are you? How many settings for Dalway?"

"Twenty."

"I'll have thirty, and a dessert service, too." He snatched up the egg cup again. "*You*, Mrs. St. James? You formulated this color?"

"Yes, sir," she repeated. "I formulated most of the glazes for Perusia."

The duke gave her a long look. "I always knew you were a sly one, St. James."

Max began replacing the dishes in the chest. "As you say, Your Grace."

"In ten years, I've never known you to place a losing bet." The duke shook his head. "Incredible. And now I hear rumors Carlyle is ill."

Max paused. "Is he?"

"Yes, more ill than usual." Wimbourne eyed him closely. "You're his heir, are you not?"

"Second," said Max. He cleared his throat and closed the lid of the chest, motioning for the waiting Lawrence to take it away. "Captain St. James, my cousin, is heir presumptive."

"Right, right." The duke tapped a quick tattoo on his knees with both hands. "Still, one never knows. An army fellow, isn't he? In Scotland? Dangerous country, Scotland."

"Yes."

"Imagine a Scottish army captain becoming duke! Wouldn't that set London on its ear?"

"Stranger things have happened, I've no doubt."

Bianca watched the conversation with interest. Max had never said a word about the Duke of Carlyle, beyond whispering his family connection in her father's ear. At first she had assumed it would make him arrogant, and then she had suspected he didn't mention it to avoid provoking her. And now she had the distinct thought that Max did not want to discuss it at all.

Which was . . . odd, for someone who had used it so blatantly.

"Stranger, yes," said the duke thoughtfully. "Not

as odd as the Durham case, I grant you. The heir was practically a shopkeeper!"

"He seems to have pulled it around rather admirably. As I expect the captain to do, when His Grace finally departs this mortal vale."

"No doubt," agreed the duke amiably, rising. "Ah—I almost forgot to inquire after Mrs. Bradford! I hope she's well."

Max had already got to his feet, ready to leave. At the name, he stiffened with a jerk. "Yes." He bowed. "Thank you for seeing us, Your Grace."

"Excellent. Give her my best regards." Beaming, the duke bounced on his feet, offering Bianca his hand. "My thanks for bringing your lovely wife and those incredible dishes. Did you *really* create that glaze, madam? It's perfection."

"It is," said Max, his voice clipped. "Good day, Wimbourne."

"And to you," replied the duke, amused. He bowed to Bianca. "Good day, Mrs. St. James."

Bianca almost had to run to keep up with Max's strides. By the time they reached the carriage, she was out of breath. "What happened?" she managed to ask, fanning herself.

"Wimbourne ordered thirty settings of Perusia ware." Max slammed the carriage door behind himself and rapped on the roof to start. "A triumph for your work, my love. He has a discerning eye."

"Yes, but—" She gazed at him in bewilderment. He was facing straight ahead, his expression calm but somehow forbidding. "Who is Mrs. Bradford?"

Max was as still as stone. "My aunt."

Bianca's eyes widened. His aunt who took him in after his mother's death. Bianca had assumed the aunt had also passed away, but apparently that was not the case. "Why did His Grace ask about her?"

"She came to visit me in Oxford a few times, and once Wimbourne met her at the theater." There was something oddly mechanical about his words. "Wimbourne never forgets a woman. He'll be asking about you until his dying day."

"But . . ." She tried to restrain her curiosity and her dismay, that he'd offered to tell her anything about himself at Vauxhall, and yet barely mentioned his aunt. "Are you estranged from her?" she finally burst out in unbearable curiosity.

"I've not seen her in a long time," he said after a moment.

And Bianca suddenly understood. He'd been a rake and a gambler. His aunt, who had tried to get him a start in a respectable profession, must have been deeply disappointed by that.

That softened her temper, and revived her sympathy. He'd lost his mother, his grandfather, and then his aunt had turned against him. She put her hand on his. "I'm sorry Wimbourne asked about her."

His fingers convulsed around hers. "He's got no tact at all. I'm surprised he didn't ask something worse, like if we'd care to join him and his latest mistress at the opera."

Bianca smiled, squeezing his hand. Max smiled, too, a trifle ruefully. "I would have said yes," she confided. "I've never seen an opera."

"Ah." His thumb rubbed her knuckles as he smiled at her, looking more like his usual self. "I can remedy that, and without having to endure Wimbourne's ceaseless prattle."

She laughed, and he grinned back. When she made a point of resting her head on his shoulder, she felt the tension melt out of him. And as they drove back to the house in Farley Street, she made a silent promise to her husband that she would never be so faithless or disloyal, as his family had been. Tates were made of sterner stuff. Together, they would build a new family, and find happiness there.

Chapter Twenty-Five

Their London trip was over. Bianca had already written to her father that the visit had been a great success. They had taken a number of orders from prominent people, which would please Papa immensely. Both the showroom near Bond Street and the little shop in Cheapside had been let, and builders engaged to refurbish both. Max had even got Bartholomew Markham to settle his bill, and delivered the dinnerware they had borrowed for the party. Despite all that, though, Bianca could not deny that she was glad to be going home.

She wondered more than ever about her husband and his history, but at the same time she knew she had misjudged him in the past, and that now she owed him some patience. After what he had related about his family, she sensed it was not a happy story, and it would be unfair for her to pry into it and make him tell her.

For his part, Max wished intensely that Wimbourne had kept his damned mouth shut. It had made Bianca look at him with pity and concern, which he didn't deserve. It was still better than the alternative, the look of horror and revulsion he feared she would give him if she knew the truth, so he said nothing, even though it felt like a lie.

Damn it. He hadn't wanted Bianca to know anything about his aunt, not yet—perhaps not ever. Half of him still argued for winning her heart first and then telling her all. Half of him wanted to take every word to his grave; it was an ugly story, and as things stood now there was no reason Bianca needed to know.

He had heard nothing more of Croach, nor had Leake found any sign of him. If the man was in London, he was lying lower than usual. When their coach rumbled out of London, north toward Staffordshire, Max breathed a silent sigh of relief. The notes he could ignore, and there was every chance the man outside the shop in Cheapside had been someone else entirely.

They reached Stoke on Trent and found the quaint little market town transformed. Large tents ringed the green, and nearby shops had thrown up awnings and set out tables. Pens of livestock were visible beyond the tents, and crowds thronged the streets, spilling from taverns and dancing to the tune of some fiddlers and cheering at an exhibition boxing match on the green.

"Oh my," gasped Bianca in surprise, throwing up the window shade and leaning out. "I forgot about Stoke wakes!"

"Wakes?" Max moved to the opposite seat, to see better.

"A country fair," she explained. "I suppose it used to be a saint's day but now it's nothing to do with the church. Oh, Papa must be beside himself!"

"Why?" Max gazed out with interest. He'd been

to a country fair only once, the year they lived with his grandfather. Old Maxim had gone for the ale tent, and Max's mother had taken him to see the races and bought him hot cross buns from a man with a cart. She had denied him watching the cock fighting, but paid sixpence for a hoop for him to race with the other children.

At his question, Bianca sighed. "All the workmen will be here and not at the factory. There is nothing Papa can say to deter them. He offered extra wages to anyone who worked, or more days free at Christmas, all to no avail. And we've brought so many new orders, too."

"How long do the wakes last?"

"At least a week. After a few days, when everyone will have spent their money, some will come back to work." She made a face. "Some will stay until they've drunk it all away, and will be useless for work for some time." She shook her finger at him. "And it shall hurt your Fortuna ware, you know. Every man you might have taken on for it will be drunk and indolent for at least a fortnight."

Max laughed. "Everyone deserves a spot of fun." He looked at her mischievously. "Let's stay a bit."

She blinked. "What? Before going home?"

"It's early still," he countered. "Send the carriage and servants on to Marslip. We can hire a gig." It was only five miles to Marslip, and on a fine summer day, they could walk if necessary.

Her lips parted, and then she slowly smiled. "All right. Let's!"

They stopped at the inn, to change clothes and freshen up. Max told Lawrence to send back the gig after he got everything else to Marslip, and gave him and Jennie permission to return to the fair. From the man's wide grin, Max thought Percy Willoughby would never get back his valet.

Although he had savored the sight of Bianca in her London finery—particularly that black gown she'd worn to Vauxhall—Max thought he'd never seen her look better than when she came down to the tap room, wearing one of her old day dresses with her hair tucked up under a cap and broad straw hat. She was just as beautiful as ever in faded linen.

At the sight of him, she smiled broadly—and his heart felt strangely light in his chest. He realized he was smiling back at her when she stopped in front of him.

"I hardly recognized you, out of your velvet coats," she teased.

He grinned. He'd also put on an older suit of wool and linen. If the Stoke wakes were anything like the Lincolnshire fair, it was not a place for fine clothing. "And now I look a dreadful fright to you?"

She blushed. "No!"

He leaned closer as he led her out the door, back into the bustling street. "I very much hope not. You, Mrs. St. James, look perfectly splendid to me."

They strolled through the town. He bought meat pies from a peddler, ale from the tavern, and they wandered through the tents set up on the green with all sorts of things. They laughed at a man with a monkey, nibbling their pies, and placed penny bets on a horse race, which they both lost.

Bianca was stopped every few feet by someone from the factory, and she introduced Max easily and warmly. *My husband*, she said, over and over, with a smile and sometimes a fond glance at him. Her hand was on his arm, and when the monkey leapt at her, she pressed closer to him and laughed. Max's heart was weightless, suffused with light and something he hesitated to name.

And then they came upon the cricket pitch.

A group of people were milling around the open ground before the woods, some with bats in hand. Three men were laying a rope for the boundary while others set the wickets. There was an air of anticipation, and one person was collecting wagers.

Bianca stopped in her tracks. "They're still forming sides," she said, waving one arm in the air. "Amelia!"

One of the young women looked up, and came running over. "You're back! And just in time, too. We need good bowlers. Gemma can't play this year." She waved one hand at another woman, who held a baby in her arms.

Bianca laughed and began tucking up her skirts. "I'm lamentably out of practice."

"We'll be forced to rely on Anne if you don't play," retorted her friend.

"You're going to play?" Max asked in astonishment. He had heard of an all-female game of cricket, several years ago at Hambledon, but never women playing with men.

Bianca took off her hat and handed it to him. "Of course! We go against the Mannox potteries every year."

"Those are Mannox men?"

"And women," put in Bianca. "Mostly Mannox workers, although they always get Tall Bob the bargeman to join them."

"Tom Mannox is playing," added her friend. "He asked about you, Bianca."

Bianca rolled her eyes, and Max paused. "Why?"

"He fancied her," said Amelia with a giggle. "And only partly for her bowling."

"Amelia," said Bianca in exasperation.

"Right! Are you a better batsman or bowler, sir?"

Max began to smile. "Batsman."

"Oh my, George will be delighted by that!" The woman, Amelia, clapped her hands together and ran back to the group, calling out that Miss Tate—she swiftly corrected herself, to Max's private pleasure— and Mr. St. James would play as well. The pace of wagering grew considerably brisker.

"Are you any good?" Bianca asked directly. She had pulled up her skirts into her pockets, and re-tied her fichu, winding the long ends around her back. It outlined her figure beautifully.

"Tolerably." Max shed his coat and waistcoat, dropping his hat atop them.

She didn't look satisfied. "I want to win, you know. If you're only tolerable—"

He laughed and snatched her hand to his lips for a swift kiss, which seemed to shock her. "Trust me." He strode off toward the fellow with the bats, turning up his sleeves.

They had enough interested players to form a full eleven, and a coin toss relegated the Perusia players, under the captainship of George Tucker from the throwing house, to the field. There was a brief argument about the wickets, with some alleging they were too close together, but that was resolved and the first innings began. Gemma Tucker with the new baby settled down to keep score under the gaze of an interested crowd and the oversight of the umpires, namely the butcher and the head groom from the Two Foxes tavern.

Mick, one of the Perusia modelers, bowled the first over. He had a strong arm, but the Mannox batsman scored five before being bowled out. The second swung a good bat, and made a respectable fourteen before being retired.

Bianca, assigned to the end of the field near Max, darted up to him as the next man strode to the crease. "That's Tom Mannox," she reported breathlessly. "He has a strong bat."

"Has he?" Max smiled grimly, and settled in to watch the fellow. He did bat well, but when he'd made twelve already, he whacked the ball hard toward Max. Max fell back, eyes fixed on it. It was heading toward the boundary, which would be another six, unless he managed it—

He leapt at the last second, straining upward, and snatched the ball in his fingertips. Behind him he heard the roar of his teammates, including Bianca's whoop of delight. He lobbed the ball back to the bowler, and made a bow toward the applauding crowd as Mannox stormed off the pitch.

The next several batsmen came and went, and the score reached seventy-eight before disaster struck. Mick slipped on the flattened grass and went down hard on his throwing arm. The crowd behind Gemma erupted with cries of concern as he was taken off, and George Tucker grimly waved Bianca in.

Unbidden, Max went, too. "Can you bowl fast?" He didn't think it likely, or she would have been put in earlier.

Bianca pushed the hair from her face and gave him a severe look. "Fast enough, sir."

He backed off, hands up, grinning in delight. "Go to it, then."

She bowled respectably. Max, having never had the pleasure of playing cricket with ladies, found himself captivated by the sight of his wife running forward to fling the ball toward the wickets, as fierce as any bloke at Balliol. She wasn't the fastest bowler, but she was, as she had said, fast enough. She gave up two paltry singles in her over, and Max roared in appreciation as she yielded to the next bowler.

"Well done!" he said as she came back into the field. Flushed but smiling, she curtsied.

The Mannox side was eventually dismissed at one hundred and one runs. There was a short interlude, with fresh mugs of ale and buns from a cricket-enthusiast peddler, during which Tom Mannox sidled up to Bianca. Max, fetching ale, watched intently. He was a thick-set fellow, shorter than Max, with fair hair and a ruddy face. Bianca gave him a withering look and said something that made him turn red and stalk back to his side.

Max crossed the grass and handed her a mug. "Is Mannox unhappy about something?"

Bianca made a face and took a drink. "Every year he used to propose I marry him, because with my bowling and his batting we'd be sure to have a son who would be legendary on the pitch. All Tom cares about is cricket." She took another sip. "As if Papa would have even let him in the door! Mannox steals our workers and then tries to claim his wares are better than Perusia. I'd lock myself in a convent before wedding Tom Mannox."

"Ah." Max savored his own ale, watching the Mannox side. A few big fellows, and one tall, raw-boned chap whom Max felt was the real threat. "Is Mannox a strong bowler?"

Bianca set aside her mug. "No. He throws hard, but if you outlast him he throws wild. Tire him out, and he'll melt like butter."

The Perusia innings did not begin well. Mick, who had bowled so well, hooked one ball around his leg and scored a single, while the other players suffered from extreme bad luck in hitting the ball directly at men in the field. They had made a paltry forty-nine when Bianca took up her bat and went to the crease.

The bowler was a short, pugnacious fellow, though he did doff his cap when Bianca raised her bat. Then he charged forward and threw the ball at her feet. She tried to block it, but it ran up the edge of her bat and over her hands. The ball arced into the field, where it was very fortunately fumbled, but Bianca was clutching one hand in the other. Max stepped forward in concern, but the look on her face stopped him. Shaking and flexing her hand, she retrieved her fallen bat and faced up to the short fellow with fire in her eyes.

Never had Max found a cricket match so thrilling, not when he was a boy playing on the packed-dirt Marylebone fields, nor on the viciously competitive Oxford pitch. The fellow taking wagers circulated through the crowd, and Max—eyes fixed on his wife at the crease—laid fifty pounds on the Perusia side. Down by fifty-two with only three batters left, the odds were long.

The next ball Bianca sent to the boundary for four. She added a single a few balls later, only to see Amelia, who had preceded her at the crease, called out by the butcher for stumbling into her wicket. She staggered off the field, head in her hands, as the Mannox side cheered and the Perusia side heaped imprecations on the butcher's head.

That brought Max to the wicket. He selected his bat carefully and took a few test swings. Bianca waited at the opposite wicket, poised to run. It sent a charge up his spine to see her so nakedly hungry to win, her eyes darting around the oval before fixing on him. He gave her a slow smile. She nodded once.

By God, I love that woman, he thought fiercely.

Then he settled in to win the game—for her.

Bianca had told him what he needed to know. Tom Mannox threw hard, but like most hard throwers, his aim degenerated over time. By now, Max expected him to throw wide, and he did. With almost brutal ease, he blocked the first few balls before Mannox buckled down and threw hard and straight. Max dug in and stroked it well over the boundary for six. The next ball he hit for four, and then another six to finish the over.

Mannox retired, glowering. The tall lanky fellow came in. Max blocked his first three balls, waiting for the one he could loft. Unfortunately his eye caught on Bianca, hovering at the opposite wicket, and so he just missed the ball, lobbing it weakly over the wicket-keeper's head. After his last few swings, the fieldsmen had moved back to the boundary, and the ball hit the ground harmlessly in front of them.

"Run," Max roared, taking off for the other wicket, and Bianca sprinted past him. They barely made it, and now Bianca lifted her bat. She blocked several balls before ending with a three.

He jogged forward to meet her on the pitch as they traded places for the next over. "Splendid work, darling," he said in passing.

"Notch some runs!" she returned.

Max laughed and stepped to the crease. Mannox had the ball again, to Max's satisfaction. He bided his time, blocking the first few balls. Mannox, frustrated, threw directly at his feet. Max squared his shoulders and stepped into his swing, sending the ball hurtling over the boundary. The Perusia side erupted in screams.

Mannox tried again, throwing high this time, but Max wasn't about to have that. He twisted his bat and clubbed the ball deep and far, sending the fieldsman almost into the woods to retrieve it.

The bat was beginning to feel right in his hands. He could swing for hours like this.

Had Mannox not been the captain of the team, he would have been taken off, but he kept the ball, and this time he hurtled toward the wicket as if he meant to fling the ball into Max's face.

Max sent this one to the boundary as well, for four. The deficit had shrunk to eleven. "Why did you put him ninth?" Amelia was shrieking at George Tucker. "We've never had such a cricketer!"

Max passed Bianca again on the pitch. "Tolerable?" she said, brows raised.

He winked. "Not done yet, love."

After a hurried conference, Mannox sent a new fellow to bowl. Tall Bob the bargeman, Bianca had called him. His wrists stuck out of his sleeves, and he moved with a rolling stride that seemed aimless and slow.

The sight of those wrists, though, put Max in mind of Wimbourne. The duke had bowled enthusiastically at Oxford, and his long, loose limbs enabled him to put a twisting spin on the ball. Wimbourne's balls were liable to sink and hit the dirt, or sneak under the bat and take the wicket. Max had only figured out how to hit Wimbourne by watching the man's thumb.

And thanks be to God, Tall Bob bowled the same way. His thumb rolled over the top of the ball, sending it spinning down toward the ground—and the wicket. Max blocked two, watching carefully to learn the man's movement.

The next ball he lifted as one might launch a tennis ball, up, up, into the setting sun and over the boundary for another six. The Perusia side was making so much noise he could hardly hear Mannox screaming at his players in the field.

Tall Bob's next ball was thrown even harder. Max gripped the bat, and stepped into his swing with all his strength. He'd never hit a ball that hard in his life, but he'd got under it, sending it more up than out. Up it went, and out—Tom Mannox was racing backward, toward the boundary—Max held his breath and unconsciously waved one arm, urging the ball to fly a little farther—and the ball bounced off Mannox's outstretched hands to land on the grass outside the rope as Mannox himself sprawled face first into the grass.

The game was won.

Bianca bolted up the pitch, shrieking, "You did it!

You did it!" Max flipped aside his bat and caught her as she flung herself into his arms.

"*We* did it," he said roughly, and then he kissed her, hard, on the mouth, not caring that half of Marslip was watching, that the players streaming forward to celebrate were gasping in scandalized astonishment, or that Mannox and all his side were protesting loudly to the umpires that the last ball had not actually cleared the boundary.

Bianca was kissing him back. Hungrily, desperately, her fingers in his hair and her body straining against his.

By God, he *loved* her. He was mad for her. And tonight he was going to make love to her.

Chapter Twenty-Six

Bianca wasn't sure how they got home to Poplar House. The thrill of defeating Mannox—for the first time in four years—carried her in a blaze of elation through the celebration at the Two Foxes, through the triumphal procession back to Perusia Hall, even through her father coming out to hear the news and bringing out a barrel of ale and tapping it, no matter that he was contributing to the drinking that would idle his factory another day. Papa hated to lose at *anything* to Mannox. When Max gave him the small pottery vase that was the victor's right—which Tom Mannox had handed over very ungraciously at the Foxes—Papa lifted it above his head with a shout of victory, and the crowd of his workmen and neighbors roared back.

Then she and Max were stumbling home, arm in arm, a little bit tipsy and still reveling in the victory. The servants at Poplar House had heard the news as well, and they were waiting to give one last cheer. The stable lads wanted Max to relate every bowl and strike, and Bianca went inside to do the same for Jennie, who had gone home early to see her mother and was beside herself, in tears to have missed the match.

By the time she finished the tale, Jennie had brushed out her hair and helped her change into her nightdress. Bianca dismissed her but was too excited still to sleep. She paced her room restlessly, recalling in exquisite detail how Max had looked with his bat at the ready, how easily he'd sent that last ball for six, how he'd snatched her off her feet at the end and kissed her.

That was why her heart hadn't yet slowed down: the way he'd turned to her, his arms open and ready to catch her, the way he shared his triumph with her, the way he kissed her as if he didn't give a damn who saw.

When she finally heard his voice in the adjoining room, she flung open the door without so much as a knock. "Why didn't you tell me you could bat like that?"

He looked up. His dark hair was wild around his face, having escaped the tie long ago. He had never put his coat and waistcoat back on, and his sleeves were still rolled up over his forearms, as when he'd strode to the crease like Colossus and punished Tom Mannox's bowling with savage precision.

"You never asked about my cricket abilities," he replied to her question. He motioned at Lawrence, and the valet withdrew silently.

Bianca gave an incredulous laugh. "I never thought to!"

He grinned as he pulled loose his neckcloth. It was limp and bedraggled, and he threw it on the chair. "Now you know."

"What else have you kept from me?" she demanded. "Are you a master at chess? A skilled archer? Will I discover you're a sculptor or a celebrated musician?"

He leaned back, spreading wide his well-muscled arms. "Will you? Only if you look hard enough, I suppose."

She raised her brows. She did look. She liked to look at him; it had vexed her from the start, but now she gave in and openly admired him. As beautiful as he'd been in London, sleek and dangerous in his black domino on his knees in front of her, this Max—rumpled and sweaty and unabashedly male—obliterated her remaining resistance.

With a clink she set down the cup of tea Jennie had brought, and closed the door to her bedroom. "How closely should I look?"

His eyes were almost black. "As closely as you want," he replied in a low voice.

She laid her palm on his chest, feeling the beat of his heart. "You promised I could touch, too."

His expression didn't falter, but his breathing sped up. "Yes."

Bianca undid the remaining button at his throat, then paused. "Don't you want to touch me? Or kiss me?"

"I want you to want me," he growled. "I want to hear you say you want to be here, in my bed, for the rest of this night and every other night of our marriage." He inhaled roughly as her eyes widened. "Until then, I don't dare touch you or kiss you, because I might combust on the spot if I can't have all of you."

No one had ever spoken to her like that. No one had ever looked at her this way. It made her feel wild and beautiful and powerful, that *this* man wanted her. She had wondered why, after Vauxhall, he hadn't pursued her, why he hadn't pressed her for more even as he watched her with banked desire in his eyes. After Vauxhall, he could have persuaded her, far more easily than she would have admitted to anyone.

Someday you'll come to me . . .

Deliberately, with both hands, she pushed his shirt open and pressed her lips to his bare chest. "Yes," she whispered. "I want you."

His chest heaved. He lifted her face and kissed her, lightly at first but quickly growing feverish. Bianca kissed him back, sucking on his tongue and holding on to his shirt as if for dear life.

Suddenly she couldn't be too close to him. She was on her toes, clinging to him, meeting his ravenous kisses with her own. She barely felt him strip off her dressing gown, though she quaked when his broad hands stroked firmly down her back, lifting her against him.

She yanked at his shirt, wanting to touch him as promised, and when she got it loose, Max broke the kiss long enough to whip it over his head. Bianca slid her hands over his bare chest, marveling at the heat pulsing from him. No cold stone statue, as Lady Dalway and Mrs. Farquhar had tittered over in the gallery, but a hot blooded man of firm muscle and ragged breath, pulling loose the tie of her nightgown and cupping his hand around her bare breast.

Bianca gasped, her hands closing convulsively on Max's arms.

"You can stop me with a word," he breathed against her temple, his thumb rolling over her nipple.

Bianca raised her head and looked him in the face. "More," she whispered.

It took mere moments to strip him of his breeches and drawers. Max muttered curses as he peeled off his stockings, his eyes fixed on her as she shrugged off the nightgown. The sharp burst of embarrassment, to be naked in front of a man, lasted only until Max's scorching gaze slid over her. He flung aside his second stocking, and caught her to him with a groan of joy.

Together they tumbled onto the bed. Bianca couldn't touch him enough, and she wasn't shy about urging him to do the same. Her body remembered, intimately, every wicked thing he'd done to her in Vauxhall, and wanted all of it, all over again. He was the one who laughed quietly and whispered that there was no rush, he meant to please her from now until dawn. But when she spread her legs in mute, shameless appeal, he went still, and his languid whispers grew short, and when he slid down and put his mouth on her, Bianca gripped his hair in both hands and begged for more.

"I love you wild like this," he said in a guttural whisper, sucking at the flesh of her inner thigh. "And this." His fingers were inside her, tormenting her. "And this." He moved over her, pausing to lick her breast until she shivered. "And this . . ." He shifted his hips and edged inside her.

She strained against him. She had thought of this every night. "Max," she pleaded. "More."

He pushed forward in a sudden motion. For a moment he was still, and then he let out his breath and began to move, riding her with long hard thrusts that made her gasp. His hands roved, stroking, squeezing, holding her in place for his ravishment.

She came, almost too soon. She had wanted him so much, and been so worked up by the cricket, he hardly had to do anything to make her succumb to that tidal wave of feeling. She clung to him as her body convulsed, and she sobbed against his chest.

Max held her tightly until the storm subsided, then pushed up onto one arm. "That was for you, darling," he whispered, smiling down at her with predatory intent. "This one shall be for us."

"What?" She could barely speak, her toes still cramped and her heart still pumping furiously.

He lowered his head until his nose touched hers. "Now I intend to pleasure you thoroughly."

Bianca couldn't comprehend his words. She was already glowing. What else could he possibly do?

He showed her. Even though he was still hard and thick inside her—and reminded her how hard and how thick, with long languid thrusts of his hips—it was his hands and mouth that laid waste to her body. Tears ran down her face as he suckled at her breasts. He bid her hold her own knees apart to bare herself for his touch as he kept up his relentless, maddening strokes into her while he parted those damp curls and made her shake and twist.

"Max," she sobbed, lifting her hips to meet him in desperation.

"Yes, darling?" He nipped at her throat, his fingers driving her mad.

"I want you," she babbled. "God help me, I do—I want you, I want this, *please*—"

He rose up, hooking first one then the other of her

legs around his waist. He braced his arms on either side of her head and gazed fiercely down at her. The tendons in his neck stood out, and his arms were like iron. "Touch yourself," he commanded between his teeth. "As I did."

She blushed furiously but did it; her body was throbbing too urgently not to. She slid both hands down her belly and did as he told her.

Max growled; his eyes glittered in the lamplight, and his hair fell in damp ebony waves around his face. His thrusts grew hard, sharper and faster. Bianca's breath solidified in her chest as she stared at him, at his beautiful face so ferociously hungry for her, stroking herself until another climax came upon her.

At her first convulsion, Max sucked in a deep breath and drove all the way inside her, holding her until she collapsed, utterly spent, beneath him, as he shuddered in his own release.

Sometime later he slid trembling arms around her and rolled them both over, leaving her draped atop him. He was still inside her, and when she moved a little, his entire body quivered. But he pressed a kiss to the top of her head and folded his arms around her, and Bianca thought she had never felt so blissful in her life.

Eventually, even pressed up against the heat of him, she grew cold. When she shivered, he raised his head. With a low whisper, he sat up and eased her off him. Bianca huddled against the pillows and watched as he got up, naked, and moved about the room, putting out the lamps and closing the window against the night air. Then he flung back the blankets and held out one hand, inviting her to stay.

Without hesitation she did so, and he slid under the covers, lying on his side, facing her.

"Why didn't you seduce me like that in London?" she whispered, tracing one finger down his chin.

His mouth curved. "Who seduced whom, madam? You came into my room, you unbuttoned my shirt, you kissed me."

She smiled. "I did. You're fiendishly handsome, you know."

His amusement faded into a brooding, almost wistful look. "But not half as beautiful as you, love." She pursed up her mouth at that empty flattery, and he laid one finger on her lips, as if to forestall any argument. "By God above, I mean that. You have an inner fire that makes you entrancing. Everyone in London saw it. Why do you think Serafina Dalway and Clara Farquhar put you in that dress for Vauxhall? They were laughing at me the whole night, knowing my brain was melting with lust every time I looked at you."

"Was it?" She couldn't stop a small smile, even though it was shocking to hear him say that. "Now I'm sorry I returned the gown."

Max gave a rough laugh. "It's not the damned dress. I wanted you even more when you lifted your bat tonight after the short fellow hit you on the hands. You looked determined to send the next ball right into his forehead, and I've never been so aroused by a woman."

Bianca snorted with laughter. "You must have played a thousand cricket matches! No one bats like that their first time. We must have seemed terribly inept to you. It was magnanimous of you to join our side at all."

Instead of laughing, too, he grew serious. He stroked the hair back from her face, and studied her for a moment. "No," he murmured. "Not at all. It was the finest match I've ever played. Not merely for the triumph of topping Mannox, as much as I relish that, but for being part of the Perusia side. I gather the same people play every year?"

"Yes," she said, startled. "Usually. Sons replace fathers, daughters their mothers . . . We only play for that ugly redware vase, and of course pride of winning. It's been a tradition in Marslip since my father was a young man."

Max's fingers tightened on her nape. "I like that," he said softly.

It hit her that he'd never had that—a stable home where the same things happened every year, with the same people. Bianca, who had rarely left Marslip or Stoke, had found it comfortable, if a bit stale. Some years she wished they could take off a number of players and get new ones, as everyone knew everyone else so well it grew dull at times. But to a young man at the whim of family caprice and always keeping poverty at bay, it might seem utterly appealing . . .

Before she could form a reply, though, Max's face relaxed into a grin more like himself. "Don't say you play for only a lopsided vase and pride. I won forty pounds on that match."

"What?" She blinked. "When? Why did you make a wager?"

He winked, pulling her back into his arms. "When you made your way to the crease, I thought to myself, *she looks capable of fifty notches at least*, and I wagered fifty pounds on Perusia to win. We were trailing badly at that point, so I got good odds. My fifty paid ninety."

"You did not!"

"I did, and the winnings are in my pocket," he countered.

"Mr. Falke ought not to have let you wager at all," she protested, "since you were playing! And you knew how good you are!"

"If I'd fallen short he would have happily kept my money and I wouldn't have argued." Max lifted one shoulder. "I didn't cheat, and he watched me field. He knew what he was doing. It was a fair wager."

She looked at him for a long moment before finally laying down her head with a sigh. "I suggest you savor it. He'll never take your money again, now that he's seen you play."

Max grinned as he pulled her close. "I'll gladly suffer that, for the right to play again."

Bianca nestled against him. She felt . . . peaceful. Not only from the euphoria of winning, not only from the bliss of lovemaking, but from feeling, for the first time, truly at ease with her husband. He was so completely different to what she had thought he was, and all for the better.

Perhaps . . . just perhaps . . . this ill-begotten marriage would turn out to be a brilliant match.

Chapter Twenty-Seven

Max woke, thoroughly frozen, because Bianca had stolen all the blankets.

It took him a moment to sort that out. At first he almost thought it was a dream, that he had been in an agony of arousal for so long, his mind had snapped and imagined that he'd spent the night making love to her in his bed at Poplar House, when really he was sleeping rough in a London doorway again.

The figure sprawled in his blankets, though, was no dream, but a flesh and blood woman. A *naked* flesh and blood woman, lying on her stomach with one arm flung across the pillows. Her long hair had come loose from the braid and trailed around her like Medusa's, the golden-brown locks curling invitingly across the smooth expanse of her bared shoulders.

He hated to disturb her. It was early still, and from the light it looked to be a gray sort of day. But she had wound the blankets around her, and the alternative to waking her was to get up and dress. Max slid across the mattress and kissed the back of her neck.

"Wha—?" She reared up, all that hair flying. Max

seized the chance to yank free a fold of blanket and press up against her. She was soft and warm, making him aware of how chilled he was.

"You're cold," she said thickly, swatting away her curtain of hair. "What— Why are you here?"

He grinned at her last statement, half alarm, half bemusement. "You're in my bed, love. And you've taken all the blankets and left me to freeze." He slid his leg between hers, genuinely cold but unashamed to take advantage.

She blinked at him for a moment, then relaxed into the pillows again. "Move over," she mumbled before draping herself across him.

Max stroked her hair and let his hand drift down her back. Like him, she had fallen asleep naked. Her breasts were plump against his chest, and her legs tangled with his, her thigh atop his. It was tender and moving and unbearably arousing.

"Are you awake?" he murmured against her temple. Lightly he cupped her bottom, marveling at the smoothness of her skin.

"No," she grumbled.

"Hmm. Pity." He stroked upward. "It looks to be a damp, rainy sort of day, no good for going out. And no one will be at the factory anyway, because of the wakes. Hardly a day to get out of bed at all."

"Only laggards lie abed all day."

Max smiled. "Do they? It needn't be lazy."

She raised her head and propped her chin on his chest. Her eyes were still heavy-lidded with sleep, but sparkled with incipient desire. "Are you encouraging sloth and other wickedness?"

He clicked his tongue as he turned onto his side, tugging her knee up to his waist. "Not at all. It's not wicked, and decidedly not sloth." He was already hard and ready, and Bianca moaned softly as his length pressed between her legs.

"Jennie will come in," she said, her mouth against his.

"Lawrence will keep her away," he countered.

She smiled, opening her glorious eyes, fathoms-deep ocean blue. "Then say good morning properly to your wife, Mr. St. James."

With a tilt of his hips he pushed inside her. She gasped, but she was already slick and ready. Leisurely Max moved against her, exploring her body as he'd dreamed of doing for weeks. He lavished attention on that beauty mark, now freely displayed to him. She was ticklish on her ribs but threw back her head in pleasure when he kissed her neck below her ear.

When she was clinging to him with arms and legs, Max flipped them over. She sat up, a wanton goddess with her hair wild around her. Heart hammering, climax building inside him, he shoved himself up on the pillows and touched her, burning to feel her come.

And his wife clasped her hands behind his neck and rocked back and forth until the color rolled up her face and she gasped in ecstasy. He seized her hips and felt his soul come apart with his climax.

Shaking, he pulled her to him for a deep kiss. Never, not even in his most fanciful dreams, had he imagined it would be this way. He'd wanted Perusia for the occupation, for the chance to prove himself not a useless fribble and to find some benefit in his rake's history. He'd wanted a marriage for the fortune, so he would never be penniless again, jerked about by the Duchess of Carlyle's whim. He'd thought it would be distant, polite, perhaps cordial.

Instead he gazed helplessly into Bianca's glowing eyes and wondered how he'd ended up so deeply in love without even noticing he was falling.

"I've wondered about one thing," she said, smiling dreamily. "When we were first married, you were downstairs every morning before I was. Do you always rise appallingly early?"

"Ah. That." He chuckled, sliding down the pillows again. Bianca curled up against him, stretching her legs over his. Max thought he would never find a petite woman attractive again, after having her long legs wrapped around him. "Rather amusing, really. This wall"—he reached up and knocked his knuckles on the panel behind his head—"is not so thick as it looks. When Jennie brings your morning wash water, the door makes a particular squeal—"

She sat bolt upright. "Do you mean to say—?"

He folded his arm behind his head and smiled modestly. "As soon as I heard her come in, I would leap out of bed and hurry into my clothes, so that I would be ready to greet my wife at the breakfast table . . ."

She slapped his shoulder. "I thought you must not need sleep! Every morning—!"

Max gave her a sly look. "The back stairs are very conveniently near my door, and in stockinged feet, it's possible to creep down without a sound."

"Oh!" Eyes flashing, she flung herself onto the other side of the bed. "How perfectly vile of you!"

"Once," he said, crawling after her, "I barely made it—if you'd looked closely, you would have noticed my shoes were thrown under my chair instead of on my feet—"

"I rose earlier and earlier!" she cried. "It was still *dark*!"

Laughing, Max wrapped his arms around her. "And you were a vision of beauty every morning, even with that piqued little frown on your brow. Well worth scrambling down the stairs without a candle."

"Why?" she demanded in indignation. "What did you win?"

"My dear Mrs. St. James," he teased, "was our marriage a contest to you?"

She flushed pink. "You know it was! That's why you ran down the stairs, in the dark, without your shoes, just to be there before me. You wanted to prove that no matter what standard I held up, you could meet it." She punctuated the last few words with a finger to his chest.

Max gave her a sinful smile in reply. "No, madam, you are wrong. I meant to show you I would *exceed* them, each and every one."

"So it *was* a contest!" Finally she laughed. "Wretched man," she said, letting him hold her closer. "I was exhausted."

"I promise not to wake so early again," he told her. "Or perhaps I will have more reason to stay abed later in the mornings . . ."

She laughed again, twisting in his arms to face him. Still smiling, she put her hand on his cheek. Her hair was wild and her face was glowing and her eyes were warm. She was the most beautiful woman he'd ever seen, and so precious to him it was almost painful.

Max barely breathed; the words seemed to be swelling inside him, about to burst from his lips. He'd never told a woman he loved her, not since his mother . . .

"This is not what I imagined," she said softly. "When I helped Cathy elope."

Max let out his breath. Her sister. What a brilliant stroke of luck the quiet sister had been in love with someone else. If Catherine Tate had dutifully walked down the aisle to meet him . . . "I am unspeakably happy that you did."

Her face stilled. "Are you truly?"

He nodded. "I hope she is very content with her marriage. Just as I hope you are . . . pleased with ours."

She gazed at him for a long moment, as if she'd heard his tiny hesitation before *pleased.* Max's heart turned to ice. Thank God he'd not said anything— perhaps love was too much to ask for, after the way they'd begun . . .

"I am," she said in a low voice. "Pleased beyond measure."

He smiled, the moment of fear passing. He kissed her again, and began teasing her about forming a cricket club in Marslip.

But he didn't tell her he loved her. Not yet.

Chapter Twenty-Eight

For the next several days, Bianca walked with a spring in her step and a song in her heart.

She had never planned to marry because she had never thought it looked like fun. Her parents had been affectionate, but her mother's long illness had of course cast a pall over the last several years of her life. Papa had been loving and caring of Mama, but the toll it took on him had been clear to all. Even now, he didn't come to Poplar House, where they had all lived together; when he wanted something from her or Max, he sent a note or visited her in the workshop.

The marriages of cousins and friends, as happy as some of them were, appeared to be comfortable and convenient rather than passionate and thrilling. Aunt Frances's marriage, on the other hand, might have been designed purposely to put anyone off the institution. Bianca had cast a critical eye on all the eligible men within fifteen miles of Marslip, assessed the chances that she would be happy in close proximity to any of them for more than a month, and decided marriage was probably not for her.

Of course, she had thought the same about Max, and now he was proving her wrong in innumerable ways. Not only had he allayed all her suspicions that he would know nothing about Perusia ware or how to sell it, he had secured orders from the Duke of Wimbourne, the Earl of Dalway, and almost a dozen other aristocrats. Papa even showed her a few letters he'd received from other noblemen, who had seen or heard of the new wares, inquiring if they could visit his factory themselves.

"I knew that fellow had a clever head," he said, watching her keenly. "Admit it. He's improving on you, isn't he?"

"Yes," she said primly, though she blushed to think how much Max had improved on her.

"Are you happy, Bee?" her father prodded.

"Of course. Look at these orders, especially for the new scarlet ware—"

"I mean with him." Papa leaned forward, refusing to let her evade the question. "Are you?"

She met his gaze. There was a trace of uncertainty in his hopeful expression. "Once you said that you and Mama had no choice but to make the best of things. What did you mean by that?"

A veil came down over her father's face. He sat back in his chair. "When did I say that?"

"When you urged me to make the best of things with Max."

"You should do that," he told her. "Always try to make the best of your lot."

"Papa."

He sighed. "I was very fond of your mother. She was a loving mother and a good wife."

"I thought you loved her," said Bianca slowly.

"Oh, I did, I did!" Papa nodded. "But . . . not . . . perhaps not as much as she loved me." He sighed, looking away. "I tried to do my best by her, and she bore up under my faults with admirable grace. Cathy is so like her—although your mother never would have run away in the middle of the night," he added, sounding grudgingly impressed.

"I suppose Cathy got *that* from you," said Bianca.

He glanced up sharply. "Aye, you would think so! Well, I suppose you were right to encourage her. I see now that St. James is a much better match for you than he ever was for her."

Bianca blinked. "What?"

"Look at this!" Papa swept his hand over the desk, where the ordering papers lay. "Cathy never would have gone off to London with him. He tells me you impressed the Duke of Wimbourne to no end, and won over Lady Dalway and Lady Carswell. He gave all the credit for the visit to you, my dear."

Bianca sat with her mouth open. "Oh—oh no," she managed to protest. "That's not true! Max knew just how to approach Dalway and Wimbourne— who were both his friends for many years—and while they admired the scarlet glaze, it was his efforts that caused the orders! He found the show-room, and the Cheapside shop where he proposes to sell his Fortuna ware, and he even got Sir Bartholomew Markham to pay his bill—"

Papa was grinning from ear to ear. "As I said," he said proudly, "a much better match for him than Cathy. The two of you are a splendid pair, perfectly suited to each other! St. James is damned lucky that curate finally screwed up his courage."

She frowned at him. "You could have prevented all that if you had listened to Cathy."

He rolled his eyes. "She barely said a word against

him! How was I to know it wasn't just maidenly nerves? Frances assured me young ladies have such fits of passion, and when they recover no one, even they themselves, can recall what the fuss was. She was certain Cathy would get over her fit and settle down contentedly with St. James."

"You consulted Aunt Frances about us?" Bianca was incredulous.

"Who else?" he asked in surprise. "What other woman should I ask for help with my daughters?"

Bianca was speechless. Frances cared for them, but she was also a quarrelsome old lady who'd been disappointed in love herself. Frances was the last person whose counsel she would ask when it came to marriage or happiness.

Papa waved one hand. "I'm not above admitting I was wrong. Neither is Frances."

"She isn't?"

He laughed at her dry remark. "Not in so many words, of course."

"You're in an expansive mood today," she couldn't resist saying.

Papa grinned. "Am I? It must be because your sister's written to me."

Bianca gasped. "She has? You never said! Is she well?"

He nodded, beaming. "She says so. Mr. Mayne has been writing to his superiors, and has finally been assured he may come back to his living here. I gather the bishop was displeased with his actions, but has decided it will all come out well."

"I hope it was because you wrote to the bishop that you now approved of the marriage," remarked Bianca.

Papa grunted. "Well, your sister asked it of me, and since all came out so happily for you, I could hardly refuse her."

Bianca shook her head, but with a smile. She'd known Papa would forgive Cathy anything. "So she's coming home?" She was both anxious to see her sister and nervous of the reunion, and the explanations that would be required. In her letters to Cathy, she hadn't been able to find the words, and finally gave it up as hopeless, promising herself she would explain much better in person.

"I have every confidence she'll come soon," her father promised. "Especially once she hears of your marriage!"

"You . . . you told her?" Bianca asked after a moment. "What did you say?"

"That you married St. James in her place, much to the advantage of everyone." Papa rose. "I expect you'll want to fill in the details, but I thought you might like someone else breaking the news to her."

She gave him a sour look, and he laughed, patting her on the shoulder.

When she met Max at the factory gate later that day, it was the first thing she told him. Max raised a brow. "You hadn't told her already yourself?"

"No." Bianca cringed. "I should have. What shall I say now?"

They strolled along, arm in arm. Bianca was a little astonished at herself; she'd been thinking of this all day, craving his advice. She, who was so decisive and who trusted her own judgment.

"Is there a reason not to tell her the truth?"

She blew out her breath. "She'll be so disappointed in me."

He squeezed her hand. "Would her feelings matter more than your own?"

Bianca paused. She hadn't let Cathy's opinion stop her before. "I fear the truth is not my friend this time."

He cut a sharp look at her.

"I can bear her disappointment at how I argued with Papa," Bianca explained quickly. "I can bear it when she learns how I . . . I agreed to our marriage in a fit of temper." Her cheeks were burning. "I shall hate to tell her how long I blamed you and called you the worst sort of fortune hunter."

"You could omit that bit," he suggested after a pause. "Or make light of it. Surely what matters most is how we get on now."

Warmth flooded her at the thought of that. She squeezed his arm and gave him a teasing smile as they reached Poplar House. "How *do* we get on now, sir?"

"Very well, madam, very well indeed," he murmured, opening the door for her. "One might even say . . . passionately."

Bianca all but purred at his gleaming glance. They had passion in abundance. More than passion, even; she looked forward to seeing him every day. She had come to respect him, she admired him, and she was desperately attracted to him. She liked being with him— enormously. She liked *him*.

Enormously.

Her hands slowed as she removed her hat and gloves, barely noticing when Mary took them. Max had not followed her; Lawrence had intercepted him at the door, speaking in a low voice. Bianca couldn't see Max's face, but just the rumble of their conversation made her heart swell. She even loved the sound of his voice.

And she knew then how she would answer her sister's inevitable question, the answer that would forestall any tears or remonstrances and elicit instead delight and congratulations. Once again, Max was correct; she didn't need to lie to Cathy at all. The truth was far better.

Cathy, I fell in love with him.

She turned on the stairs to look back. Max still stood in the doorway below, head together with Lawrence and poring over a letter. Upstairs Jennie was humming, and from the kitchen came the murmur of the other servants' voices, preparing dinner. It was the sound of a happy home once more.

Bianca put a hand on the wall to steady herself. How had she been so blind? Why had she not admitted to herself that this was what she wanted? Max was not her vision of an ideal husband; he surpassed it in every way. He shared credit for their successes, even when the idea had begun with him. He never once argued against her working on the glazes, but congratulated her and encouraged her. He looked at her as if she were beautiful and alluring. He even wagered on her at cricket.

He said something to Lawrence, who nodded and slipped out the door. For a moment his dark head remained bent over the letter in his hands. Then he looked up.

Bianca's smile withered at the sight of his expression. "What's wrong?" She descended a few stairs.

His face was stark. "I have to go out."

"Now?" She was astonished. "Why?"

His gaze dropped to the letter. "Yes, now. I'm sorry."

Bianca clattered down the remaining steps. "Why? What is wrong? You're as pale as death, Max!"

His eyes closed. She put her hand on his in concern, fearing he might fall unconscious, and he jerked violently away from her touch. "I have to go," he repeated, breathing hard. He crumpled the letter in his fist. "I'm sorry." He brushed past her and took the stairs two at a time.

Bianca ran after him, following him into his bedchamber. It had been *their* bedchamber for the last week, where they talked and laughed and kissed and held each other and made love to each other. Now he was flinging off his clothes, pulling on riding breeches and boots and determinedly not looking at her.

She lowered her voice, mindful of the servants. "What is wrong? Tell me something."

He yanked on one boot. "It's a family matter."

Her mouth fell open. "Family? Is—is it the Duke of Carlyle?"

His gaze flashed toward her, then just as quickly away. "No."

"Mrs. Bradford," Bianca guessed after a moment's frantic thought.

Max's head came up. "What did you say?"

She blinked in astonishment at his tone, practically a snarl. "Your aunt. Is it about her?"

He jammed his other foot into a boot and rose. He came to her and cupped her face in both hands and for a moment, appeared to struggle for words. "I—I don't have time to explain now." He looked anguished. "Can you trust me?"

"Yes," she replied at once. She was done doubting him.

He gave her a scorching kiss. "Thank you, love," he breathed, and then he was gone, his boots echoing on the stairs, calling for Mary to bring his greatcoat and hat.

Bianca hurried after him in time to see him swing into the saddle of his horse. He wheeled the animal around, saying something to Lawrence. He caught sight of her and touched his hat before riding out of the yard.

She was left staring after him, her hand still upraised and her mind a whirl. "Lawrence," she demanded as the valet retreated to the house, "where has Mr. St. James gone?"

"Stoke on Trent," he replied. "'Tis all I know, madam. He bade me send for his horse, and questioned me about the man who brought the message."

"Who brought it?"

"Someone from Mr. Leake, madam." Lawrence must have guessed her next furious question, for he put up his hands. "Mr. Leake is a man from London, an investigator of sorts. Mr. St. James hired him some time ago, and has been waiting for his report ever since. He told me I was to notify him immediately if anything came from Leake, no matter the time."

"A man from London!" Bianca was staggered. "Has this man been working for Mr. St. James since we were in London?" she demanded.

Lawrence's gaze veered away from her. "Aye, ma'am. Since well before, I think."

That meant Max had hired him months ago—and to search for what? Even if he'd not had time to explain tonight, he might have mentioned it last night, or the night before, or any of the dozens of other times they'd talked since arriving home. Since consummating their marriage. Since Vauxhall. They had spent hours pleasing each other, whispering to each other, laughing together. They had discussed mundane things, important things, matters dear and sensitive.

But not this.

"He bade me not tell you anything," Lawrence said in apology. "I understood it was a matter of very personal importance to him."

And Bianca was left to wonder, in the deepening shadows of twilight, just what her husband had kept from her.

Chapter Twenty-Nine

It's not like St. James," grumbled Papa. "I can't believe he's run off!"

"It's unpardonable," said Aunt Frances tartly. "Mark my words, he's up to no good, see if he isn't!"

Bianca picked at her plate and said nothing. She had no earthly idea what *to* say.

It had been two whole days since Max bolted out of Marslip with nothing but the clothes on his back. She had sat up waiting until the clock striking midnight had startled her awake, and Jennie had come, in her nightdress and yawning, to urge her to go to bed. She assured Bianca that someone would wake her the moment he returned, and Bianca had slept, fitfully, in her own bed for the first time in several days.

The next morning she'd sent Lawrence into Stoke on Trent, intent on getting at least a word of explanation. She told the valet to ask four specific questions, and not to come home until he got answers. She paced Poplar House all morning, unable to concentrate on anything, until Lawrence returned to say that Max was not in Stoke at all.

"He left at dawn with the same bloke who brought the message," Lawrence had reported. "Mr. Barkley at the Foxes said they asked for their horses to be made ready at first light, and a sack of provisions left waiting. He never saw them go. The stable boy says Mr. St. James gave him a shilling and told him to go back to sleep, but said naught of where they were going."

Max had left no word, sent no note. And again he didn't come home.

For the first time in years, Papa had come to Poplar House, when neither she nor Max went to the factory the second day. His concern that there was illness in the house dissolved into amazement and then outrage when Bianca confessed she had no idea where her husband was or why he'd left. Papa told her to come to Perusia Hall for dinner, and, listless, she had agreed.

She had regretted every moment of it, though.

"I don't know about that," argued Papa with an uneasy glance at Bianca. "But it's very strange. Are you certain the valet has no idea?"

Bianca shook her head.

"A man's valet always knows more than he lets on." Frances took a bite of roasted goose, and then fed a piece of the same to Trevor, who sat panting beside her chair. "Bring the man in and we'll demand some sense from him."

"I am persuaded he does not know," said Bianca quietly. Lawrence had grown sweet on Jennie; in the course of the last two days, as Max's absence grew long and strained, he had pleaded not to be turned off, and become a font of information.

Afraid of being dismissed, Lawrence had sworn he had no idea where Max had gone or why, and offered up that Max had indeed led a wild and debauched life in London before proposing to marry a Perusia heiress. He told her all about his previous employer, a friend of Max's who had lost twenty-eight thousand pounds in a single night at the Vauxhall gaming tables—in company with Max—and been forced to flee London. He confessed that the lease of their house in London had been held by Lord Cathcart, for his mistress, and that the house had required extensive cleaning to be habitable, after the scandalous parties held there—some of which Max had attended. He admitted that Max had sent him to Cheapside when Bianca was measuring the shop there, with a directive to watch out for a man Lawrence knew only as a person from Max's past who posed a threat.

He admitted he had been told to keep watch for any letters from Reading, which were to be delivered immediately, and he said they had upset Max, though he claimed not to know why. And he confessed that Max had strictly instructed him never to let anyone, most especially Bianca, know about any of it.

That last had cut deeply. Bianca had known her husband had a scandalous past—the women in Vauxhall proved that—and she was not surprised that his friends were scandalous, too. While he might reasonably have kept quiet about it in the early, difficult days of their marriage, she had thought they were honest with each other now.

Yet Max had never said a word.

"He must know something!" Frances refused to let go of her belief that Lawrence was lying. She aimed her fork at Bianca. "You are too soft on your servants, my dear. Question him sternly!"

Bianca, who knew her great-aunt was not harsh at all to her own servants, gave her a jaundiced look. "I did. He knows nothing."

"I still have confidence there will be a good explanation when St. James returns," put in Papa. "He's not been disloyal or untrustworthy before."

Trust me. Max had asked her to trust him, time and time again. He had never betrayed her before, but she was struggling to continue trusting. Surely there must be a good reason for this; there *must* be. She sipped her wine in silence.

"I've had another letter from Cathy," said Papa in forced good cheer, trying to change the subject. "She is coming home."

"It is about time," said Frances. "Gallivanting about Staffordshire without a thought for her people at home!"

Bianca roused herself. "When do you expect her, Papa?"

"Oh, soon, soon," he assured them. "Within the fortnight, I expect. She seemed intent on it. Expressed her astonishment at all that's happened here."

Meaning her marriage. The one she could no longer explain with professions of love for a man who had, apparently, abandoned her. Bianca drained her wineglass and beckoned the servant to refill it.

In the taut silence came the distant crunch of carriage wheels. Bianca twitched to alertness. It was unusual for visitors to arrive at this time of evening. Twilight was fading, and the roads around Marslip were treacherous enough in the day. Max had left on horseback, but a carriage might be safer now . . .

Papa heard it, too. He glanced at her as he helped himself to more goose. "What a fine joke if that should be your sister already, eh?" He chuckled, too heartily. "Summoned by the mention of her name! They must have made excellent time from Wolverhampton . . ."

Bianca was listening as intently as any pointer. Frances began muttering and clucking to Trevor, who was growling, and Bianca hissed at both of them to be silent. Shocked, the older woman glared at her.

"Maxim," wailed a voice outside. A female voice.

With a lurch Bianca leapt up from the table and ran. Papa followed at her heels, as Frances shouted at them to wait for her. She flew out of the dining room and down the corridor, into the spacious front hall, where she stopped in astonishment.

The butler was attempting to force a wild woman out the door. Her black hair trailed past her waist in a tangle. Her coarse gray dress was virtually rags, slipping off her shoulders and hanging loosely around her figure. She was as thin as a stick, her collarbones prominent as she writhed like a feral creature in Mr. Hickson's grip.

"What the devil?" exclaimed Papa.

"Maxim," wailed the woman again, her long, wraithlike arms flailing. "Wo ist er? *Maxim!*"

"Merciful heavens," said Frances, nonplussed.

In a trance Bianca walked forward. "He's not here," she said clearly to the woman. "Who are you?"

Tears filled the stranger's eyes. "Maxim," she screamed once more, before collapsing like a puppet whose strings had been cut, sliding through

Mr. Hickson's arms into a shaking huddle on the floor.

Aside from her sobs, the hall was deathly silent. Mr. Hickson hovered uncertainly over her, but now the woman looked defenseless and broken. Papa appeared thunderstruck, and Frances had both hands clasped to her bosom in shock.

Maxim. This woman knew him. Bianca's breath rasped in her lungs. Slowly she went down on her knees and touched the woman's shoulder. It set off another scream, and the woman scrambled backward until she hit the wall.

A big fellow lumbered into the open doorway, panting hard and clutching a handkerchief to his cheek. Blood spotted his waistcoat. "Sorry, mate," he said to Mr. Hickson as he reached down for the woman. "Come on, now. Here you are, ma'am." He spoke kindly enough as he tried to lift her from the ground.

"Wo ist er?" sobbed the woman, flinching from his touch. "Fass mich nicht an!"

"What the devil is this?" Papa recovered from his surprise and strode forward. "Who are you, sir?"

"William Leake, at your service," said the man. He removed the handkerchief from his face to bow, and Bianca's eyes widened at the deep scratches that still ran red with blood. "Here to see Mr. St. James, if you please."

"He's not here," said Papa indignantly. "Who are you, and who is this woman?"

Mr. Leake did not appear pleased by Max's absence. "This is Mrs. Margareta Croach," he said. "Where might I find St. James?"

Bianca had been staring at the woman. Beneath the dirty and bedraggled exterior, looking past the hollows in her cheeks and the jutting bones of her arms, she must have been a beautiful woman once. She could not be more than forty years old. Tears had left tracks in the dirt on her face, and when her head lolled back in despair, Bianca caught her breath as a sudden thought struck her.

"He's away from home," she said, softly but clearly. "Away. Do you understand?"

The woman's lashes fluttered, and she stared at Bianca with dull onyx eyes.

"Greta," said Bianca. The eyes flickered again, and fastened on her. "Are you Greta?"

A deep breath shuddered through her. "Ja."

"A German woman?" whispered Papa loudly. "What is this?"

Gingerly Bianca stretched out her hand. The woman, Greta, eyed her warily. "I am Max's wife. Maxim. Wife."

With a jerk the woman seized her hand. "Maxim . . ." she whimpered.

"Bianca," said Papa plaintively.

She held up a hand to quiet him. "Mr. Leake," she said, eyes fixed on Greta. "Did you send for Max two days ago?"

"Aye." Leake let out his breath. He had gone back to trying to staunch the blood still welling from his face. "I told him to wait in Stoke on Trent but he's not there. If he's not here, either . . . I suppose he couldn't wait and took off after me."

"I suppose so." Slowly, still holding Greta's hand as if the woman might wrench away, Bianca rose. "Won't you come in?"

Mr. Leake frowned. "Not sure I'd take her inside, ma'am. She flew into a fit when I said we were going to find St. James. Until then she was docile. His name set her off."

"Well, he's not here, and I cannot put her outside," said Bianca, keeping her voice soft and even. Nothing to startle Greta, who struggled awkwardly to her feet. "Come sit with me," she urged the woman, leading her slowly into the sitting room nearby.

"Bianca," said Papa sternly.

"Shh," she said. Greta had flinched at Papa's voice. "We'll wait for Max. Are you hungry?"

Fear filled Greta's face. She shook her head.

"All right. Sit here." Bianca guided her to the settee. Greta perched warily on the edge. To Bianca's surprise, Aunt Frances stepped forward and swung her own shawl around the woman, tucking it gently in place. Bianca glanced at her in gratitude, and her aunt stepped back, her expression unreadable.

"Where is St. James?" Papa was demanding loudly of Mr. Leake, in the hall outside the parlor.

"I got no idea," replied the other man. "When he wasn't at the Two Foxes, I thought he must have come home. It took a fair bit longer to reach this place than I thought. Your roads are an abomination."

"And who *are* you?" Papa was so agitated, he didn't even agree about the roads.

"William Leake, thief-taker," was the answer.

Papa stormed into the doorway. "Bianca, come away from that woman at once!"

"No, Papa," said Bianca. "Aunt Frances, send for a glass of wine." She continued holding the woman's hand as her aunt rushed for the bell.

"What the bloody hell is going on?" Papa barked.

Bianca didn't blink at his curse. "Be calm, Papa. I believe I know who she is. But we should wait for Max." Jane scurried in, wide-eyed, with a small glass of claret, which Bianca handed to Greta.

"And where has he gone?" Papa retorted. "Two days, and not so much as a message to his wife!"

"I have every confidence he'll be here soon," she said evenly. This was the person Max had been seeking, whom he had raced off to find without even pausing to explain. Indeed, she thought she heard hoofbeats approaching now.

A few minutes later she was proven correct. Hickson's voice echoed in the hall, and running footsteps. Max caught himself in the doorway, let out an exclamation of relief and rushed forward.

At the sight of him Greta made a noise like a lamed animal. She dropped the glass and scrambled off the settee.

Bianca lunged for the claret, setting the glass aside with only a small spill. Greta had flung herself at Max, collapsing to her knees and throwing her arms around his legs. At once Max sank down, his greatcoat pooling around them. He clasped Greta to him, resting his dark head next to hers and murmuring to her as she sobbed in renewed vigor.

"St. James," said Papa, sounding dazed. "Explain this."

Still stroking the woman's hair, Max raised his head. He looked terrible, his complexion gray and exhausted, his hair flattened and filthy, every inch of him covered in dust. "This is my aunt. My mother's sister, Greta."

"Your aunt!" Papa reared back. "What's happened to her?"

"You've been searching for her for months," said Bianca numbly. "Why didn't you tell me, Max?"

He turned desolate eyes to her. "Can't you guess? Because she's mad."

Chapter Thirty

It took some time to settle the household.

Max explained in spare terms. His aunt had taken ill after her second marriage; a severe melancholy, the doctor said. She drank to excess, and fell into stupors that lasted days. There had been doctors and treatments in three spas, to no improvement. Greta wasted away and began speaking only German, the language of her youth. Her husband had her confined to an asylum.

Bianca thought there was much more to it than that. Max handled his aunt as protectively as if she were a child, and indeed she seemed as defenseless as one. She sagged heavily against Max's side on the settee, her hand clutching a handful of his coat. Under his urging she ate a few bites of bread, and then fell asleep with a suddenness that astonished everyone.

Papa took himself off, saying he needed some port to calm his nerves. Frances slipped out of the room as well, and came back several minutes later to report that she had told the maids to prepare a room for Greta.

Max roused himself. By the end of his story he looked half-asleep himself. "No," he said, his voice rusty. "I'll take her home." He stopped, and looked at Bianca. "If you'll permit me to take her there."

"Don't be ridiculous," said Frances with her usual brusqueness. "This woman is exhausted. Let Ellen wash her and put her to bed."

Max shook his head. "I can't leave her."

"Of course not," replied Frances tartly. "I've already sent for Jennie and your man. You shall have Bianca's old room."

"I'll go with her," offered Bianca as Max kept his arm around the sleeping Greta. "If you think that would help her."

For a moment he stared at her, before blinking with a start. He was nearly asleep on his feet, she realized. "Yes. Yes, I think it would. Thank you."

Greta woke with a panicked cry, but Max calmed her at once. He spoke to her for several minutes in a low, hushed voice. Bianca heard her own name, and saw Greta's terrified eyes dart her way.

Even though she didn't understand and still smarted under the sting of Max's secrecy, she felt her heart move at the way he treated his aunt. Whatever the state of Greta's mind, she had been treated abominably. It was clear she hadn't had a bath in weeks; her clothes were rags, and she was half-starved. She kept plucking Frances's shawl over her shoulders as if she hadn't been warm in forever.

She sat quietly waiting until Greta looked at her again. Max smiled encouragingly. "Meine Frau," he told his aunt. "Bianca."

Slowly, Greta nodded once. "Schön," she whispered.

"Sehr schön," murmured Max with a ghost of a

smile at Bianca. He helped Greta to her feet, and
put his arm around her as he guided her from the
room. For the first time Bianca noticed her feet
were bare, scratched and scabbed. She told Aunt
Frances to send for some salve, and wondered uneasily what Max meant by *mad*.

Max must have convinced Greta she was safe. The
woman went into Cathy's old bedroom with Bianca,
only jumping uneasily when the door closed. Ellen
came in with a bucket of warm water and Greta
started to shake again, whimpering.

"Set it down and go," said Bianca swiftly. "Go!"
Looking startled, Ellen put down the bucket by the
hearth and fled. Bianca heard her voice in the corridor, and the weary rumble of Max's reply, followed
by Frances's tart admonition to Ellen to fetch more
water for Mr. St. James's bath.

Greta cowered from the hip tub, so Bianca abandoned the idea of bathing her. She settled for wip-
ing away as much dirt as she could with a damp
cloth, speaking softly and soothingly the whole
time. She began to brush Greta's hair, but the mass
was so tangled and filthy, the brush made no progress. They would have to wash it and probably cut
it, but that was for another day. Finally she coaxed
Greta into a clean nightdress, and then into bed.
The woman looked so childlike, clutching the blankets to her chin, her eyes roving the room.

When she was asleep, Bianca slipped out of the
room. To her surprise, Frances was waiting. "How
is she?" asked her aunt.

"Asleep. Aunt Frances, there are bruises all over
her body. Her feet look as though they were whipped.
Her hair is so matted, we'll have to cut it—"

"Yes," Frances said quietly. "Madhouses are terrible places, my dear."

Bianca hesitated. "Is she mad? She looks a fright, but she understood what I told her to do, and she cooperated . . ."

"I do not know," was Frances's answer. "But now you must go to your husband. Assure yourself he has not fallen asleep and drowned in his bath. I will stay with her."

Bianca nodded gratefully and went to her old bedroom.

Max had indeed fallen asleep in the bath. Of course, he was much too large for the bathing tub, so his head lolled on his shoulder while his knees stuck up out of the water. For a moment Bianca stared at his face in the flickering firelight.

Why hadn't he told her about Greta? Or rather, why hadn't he told her *this* about Greta?

Madness, of course, was terrible. A lunatic in the family was something most people would keep hidden. If Papa had known there was madness in Max's family, he would never have invited him to dinner, let alone entertained a marriage proposal.

But *Max* was not mad. No, not at all; he was the most logical, sensible, driven person she knew . . . and that meant he had known full well how people would have reacted, if he'd told. How Papa *had* reacted tonight. If Bianca hadn't realized who Greta was and gone to her aid, Papa would have thrown her out of the house and barred the door.

And she was no better. If Max had told her of Greta in the early, antagonistic days of their marriage, Bianca knew she would not have taken it well. Not out of fear of Greta, but fury at him.

You kept her a secret so you could save her, she thought as she gazed at her exhausted husband. He clearly cared for his aunt. Greta had taken him in when his mother died, she had sent him to university, and she had tried to get him started in a respectable profession. Lawrence said Max had hired Mr. Leake to look for her months ago.

But had he meant to conceal her existence forever?

Bianca sighed. There was no use pondering these questions on her own. She took up one of the towels left to warm by the fire and draped it gently over his shoulders.

"What?" He startled awake before subsiding. "Greta. Is she—?"

"Asleep in bed, with Aunt Frances standing watch."

He scrubbed his hands over his face. "Thank you."

He got out of the tub and dressed. Much as she had done with Greta, Bianca put him to bed, too. Max went as docilely as a child. "When did you last sleep?" she asked, sitting on the bed beside him and brushing the damp hair from his forehead.

"A long time ago," he said on a sigh. He groped for her hand and brought it to his cheek. "I'm sorry, love."

"For what?" She kept her voice calm and soft. "For haring off without explaining why? For letting me think you and Greta were simply estranged? Or for something else I've not discovered yet?"

He looked at her in despair. "I've much to beg forgiveness for."

She sighed. "Let's start with this. How long have you been searching for her?"

He hesitated. "Three years."

That was much longer than Bianca had expected. "My," she said. "Why so long?"

"Her husband hid her away," he said, his voice sinking into a drowsy rumble. "He put her in a prison and refused to tell me where. He taunted me and extorted me until I had no more money to give, and still he would not tell me where she was."

She stroked his hair. "Will you tell me more later?"

"Yes," he sighed, pressing her hand, still in his. "Everything."

"What did she say?" asked Bianca on impulse. "When you told her I would help her. Schön?"

His sleepy smile held a hint of his usual wickedness. "Beautiful," he said softly. "And I replied that you are *very* beautiful."

And with that, he fell asleep, and Bianca lay next to him for a long time, unwilling to pry apart their hands.

MAX WOKE WITH a jerk, bolting upright. He could swear he heard screams, just like the ones at Mowbry Manor. He was half out of bed before Bianca caught his arm.

"Stay," she mumbled. "Greta is well."

Heart thundering, he paused, every muscle tensed. "How do you know?"

His wife rolled over and yawned. She was fully dressed, asleep on top of the coverlet. "Aunt Frances and I traded turns sitting with her all night. When she woke this morning, Frances read to her. She seemed to enjoy it."

"Oh." Slowly he collapsed back into bed, still trembling from the moment of fearful fury.

"When last I went in, Aunt Frances had persuaded

her to let Ellen wash her hair. Can you guess how?" She smiled. "No, you never will. Frances had Ellen wash *her* hair in the basin, to prove it was safe. Ellen and Jennie were fussing with the combs when I left."

"How very kind of Mrs. Bentley."

"Max." Bianca turned over to face him. "What happened to her?"

He hesitated. Originally, his plan had been to conceal Greta and her condition forever. He'd taken the Duchess of Carlyle's money and hired Leake, unwilling to abandon his aunt to the clutches of her viper husband, but also desperate to keep his family stain from anyone's knowledge. As long as Croach had Greta, he had leverage over Max, able to turn up and make a spectacle of Greta in one of her fits.

Now . . .

"She was not mad years ago," he said slowly. "She was charming and beautiful and lighthearted. She looks so much like my mother, her older sister. When I was a child she would run in the fields with me. She taught me to play cricket, in fact. I thought she was wonderful," he finished wistfully.

"Nothing seemed wrong until Thomas Bradford, her first husband, died suddenly. They had been happy together, and Greta felt his death very keenly." Max sighed. "I ought to have given her more support, but I was a young fool, irked at being turned off from Bradford's law office and yearning to keep pace with my mates from Balliol—Wimbourne and Dalway and that lot. It was impossible, of course, and I ran myself into such trouble . . ." He closed his eyes for a moment. "I didn't know she began drinking gin, in the mornings and at nights. I neglected her, and she—still beautiful, still young, possessed of Bradford's money and my grandfather's farm, but desperately lonely—married Silas Croach."

"When did he put her in an asylum?"

Max felt his face harden. "Not immediately. He was canny—he outfoxed me, for certain. I thought him a rum chap, devoted husband and all that. He appeared to fuss over her, and would declare he was taking her to Bath or to Cheltenham for the waters. Every few months they were off to a different spa. Doctor after doctor was brought in to consult, and Croach told me their reports of her condition were relentlessly grave."

"Did you never see her yourself?" Bianca asked softly.

"Yes," he murmured, remembering. "Croach said visitors upset her, so I was not to come often. When I did, she would be raving about the blue hedgehogs living under the furniture, or sunk in a stupor so low, she couldn't respond to any conversation. I believed Croach." Max paused again, swallowing bile at how bloody stupid he'd been. "I agreed when he said she must be put into a hospital for her own benefit."

"What do you suspect him of doing instead?" asked his wife—his beautiful, intelligent, clear-eyed wife. Max smiled sadly. If he'd had her then, she would have seen through Croach's lies, and smacked some sense into Max himself.

"I think he encouraged her to drink beyond reason. I think he drugged her— No," he corrected himself. "I *know* he drugged her. With my own eyes I saw him dose her, and I thanked him for it.

I thought it was medicine to treat her, but now I suspect it was to make her worse."

Bianca's lips parted.

"Greta was not an heiress, but neither was she poor," he explained. "Bradford left her a respectable widow's portion, almost four thousand pounds. And then my grandfather died, and she inherited the income from the farm in Lincolnshire. Grandfather was wily enough to leave the land to me, but a life estate in the income to her. And Croach knew it."

"So he spent all her money?" asked Bianca in outrage.

"No, I believe now that he hid that away. But he told me he had spent it—all those spa visits, you know—and that he needed more to pay for the doctors and the hospitals." Max shrugged. "So I took myself to the gaming tables and I got it for him."

He'd told her that. She knew he'd been a gambler and a rake. He'd simply never said why.

"You said you were brilliant at it . . ." Of course she remembered that, from Vauxhall.

Max grinned slightly at that memory. "I was. My best year I cleared nine thousand pounds."

Bianca's eyes rounded, as he had expected. That was a very handsome sum of money.

"You're thinking I only gambled so I could give it all to Croach," he said. "Don't. I spent as carelessly as any young man, loosed upon town with no one to say me nay. I lived well when the cards fell in my favor, and then I lived rough when they did not. It was all sport to me. But I did dutifully give Croach money, every quarter." Max's voice grew bitter again. "He lectured me of cures, of medicines, of doctors! She was trying to harm herself, he said, and attacking the servants. If I didn't help him care for her, he would have no choice but to have her confined in Bethlem Hospital with the lunatics."

Her face softened. "What made you think he drugged her?"

"She began speaking German to me, instead of English, when I visited," he said slowly. "It was . . . odd. Her parents spoke nothing else but Greta spoke English. I know only enough German to get by. But Croach couldn't understand any, and she asked me to take her away. I began to suspect him of being, if not the cause of her malady, at least no help, and that's when he abruptly put her away in a private madhouse."

He remembered that as if it had happened an hour ago. He'd gone to visit Greta, armed with more information than usual as his suspicions grew. He'd asked a couple of friendly apothecaries, who had told him what to look for. He'd asked his aunt, in German so Croach couldn't know, if her medicines made her feel worse. She said they made her soul split in half; Max promised he would come back for her the next day. And by the next morning Croach had bundled her off to God knew where.

"Why didn't you tell me any of this?" Bianca's betrayed tone pierced his heart.

Max turned onto his back, staring at the ceiling. "I told no one. Nor did I ever intend to. Who would want a man with lunacy in his blood? Your father would have shown me the door and locked it behind me. You didn't want me at all. What would a mad relation, locked up in an asylum, have done to your feelings?"

She was quiet for a long time. Max felt drained of all emotion. This was why he had planned never to tell anyone. He had hoped to find a hospital—a good one—and make Greta as comfortable as possible. He had planned to visit her as often as he could. But he had accepted that her condition, even her existence, must be kept secret.

"I don't know," Bianca said at last. "Heaven knows Aunt Frances is terrible enough, and we let her walk about freely. Madness is different, of course . . . Are you certain she *is* mad?"

Max paused. "I fear so. She had flashes of sensibility, but you saw her—"

"She's been starved and whipped, dressed in rags and locked in a madhouse. I shudder to think what any of us would be like after enduring that." She went up on her elbows and looked at him. "Perhaps kinder treatment will improve her."

"She shall have kinder treatment for the rest of her days, even if her mind is irretrievably broken," Max vowed. "I'll tear Croach apart if he tries to take her again."

"As he's the one who allowed her to be treated this way," said Bianca, "I'll gladly help."

His heart swelled. When he'd realized Leake must have brought Greta to Perusia, Max had braced himself to be reviled and rejected, thrown out and even divorced. Instead of scenes of horror and revulsion, though, he burst into the house to find Greta sitting on the settee, a fine shawl around her shoulders and Bianca's hand in hers. Even after his secrecy, even when he'd gone off and been too afraid to send her a note, even after he'd decided, with a sinking heart, that he must try to save Greta even if it cost him his wife.

His wife had been more insightful and compassionate than he deserved. Before he could think, before caution could rear its head and silence him, he pulled her to him and kissed her. "I love you," he breathed. "I love you."

She slid her arms around his neck. "You frightened me half to death."

"I know," he said. "I'm sorry."

"You had better never do it again," she added with a tug at his hair.

"Never," he promised. "I am the poorest excuse for a husband in all Britain."

"As long as Silas Croach walks the earth, you can't be the worst husband anywhere."

He kissed her. "You are the very best of wives to endure my many faults and failings, and I shall spend the rest of my days atoning for being such an idiot to have doubted you."

She took his face in her hands and kissed him back, softly, deeply, completely. "You had better make love to me so I forget how you didn't trust me, after asking *me* to trust you so often . . ."

"Always." Max yanked off his nightshirt and moved over her. Primed to iron, he plowed up her skirts and pushed inside her. Her fingernails dug into his back, and he shuddered at the sight of her beneath him, her eyes shining like silver and her hair dark bronze around her.

"Yes," she moaned. "Yes—*Max*—"

It was the hardest, fastest bout of lovemaking he'd ever had. Neither needed soft tender touches;

Bianca clutched his arse and urged him to harder, deeper strokes. She writhed beneath him, tossing her head from side to side and whispering incoherent words of encouragement, passion, even something like love.

Love.

He fought back his own release until he felt her come. Her climax was a glorious sight to his eyes, and this morning it seemed tinged in shades of rose and gold, like everything about her.

The biggest gamble of his life had paid off beyond his wildest dreams. Not only had he proved himself capable of running a business, he had found Greta and rescued her from the hell Croach had cast her into. He was no longer a penniless rake, living from wager to wager; he was a gentleman of property and purpose. And he had Bianca—fiercely intelligent, passionate and loyal, a match for him in every way.

He had everything a man could ever ask for.

Even if she never loved him back.

Chapter Thirty-One

To the surprise of everyone at Perusia, Frances took Greta protectively under her wing in the next few days. She sent a stream of requests to Cook for various dishes she thought would be beneficial. She refused to allow Greta any spirits or wine, only strong tea—but in great quantities. She plied her with eggs and beef broth with fresh vegetables and fresh fish, but no pudding. When Bianca wondered where her great-aunt had gone one morning, she found both women in the kitchen, toasting bread on forks at the hearth.

"And when it's nicely browned, we'll put some of this lovely cheese on top," Bianca heard her confide, sounding unusually warm and inviting. Greta, looking much better in a proper dress with her hair combed and braided, smiled slightly, swaying on her feet as she held out her fork.

Max looked askance when she relayed the scene. "Should they give Greta a toasting fork? She has a history of attacking—"

"Does she?" Bianca raised her brows. "Did you ever see it?"

He closed his mouth in chagrin. "Of course I didn't."

"If she hits Frances with the fork, it won't be anything Aunt hasn't had coming for years," Bianca added. "But I expect my aunt can look after herself."

Max laughed, his eyes warm and full of love.

Bianca smiled and looked away. She'd heard it, when he said he loved her, but she had not responded to it, and he had not repeated it.

She thought she loved him, but his secrecy had been a blow. Even worse, he had planned never to tell her about Greta at all. Part of her understood completely, and part of her was angry that he would think that way, even after their closeness. If he had said he meant to tell her later, if he had confessed that he hadn't known *how* to tell her and that had kept him silent, she would have believed and forgiven all.

But he had said *never*, and that was a very long time to keep something so significant from her. She still didn't know how to talk to him about it.

"I'm going to Poplar House," she told him. They had remained at Perusia Hall, as had Frances, to avoid upsetting Greta again. Despite being closely monitored every hour of the day, so far Greta seemed more like someone who had survived a terrifying ordeal than a madwoman. Max had reminded her, grimly, that it guaranteed nothing, but even he agreed it was a promising sign that Greta hadn't been violent or wild.

"Will you return before dinner?" Max asked, looking a little disappointed that she was leaving.

"Likely not. I have so many letters to write." Not only had Lady Dalway and Mrs. Farquhar sent very gracious notes, she had decided to tell Cathy everything. Hopefully that would cause the wave of astonishment and dismay to break before Cathy came home, and spare Bianca the worst of it, but either way she had to be honest with her sister. After being so hurt by Max's lies by omission, she had resolved not to commit the same sin herself.

"You could write them here," he offered. "I promise to be very quiet and not rustle my papers."

She laughed, but shook her head. She needed a little space from him, for what she had to write.

"Very well. I'll be here." He masked his disappointment gallantly, gesturing at his papers on the table. Bianca recognized his plan for Fortuna ware. They had discussed it often since London, and she knew he hoped to get her father's approval soon.

Max caught her hand to his lips, then turned it over and pressed his lips for a longer kiss on the inside of her wrist. "'Til then, my love."

She smiled and touched his cheek. Yes, she did love him. No one else made her smile like he did.

MAX WATCHED HER go, his chest brimming with love—and tight with longing. Bianca had been kinder and more compassionate to Greta than he could have ever hoped. If he'd thought himself in love with her before, now he realized how boundless and deep it was, to love someone the way he cared for his wife. After a lifetime of keeping everyone at arm's length, warding them off with caustic humor and rakish wildness, he had found someone who stood by him even at the risk of madness and lunacy. He desperately wanted to see her turn to him with that warm, glowing smile on her face, the way she had after the cricket, when he could swear love had been hanging in the air between them, unspoken but real nonetheless.

But he'd made a mistake not telling Bianca about Greta, and a bigger one by asking her to trust him before impulsively haring off after Leake instead of biding his time in Stoke. Leake's message said only that he'd discovered where Greta was; he'd told Max to wait for him in Stoke, while he made a rescue and spirited Greta there. He hadn't said where she was being held, or how he meant to get her. And like an idiot, Max had bullied the information out of Leake's man and taken off after the thief-taker, both from impatience and from panic that he'd not had time to arrange what to do with Greta when he found her.

In one way, he was glad he'd gone and seen for himself the bleakness of Mowbry Manor, the private hell where Greta and several other people were confined. It had persuaded him fully that he would indeed kill Croach, prison be damned, if the man tried to send her back to a place like that. The screams of the poor souls locked up there would haunt him forever.

But going had turned out to cost him any chance of breaking the news delicately to the Tates. Leake had handily bribed one of the keepers to sneak Greta out, and then he'd brought her to Stoke—and then right into Perusia Hall, without any warning at all, because Max had not been waiting for him at Stoke, where he should have been.

Well. He could not change any of that. His only choice was to continue onward, proving himself a hundred more times if he must. It had been such a terrible mistake, he deserved to suffer. He meant to atone for his stupidity by being the husband Bianca deserved, and proving he'd meant his apologies in every way. And he would wait, to the last iota of his patience, for her to trust him again, no matter how hard it was to keep from professing his love every day.

As Bianca's footsteps faded, Max reviewed some of his notes, and went back to work on the Fortuna plan. This was the only way he knew to restore Samuel Tate's confidence. After Bianca's, Samuel's was the faith he craved most. His father-in-law hadn't spoken to him since that dreadful night, which had been a sharp reproof. It was too late to undo the marriage, but Samuel could easily push him out of Perusia, not to mention deny him a chance to launch Fortuna.

He had worked for some time when the door burst open and Greta flew in, her face a mask of terror. "What's wrong?" he demanded, leaping to his feet.

But he knew.

The keeper at Mowbry Manor had screamed at him, as Max strode away after punching the man in the face, that Mr. Croach would see to him, see if he wouldn't. Max had been waiting every hour since then for Croach to appear in some way, staying in Perusia Hall protectively near Greta, working in the sitting room instead of going down the hill to the offices. Now it appeared the viper himself had come.

Announced only by the sound of a footstep outside the door, Silas Croach appeared. He had once been a handsome man, tall and lean with an oily charm to him. He looked a bit older than Max remembered, but his eyes were the same icy pale green, and his thin smile was as cold and threatening as ever. Greta flung herself behind Max with a low moan.

"Mr. St. James." He made a slow bow that was somehow ominous. "I began to fear for your health, when you did not reply to my letters."

"As you see," replied Max, "I am in perfect health. I simply had nothing to say to you."

"Hmm." Croach smiled wider. "One hopes you will continue to enjoy such excellent health, in Newgate. Kidnapping a woman is a serious offense, particularly when that woman is in desperate need of the care she was receiving."

"A point of fact," said Max. He widened his stance and let his hands curl into loose fists. "I did not kidnap her. Nor, I believe, did anyone, as she came away quite willingly."

"She has no free will," said Croach sharply.

"Not when dosed with laudanum," agreed Max. The local doctor, who had come yesterday morning, said Greta showed signs of poisoning, including laudanum. "And something else that made her see horrific visions. Belladonna, perhaps?"

From Croach's small twitch, Max thought the doctor's guess had been right. "When she flies into madness, laudanum is the only way to calm her. Don't interfere with what you don't understand, my boy."

Greta, who had gone stone-still at the mention of the drugs, now poked Max in the back. He put his hand behind him, trying to reassure her without diverting his attention from Croach. Where had Frances Bentley gone? Bianca had said the two of them were making cheese toast this morning. "You're lying."

Croach simply smiled at this accusation. "She was under a doctor's care," he said. "I only gave her what she needed."

"Close your mouth," he growled. Greta's fingers dug into his back, as if preventing him from attacking Croach. "I promised I'd kill you if you hurt her, and I'm a man of my word."

The other man's gaze was chilling. "Are you? I suppose you might try. If you strike me, it would look very unfortunate to the court. But then . . ." He looked past Max to Greta, and his face grew terrifying. "Madness does run in your blood. A fit of violence is to be expected in these lamentable circumstances. Your aunt is the same way when she becomes overwrought. Perhaps you should both be confined, for the safety of all."

Greta wheezed. Max reached behind him to comfort her, wishing Bianca or Frances were here to take her away. Not only should she never have to see Croach again, she was clinging to his back with a grip of iron. "Get out of this house," he told Croach in a low voice.

The other man raised his brows. "As you wish. I shall take my wife with me, of course." He held out his hand and Greta shrank behind Max, shaking like a leaf. "I expected you would be troublesome about it," he said to Max. "Some men from Mowbry Manor are waiting outside, to convey her safely back to her room there. And I expect Dr. Hawes will have something to say about your attack on him as well, to the magistrate."

"Summon him. I shall appeal for assistance from the Duke of Carlyle," replied Max. "My cousin."

For the first time Croach seemed to understand

that he did not hold an unassailable position. He advanced on Max furiously. "She's *my wife*," he snarled. "Either she's mad, and should be confined for her own safety and that of everyone around her, or she's recovered, in which case I demand her return, so she can fulfill her wifely duties." He smiled at Greta, poisonously. "Come home with me, my dear."

"Nahhhhh," cried Greta.

"Try it." Max spread his arms invitingly, ready to make good on his promise. "Come take her from me."

"Get out!" screamed Greta, suddenly lurching out from behind him. "Get out!"

Croach stopped in his tracks. Max tried to hide his astonishment; he hadn't heard an English word from her in years.

"Merciful heavens," said Frances Bentley irately. "Will someone whip this revolting man from the property, or must I shoot him?"

She had come in from the side door. She held a pistol in her hand. And Bianca was with her.

As Croach stared at her, obviously trying to decipher her role in this scene, Frances added, very matter-of-factly, "I've already had the footmen chase off those men who came with him. Beastly characters, both of them. They seized poor Hickson and dragged him outside, which is disgraceful. They won't be back, not unless they wish to be shot as well."

"Well done, Aunt Frances," said Bianca. "Are you hurt, Greta?" Slowly Greta shook her head. Bianca smiled encouragingly. "Won't you come upstairs? You don't have to see this man ever again."

Croach's veneer of civility dropped. He took a step toward Greta, but stopped when Aunt Frances cocked her pistol. "What you both fail to comprehend," he spat, "is that Margareta is mine. She is my wife, and by God's will she belongs to me. This man has attempted to cheat me of my rights under law!"

"Bosh," said Aunt Frances scornfully. "Marriage laws are such rubbish. I never liked them before, and don't see why I should start now."

"I don't think Greta's mad at all," remarked Bianca. "But I do think you've been abusing her, sir, dosing her with poisonous drugs so you could confine her to an asylum. I suppose you did that to be able to spend her fortune as you pleased."

"Shut your mouth," snapped Croach. "I acted in her best interests. You know nothing about madness or poisons or drugs!"

"No, I don't know about madness," said Bianca thoughtfully. "But I do know a bit about poisons, after working with all those glazing compounds. Chemistry is such an interesting study."

"All right." Croach was breathing hard but trying to maintain his control. "You chased off Dr. Hawes's men, and you think an accusation of poisoning will frighten me away as well. It won't. I have rights, damn you, and the law is on my side!"

"I suppose it will have to be murder, then." Max stripped off his coat. He felt delusional himself, but also drunk on the thought of beating Croach to a cinder, whether or not it became murder. He'd *dreamed* of this. "Bianca darling, will you fetch a shovel?"

"Don't be ridiculous," said Bianca. "We'll put him in one of the kilns."

Max blinked, startled. He had not expected that.

Croach laughed after a moment. "I say, Maxim! A bloodthirsty little slut, ain't she?"

"Not really," said Bianca, as calmly as before. "There's no reason to make such a mess. One good blow should incapacitate him long enough to carry him down the hill. Kiln four is ready to fire. Have Lawrence take his horse to Lichfield to sell, and no one will ever know he was here."

This set Croach back on his heels. A frown creased his brow. "Be careful what you say, madam. Making threats will not stand you well."

In reply she lifted the fire tongs she had been holding behind her skirt. "Our kilns are hot enough to melt glass, sir. In four days' time there won't be anything left of you but a pile of ash, nothing at all for a magistrate or coroner to investigate. It is not an empty threat."

Croach glanced between them.

"If I were you," said Max, "I would run."

"Far, and fast," added Bianca.

"Get out," repeated Greta in a low growl.

"I wouldn't mind shooting him," announced Frances. "I have never liked this carpet and if we have to burn it in the kiln with the body, so much the better."

Bianca's lips twitched. Greta suddenly laughed. "Burn, burn, burn," she declared in delight. "Silas will burn!"

That, more than anything, seemed to unnerve Croach. "Silence," he snarled at her, but Greta took a step toward him, and he stopped.

"You poisoned me," she said, slowly but clearly. "You can burn."

"For pity's sake. Hold my spare," said Frances to Bianca, handing over her second pistol. "Goodbye, Mr. Croach." She raised her pistol, and Croach gave a shout before sprinting from the room. Max took off after him, only stopping when Croach was galloping away, glancing behind him with a mixture of terror and hatred.

He stood, breathing hard, and watched until Croach was out of sight. It wasn't the last of the man, unfortunately, but Max would be ready for him next time. Leake had uncovered some of the mad doctors Croach had hired, at least one of whom stood accused of poisoning a man into madness at the instigation of his mother, over a planned engagement the mother disapproved of. Dr. Hawes at Mowbry Manor would also no doubt suffer an inspection by the local justice of the peace.

Max turned back toward the house. God above. Never had he been so astonished in his life, between Mrs. Bentley threatening to shoot Croach and Bianca coolly planning to shove the man's corpse into a kiln to dispose of it.

And Greta had spoken English. Combined with the doctor's diagnosis that she showed signs of laudanum dosing, perhaps Bianca was right, and Greta wasn't really mad at all. She'd stood up to her husband after he'd almost killed her.

Feeling lighter than he could ever remember, Max walked back inside. He found Greta on the settee with Frances Bentley, chattering away in a mixture of German and English, more animated than he'd seen her in . . . forever. The pistols lay on the side table, and Bianca was pouring small glasses of port for all of them. At his entrance, she grinned and handed him one. Max was astonished that his hand shook, while hers were steady. He threw back the drink with one gulp.

Greta leapt up. "Silas?"

"Er ist gegangen," he replied, then again, "He's gone."

"Gut," she said. "Good!"

Max laughed, relief and joy.

"Good for him, you mean," remarked Frances, sipping her port.

"And I hope he knows it," added Bianca. "Would you really have shot him, Aunt?"

"Of course I would have!" The older woman frowned at her. "I looked forward to it, if you must know."

"Right," murmured Max. He picked up the pistols. "I'll take care of these."

"They aren't loaded," said Bianca.

"The first one is," retorted Frances. "I haven't loaded a pistol in years! It took too long to do both."

Bianca laughed. "Well, I am sure Papa will be relieved that we didn't shoot indoors, and aren't going to burn the carpet. He would have to buy a new one, which he would complain of to no end."

"He could hardly choose an uglier one," murmured Frances with a sniff. "I shall have to hope someone spills a decanter of wine on it, I suppose." Greta broke into peals of laughter.

Max stood in silent amazement, a pistol in each hand, watching the three of them. He had feared they would revile him for bringing a madwoman into their family. Instead there sat Greta beside them, supported even to the point of violence, and her venomous husband was the one chased off the property. "You are the most remarkable women I've ever met," he said, humbled.

"Yes," said Frances serenely. "I trust you won't forget it again."

Chapter Thirty-Two

The furor over Croach had barely died down two days later.

Papa, ranting about dangerous villains, instituted a patrol of armed watchmen around all the grounds of Perusia, including Poplar House and the village. He upbraided the servants as well, including a despairing Mr. Hickson, who had been lured outside and kept there by Mr. Croach's madhouse conspirators. Aunt Frances told him off for that, but Papa didn't relent until Greta appealed to him for understanding.

Bianca thought her father was developing a soft spot for Greta. As her health recovered and her English improved, Greta was a very striking woman. Bianca caught Papa sneaking looks at her during dinner.

Aunt Frances had overruled Max's protests and decreed that Greta would stay with her. "Everyone is at the potteries all day except me," she said. "She would be desperately lonely at Poplar House. Why shouldn't she take my second-best bedchamber? If that horrid Croach comes sniffing around again, she'll be out of sight at Ivy Cottage."

Then Frances hired four new footmen, tall brawny lads from Stoke. Bianca thought she must have been wanting to do that for years, and now saw a perfect justification. But it was genuinely moving how kind and supportive Frances was with Greta, and the footmen did set Max's mind at ease.

As for herself . . . Bianca could not deny that her hurt was fading rapidly. The more Greta spoke about her ordeal, the more appalled everyone at Perusia was, but especially Bianca. She could see that every word was an arrow in Max's chest; once he had physically hunched over as Greta described how Dr. Hawes sent his inmates running for hours over gravel in bare feet, driven onward by keepers with whips.

Bianca had wondered, what would she have done, had it been Cathy in such a place? If she had feared for her sister's life, but been uncertain that anyone else would care about Cathy—or if they might even quietly wish her dead? Secrecy, lies, desperate midnight races across the county . . . yes, she thought she could have done all that and more, to save her sister from the nightmare Greta described.

She had been thinking of her sister a great deal lately. Not only was this the longest they had ever gone without speaking, it seemed as if so much had happened since Cathy's elopement that Bianca thought she might burst from not having told her any of it. The long explanatory letter had been written and dispatched, but it was not the same; her sister was not there to respond, and question, and tease, and wag her finger in Bianca's face before folding her into a comforting embrace. More than ever she needed a confidant, and this time Max would not do—because he was the topic she desperately wanted to talk about.

He called her his love every day; he made love to her at nights with a passionate tenderness that made her skin glow and her heart swell. He told her he was wrong, and that he was sorry beyond words that he hadn't told her everything. She said she forgave him, and she did—she had.

She loved him.

But somehow those words never came out.

She asked herself why as she stood waiting for him after the horn blew, just inside the tall gates of Perusia. He had been closeted with Papa all today, presenting his plan for Fortuna ware. He had asked if she wanted to go with him, but Bianca had laughed and said no; she had already told her father she thought it was a brilliant idea, and all Max had to do was lay it out.

Even she had been startled by the breadth of his intentions and planning. Not only did he have a list of wares to produce, complete with sketches, he had sample price lists, proposed lists of shopkeepers who might carry it in Liverpool and Birmingham, and suggestions for how to advertise. He had a list of workers to divert to Fortuna and a plan for assigning and promoting workers in both Fortuna and Perusia.

And at the end, he proposed a small production of porcelain items, pretty and delicate, aimed at the boudoirs of ladies of less expansive means. Darling little pots for rouge, light simple dishes for powder— with matching brush handles—even chamber pots that served their purposes attractively, and with close-fitting lids.

Bianca knew the porcelain was for her. Papa had disdained paste, and without his approval she couldn't work with it. But if Papa approved this plan, they *would* be making it, and she would get to experiment with it to her heart's delight.

Bianca had been bowled over by how deeply Max had thought out everything. Papa, who was accustomed to approving a new idea or suggestion on the spot when presented with a sample of it, would be awestruck.

At last, Papa and Max emerged from the office, still deep in conversation. Bianca went up on her toes to see over the crowds of workers leaving for the day, and caught sight of her father's beaming smile.

Her heart soared, and she clapped a hand to her mouth to keep from bursting out in delight. Papa was pleased. Max was smiling, too; Papa had approved and given his blessing. After so many weeks of discussion with Max, Bianca had almost come to think it already had been, but today she realized how anxious she—and Max, no doubt—had been about it.

They joined her and she couldn't hold back anymore. "Did you support his ideas, Papa?" she demanded.

He chuckled. "How could I not? I've never seen a more complete plan for anything, including this factory. Of course I did. Only an idiot wouldn't be willing to give it a go."

Bianca laughed, already looking to her husband. "Congratulations," she said softly.

He took her hand and kissed her wrist, his eyes twinkling. "At least half of it is due to you."

"You're too generous," she replied.

"No, I'm too fortunate by half," he said as they started toward home, Papa striding in the lead. "I told him which parts were your ideas."

"Nothing is surer to invite his critical eye," she said, but at the same time she blushed with pleasure.

"Mr. St. James! Mr. St. James!" John, one of the young workers in the modeling workshop, was pursuing them. "I tried to catch you, sir, to see if you'd want to see the pots you told me and Bobby Jenkins to throw for you."

Max hesitated. "Go on," Bianca said, untangling her arm from his. She knew he'd been waiting to see those pots. John and Bobby were atop his list for workers to bring into Fortuna, and their ability to do what he asked was key to its success.

"Just a quick look," he said, giving in. "I'll see you at home?"

She nodded, and to her surprise he leaned down and kissed her, lightly, quickly, on the mouth. "Thank you, love," he whispered, then turned and strode off with John trotting beside him.

"A hard worker, that one," said Papa as she joined him on the path up the hill. "How long has he been at this Fortuna business?"

"I expect since he arrived at Perusia. Certainly he had a fully composed idea when we went to London."

Papa grunted. "I knew I was right about him! Got Markham to pay in full, and by the end of this year Perusia wares will be serving a duke and two earls. He's got a nerve, you can't deny that."

She laughed. "And you've not even mentioned his greatest contribution to Perusia."

Papa brightened at this teasing mention of the redware cricket vase. "True, true! I give it a fond pat every morning and reflect with pleasure that Mannox does not have it. I mean to hold on to it, too, you know. St. James had better practice his batting before next year's wakes."

"He suggested we form a cricket club."

"A fine idea," exclaimed Papa. "There's a fair prospect for a pitch below Frances's terrace . . ."

They were still laughing when they reached Perusia Hall, where Hickson came out to meet them. "Miss Tate has returned home, sir," he said, his face bright with eagerness. "Oh no—I do beg your pardon—Mr. and Mrs. Mayne!"

Bianca had already run past him into the house, darting down the corridor toward the sound of voices. At her entrance, Cathy and Mr. Mayne looked up from the tea tray in front of them.

"Bianca!" Cathy rose and opened her arms, and Bianca flew to her sister with a cry of delight. "Oh my dear, it's been so long," Cathy said, laughing and crying at the same time. "Let me look at you!"

Bianca stepped back, keeping her grip on Cathy's hands. She knew what had caught her sister's eyes. "Do you like my hair? Jennie learned it in London."

"It's beautiful." Cathy smiled. "Jennie must be so pleased to be a lady's maid at last! She and Ellen skirmished regularly . . ."

Bianca laughed. "Wait until you see the gowns I ordered in town! I declare the dressmakers there are so artful, they made even me look handsome."

"Bee," said Cathy with a helpless smile of reproach. "Of course you're lovely!"

Bianca grinned. "And *you* look blissfully happy."

"I am, Bee, I am." Cathy did look blissful. There was a glow to her face that hadn't been there before. For a moment the joy of seeing her sister again almost made Bianca shed a tear.

Cathy's face went still, and she released Bianca. Bianca turned her head, even as she instinctively stepped aside.

Papa stood in the doorway, one hand on the jamb as if to hold himself up. Cathy's chin trembled. She started forward, hands outstretched. "Papa," she said in her soft pleading voice.

Their father broke. Two swift steps forward and he swept her into his arms, holding her tight. Cathy's arms were around his neck, and Bianca guessed her sister was sobbing her apologies into his shoulder. Tactfully she went to greet Mr. Mayne, who had remained quietly to the side, and offered him her congratulations and welcome.

Of course Papa forgave Cathy instantly. After a few minutes they came to the table together, with Papa fumbling for his handkerchief as tears sparkled openly on Cathy's cheeks. "And you must forgive Richard, Papa," she said, reaching for her husband to come forward.

"Mayne," said Papa gruffly, extending his hand. "I suppose there's nothing for it but to welcome you to the family."

Mr. Mayne's face eased. "Thank you, sir. I am deeply sorry for the dismay and pain we caused here, but I love your daughter to distraction. I hope we have your blessing."

"Aye, aye," muttered Papa, swiping at his eyes. "But here—you must be wondering how Bianca is! And you'll want to meet her husband again, too. I hope you're not upset about that, Cathy, with your sister marrying the fellow."

Cathy bit her lip. Mayne looked downward. Bianca realized with a jolt of dismay that her long letter, explaining everything, couldn't have reached her sister. It had been sent to Wolverhampton only yesterday. She cursed herself for a coward, putting it off so long. "Max should be right behind us," she said in the silence. "He was delayed at the pottery, seeing to some new wares."

Cathy moved to the edge of the settee. "Bianca . . . I have been in agony since Papa's letter. My dear, when you agreed to help me, I never—I didn't dream—oh, I am so sorry!"

"Bosh," she said uneasily. "There's nothing to apologize for! I'm not sorry I helped you elope . . ."

"But look at the price you paid!" cried Cathy. "Coerced into marrying that conniving, fortune-hunting rake!" Bianca blinked. Papa scowled and opened his mouth, and Cathy turned on him wrathfully. "You knew he was, Papa, when he first turned up! When he wanted me, your main argument in his favor was his connection to the Duke of Carlyle. He had no fortune, no profession, nothing to recommend him but that one connection!"

Papa stirred uncomfortably. "Well . . . Come now, Cathy . . ."

"And in exchange for that you sold your daughter into marriage to a man she didn't know, who didn't even want her!" Cathy was in full roar now, hands waving and eyes flashing.

Bianca lowered her voice. "Cathy, let me explain—things are different now—"

"Yes, so I understand. Ellen was telling me all about it, how his aunt is a raving madwoman and he brought her here, provoking the poor woman's husband to come and threaten Aunt Frances and Bianca both!"

Bianca cursed Ellen's wagging tongue. "That is not the full story—"

"Bianca." Cathy seized her hands again. "It does not matter. As soon as Papa told me what happened, I went to Richard. He's a man of the church, and he knew precisely what questions to ask. Tell her, Richard. Tell her how she can be free of this man."

Bianca's mouth fell open in shock. "*Cathy . . .*"

Richard Mayne sat forward. He was a tall, rangy fellow, quiet and reserved. His shaggy brown hair fell over his forehead like a boy's, but he had a calm, quiet way of speaking that commanded attention. "It's not a legal marriage."

Now Bianca was quite literally speechless.

"What?" barked Papa.

"It's not a legal marriage between Bianca and Maximilian St. James," repeated Mayne. "I explained as much as we knew to my superior, Mr. Williams in Wolverhampton, and he concurs. The license was issued to St. James and Cathy." He couldn't stop a fond glance at his wife. "The fact that he wed Bianca instead means there was no valid license, and of course there were no banns called, since it happened on the spur of the moment."

Bianca's heart felt like a silent boom inside her chest. Good God. She'd never thought of that. She could barely speak, her lips and throat had gone so dry. She pulled free of her sister's grip. "But since then—Cathy, we were married in *church*. Everyone came to the wedding breakfast. We have lived as man and wife . . ."

In every way. Her skin flushed at the memory of how intimate she and Max had become.

Was it all false? Were they not really married?

Richard was still speaking. "It is an obstacle, but not an insurmountable one. A claim of fraud will do, and Mr. Filpot will testify that he was asked to wed St. James to Cathy, not to Bianca. I daresay the license will show signs of being altered as well."

"But Cathy bolted," protested Papa. "And Bianca agreed to it!"

"That does not matter," replied Richard somberly. "The lack of a proper license invalidates the marriage."

No. She did not want her marriage invalidated. Bianca shook her head, her thoughts flying too rapidly. "No— Wait— Are you certain? Can that be true?"

"By Church law it is," said Cathy, seizing her hand again. "Oh, Bee, I remember how you scorned him! I remember how you portrayed marriage to him— how I must subjugate my desires to his own, suffer *his* temper and indulge *his* vanities, from now until the day I died! I know you would never wish that for yourself, you who swore marriage was not for you! None of the kind, amiable gentlemen who asked to court you pleased you, and then you were coerced into marriage with a man who is everything you despise!"

Bianca squirmed at having her own angry words turned back at her. "Cathy, don't . . ."

"Coerced!" blustered Papa indignantly. "Hardly that!"

"Papa. I know you, and I know Bianca," said Cathy with a severe look. "You told her Perusia would be lost to her, didn't you—Perusia, the only thing she's ever truly loved."

Bianca jerked in astonishment. That was not true. Good heavens, is that what her sister thought?

But Cathy rolled on in a passion. "You were angry, Papa, and you made *her* angry, and she agreed to it in a fury—I know you both, please don't argue," she said, flinging up her hand as both opened their mouths to do just that. "And in that fit of anger, neither of you willing to back down and lose face, Bianca was wed to a stranger whose main interest is Perusia. Papa, don't you see it?" She swiveled to Bianca as their father turned red in the face. "And Bee—I know you did it for me. I never wanted you to pay such a price! No, I never would have gone if I'd thought this would happen! I would have stayed, and refused to speak in the church." Tears welled in her eyes for a moment. "But don't worry. We will make it right for you. Richard has spoken to everyone, and they are all united in their opinions. The marriage is invalid, and can be wiped away as if it never existed."

In the sudden, frozen silence after this speech, Bianca's reeling senses still caught the sound of a quiet footstep. Then another and another, retreating from the door, and with a sinking heart she knew that it was Max, and that he had heard.

She wrenched free of her sister's grip. "You're wrong, Cathy, *all wrong*," she managed to say, and then she was running after her husband, her heart like lead in her chest.

Chapter Thirty-Three

Max climbed the hill with a spring in his step. John and Bobby had produced a run of teapots that were precisely what he wanted: simple, clean, and perfect. By now he knew what flaws would catch Tate's eye, and he had satisfied himself there were none. Tate had been impressed by his plans today, but had warned that he still needed proof the workers could produce wares of high enough quality to put his name on them. Only if Max could demonstrate that the less experienced workers could produce wares of high enough quality would Samuel approve.

John's and Bobby's pots meant Fortuna wares would get a start.

Hickson met him at the door and informed him that Mr. Tate and Mrs. St. James were in the parlor, with Mr. and Mrs. Mayne. "Ah," said Max in pleasure. He knew Bianca had missed her sister, and everyone had been expecting them any day now. He headed toward the parlor, where the door had been left open.

". . . not a legal marriage," said a man's voice.

Max paused.

"What?" exclaimed Tate.

"It's not a legal marriage between Bianca and Maximilian St. James," repeated the unknown fellow.

Max's feet rooted to the floor as the man—presumably Catherine Tate's curate—explained the fault in the license, the requirements of the law, the grounds for invalidating Max's marriage.

He couldn't find a flaw in the fellow's argument. But even worse, he didn't hear Bianca protesting that it *was* valid, that she didn't give a damn about the license, that she wanted to be wed to him now, no matter what she'd thought and said weeks ago.

You damned fool, he thought to himself. He'd been cynically amused at the time about Tate bribing the visiting vicar to amend the license; he hadn't realized it would be the trap door to release Bianca from her vows.

There—that was it, his fevered brain thought. Tate bribed the vicar, making both of them complicit in any wrongdoing. Surely neither would want to stir up trouble now . . .

But still he listened for Bianca's outburst, and heard nothing but confused questions from her, testing the argument.

Slowly he backed away, not wanting to hear any more but unable to close his ears to it. *I remember how you scorned him . . . a man who is everything you despise . . . Perusia, the only thing you've ever truly loved . . . The marriage is invalid, and can be wiped away as if it never existed.*

Finally he turned and slipped out the garden door. He was halfway home before the full impact hit him.

Poplar House, standing before him with its welcoming blue door, wasn't *home*; it wasn't his. The marriage contract had been signed after the wedding, properly amended with Bianca's name in the right places. But if Samuel Tate meant to invalidate the marriage itself, the contract—complete with possession of Poplar House and his stake in Perusia—would be next.

Max would be penniless again, homeless and discarded. And this time with his heart in broken shards too small to put back together.

He had lost everything before, when he had little enough to lose. He had laughed it off, cursed at Fate, charged belligerently back to the tables the next night, intent on swinging his luck around. This time . . . this time he was numb. He'd had everything he ever wanted—no, far more—and he'd lost it, through some stupid error that hadn't even been his doing. How did a man come back from this?

He went inside and dismissed Lawrence. Leave it for tomorrow to tell the man he was being turned off again, let go by another employer who'd risked what he could not afford to lose, and lost everything.

He was standing in his bedchamber—which had been *their* bedchamber—staring out the window when Bianca finally came home. Her voice echoed in the stairwell, and then her footsteps pounded up. Was she coming to throw him out? Fortune hunter, liar, lunatic . . . which would she call him?

"Max!" She flung open the door and let out a gusty breath. "Thank goodness. There you are."

"Yes." Thin puffs of smoke rose over the hill, white against the twilit sky. It was the kilns, firing the first pieces of Wimbourne's order. He wondered if

Bianca would deliver it to the duke herself. Wimbourne would enjoy that. "Here I am."

"I thought you'd gone to Greta—Hickson said he thought you'd gone that way, but he was wrong . . ." She was gasping for breath between words. "I ran all the way to Ivy Cottage, and then all the way here . . ."

"No," he murmured. God. Would Mrs. Bentley allow Greta to stay, at least until Max could scrabble together something suitable? He'd have to do it quickly, before Croach got wind of things and realized Max was helpless to stop him from snatching her again.

"You heard—I know you heard what Cathy said," Bianca said, coming toward him.

"Yes." He'd read enough law to suspect Richard Mayne was correct. The license had been altered improperly, and that was probably enough to invalidate his marriage. All Bianca would have to say was that she hadn't wanted to marry him.

And perhaps he shouldn't fight it. All those things Mrs. Mayne had said about Bianca—that Max had been everything she despised, that she'd only married him to keep control of Perusia, that she had done it all in a mindless fury—those were true.

Silas Croach had also spoken truly when he said Greta belonged to him, under the law. Max hadn't cared. Greta didn't want to live with him, and Max had been willing to beat Croach to a cinder to prevent his aunt being forced back into a marriage she didn't want. He could hardly ask Bianca to stay with him, if she wanted out.

"She's correct, you know," he said, watching the

smoke dissipate on the breeze. There was a blazing fire below, but a few hundred feet later, nothing remained of it. "About the validity of the license, and hence the marriage."

"Well, that's ridiculous," she exclaimed. "We've been married for more than three months! How can that be invalid?"

"The law cares naught, my dear. If you wish to have it swept away like so many shards of broken pottery"—he flicked his fingers in illustration—"it shall be."

"Max." She caught his arm and made him turn to her. "What are you going on about?"

He looked at her face, so beautiful and beloved, so flushed from running after him. "If you want to invalidate the marriage, I won't protest it."

"What?" She looked outraged. "Why not? Curse you, don't tell me you don't care!"

Gently he laid his hand on her cheek. She clasped his wrist as if she were drowning. "I care," he said softly. "Too much to hold you, if you want rid of me."

She flung his hand aside. "Then I expect to hear some sign that you want to stay!"

His temper stirred, and this time, recklessly, he didn't force it back down. "Do you need more? Have I not shown you all this time?"

"You have," she said wrathfully. "And you've been so bloody patient, waiting for me to get over being hurt about Greta—"

"You saw Croach," he charged. "You heard what he said about her—about me. Madness is in our blood! How could I tell you that and bring that sort of darkness into your home, your family?"

"Well, I suppose now I see that you don't think I'm strong enough to hear such news without falling into a fainting fit!"

"Strong enough! You! You, who could run this entire factory and win the cricket match to boot!"

"I bloody well could! And *you* didn't trust me!" she shrieked.

Max's blood was running furiously. He'd never let his temper loose like this. "Didn't you hear me—I told *no one* about the madness in my family. I didn't keep it from you for a laugh, I kept it from you because I thought it would send you screaming in the other direction!"

"I don't even think she's mad! You should have told me about her, if nothing else!"

"I couldn't bear to lose you," he fired back. "I wanted to put it off until you cared for me, and could overlook it. More fool me!"

"Yes!" She smacked his arm. "Because you're too big an idiot to see that I *do* love you, even after you took a piece of my factory and had cleverer ideas for it than I did and risked your life to save Greta and made forty-five in the cricket and told me I'm beautiful when I'm not—"

Max threw up his hands. "I don't know why I bothered! You're clearly just as mad as I am! It is the only earthly explanation for why I would allow you to provoke me into this ridiculous screaming argument over how desperately in love with you I am, and always will be, and if you think you're going to invalidate our marriage, *you're* mad, and I'll fight it 'til the end of my days because we belong together!"

"That's the first sensible thing you've said tonight!" She seized his head and pulled him down for a fierce kiss.

Recklessly he kissed her back. With two steps he pushed her to the wall, clawing up her skirts. She yanked at his breeches, sending a button flying before taking him in her hand, so firmly he gasped.

"Mine," he growled, hooking her leg around his waist and pulling her higher.

"Mine," she retorted, pulling the tie from his hair and taking hold of a handful.

He bared his teeth and thrust into her. Bianca curled her legs around his waist and arched her back, and he needed no more encouragement.

Having been wrought to a fever pitch of arousal and passion, both were on the brink. Max felt her come within moments, hot and tight around him, and he reached his own climax instantly, so violent and sudden his vision dimmed.

"I told you," Bianca panted, shaking in his arms. "Someday we would shout at each other . . ."

Max gave a wheezy laugh. "Our servants must be huddling under the table in abject fear."

"Oh goodness, let them." Eyes glowing, she kissed him. "I love you," she said softly. "I love you, Max, I do. Cathy caught me off guard—"

"I know." He kissed her back.

"I should have told you sooner," she went on as his mouth drifted over her eyebrows and temple. "I was so hurt you didn't tell me about Greta, and I was so frightened those two days you were gone—"

"I was entirely at fault. I will never do that again."

She pulled his face level with hers. "I was wrong to be so cold to you in the beginning. I agreed to the marriage on impulse, but once it was accomplished, I ought to have made the best of things. Instead—"

"I do not hold anything against you," he said, laying a fingertip on her lips. "Nothing. I have no stones to cast, having kept a large secret of my own."

She smiled hesitantly. "Then we shall start anew?"

"Anew?" Max quirked a brow. "And lose all the ground we've gained? No, I think we should continue on from this moment, mindful of our own faults and considerate of the other's sensibilities. What do you say, love? Will you carry on with me, in spite of our faulty marriage license?"

A slow, enchanting smile curved her lips. "I will. This time pledging my whole heart to you in true love and honesty."

"And I do pledge my whole heart and honesty to you." He rested his forehead against hers. "'Til the end of time."

She kissed him. "That's a fine start."

Chapter Thirty-Four

❧⸱❧

Five weeks later
Carlyle Castle

They saw the castle long before they reached it.

Bianca alternated between hanging out the window in astonishment and stealing amazed glances at him. Max, who had seen it before, was content to enjoy her awe.

"And you're really heir to all this?" she finally asked, settling into the seat beside him. They had been on Carlyle property for almost the last hour, and the castle itself still loomed ahead of them.

"Second," he said. "A distant cousin, an army man, outranks me. The chances of my ever sniffing a dukedom are vanishingly small, love."

"This is a vast deal closer than I ever thought to come to one." She looked out the window again. "We're here."

Up close, the castle was even more impressive. The gray stone walls towered above them, and they drove through a narrow stone arch into a courtyard so large, there was a neatly kept garden in the center.

Max stepped down, waiting for the onslaught of tension or apprehension at facing the duchess again, and felt . . . nothing.

Well—not nothing. He felt a burst of pride as Bianca stepped down in her beautiful cream gown from London. They had stopped at an inn a few miles ago to refresh themselves, and Max had had a hard time keeping his hands off her since. She was breathtakingly beautiful, even before she sent him a mischievous glance and wrinkled her nose ever so slightly and sniffed.

He could only smile back at her.

Her hand on his arm, they walked up the shallow steps to the butler standing at the open doors. After showing them to a more handsome guest chamber than the last one Max had inhabited, the butler conducted them through elegant corridors quieted by lush carpets, through a paneled great hall lined with tapestries and paintings, and up a grand staircase of intricately carved stone into what Max privately referred to as the Audience Chamber.

The duchess was waiting there, as plump and gray as Max remembered. Her companion sat quietly behind her, a large ginger cat on her lap. "So," the duchess remarked, after the introductions had been made, "you certainly did not waste any time, Mr. St. James."

He bowed. "No, Your Grace."

Her gaze transferred to Bianca. "You must know about your husband's connection to Carlyle."

"Yes, Your Grace," said Bianca. She stood erect and gazed forthrightly back at the intimidating duchess. "I was very sorry to hear of your son's passing. My heartfelt sympathies on your loss."

The duchess blinked in surprise. "Yes. Thank you. That is very kind, Mrs. St. James." She turned her head to glare at Max. "I suppose you are here to demonstrate that you have made yourself more respectable."

He smiled. "I have come to thank you, ma'am. Your generous offer provided the means I needed to do just that. And now, I have come to say, I am no longer in need of your assistance."

"What?" she demanded after a shocked moment. "What do you say to me, Mr. St. James?"

"I am determined not to be a burden, Your Grace. You need not pay the allowance you offered me the last time I was here."

She pursed up her lips in displeasure. Max was sure he knew why; now she had no leverage over him. "As you wish, sir. Far be it from me to force an income upon a man!" She turned back to Bianca. "You are of the Staffordshire Tates, are you not?"

"Yes, ma'am. My father is Samuel Tate, of Perusia."

"Hmph." The duchess looked at her with unwilling interest. "My solicitor tells me you work in the factory."

Max could see how surprised Bianca was, but he doubted the duchess did. His wife was as poised as ever, confidently answering questions from the older woman. "I do, ma'am. I formulate the glazes used in our finest wares."

"Glazes!"

"I recently developed a brilliant scarlet red glaze. We have only just begun filling orders for it."

Again the duchess's lips pursed. "And what is your part in this endeavor, Mr. St. James?"

"I have taken it upon myself to arrange viewings

for interested parties who might wish to order a service of dinnerware," he said. "His Grace the Duke of Wimbourne recently ordered thirty settings." He paused, then added, "Wimbourne and I were at Oxford together."

"Wimbourne!" The duchess made a face. "Not even married! What use has he got for a dinner service?" She leaned forward. "I want to see these dishes. If you came all this way, I expect you've brought a few."

Max smiled. "Yes, ma'am. We have indeed brought a tea service in the new scarlet glaze, and hope you will accept it as our thanks for your generosity."

That had been Bianca's idea. "Without her, we would not be here, together," she'd told him, and Max had packed up the service without another word. If it came down to thanking the duchess for enabling him to approach Samuel Tate with his audacious marriage and business proposal, Max would send a new service to Carlyle House every year, and bear the expense himself.

It seemed to astonish the duchess. "Well," she said, then again, "Well. That is thoughtful of you. Miss Kirkpatrick, see to it." The companion silently rose and slipped out. Max had left the crate, each glittering ruby piece nestled in a black velvet box, with the butler. Max and Bianca were invited to sit, and the duchess quizzed them about the factory, Bianca's family, and Max's role in it.

Unbidden he told her about Greta. In the month since being rescued, his aunt had improved a great deal. She spoke mainly English now, had put on some healthy weight, and took long rambling walks in the country with Frances and a pair of the handsome footmen. She was returning to the woman Max remembered, and he knew it was due to Bianca and her family, who had taken her in with unfaltering support and kindness.

The duchess was gratifyingly angry over Greta's treatment. "A madhouse!" she declared indignantly. "How dare he! If he returns and gives you any trouble at all, I trust you will send Mr. Edwards after him. Edwards knows how to tear a person apart without leaving a mark."

"Thank you, ma'am, I shall bear it in mind."

Miss Kirkpatrick returned some time later, followed by a maid carrying a large tray with the new tea service on it, replete with cakes and pastries. "Ah!" The duchess gazed with interest on the teacups and the teapot, one of the finest Perusia had ever produced, with a fluted rim and embossed lattice-work handle. "I commend you, Mrs. St. James. I would have thought it was genuine rubies."

Bianca smiled modestly. "Thank you, ma'am."

After they had left the duchess—in a noticeably warmer mood—they toured the house. Max thought Bianca might like to see it once, although as her eyes climbed the tall, narrow windows in the dining room, a relic of the castle's Norman past, he thought he might have let himself in for some teasing as well. They visited his ancestor's portrait, and Bianca agreed he looked a bit of a rogue.

"Then again," she whispered to him as they strolled out of the gallery, "I have a greater fondness for rogues now . . ."

They did not see Mr. Edwards, the solicitor, until the day they left. While the luggage was being stowed in the carriage, they had walked outside the castle walls to the rose garden, terraced on the sunny southern side of the motte. Mr. Edwards begged a moment of Max's time, and so they left Bianca admiring the roses.

"Her Grace tells me you have refused further payments under her proposal," said the solicitor once they had reached his office.

Max bowed. "You have the right of it, sir."

"If I may be so bold, sir," said the solicitor, "do not be an idiot."

Max raised his brows. "I beg your pardon."

"Despite what you might think, Her Grace did not offer the income to hold you under her thumb." Edwards put up his hands at Max's cynical look. "Not entirely to do so," he amended. "It was her fondest hope that it would rouse your interest in Carlyle as well. Becoming duke would be an enormous challenge, and she did not wish to see you struggle under the weight of it. Any preparation at all would be invaluable."

Max frowned. "We both know the odds that I'll inherit are vanishingly small."

Mr. Edwards coughed delicately. "*Do* we know that, sir?"

"Yes," said Max slowly, staring at him. "I understand the current duke is in declining health, but Captain St. James is hale and vigorous."

Mr. Edwards folded his hands on his desk. "Yes. You are correct about His Grace's health, lamentably. However . . . I would not brush off all expectation, sir."

"Why?"

"We've not heard from Captain St. James since he went north," said the solicitor. "He intended to visit

Scotland to inform his mother and sisters of his good fortune, and then return. We expected him weeks ago. Unfortunately, he has not returned, nor has he sent word."

Max's brain froze. The St. James family tree rose in his memory, stark and spare with all those stunted branches, bare of heirs. "I see," he murmured.

Mr. Edwards smiled. "I am relieved to hear it. Her Grace was very pleasantly surprised by your visit. Managing a factory, while hardly comparable to a dukedom, is at least a step in the right direction."

"You'll let me know, won't you?" Max demanded, ignoring the slight to his new profession. "If you hear from the captain?"

Edwards bowed his head. "Of course, sir. And I shall continue paying your income."

In a daze Max walked back out to his wife. In the sunlight, in this magnificent garden, she was unbearably beautiful, her hair shining like honey under her straw hat, her gloved hands trailing through the last of the summer roses.

At his approach, she smiled. "What news? Have they decided to banish us back to Staffordshire?"

He didn't smile back. "They've not heard from Captain St. James in weeks. He returned to Scotland and hasn't come back as planned."

Her eyes grew wide. "But then . . . that means . . ."

Grimly he nodded. "This could be ours."

"No," she said, stricken. "What about the showroom in London, and the Cheapside shop? What about Fortuna?"

"I'm afraid," he said, "if they cannot locate my cousin the captain, and the duke departs this mortal vale, there may be no choice."

Together, silently, they surveyed the castle. From outside the main walls, it rose forbidding and impregnable, ancient and commanding. Max had never wanted it, although he had once thought the power and wealth that came with the castle wouldn't be unwelcome.

Now, though . . . Now he already *had* everything he wanted—his aunt, restored mostly to herself. A home of his own, not nearly so grand as this one but happy and comfortable. A purpose to his days, with people who respected him and depended on him. And Bianca, who surpassed everything he'd ever thought a wife could be, at his side and in his heart.

What the bloody hell would he do with Carlyle, if the captain had met an unfortunate end and ceded his place in the succession?

"Well," Bianca said after a long pause. "It looks like a prison to me. You're very fortunate I love you so much."

Max laughed, his somber mood breaking. "That is in fact the most fortunate thing about me, my love. And if I must inherit this monstrous pile of stones and become as stuffy and priggish as Wimbourne, I shall only bear it because of you."

She laughed, and he kissed her. "I think we had better run for it while we can," she confided.

Max glanced again at the imposing stone walls as they turned toward the carriage. A prison, indeed. "And pray very earnestly for Captain St. James's health and safety."

Next month, don't miss these exciting new love stories only from Avon Books

Suddenly You by Lisa Kleypas

Novelist Amanda Briars wasn't about to greet her next birthday without making love to a man. When Jack Delvin appeared at her door, she believed he was her gift to herself, hired for one night of passion. Unforgettably handsome, irresistibly virile, he tempted her in ways she never thought possible . . . but when fate conspired for them to marry, their worlds collided with a passionate force neither had expected . . .

Dark Guardian by Christine Feehan

Jaxon Montgomery is a woman hunted. Trained by the Special Forces, honed by a traumatic childhood, she is a policewoman with an undisputed reputation. She meets her match when she is set up to be murdered by an enemy. Hunted on all sides, she can only turn to Lucian Daratrazanoff, the strangely seductive, piercingly erotic stranger who seems more dangerous than any other she has ever known.

My Highland Rogue by Karen Ranney

Since she was a little girl, Jennifer Adaire, daughter of the Earl of Burfield, has loved Gordon McDonnell even though he was below her station. After Gordon was forced from Adaire Hall, Jennifer has waited patiently for him. Now, finally back in Scotland after five years, Jennifer doesn't know if she can manage seeing again the man she loves—but can never have.

REL 0720